Fallout

By

JP Guppy

With Best Wishes,
Jonathan Guppy

Fallout

ISBN: 978-1-4092-3973-4

Copyright © Jonathan Pennant Guppy 2008

Jonathan Pennant Guppy has asserted his right under the Copyright, Designs and Patents Act 1988 to be identified as the author of this work.

All rights reserved.

Any unauthorised broadcasting, distribution, copying or reproduction will constitute an infringement of copyright.

The events, institutions and individuals referred to in this book are fictional and purely a figment of the author's imagination. Any misrepresentation of institutions or individuals is entirely unintentional. Where actual people or institutions are referred to, they appear as part of a fictionalised account of events, or fictionalised versions of themselves.

About the author

Jonathan Guppy was born in 1976 and lives in Shropshire with his wife and two daughters. His previous careers have included City finance practices, the wine industry and property development. After building his own house, a conversion of a disused old granary, he divides his time between his family, property renovation, studying, involvement in local politics and writing. He spends his free time pursuing hobbies including wine and beer making, shooting, and messing around on old tractors.

Acknowledgements

There have been numerous contributors to this book, many unaware of the inadvertent help they have lent. Mr Colin Chapman, Flt Lt D E Thresher RAAF, Flt Lt J S Durham RAF, Mr James Wilson, Mr Steven Jones and PC Royston Alderwick certainly deserve a mention, whether it be for their technical advice or kind words of encouragement. As does the Freedom of Information Act, which has helped lift the veil of secrecy that hides much of the working of government from the very people who pay for it.

Finally, this book would not have been completed without the loving support of my wife.

Preface

The Cold War reaches out from the past....

April 1986: Reactor No. 4 of the Chernobyl Nuclear Power Station explodes. A deadly cocktail of radioactive materials blows across Europe leaving a swathe of contamination in its wake. The fallout finally reaches Britain three days later, as the world slowly wakes up to the catastrophe. It is the worst nuclear accident in history...

Two decades later, four retired British civil servants are found dead. The deaths do not appear suspicious and the men seem unconnected. Then an old man commits suicide. Before he dies, he sends a document to a young journalist. It reveals a terrifying secret at the heart of Britain's nuclear establishment, a secret that people are prepared to kill for. A secret worth billions. A secret vital to Britain's security.

James Hudson is a struggling journalist, his career going nowhere. But after an unsettling encounter with an old friend, he begins investigating the legacy of the Chernobyl fallout. Has the government covered up the true effects of the cocktail of radioactive dust that settled across Britain? And why?

Hudson stumbles across the horrifying truth, far worse than his wildest suspicions. As others are ruthlessly silenced, Hudson discovers the stakes could not be higher. The race is on to tell the truth, a race of life or death.

"We knew the world would not be the same. A few people laughed, a few people cried, most people were silent. I remembered the line from the Hindu scripture, the Bhagavad-Gita. Vishnu is trying to persuade the Prince that he should do his duty and to impress him takes on his multi-armed form and says, 'Now, I am become Death, the destroyer of worlds.' I suppose we all thought that one way or another."

J. Robert Oppenheimer, interviewed in 1965.

Prologue

April 26th, 1986. Chernobyl Nuclear Power Station, Ukraine (USSR).

The operator was sweating profusely, fear and adrenalin coursing through his body as he desperately tried to bring the reactor back under control. His superior, the Chief Engineer, was leaning over him, monitoring the banks of dials on the vast control panel, his face ashen. The tension in the large Control Room was palpable, with all eyes on the readings for Reactor Number Four. There was hardly a sound except for the distant hum of massive electrical equipment and machinery from deep within the bowels of the enormous building.

As the sweat trickled over his brow, Vladimir Kravchenko cursed his own stupidity. *If only he hadn't forgotten to reset the water controller.* They were meant to be carrying out a safety test on the reactor. It should have been simple: Reduce the reactor power to 30%, switch off the steam supply to the turbines and measure how much electricity they produced whilst spinning under their own momentum, then see if it was enough to power the critical safety circuits before the emergency generators came online. It should have been perfectly straightforward.

But it wasn't.

Not long after they began reducing the reactor output in line with the test procedure, the electricity grid controller for Kiev had suddenly demanded more power from Chernobyl. The test had been suspended for several hours, and the first shift of operators had gone home to be replaced by the nightshift at midnight. Vladimir and the rest of the nightshift then had to pick up where the dayshift had left off, and try to finish the test. But they couldn't do anything until Kiev gave them the go-ahead. Until then, it was a waiting game.

At 12:28 am, Vladimir was just heading off to enjoy his first cigarette of the shift when the call finally came through from Kiev: They could reduce power and carry out the test. Whether it was because his attention was dulled by boredom, or the fact that he was distracted by the irritation of having his cigarette break interrupted, Vladimir made a simple but dreadful error: He forgot to reset a critical water controller for the reactor. Moments after commencing the shut-down procedure, this error resulted in the reactor being flooded with water, its output crashing to just 1%. However, far from being safe, past experience had shown that the reactor became dangerously unstable at such low power, a situation he was now trying desperately to rectify, with the help of the Chief Engineer, whilst emergency warning lights flashed across the console in front of them.

'Remove the manual control rods, try to get the power back up,' ordered the Chief Engineer, panic creeping into his voice.

'What? All of them?' Vladimir asked, incredulous.

'Yes! Hurry up! Keep on removing them until the power starts to increase, then stop.'

Vladimir was frightened. He knew that the reactor should never be left with less than fifteen manual control rods. But he followed the instructions. He removed the rods until there were fifteen left, the critical level for safety.

Nothing happened.

'Keep on removing them,' the Chief Engineer whispered, swallowing deeply. Vladimir removed another five, by which point the tension in the room was unbearable. All eyes were riveted to the output dial.

Still nothing.

'Keep going,' ordered the Chief Engineer hoarsely, drawing his hand over his mouth anxiously. They were in unchartered territory now. With mounting fear, Vladimir carefully removed two more control rods. There were only eight left now, way below the minimum permitted for safety. If they lost control of the reactor now…

Suddenly, the output dial quivered.

Yes! It was working!

'Power's increasing,' he breathed, with considerable relief. The sighs of the other technicians were clearly audible. Vladimir watched the output dial creeping up from 1% to 5%. It edged up past 10%, back into safe operating range. Vladimir let out another deep breath. It was going to be fine. His mistake with the water controller might be overlooked now. There was nervous laughter and smiles amongst the other technicians. They had got away with it. Vladimir sat back in his chair with relief, his white technician's overcoat stained with wet sweat patches, watching the dial steadily creep up. He definitely needed a cigarette now. The reactor was safe.

Then Vladimir noticed something. He blinked and leaned forward to study the power output dial. Then it happened again: A twitch in the needle. A twitch that shouldn't be there.

'Chief?' he murmured in alarm, his eyes fixed on the dial. The Chief Engineer, turned back and inspected the dial. It happened again. This time, the needle dipped dramatically, then recovered.

'What's happening?' asked Vladimir, feeling the fear return.

'It's becoming unstable! Regulate the water flow manually. Quickly!' the Chief Engineer snapped in a shaky voice. The panic was also evident on his strained, thickset features, and he ran a hand nervously through his greying hair as Vladimir began adjusting the water supply, trying to smooth out the fluctuating power output. Vladimir tried to swallow, but his mouth was incredibly dry and his tongue caught on the back of his mouth, nearly making him retch. His heart was pounding and his legs felt weak. Sweat glistened on his low Slavic forehead and heavy brow. It occurred to him that they wouldn't be able to shut down the reactor rapidly if an emergency arose. They had removed too many rods. And they had deliberately disabled the automatic shut-down safety systems in order to carry out the test. He kept his eye on the power output dials, which continued to fluctuate alarmingly.

'It's no good, Chief,' he gasped. 'I can't control it!'

'Keep trying. You have to!'

Vladimir concentrated as hard as possible, tweaking the water supply, trying to anticipate each power dip and spike.

'Come on, you're doing it,' the Chief Engineer encouraged him.

The operator was bathed in sweat by now. Try as he might, it was nearly impossible to eliminate the power fluctuations. With most of the control rods removed, the only way of regulating the reactor was with the water flowing through its core. The entire stability of the reactor now depended solely on his skill in regulating the water flow and, with the emergency systems deliberately disabled, there was simply no room for error.

Eventually, however, after persevering for several more minutes, it looked like he had brought the reactor back under control. He had to keep tweaking the cooling water supply every few seconds, but the power output remained fairly constant.

'I think I've done it,' he announced finally, sighing with relief. The dark patches of sweat on his laboratory coat bore testament to that. The power output was back up to 20% and the fluctuations had diminished, though they hadn't gone away entirely. He checked the clock; it read 1.22 a.m. The Chief Engineer turned towards him and gave a tight smile, the stress evident in his features.

'We should start the test. Let's get it over and done with, then we can get the reactor back up to normal. You need to keep all the automatic safety circuits switched off, otherwise the test will set them off and we won't be able to complete it. We won't have another opportunity to get it done after tonight.' He didn't have to explain himself further. They all knew that the Chief Engineer had been placed under considerable pressure by his superiors to get the test done, and he was keen to avoid antagonising them. Such things were foolish in the Soviet state, and he didn't wish to spend his retirement in a labour camp.

'What about the emergency shutdown system?' asked Vladimir. 'Shouldn't we leave that on, just in case?'

'No. You'll have to keep that switched that off as well, otherwise it'll keep kicking in when you're doing the test.'

'Are you sure? The reactor's not stable.'

'Yes. We have to get the test done. There's no other option. You'll still have the manual override.'

'*Da, tovarisch.*' Vladimir did as he was told, and closed off the steam supply to the turbines, so that they were spinning solely under their own momentum. The other technicians began recording the slowly, but exponentially, falling electricity output as the massive turbines wound down. The power station relied on its own output to power the critical safety systems that kept the nuclear reactors safe. In the event that the steam supply failed in an emergency, they needed to assess whether the turbines kept spinning long enough to power these safety systems before the emergency back-up generators came on line. As the massive turbines slowed down, Vladimir kept a close eye on the bank of dials in front of him.

Suddenly, a shiver of fear went through him.

'*Chyort voz'mi!*' he cursed, 'Shit! Steam production's rising!' Before his eyes, the gauge was showing the steam production running out of control inside the reactor. But the automatic safety systems had been switched off, so did not respond to the danger.

'Shut it down! Quick! Use the manual override!' yelled the Chief Engineer frantically.

Vladimir lunged forward and hit the button to reinsert all the control rods at once. That should have stopped the nuclear reaction.

It didn't.

A fatal reactor design flaw had been deliberately concealed by the labyrinthine Soviet bureaucracy. Rather than slowing down the nuclear reaction, a peculiarity of the Chernobyl reactor design meant that an emergency reinsertion of all the control rods always led to a short power spike before they took effect. A similar test performed at a plant in Lithuania in 1983 had resulted in near catastrophe, though nobody had deemed it necessary to pass the information on, and the incident had been quietly filed away.

'Power surge!' Vladimir yelled in terror. The power output dial flicked around into the red and past 100%.

Two seconds later, at the time of precisely 01:23 and 44 seconds on the morning of April 26th, 1986, Reactor Number Four reached 120 times its full power. Inside the control room, they heard a loud bang, followed by a second, far larger explosion which sent shock waves through the room.

Then there was total silence.

Vladimir turned and stared into the Chief Engineer's eyes with a look of horror. *What have we done?*

The lengthy investigation that followed determined that all the radioactive fuel rods had disintegrated and pressure from the steam created by the boiling water broke every one of the pressure tubes and blew off the entire concrete top-shield of the reactor, exposing the superheated graphite core to the atmosphere. This then caught fire, burning for several days. Only the suicidal heroics of the Soviet emergency workers prevented a far more serious subsequent blast, as the molten reactor core burned through the concrete floor towards the pool of cooling water beneath it. If the two had come into direct contact, not only would it have resulted in a huge steam explosion, but there was the very considerable risk of a nuclear detonation with the potential to devastate a vast swathe of Ukraine. To avert this, two Special Forces divers descended into the pool and opened the valves that allowed it to drain. Both had understood their likely fate before entering the highly radioactive water, yet they volunteered without hesitation. They are remembered as heroes, of the highest order.

It is estimated that all of the xenon gas, about half the iodine and caesium-137, and at least 5% of the remaining radioactive material in the core was released. Most of the nuclear material was deposited within the local vicinity, but a cloud of lighter materials, including the caesium-137 and iodine-131, was distributed across Europe. Desperate to avoid adverse publicity, Soviet authorities kept details of the accident hidden from the West for three days, by which time the cloud had already passed over Britain.

It was the worst nuclear accident in history....

*

Whitehall, London, 1986

His footsteps clattered on the polished linoleum-tiled floor as he rushed down the corridor, breaking into the occasional running step, such was the urgency. Out of breath, the secretary reached the outer office of the Minister of State for Trade and Industry. The Minister was covering for his immediate boss, the Secretary of State, who was attending a European trade summit in Brussels. As usual, the Minister had attended all the dreary preliminary meetings, along with his counterparts, and now it was time for their respective Secretaries of State to meet at the end and finalise business, whilst enjoying legendary Brussels hospitality. Such was the prerogative of rank.

The young Minister had been kept at his desk all evening, having been alerted earlier to the impending nuclear crisis. The Secretary of State had been fully briefed, but had delegated decision-making authority in the matter to the Minister. The Minister knew that he had been handed a poisoned chalice by his boss, who had an acute nose for political risk. *Bastard.* It was obvious that the Minister would be made the scapegoat. Therefore, for the sake of his own political career, it was imperative for him to find a way out of the mess that had been presented to him earlier on under conditions of the utmost secrecy.

The secretary rushed through the outer office and burst into the Minister's room without knocking. Shaking and out of breath, the secretary presented him with the secure communication, clearly marked *Top Secret*. The Minister's first instinct had been to berate the secretary for his impudence, but one look at the man's face stopped him in his tracks. Taking the message, he read it with a growing sense of alarm, feeling the blood draining from his face. He read it again, after which his pallor was distinctly grey. He was out of his depth on this one, way out of his depth.

'Get me Symonds on the phone now…no, tell him to come here right away,' he ordered. Symonds was the Permanent Secretary, the most senior civil servant in the department. He was somewhere inside the vast 1960s-era office block that housed the department.

'Yes sir,' the office secretary replied, scurrying back towards the door.

'And see if you can get hold of Heathcote in Brussels!' the Minister shouted after him.

The secretary skidded to a halt.

'Sir, that might be difficult, they're in the middle of the final meeting, it's been going on all night.'

'Tell him it's a bloody emergency!' the Minister bawled.

Symonds arrived five minutes later and read the communication as the Minister paced up and down the short run of cheap nylon carpet behind his desk, drawing deeply on a cigarette. Frowning, he gave the document a careful second reading. Upon finishing, he laid it carefully on the wide, paper-strewn desk, with almost effeminate deliberation. And grimaced.

Years of crisis experience had taught him the useful lesson of first garnering all the facts, then making a careful consideration of them before venturing an opinion. However it was clear that even his normally calm composure was disturbed by what he had read. His intelligent eyes flickered with concern.

'What the *hell* are we going to do?' the Minister demanded.

'What about Heathcote?'

'Doesn't know about it yet, we're trying to get hold of him at the summit.'

'I see,' Symonds murmured. He inspected his hands, then nibbled a small fingernail thoughtfully.

Symonds could be infuriating to the point of distraction, but the Minister held his tongue, knowing full well that the old civil servant was utterly indispensable when it came to getting him and his boss out of a crisis. Instead, he mashed his unfinished cigarette furiously in the overflowing ashtray and lit a fresh one. He tried not to look at Symonds who was now touching his pursed lips with the tips of his fingers, as he pondered the options. He seemed to be grappling with some inner turmoil. Finally, a flicker of a smile cracked Symonds' starched, usually humourless, features.

'Who else knows about this so far?' he asked the Minister.

'Only those in the nuclear incident reporting chain. At the moment, we're at the top of that chain.'

'We need to keep it that way for the time being.'

'*What?*' snapped the Minister. He wasn't in the mood for Symonds' crypticism.

'The radiation has already passed overhead. The population has already been exposed; even if there was something we could do, it's too late. You would create panic on a massive scale, it would lead to civil unrest and the emergency services would be overwhelmed. Someone would be held responsible.'

Likely to be anyone but you, thought the Minister. Unwritten Westminster protocol demanded that the elected politicians always took the blame for scandals in their departments, irrespective of whether it was their fault or not. The anonymous civil servants were usually left unscathed, perhaps transferred sideways into other departments. Some were even promoted.

'So you're proposing we do nothing?'

'Not exactly….' Symonds hesitated.

'Well, *what* then?' demanded the Minister, irritably.

Symonds shifted in his seat. 'There is something…An idea that was shelved a few years ago. At the time it was considered…*inappropriate*. But I think it might be rather suitable for our little problem now.'

'Go on.'

'If you'll forgive me, I've already taken the liberty of digging out my copy of the original report. I could never bring myself to destroy it. Just in case, you understand.'

Symonds reached into his attaché case and pulled out a brown manila folder, held together with parcel string. He undid the string and slid out a red folder. The Minister raised his eyebrows. Symonds slid the opened folder across the table and the Minister began flicking through the yellowed pages, noting the *Top Secret* and the highly restricted circulation list stamped across the top of each one. When he had finished reading, he sat back and studied Symonds, who remained inscrutable.

'You're serious about this?'

'Why not? The Red Dawn proposal is perfect for this situation. We should use it.'

'But this was written in 1958.'

'I know. I prepared it.'

'*What?*' The Minister was incredulous. The extent and longevity of Symonds' career never ceased to amaze him. Another reason why the man was indispensable.

'Obviously a degree of adaptation is necessary, but the fundamental plan is the same. But we need to act quickly if we are going to use it.'

There was a pause as the Minister digested the proposal. 'You really think it would work?' he asked, finally.

'I'm reasonably sure, yes,' replied Symonds cautiously, ever the civil servant.

'You realise what would happen if it went wrong?'

'Yes. But the decision is up to you. We haven't time to wait for Heathcote to come back from Brussels and make his mind up. We have to act now.'

The Minister fished out a fresh cigarette, lit it and inhaled deeply. He stared at his reflection in the glass of his office window, the bright lights of London glistening outside. A city oblivious to the awful possibilities lying on his desk. He exhaled a steady stream of smoke. The full weight of responsibility lay on his shoulders. The wrong decision would have far reaching consequences for both him and his immense political ambition. And for thousands, perhaps millions, of his countrymen.

'What other options do we have?'

'We come clean about it; issue full guidance to the public, instigate a treatment programme for those affected. It would be messy, cause mass panic and achieve little. It's too late to do anything effective. But the public would still hold you responsible. Remember, there's an election next year.'

It was an unenviable decision to make. Either way, the Minister could find himself in trouble. On the one hand, he would be setting himself up as the fall guy for events that had been beyond his control, or he would be a party to Symonds' monstrous scheme. But at least that scheme held out the possibility they could get away with it. Doing nothing was far worse.

'How many people would know about it?'

'The absolute minimum required to implement it.'

'That's not an answer.'

'We can keep the numbers small, but I can't be definite at this stage. I have a list of those of who need to know immediately, but there may be others who have to be included later on.'

'What about the Prime Minister?'

'You wish to implicate her?'

The Minister most certainly did not. That would do him no favours. He realised that if the Prime Minister was briefed on the scheme, it would be the end of the matter. She would not wish to be associated with it. But still the Minister sought higher approval, or at least the support of others.

'This should be discussed at COBRA.' He was referring to the Cabinet Office Briefing Room A, where ad hoc crisis management was carried out by specially chosen committee, the composition of which depended entirely on the nature of the crisis.

Symonds nodded wearily. He had expected as much. He picked up the telephone and quickly made the necessary arrangements. They didn't have much time.

*

The COBRA meeting had been convened at great haste. Rather than taking place in the eponymous room located in the basement of Number 10, a secure site in another nondescript Whitehall building was being used. There were several alternative locations dotted around the capital; Number 10 was to be distanced from this operation.

The relevant delegates were all present, in line with the well-established protocol. They squeezed around the slightly tatty conference table. It was a cheap reproduction piece; the mahogany veneer was already peeling from the edges of the leaf extensions that had been hastily fitted to accommodate the large gathering in attendance. The faces of the entirely male complement sat around the table were ashen. A pall of blue smoke hung over the proceedings, combining unpleasantly with the aroma of cheap coffee and the musty odour of rain-sodden suits in the poorly ventilated room.

The chairman of the meeting, the Minister of State, had just finished speaking and what they had heard had shaken them to the core. The proposal put forward by Symonds had been relayed to the assembled group, all of them associated with the nuclear industry and its regulatory bodies. The Minister finished his statement by announcing that the doors of the room would remain locked until they had reached a unanimous conclusion, one way or the other, on the proposal. Once the doors were opened, all discussion hitherto undertaken would be subject to the Official Secrets Act. The warning was superfluous, as everything they ever did or discussed in a professional capacity was automatically subject to the Act. But the Minister was just reinforcing the point.

After a period of nervous silence in which the various delegates weighed up the general sentiment in the room, a couple of them dared to advance their reservations. These were robustly put down. Many of those present could see the logic in Symonds' proposal, as conveyed by the Minister. After all, they were acting in the national interest, so whatever conscience they had should be assuaged by that consideration. Besides, they had good jobs. Why risk the final salary pension, especially as most were nearing retirement age? The Minister was right. Even those who had initially harboured doubts were won over to the cause.

The final show of hands was clear, and the Minister cleared his voice.

'Gentlemen, we have an agreement. In the national interest, the proposal to implement Red Dawn will be put into immediate effect. We have no time to waste, so may I suggest we make a start. I'm sure that I don't have to remind you of the need for utmost confidentiality in this matter. We will meet on a daily basis to discuss progress. That will be all, thank you.'

As they filed out of the claustrophobic room one of the delegates casually put a hand into his jacket and switched off a Dictaphone recorder. He had been using it to dictate letters for his secretary when the urgent call to attend the COBRA meeting had come through. In his haste he had brought it with him. Some nagging doubt, call it sixth sense if you will, had compelled him to switch it on discreetly during the meeting, once the doors had been closed. That single small act, the pressing of a small button, would prove momentous. It would change the course of history…

1

Thursday

(September 24th 2009, London, Canary Wharf).

The large flat screen television dominated one wall of the spacious corner office, which afforded commanding views of the Thames. The rent was punishing, but Sir Charles Millburn was of the opinion that his corporate headquarters should be suitably housed and that he, as the Chairman of Gencor Energy PLC, should have an office which reflected his status as head of one of the world's foremost nuclear energy providers.

Millburn was glued to the television, as the Prime Minister made his well-publicised and meticulously leaked speech to the House of Commons. The deep burr of his voice resonated from the television set.

"….Mr Speaker, the nuclear white paper published today sets out a clear timetable for action to enable the building of the first new nuclear power station, which I hope will be completed well before 2020.

The United Kingdom is firmly committed to reducing our carbon emissions in line with our policy to address climate change and play a leading role in this.

Mr Speaker, I remain firmly of the view that there should and will be room for all forms of low-carbon power technologies to play a role in helping the UK meet its energy objectives in the future. The energy bill will ensure we have a legislative framework enabling all of these technologies to make a positive contribution to our future requirements for cleaner, more secure energy.

Giving the go-ahead today that new nuclear power should play a role in providing UK with clean, secure and affordable energy is in our country's vital long term interest. I therefore invite energy companies to submit plans to build and operate a new generation of nuclear power stations. Set against the challenges of climate change and security of supply, the evidence in support of new nuclear power stations is compelling. We should positively embrace the opportunity of delivering this important part of our energy policy and to this end I have instructed my Chancellor to allocate £35 billion to the building of new nuclear facilities over the next decade. This is the right long-term decision for the country.

I commend this statement to the house."

The Prime Minister sat down to much cheering and waving of order sheets from his backbenchers, whilst the Leader of the Opposition sprang to his feet and attempted to criticise a policy which his own party had previously advocated. Millburn hit the mute button.

Sir Charles Millburn already knew the content of the speech. He had been sent a copy in advance by Giles Devereaux, the Prime Minister's Director of Communications. But to hear it from the man himself was music to his ears.

£35 billion. Pounds Sterling. That exceeded the entire gross domestic product of some countries. And Gencor Energy PLC was the front-runner to win the contracts. His company was virtually guaranteed £35 billion of taxpayers' money. He had it on good authority that the general sentiment around Whitehall was that such a vast sum should remain in British hands. British taxpayers should be supporting British jobs and technology. Certainly not the French or Germans. Possibly the Americans. But best to keep it British. And since the entire British nuclear industry had been privatised in 1989 under the umbrella of Gencor Energy PLC, there was really only one player left in town.

Millburn turned to the computer monitor which sat on his expansive glass-topped desk. The screen flickered with the Reuters feed from the London Stock Exchange. Gencor shares had been marked progressively higher since rumours began circulating about the intention to recommence a nuclear building programme, but with the Prime Minister's statement, the stock surged ahead. In a matter of seconds, Millburn saw the value of his personal shareholdings and share options increase by £3million as institutional investors bought heavily into the stock. Millburn safely predicted that by the end of the day, he would be enriched by over £100million. It was a staggering sum to make in a day.

Millburn reflected on his fortunate position in life. His ministerial career in the Department for Trade and Industry had spluttered to a halt in the dying days of Mrs Thatcher's premiership. His finely tuned political nose had detected the growing disillusionment within the party towards the leader and, as an ardent Thatcherite, he knew his days were numbered. There would be little room at the top table for men like him, so he took the much tried and tested exit route of a City directorship. It was only natural that his expertise and experience in the nuclear sector would lead to an appointment to the board of the recently formed Gencor Energy PLC. A cleverly engineered boardroom coup later led to his installation as Chairman, working alongside a very reliable and loyal Chief Executive who made sure that things were run according to Millburn's vision.

To begin with, it seemed a disastrous career move, only brightened with a trip to the Palace to receive his knighthood, courtesy of the Iron Lady's final Honours List. The nuclear industry was in the doldrums, politically out of favour, and saddled with huge decommissioning costs for its aged and decrepit power stations. The future looked bleak. But Millburn was no fool. He knew the case for nuclear power would one day prove irresistible, and a number of factors gradually colluded to make this outcome inevitable. North Sea oil and gas began to run out at the turn of the millennium, which made his old government's decision to invest in new gas-fired power stations after closing down the coal industry seem particularly short-sighted. At the same time, relentless Chinese and Indian economic expansion sucked in vast energy supplies, whilst Britain's own sustained economic growth had put huge demands on its generating capacity. The final factor was the growing political importance of climate change and the need to cut carbon emissions, but all this in a country which had woefully underinvested in alternative energy sources. All these factors conspired to place Gencor Energy PLC in a prime position to capitalise on the looming energy crisis. Years of extensive political lobbying, exploiting Millburn's old contacts in government, were about to pay off, spectacularly so for Millburn.

On his appointment as chairman of the board, he had insisted on remuneration in shares rather than cash. This had been approved by shareholders, who viewed it as a perfect alignment of their mutual interests, as well as representing a considerable saving. When the shares were trading so low, the terms had been generous with the result that Millburn had built up a personal stake of 2% in the company. It didn't sound much, but the market capitalisation that morning had been in excess of £11billion. Millburn's stake was now worth over £220million.

He was confident that by the end of the day's trading after the Prime Minister's announcement, the shares would be up by 50%.

He slapped the glass desk in triumph and reclined in his sumptuous custom-built leather chair, savouring the moment. He was rich beyond his wildest dreams. He didn't need to sell any of the shares: The dividends alone would amount to several million a year; plenty to live off and maintain his expensive homes in Chelsea and Surrey.

Along with his expensively appointed office, the debonair Millburn was every inch the City gent. His expertly tailored suits, by Manning & Manning of Savile Row, concealed a relentlessly expanding paunch as best they could, whilst his smooth, tanned and handsome features, with luxuriant silver hair, lent him an aura of gravitas and wealth. His taste for cigarettes had evolved into fine cigars to match his budget and, in keeping with the moment, he fished a Ramon Allones from the humidor on a side table and expertly lit it, after warming it carefully on the flame of his platinum Ronson. He blew a satisfying cloud of blue smoke across his office and smiled to himself.

Yes, life was looking up for old Charlie Millburn.

The same could not be said for the elderly gentleman studying his financial statements that morning with a mixture of dread and foreboding. The latest court summons had arrived with the early post, with a final demand for payment. His financial statements were dire. His only remaining asset lay in the minority equity stake he still held in his house, the rest having been gobbled up in an equity release scheme to pay off his numerous creditors. But it wasn't enough. He now stood to lose the house as well. There would be nothing left for his children, nothing left from a lifetime of slog and toil on behalf of Her Majesty's Government. In other circumstances, his pension could have been regarded as generous, but it was consumed by interest payments on his many debts. And all because of one disastrous investment.

The brokers, a company he had not previously heard of but with seemingly bona fide credentials, had assured him they had a red-hot tip: A small Swiss medical research firm with a block-buster patent on the way. The stock would rocket. Guaranteed. Initially sceptical, he had declined the offer, but the brokers were persistent and bombarded him with facts and figures, impressing on him the small window of opportunity that was available. In the end, the persistence paid off.

So, he had invested a quarter of a million into the penny shares. The stock did indeed rise, but he failed to appreciate that was because of his own investment. There was no patent, no medical research. Just an obscure post office box in Geneva, registered to a business in Buenos Aires. Which had since disappeared, along with his cash. He had wept when he realised how foolish he had been.

Now he was flat broke, barely able to afford the alcohol which numbed the painful daily reality of his situation.

Bleary-eyed from the whisky he had been consuming since waking up that morning, he glanced at the twenty-four-hour news channel which was carrying the Prime Minister's announcement of massive investment in nuclear energy. The same news story also reported the soaring value of Gencor Energy on the London market and the old man cursed.

That *bastard* Millburn making even more money. The world wasn't right. How could such a man, such an affront to humanity, be so successful? The old man chewed over his words for some time, muttering profanities to himself as he waded through the misery contained in the mail, meeting each demand for money with another swig of scotch.

And then he had it. The idea to solve all his problems. *Why hadn't he thought of it before?* How stupid of him, it was so *obvious*. With the zeal of the newly converted he started up his old computer and set to work.

2

Friday

After enjoying a leisurely breakfast in the painstakingly restored splendour of his Regency townhouse in the Borough of Kensington and Chelsea, Millburn arrived in ebullient form at his Canary Wharf offices, having being ferried there in the comfort of his Bentley. Investors' interest in Gencor had exceeded even his wild assumptions the day before, and the shares had closed 57% up at the end of trading. There would be the inevitable round of profit-taking this morning, which would depress the shares again, but Millburn was confident his newly-found paper wealth would remain largely intact.

Gencor Energy occupied the entire top floor of the office block, and Millburn was a well-known personality in the building. On his way up in the lift, he was treated to a round of back-slapping and handshakes as his employees and other business associates congratulated him on the news from the government. He played down their enthusiasm by cautioning that they hadn't been awarded any of the contracts yet, but there was no denying he relished the applause. Millburn was a man who demanded and expected absolute loyalty. Those who did not play by these simple rules quickly found themselves looking for alternative employment.

As he strode through the largely open-plan office to his enclosed corner suite, he was greeted with polite applause and shouts of approval from staff eager to impress the notoriously irascible Chairman. He acknowledged the praise with a languid wave and headed into his office, to be greeted by his secretary.

'Good morning, Sir Charles. Your papers and mail are ready for you.'

'Thank you, Susan. Could you bring some coffee?'

'Yes, Sir Charles.'

She retired from the office suite, pulling the plate glass door quietly shut behind her. Millburn could not abide noise. The previous secretary had been summarily dismissed simply on account of her habit of slamming shut filing cabinets.

He approached his desk to see that Susan had arranged his newspapers neatly, the FT on top as always. With a smile, he could see that the Prime Minister's statement on nuclear energy had made the front page. He sat down and revelled in the coverage, sipping at the fresh coffee brought in by Susan, who quietly slipped in and out without disturbing him. The FT editorial was firmly of the belief that Gencor would be picking up the contracts to build and operate the new power stations. The shares were recommended as a definite buy. A flattering picture of Millburn accompanied the article, describing him in the most glowing of terms. There was more of the same in the other papers, accompanied with the usual howling from the environmental lobby. *Who cares?* They weren't invited to the party.

Feeling extremely pleased with himself, he turned his attention to his mail. Susan ran a tight ship with regards to his personal correspondence, only forwarding items that she believed were genuinely personal. As a result, there was blessedly little to bother him. Most of the small pile of envelopes had already been opened by the secretary, with the exception of one, which was clearly marked *Private and Confidential, for the sole and personal attention of Sir Charles Millburn KCBE*. This piqued his interest. It was always nice to be properly addressed. Millburn flourished the silver letter-opener presented to him by his old constituency office upon his retirement from politics and fished inside the envelope. There was a single sheet of paper, which he extracted.

Two minutes later his morning had been utterly ruined.

*

Behind the firmly locked door of Millburn's office, with the blinds closed, the letter was read carefully by each man in turn. It was important not to destroy or contaminate any forensic evidence, so the letter had already been placed in a sealed transparent bag. It was printed on thick paper with a raised weave. The watermark denoted an expensive marque. The folding was neat and precise, exactly in thirds, with a perfect alignment of corners. The text was double spaced, Times New Roman, font size 12. Drearily standard. It covered two thirds of the page and was split into just two paragraphs. Each man read the letter twice just to make sure that they had digested the contents accurately, before passing it on. The last line in particular appeared to cause the most consternation. There were four men in total. It was a very select gathering.

'This *is* rather inconvenient for you,' murmured Peter Kroll, after he had finished reading it. Millburn had called his Director of Security as soon as he had recovered from the shock of receiving the letter.

'It's pretty inconvenient for you, too,' snapped Millburn angrily, searching for a packet of cigarettes. He found a fresh packet in the drawer of a side cabinet and peeled off the cellophane.

'I suppose you're right, there,' Kroll drawled with Old Harrovian languidness. 'And, by the way, I'd appreciate you not lighting that.'

'Piss off, Peter' mumbled Millburn through pursed lips as he spun the wheel of his monogrammed platinum lighter. Kroll, Gencor Energy's Director of Security and head of Kroll Associates Limited, a rather special and exclusive security consultancy, could be just as irritating as old Symonds had been. Probably why they had once been friends, before the old civil servant had died, or it might simply be a quality the Civil Service Recruitment Boards looked for. The other two men in the room went by the names of Trevor and Julian. Millburn did not know their surnames and had had never bothered to ask. It was of no concern to him. All he knew was that they worked very closely with Peter Kroll and were highly efficient in what they did.

A smile flickered across Kroll's pinched, humourless features as Millburn blew a cloud of smoke in his direction. Whilst Millburn's volcanic temper was legendary, Kroll prided himself on remaining calm in a crisis.

'I never thought I would hear Red Dawn mentioned again,' observed Kroll. 'Any idea who's behind this?'

'Of course not. Why the hell do you think I called you?' snapped Millburn.

'You've got no idea at all?'

'*No!*' he insisted with some exasperation, before standing up and pacing behind his desk.

After he had recovered from the shock of reading the letter, Millburn had realised that he had three options: Ignore the letter and call the sender's bluff; secondly, acquiesce to the letter's demands and therefore keep his secret past hidden; or, thirdly, call the police and report the blackmail attempt.

The first option was always tempting for blackmail victims. Pretend he had never received it; hopefully the problem would go away. This was hopelessly unrealistic, though. Whoever had sent it knew about Red Dawn, knew that they could destroy him and Gencor. Very, very few people knew about Red Dawn, and he knew whoever was behind the letter was not bluffing. They had provided enough information in two paragraphs to convince him of their credibility and seriousness. The letter could not be ignored.

The second option offered an exit route, of sorts. If he paid the requisite sum of money into a numbered account held at an obscure family-owned bank on the Isle of Man he was assured that the sender would go away quietly. Good old fashioned blackmail. Considering what was at stake the sum was actually quite modest, a mere million. He had the cash; that wasn't a problem. His personal bank accounts contained many multiples more. It was both the principle and the practicality that bothered him. Millburn was damned if he was going to be subjected to something as humiliating as petty blackmail and, at a more practical level, any self-regarding blackmailer would not be able resist a second bite of the apple. The million would be a taster, to whet the appetite and gauge the final sum to be extracted. It could go on for ever. Payment was therefore out of the question.

He had then moved onto the third option. Which wasn't really an option at all. Reporting the matter to the police was a laughable proposition. Red Dawn was an extremely closely guarded secret and it was going to remain that way. Therefore Millburn had resorted to the fourth option: He had called Peter Kroll, and his 'associates'.

Kroll was fully aware of the Red Dawn programme. He had been briefed at its inception, in his capacity as the Security Service liaison officer. His job had been to ensure the utmost secrecy was maintained, to prevent knowledge spreading beyond a tightly controlled group and to vet any new potential members. When Millburn had left politics to join the board of Gencor, he had made Kroll a very tempting offer. As agreed, Kroll had formed his own nominally independent security consultancy, but in reality all his invoices were paid by Gencor. His rather underhand research had helped Millburn outmanoeuvre his rivals on the board, paving the way to the Chairmanship. In return, Millburn had made Kroll an associate director, with a very handsome remuneration and reward package, along with a long-term and highly lucrative contract for Kroll Associates to undertake the firm's internal security. Kroll was a multimillionaire in his own right, a happy circumstance he owed entirely to Millburn. His loyalty was without question.

Up until this moment, Kroll's ability to keep Red Dawn secret had also been without question. This was the first ever breach.

'It seems we have quite a problem,' Kroll pronounced. 'Someone's been talking to the wrong people, or they have suffered an unfortunate lapse in judgement. Either way, we need to identify who it is and put a stop to it. We don't have much time, if this deadline is serious. I can ask my old contacts at Thames House to have a look at the letter, see what they come up with?'

'No. I want this kept in-house for now. The last thing we need is another leak.'

'Then we need to go back to first principles. We need to start with the original membership of Red Dawn.'

'I agree. But there were thirty one.'

'Yes, but a lot have died since then. It was over twenty three years ago. Remember, you were one of the youngest.'

'How many are left?'

'Of the original group, seven. Including us. Obviously, Trevor and Julian know about it as well, but they don't count.' The two burly men shifted uncomfortably in their seats, remaining silent, not sure if they liked the implication of Kroll's words. 'Therefore, that leaves five people outside this room who know everything about Red Dawn.'

Of course there were more than thirty one involved; there had to be. The scale of the programme was such that it would have been impossible otherwise. But only five other people knew all the details of Red Dawn, knew enough to put the disparate strands together into one coherent picture and destroy Millburn and Gencor. They were the only people who even knew that the programme was called Red Dawn, such was the secrecy that surrounded it. This was why Millburn knew the letter was no joke.

'Well then, surely we can set about finding out which one of them it is and make sure they are silenced,' Millburn announced.

Kroll paused, before clearing his throat. 'Normally that would be the case, I agree, but in this particular situation I don't think we have the luxury of time. The letter gives you a deadline for payment. I'm not sure we could identify which of the five was behind it before the deadline, without tipping them off that we were looking. We would need to mount a simultaneous surveillance operation against five people, and we simply don't have the resources for that. Especially if you want this kept strictly in-house.'

'So what do you suggest then?'

Kroll glanced at Trevor and Julian before clearing his throat again and speaking. When he had finished, Millburn sat back in his chair. It was a big decision to take, and there would be no going back from it.

'There's no alternative?' he asked after a while.

'No. We've been backed into a corner.'

Millburn nodded. 'Is there any risk…?'

'No. It will be done as discreetly as possible.'

Millburn took another long pull on his cigarette, casting his gaze out of the window. Kroll was right. He did feel cornered. He had taken years to reach this position, years and years of painstaking work and colossal effort. And now someone from his past was threatening to take all that away from him. Some resentful, grasping little shit who had made a hash of their own miserable life and wanted him to make it up to them.

He felt his rage rising. No one did that to Charlie Millburn and got away with it. No one.

'Alright, do it.'

3

James Hudson was having a rotten day. In fact, it was merely the continuation of a rotten twenty four hours. The previous day, his girlfriend of six months had announced that they were splitting up. Hudson had not seen it coming. By way of explanation, it was nothing to do with him. Nothing at all. It wasn't his fault and he had done nothing wrong. She just needed some time to herself. He was a lovely guy and really didn't deserve her. He'd find someone better in no time.

Not that he had much say in the matter as she busied herself emptying his bathroom of a bewildering array of cosmetics. Watching her throw it into a bag, one of *his* bags he realised, it occurred to him that he couldn't remember the precise moment she had moved in – the takeover in his bathroom had been gradual, until it reached the point where every available surface appeared to be cluttered with her paraphernalia.

After the bathroom had been systematically purged, she had scoured his bedroom, removing items of skimpy underwear from various hiding places, with unnecessarily excessive zeal as far as he was concerned. The final act was rifling through the DVD racks to collect her films (which he had paid for), and assorted self-help books (which he had also paid for), then she had gone. With a bang the door had slammed shut behind her. Twenty minutes from start to finish, and she was out of his life.

As he marveled at the newly revealed tiles in his bathroom and the free space now available in his wardrobe and television cabinet, it finally sunk in. Then he heard the car outside and saw her driving off with her new 'best friend' from the call centre she worked at. Yes, he had heard rather a lot about 'Dave at work' recently, come to think of it. Certainly more than was strictly necessary.

His friends at the amateur rugby club had commiserated, rather too gleefully for his liking, and dragged him out for a beer or two which, of course, led to the inevitable binge.

The net result was the truly monumental hangover which greeted him that morning, accompanied with profound regret for his considerable dedication to the cause the night before. He contemplated phoning in sick, but remembered that his attendance record at the office was already a matter of contention with his boss. There was no alternative but to brave the elements and crawl into work. Fortunately, this was only a relatively short walk from his rented flat in the old docks area of town, as driving was clearly out of the question.

The Preston Advertiser was housed in a dilapidated office block that had long exceeded its intended lifespan. The brutal slabs of prefabricated concrete, tastefully pebble-dashed in a fetching shade of grey, were enough to dispirit even the most modernist of architects, let alone a disillusioned junior hack grappling with the near-terminal effects of his intemperance the night before. Hudson arrived ten minutes late and, before he could even pour himself a medically essential mug of coffee, had been summoned into the ramshackle cubicle that passed for the Editor's office.

He sat, or rather perched, as best he could in an uncomfortable plastic chair whilst the Editor administered what Hudson presumed was intended to be a thoroughly invigorating bollocking. The room was excessively warm, which did nothing to alleviate the splitting headache and the growing sense of nausea that threatened to overwhelm him. He suspected that he was oozing alcoholic fumes, a condition unlikely to endear him to the notoriously abstemious Donald Winston, so Hudson made a conscious effort to breathe through his nostrils rather than his mouth, in a vain attempt to minimise the contamination of his editor's office. This only made his headache worse.

Considering his diminutive, wiry stature, Mr Winston could be quite ferocious, especially when one was feeling particularly sensitive to raised voices and any noise in general. The effect was magnified by the man's broad Lancastrian accent.

'I'm sorry, James, but your performance isn't good enough. A newspaper like this can't afford to carry people. We're barely breaking even. It's absolutely vital that we raise the circulation, which means coming up with better stories. You just seem to want to sit back and wait for them to come to you. Look at this,' he brandished the previous week's copy. 'Most of your articles were written by the press officer at the council. You just copied and pasted them, and stuck your name on the bottom.'

'Er, no I didn't…'

'She emailed them to me as well.'

'Oh.'

'Look, James. I'm sorry, but you're having a formal warning.'

'*What?* Why?' was about all Hudson could muster by way of protest. He shifted in the horrible seat, trying to ward off the onset of paralysis in his legs.

'Don't push me, James. Buck up your ideas. Get out there and find the story. It's not that hard; we're only a weekly publication, for Christ's sake!' Winston signalled the end of the meeting by turning back to his ancient old computer and jabbing ferociously at the keyboard.

Hudson traipsed back to his desk feeling suitably chastened. He was the junior reporter, still on his first placement after graduation from journalism college. So far, the profession had not lived up to its glamorous image. He had found it virtually impossible to obtain his first job, and there had been over fifty applicants for this remote trainee post in Lancashire. Sometimes, Hudson was given to wonder why. The dreary, tatty office was soul destroying and there were only six other members of staff, none of whom he regarded with any particular affinity. The local news, if you could call it that, took mundanity to an entirely new art form. Boredom consumed his life, but the opportunities to escape were scarce, with the few openings on the national and regional papers being deluged with applicants. He was seriously considering a change of career, having now entered his third, and manifestly unproductive, year on the Preston.

At least it was a Friday, which meant he had nearly a week until articles had to be submitted for printing on Wednesday night, ready for distribution on Thursday. Sitting at his desk, he felt another wave of nausea and decided an urgent change of scenery would be a wise precaution.

Peering blearily into the mirror above the cracked and stained enamel sink in the toilets, his dark, ruggedly handsome features were marred by his sallow skin and bloodshot eyes, the result of the previous night's excess. On a healthy day, he looked the type more suited to the outdoor life rather than stuck behind a desk in a dingy office. Twenty five years old and going nowhere, he thought ruefully. No girlfriend, no job prospects and no money. Above all, no fun. Perhaps the alcohol was making him depressed. He splashed his face with cold water and felt the nausea subside. He only had to get through the rest of today before the weekend.

Returning to his desk equipped with a large mug of the rancid office coffee, he concentrated on writing up the bread-and-butter short articles and announcements that had been sent in by readers, sending them to his editor's electronic basket as quickly as he could to prove that he was at least doing something useful, and capitalising on the fact that activity made time pass more quickly. It would soon be Friday night, he prayed.

But the weekend did not offer many enticements, especially as the prospect of another night on the beer had lost its appeal. There was a rugby practice due on Sunday, but that was about it. Hudson also had something else planned after work, something he wasn't looking forward to: Visiting an old friend from university, currently lying in a Manchester hospital.

After work eventually finished at five, he drove down the motorway towards Manchester, arriving at the cancer centre in time for visiting. There was something he could not bear about hospitals, something that always filled him with a terrible foreboding whenever he entered them. The smell of the disinfectant alone was enough to make his stomach tighten, but it went deeper than that. The places always filled him with dread. Perhaps it was the knowledge that Death lingered in the corridors and wards, looking for an opportunity.

After enquiring at the reception, he made his way up to the radiotherapy ward, where Ben was recuperating from his latest bout of radioisotope treatment. Ben Goddard had been suffering from thyroid cancer for nearly two years. His thyroid gland and various lymph nodes had already been removed, and he had already undergone radioactive iodine therapy to eradicate any remaining thyroid cells, but his blood samples still revealed the presence of thyroxine. This meant only one thing: Cancerous thyroid cells were still present in his body, hence the latest round of treatment. The treatment was simple: radioactive iodine was injected, and absorbed by the thyroid cells, killing them off. The downside was the nausea induced by the radiation, plus the fact that Ben had to be kept in isolation, to avoid exposing others to the harmful rays he was emitting. He would be free to go only when his radioactivity dropped below a level deemed permissible for public safety. In the meantime, he just had to sit it out.

Hudson was directed towards one of the isolation cubicles after being taken through a list of precautions by a nurse. Inside the room, a pretty blond nurse was speaking to Ben from behind lead shielding. She had a clipboard and seemed to be asking questions. Ben caught sight of Hudson through the glass window and beckoned him in.

The nurse stood up as Hudson entered, and their eyes met. They were deep, almond eyes which took his breath away. She smiled and made her excuses, leaving Hudson staring after her.

'Hey, eyes off, tiger! She's mine!' protested Ben with a weary smile from the bed. He looked gaunt and had lost a lot of weight, but Hudson tried to hide his reaction at seeing him.

'It's alright for some, isn't it?' Hudson replied with a grin. 'Good to see you,' he leant forward with his hand out.

'Can't shake hands, sorry. You don't want to get zapped.'

'Oh, right. Sorry, I didn't realise,' he muttered, flustered. 'Um, how are you feeling?'

'Not too bad. Gasping for a pint, mainly.'

Hudson grinned. Good old Ben, never complaining. And always thirsty. In fact, if Hudson had learnt that his old friend had been suffering from cirrhosis, it wouldn't have been much of a surprise. But cancer; that had shocked everyone.

'Yeah, but who cares about having a pint when the nurses are like that! I'd rather be in here than the pub.'

'She's not a nurse,' Ben corrected him. 'Susannah's a cancer researcher.' He explained how Susannah had started investigating thyroid cancer at the Manchester University Cancer Research Institute, and was travelling the country speaking to patients, trying to establish a cause for what was once a very rare cancer but was now becoming increasingly commonplace. Research funding had recently been made available, due to its increased prevalence.

'It's becoming more common?' asked Hudson.

'Apparently.'

'Do they know why?'

'That's what Susannah's trying to find out.'

'Has she got any ideas yet?'

Ben went quiet, and Hudson raised an enquiring eyebrow.

'She's got a hunch, but I'm not meant to tell anyone.' Ben gave him a conspiratorial look.

'Come on, Ben, I'm your mate.'

'Yeah, and you're a bloody journalist!'

Hudson feigned mock indignation, but Ben persisted. 'It's true, James. I once told you that I fancied Claire Smith and you went and told everyone, made me look a right tit. Especially when she said no.'

'That's what mates are for, Ben. You should know that by now…Come on, what is it? I won't tell, promise.'

'Yeah, right.'

'I'm hurt. Deeply.'

Ben thought for a moment, before sighing and shaking his head. 'Alright then. But don't let Susannah know I told you. She'll go mad. It's her research project.'

'Go on then, what is it?'

Ben took a deep breath.

'Chernobyl.'

'Chernobyl?' Hudson gave him a sceptical look. 'But that was years ago.'

'I know, but Susannah thinks it's linked. Thyroid cancer is caused by exposure to radiation, and she thinks there are clusters in the areas affected by the fallout here. Thousands of people have been diagnosed in Ukraine and Belarus, mainly young people. It seems to affect children the most, but adults can get it too. She thinks the same might be happening here, too.'

Hudson frowned, but before he could ask any more questions, Susannah returned. She smiled sweetly as she entered the room, and Hudson suddenly found he was in no rush to leave.

'Sorry, but I've got to get my questionnaire finished.' She held the door open, and smiled again, but the message was clear: Get out.

'Oh, I'll wait outside, then?'

She nodded and smiled again. It was the sort of smile you would do anything for, and he found himself trotting meekly through the door. Ben winked at him, unable to conceal a triumphant smirk.

Hudson loitered around the ward, waiting for Susannah to finish. It was nearly twenty minutes before she finally emerged from the isolation room. When she saw Hudson, she rolled her eyes, turned abruptly and marched off down the corridor with him in pursuit.

'Hi. Hudson, James Hudson,' he introduced himself, walking quickly alongside her. She didn't shake his offered hand.

'Dr Susannah Harlowe,' she replied coolly. She was used to dispensing with unwanted attention, but Hudson persisted.

'I'm a…'

'Journalist. Yes, I know, Ben told me.' She headed towards the nurses' station and into the rest room that lay beyond it.

'Hey! You can't come in here!' she protested as Hudson followed her in.

'Ben told me about your work.'

'What?' She seemed angry. 'He had no right!'

'I know, I know. I tried to stop him, but he insisted. The thing is, I might be able to help.'

'Help?'

'Yes. Or we could help each other.'

'You want me to help you?'

'Yes, I want to cover your research work in my newspaper, run a feature on it.'

'What's in it for me?'

'Free publicity. And dinner. Tonight.'

Susannah laughed, showing off her perfect white teeth.

'That's outrageous. No.'

'Tomorrow night, then?'

'No!' She insisted, blushing. Hudson grinned.

'Your favourite restaurant, seven o'clock tomorrow night.'

Susannah shook her head and bit her bottom lip, trying not to smile. She knew that she should really say no, but Hudson had worn her down. And he intrigued her.

'Okay. You win. Seven o'clock. Paolo's Trattoria. Now please get out of here.'

Hudson grinned again, this time triumphantly, and left without another word. Susannah watched him go and smiled ruefully to her herself. She really should have said no...

4

Saturday

The Senior Fire Officer attempted to fight his nausea, but the acidic bile kept rising up and catching the back of his throat. It was the smell more than anything. Years of experience still did not prepare him for the sweet, pervasive tang of burnt human flesh, which always seemed to dominate the other aromas which linger around a fire-gutted building.

That Saturday morning, his crew were still damping down the remains of the small bungalow in the new estate on the outskirts of the Berkshire new town of Bracknell. It was part of a managed complex, with a resident warden to keep an eye on the mainly elderly and infirm inhabitants, who wished to retain an element of dignity and independence rather than succumb to the communal privations of a nursing home.

The Senior Fire Officer had been alerted to the grim discovery one of his men had found inside the bedroom, and he now surveyed the scene, trying to keep his nausea under control. The charred remains of the body lay amongst the blackened springs of the incinerated mattress. With any luck, the old man had died in his sleep from smoke inhalation, before the flames reached him. He was assuming it was an old man, based on the information provided by the distraught warden, though it was impossible to even determine the sex of the victim, let alone his age, without a post mortem examination. But they had no reason to believe that victim was any other than Mr Geoffrey Adams, a retired gentleman of impeccable manners, who lived alone in the bungalow.

The Coroner had been informed and an autopsy would be conducted to determine the cause of death. Just to rule out foul play. It was likely to be a formality. The Senior Fire Officer restated his belief that, in all likelihood, the cause of death would have been smoke inhalation, before the flames reached him. Mr Adams would not have felt any pain. This provided small comfort for the distressed warden, who felt responsible for the terrible events of the night.

The warden could not understand why the smoke detectors had failed. They were correctly wired, with back-up batteries, to the latest regulation standards. In fact, they had all been checked the week before. There was no reason why they should have failed.

But the warden had completely forgotten about the quick visit paid by two workmen earlier the previous day. They purported to be from the property maintenance firm contracted to look after the complex. The visit had been of no real concern to him, just part of the ordinary routine. Two anonymous tradesmen in overalls and a Transit van. Inconsequential.

Mr Adams was known to smoke. He was old and therefore liable to make mistakes with his discarded cigarettes. He was also too old to warrant much expenditure being wasted on an investigation. It was just another tragic accident.

A detailed examination of his background would have revealed that, prior to his retirement some years earlier, Mr Adams had been a senior civil servant. Furthermore, he worked for the Nuclear Installations

Inspectorate, though this fact would be deemed of little consequence to the Coroner's Inquest. High levels of a prescription sedative were found in his blood samples, but they could not draw any significant conclusion from that, as Mr Adams had a medical history of insomnia. The inquest would subsequently record death by misadventure. Mr Adams was consigned to history, his passing noted by few outside his family.

Except in a Canary Wharf office in London, where a red line was drawn across a folder, which was placed back in a drawer with four others.

5

The Director-General of the Security Service was ushered through into the Prime Minister's office for the Saturday morning briefing. Weekends constituted a normal part of the working week as far as the notoriously industrious Prime Minister was concerned, to the great irritation of his staff. Sir Mark Wellesby was accompanied by his designated replacement for the job, the current Deputy DG, Jeremy Langham. After the preliminary greetings, the Prime Minister waved them to the two empty chairs that had been placed opposite his desk. The PM's Director of Communications, the weasel-faced Giles Devereaux, lurked on a sofa in the shadows, barely acknowledging their presence, his narrow eyes flicking through various briefing sheets he had been working on.

Wellesby eased himself into the chair and sat down carefully, but the pain shot through him, causing him to grimace and close his eyes for a moment. The tumour in his lung had been diagnosed a month earlier, his reward for forty years of dedicated heavy smoking. On enquiring about his prognosis, the consultant oncologist had advised him gravely to make sure that his affairs were in order and that his family were well provided for. He would be lucky to see Christmas.

It was therefore clear to Wellesby that a replacement needed to be found, and quickly. Privately, he despised Langham, who was far too political for his liking, but he had to concede that the young, dynamic deputy was probably the best placed person to take on the job at such short notice. It was just that the man paid too much attention to his appearance, with his sharp suits and slicked back dark hair, whereas Wellesby had always been a bit more shambolic. He valued sharpness of mind above sharpness of cut. It wasn't just their sartorial differences that mattered, it went far deeper than that, but it was a good enough place to start. The corporate values and ethos of the Service had changed, and different times required different men. In the meantime, Wellesby was remaining in his position as long as medically possible in order to ensure a smooth transfer.

The PM glanced up as Wellesby coughed gently into a handkerchief, then started proceedings.

'Thank you for coming, gentlemen. First things first. As you know from my speech on Thursday, I have initiated a new phase of nuclear energy in this country. I have invited tenders from all companies but I think we all know that the preferred bidder will be Gencor Energy.

'As far as I am concerned, nuclear energy is a strategic industry and must remain under British control. I trust you agree with this.

'What concerns me, and this is where you come in, is security. I want a full security review and assessment of the risks to our nuclear industry, as they exist today and as they will exist in ten years' time when the first of the new power stations comes on line. I want to know about the threat from terrorists and the risks from sabotage or accidents. I want to make sure every eventuality is covered. Your report will be given to Gencor to make absolutely sure that everything possible is done to minimise risk. The British public must have complete confidence in nuclear power and I do not want anything to jeopardise that, understood?' They both nodded. 'Good. Right, you can carry on with the rest of the security briefing now please...'

*

As the Prime Minister's meeting got under way, William Terleski sat in the summerhouse of his walled Victorian garden and carefully tamped the tobacco down into his meerschaum pipe. Once he was satisfied with the plug, he located the pipe in its customary position on the left side of his mouth, and lit it. He squirted a stream of smoke expertly out of the opposite corner of his mouth, and settled down into quiet contemplation.

His mind wandered back to many happy times he had spent sitting here with his dearly departed wife, May. He continued the ritual out of the comfort it afforded him, but he was finding life harder and harder without her. He ached to be with her again, but his scientific empiricism made him sceptical about the afterlife. He suspected that her existence had come to a complete and utter end the day he had lowered her body into the ground. Therefore, he had reached an intellectual and theological compromise. If he was to die tomorrow, he wouldn't be unduly concerned, but neither would he go looking for his day of reckoning. Besides, there was something he had to do before that day came.

On her deathbed, she had extracted a solemn promise from him. They had been married for forty eight years and there were no secrets between them. Or so she thought.

One night, whilst he was gently tending to her, she had asked him whether he had kept any secrets from her. The question had caught him by surprise and he was unable to hide the expression on his face. Her first reaction had been that of a woman betrayed. She had cried, demanding to know who the other woman was.

'No, no, my love. There's never been anyone else but you. I promise you that,' he insisted.

'Then what *is* it, William? What have you been hiding from me?'

'I'm not sure I can tell you. It was to do with work.'

'But we have no secrets, William. Look at me. What can I do?'

He thought about it for a while, wrestling with his conscience.

'It was a long time ago…There was a group of us involved, many years ago.' He took a deep breath. 'I just feel so….so ashamed.' His eyes watered, and he avoided eye contact.

'Tell me, William, tell me,' she whispered. Terleski took another deep breath.

'I didn't have much choice, really. It all happened so fast and, before I knew it, I was involved.'

'In what?'

'A special project.'

'Most of your work was special. What was so different about this one?'

Terleski steeled himself, not sure how to continue. 'I became a scientist to help people, to find solutions for the world's problems, to make things better. But the Red Dawn programme was…it was the problem, not the solution....'

He took a deep breath and described Red Dawn and his involvement in it. His wife held his hand as he spoke, her eyes revealing the horror and revulsion she felt. When he had finished he hung his head in shame. She pulled her hand away.

'I couldn't tell you before. I thought you might leave me. I'm so sorry, but I had no choice at the time. We had to do something.'

'You always had a choice, William. You should have resigned, if that's what it took.'

'But what about the house? The mortgage on this place was crippling us, but it was the house you'd always wanted. I didn't want to let you down.'

'But you *have* let me down.'

'Please don't say that. Not now.'

'What you did was despicable. Utterly despicable.' She spat the words out, as though they were distasteful to utter.

'What can I do?' he begged, desperate to restore her faith in him, in the twilight of her life. He should never have told her, but she knew him too well. He couldn't lie to her once she had suspected he was hiding something.

'I want you to write down everything you have told me. Leave nothing out. You owe it to all those people and their families. Then I want you to go to the police, the media, anyone, and tell them what you've done.'

'I can't! It's all covered by the Official Secrets Act. It'll never be allowed.'

'Oh, William, don't be so weak,' she sighed. 'I'm not surprised they want to keep it secret. You have a moral duty to tell the world about this.'

Stung by her reaction, he had promised her solemnly that he would, and try to win back her trust and affection. He had not finished compiling his dossier before she died, but he would honour his promise to her, whatever the personal cost.

Sitting in the summerhouse, Terleski reaffirmed his pledge. Even though the sun was bright, he felt the cold autumn chill creeping up his legs so, still puffing on his pipe, he retreated indoors pulling the French windows shut behind him. The sunshine shone through the Victorian stained glass, illuminating the original tiled floor in all its rich geometric splendour. His wife had loved this house, especially in autumn.

He shuffled through to the library cum office. The casual observer would have been horrified by the chaotic nature of his filing system. Heaps of folders with yellow post-it notes protruding at all angles seemed strategically positioned to frustrate all but the most wary of visitors to the room. Bookcases strained under the weight of reams of scientific papers. But, despite the apparently anarchic nature of the office, Terleski was blessed with an impressive mental filing system. Provided nobody interfered with his papers, he knew exactly where everything was. It helped keep him mentally agile, a growing obsession since he had retired.

A magnificent mahogany desk, with a heavily worn green leather inlay, dominated the middle of the room. A smart new laptop sat, rather incongruously, amongst the clutter on the desk. This was where his dossier, a full account of the Red Dawn programme, was being prepared. His atonement, to satisfy and honour the pledge he had made to his wife.

An apology to all those who had died.

Terleski switched on a small television that nestled amongst the academic detritus on a low coffee table. He enjoyed the repetitive burble of twenty-four-hour news for company. Returning to the desk, he banged the ash out of his pipe and replenished it with fresh tobacco whilst his laptop started up. Glancing across to the television, he scowled as coverage continued on the new nuclear energy strategy. Again, Gencor Energy was tipped as the leading contender to win the government contract. All £35 billion of it.

'Not if I have anything to do with it,' muttered Terleski as a he jabbed at his keyboard.

6

That evening, Hudson arrived outside Paolo's Trattoria in Manchester city centre. He had phoned ahead and booked a table for two. All that remained was for Susannah to show up. He was fairly confident she would. He had no real justification for this optimism other than gut feeling. She *would* turn up.

Hudson had acted on impulse. It was partly because he thought her project would be a good feature for the newspaper, but this paled into insignificance compared to the main reason: She had captivated him.

To make a good impression, he had spent the afternoon researching the Chernobyl disaster. It had proved sobering reading. After the explosion in Reactor Number Four, a vast cloud of radioactive dust had blown across Europe, depositing a toxic trail along the way. Then, when the cloud had reached Britain, still before the Soviet authorities had notified the world about the disaster, it had rained. The rain had washed the cloud of dust to the ground, concentrating it over the highlands of Wales, Cumbria and Scotland. Hudson had grown up in the picturesque Lake District town of Ambleside. Smack bang in the middle of the fallout zone. He had felt a chill pass through him, especially when he discovered that livestock restrictions were still in place on several upland farms. If the livestock was still affected, then what about the people…?

It occurred to him that Ben had also grown up in the area, although they had only met at Manchester University. Hudson began to feel a very personal affinity to Susannah's burgeoning research project.

He also realised that his planned feature would certainly have resonance with his Preston readership, the town being on the periphery of the affected area.

As he mulled this over, he felt a gentle touch on his arm.

'James?'

He turned to greet her, and was greeted by her dazzling smile. He flashed a grin in return, admiring her figure-hugging outfit. Black, understated and elegant, perfectly offsetting her honey-coloured skin and blond hair.

'You look fantastic,' he complimented her, earning another smile. 'Shall we?'

They entered the busy, noisy restaurant and were ushered to a discreet table for two. The aperitifs came, followed by an awkward silence.

'I knew you wouldn't be able to resist,' he started. It was nearly a disastrous start to the evening, but she caught the twinkle in his eye.

'I'm doing it for charity,' she replied, deadpan. Then they both laughed. The ice was broken.

After that, the rest of the evening flowed well, and they established an easy rapport. She was indeed impressed with his interest in her work, and flattered by his proposed newspaper feature.

'Do you really think there's anything in it?' he asked.

'What, Chernobyl?'

'Yes, do you think the fallout's causing the extra thyroid cancer cases?'

'I'm not sure. Something's causing it. That's why I'm interviewing as many patients as I can, to try and put together a picture of their habits, lifestyles, diets. Anything really, to see if there's a common thread.'

'But you think it's quite likely?'

'I really don't know, James. I'm keeping an open mind. It's just one avenue we're exploring. The government has commissioned various reports over the years which clearly state that there wasn't any risk from the fallout, so I could be completely wrong.'

'What if the government has covered up the truth?'

'Typical journalist, looking for a conspiracy. Unfortunately for your wild imagination, I have an uncle who used to work for the National Radiological Board and *he* says that the reports were all accurate. There was no cover up, and he thinks I'm wasting my time. Happy?'

'Sorry, but if there was a cover up, he wouldn't admit to it, would he?' he stated, smiling matter-of-factly.

'Alright, know-it-all, ask him yourself.'

'What?'

'Ask him yourself. He wouldn't mind. I'll give you his number. You could quote him, add balance to your feature. Isn't that what all good journalists should do?'

'But that undermines what you're doing.'

'I'm a scientist, James. I just want the truth. I've no agenda other than finding out why so many young people are developing thyroid cancer. If it's not Chernobyl, but something else, then fine. As long as we find out.'

'Okay, fair enough.'

She handed her phone over for him to copy the number.

'William Terleski?'

'My great grandparents came from Poland, during the war. He's my great uncle, actually. My granddad's brother. He's the last one, so he's kind of my step-granddad,' she replied fondly.

Hudson nodded, as though that made complete sense, and copied the number to his phone. 'Thanks, I'll call him tomorrow.'

The rest of the evening was spent finding out about each other, and they had a remarkable amount in common, despite their wildly differing careers. It was only when the waiters began making discreet noises that they realised how late it was. Hudson paid, leaving a generous tip, and they headed outside.

'Can I give you a lift? My car's around the corner,' he offered.

'Okay,' she replied without hesitation.

It wasn't far to the Fallowfields area of the city, where many students lived. Susannah could tell that he wasn't overly impressed as they pulled into a desolate looking street of dilapidated houses and old cars.

'It's cheap and close to the University,' she explained, justifying it. 'I'm saving up for a deposit on a house…it's that house, there, on the left, thanks.'

Hudson pulled up to the kerb and there was another awkward moment.

'Thanks for a great evening,' she said, turning towards him. Then before he could say anything, she leaned over and kissed him gently on the lips. She pulled back, flashed her beautiful smile again, and climbed nimbly out of the car. Hudson was too taken by surprise to react and only just had time to shout after her that he'd call her. He watched her go safely to the door of her rented flat in the converted Victorian terrace house, waved and pulled away, pleasantly aware of the ache in his groin.

It had indeed been a great evening.

*

That same evening, Howard Roberts was in high spirits. He had also enjoyed a great evening in the company of his friends. Living at home by himself was such a bore, although he considered himself lucky to be able to enjoy retirement in the upmarket Wiltshire town of Chippenham. The only downside was that there wasn't much to do, so he had jumped at the invitation from the chairman of his local bridge club in to come round for a meal and a couple of drinks, followed by a good game.

He had indulged considerably, availing himself of several glasses of a rather sublime premier cru Gevrey-Chambertin 1990, served with roast beef, followed by sticky toffee pudding washed down with an excellent Sauternes. They were very generous friends, who had looked after him well since he had moved into the town. Howard was now the ripe old age of seventy eight, so felt that he had earned the right to indulge himself. He had given his life in unstinting service to the country. Like many who worked in the public sector, he was adamant in his belief that he had sacrificed potentially higher earnings outside the Civil Service in return for a guaranteed final salary pension. The least the country could do was to support him well in old age, which it did, in the form of a hefty final salary pension. He lived in a fine stone-built house in one of the most expensive towns in the country.

Howard enjoyed his hosts' company until the clock struck eleven. He decided that he had better go home before it got too late. Chippenham was very safe, but he held an almost superstitious belief that bad things generally happened after midnight, and he wanted to be safely tucked up in bed well before that. Spurning the offer of their company for the short walk home, he wrapped himself up warm and headed off into the drizzly night. The cool, moist air helped clear the alcoholic fumes from his head, and he took great careful negotiating the slippery cobbles on the little access lane that led to the exclusive cul-de-sac in which his house stood. As he approached the house, he noticed the security lights were on, bathing the Cotswold stone in a soft glow. *Bloody cats.*

His house was reached via a small wicker gate, set in a thick yew hedge that had been trimmed to form an arch over the gate. The path beyond was shrouded by tall shrubs. The effect was to create a short dark tunnel that had to be negotiated before he reached the pool of light cast by his security system. The bright light ahead dazzled him, ruining his night vision as he felt his way gingerly along the path, unable to see where his feet were treading, conscious of the uneven, slippery cobbles. He edged through the darkness, towards the edge of the circle of light that illuminated his front door. Just a couple more steps, then the going would be far easier.

He never made it.

Howard sensed the presence behind him a fraction of a second before the gloved hand clamped firmly over his mouth. At the same time, he felt an irresistible pressure to the back of his legs, as his assailant pushed his knee against him. Howard's legs buckled under him, he fell backwards and the gloved hand forced his head down hard, accelerating it towards the hard cobbles.

Then he was consumed by darkness.

7

Sunday

The housekeeper discovered the body in the morning, when she turned up to prepare his breakfast. The police and paramedics were on the scene within minutes, but it was obvious there was little they could do. The light drizzle had diluted and spread the pool of blood, making it appear worse than it should have been, but that did not disguise the fact that he was dead, the back of his skull shattered on the cobbles.

It was obvious that he had slipped. A combination of alcohol, light rain and darkness had conspired to take Howard Robert's life. It was a tragic end for a fine man. There were no suspicious circumstances and a verdict of accidental death would eventually be recorded by the Coroner. His friends in the bridge circle were mortified, blaming themselves for not accompanying him home.

Had the police been a little more probing with their enquiries, it may have been discovered that certain documentation was missing from the house. The housekeeper harboured a suspicion that some files were missing from one of the book cases in the office, but couldn't be absolutely sure as she rarely went inside that room. So, she didn't mention it. The hard drive of the computer in the office had also been wiped clean, though this was never detected as the whole system was password protected and the executors and beneficiaries of the estate did not see the need to waste any precious inheritance on something as frivolous as hiring an expensive IT expert to access it and check whether there was anything important on it. They just threw it away.

*

That morning, back at the Canary Wharf headquarters of Gencor Energy, Peter Kroll took a call. He listened to the terse message, thanked the caller and hung up. He sat thoughtfully in his chair for a few moments, then extracted a thin folder from his desk. Opening it up, he studied the photograph of the elderly man, snorted with satisfaction, drew a red line over it and placed it back into the folder. He closed the folder and placed it on his desk. Then he extracted four more similar folders from the desk and placed them on top. Collecting them together, he left his office to visit Charles Millburn in his corner suite.

The vast majority of the enormous office, which covered the entire top floor of the tower, was open plan. Several hundred employees, mainly working in finance and administration, normally filled the room, sitting in cubicles and clusters of desks. Signs hung down from the ceiling denoting the various functions of the employees beneath, but as this was a Sunday, the office was quite empty. Senior management were allocated enclosed glass-walled offices on the external walls. With rank came windows and naturally Sir Charles Millburn, as Chairman, enjoyed a corner suite, giving him windows on two sides of his huge office. As Director of Security, Peter Kroll could have obtained a corner suite as well, but he preferred a lower profile, though few members of staff were in any doubt over his real position within the firm.

One of the remaining three corner suites was occupied by Mike Weston, the Chief Executive. Whilst Millburn was Chairman of the

Board, setting the strategy and direction of the firm, Weston was the company's most senior manager, tasked with turning Millburn's vision into reality. He had been with the company for years, since being taken on as a graduate management trainee whilst it had still been in public ownership. He had enjoyed a slow but steady rise up the corporate ladder. When Millburn had become a director after privatisation, he had been impressed with the capable young manager who seemed to outperform his colleagues on almost every task he was given. Millburn liked competence, attaching nearly as much value to it as loyalty. Having spotted potential for the latter quality as well, he ensured that Weston's slow but steady rise became fast and meteoric.

Weston received a handsome salary, but his real wealth derived from the same share option scheme which benefited Millburn. He was a paper millionaire, a happy circumstance which did no harm for his feelings of loyalty towards Millburn. But there was one area Weston was not happy about, and that was Kroll.

Under normal circumstances, as Chairman and Chief Executive respectively, Millburn and Weston should have been the crucial partnership at the centre of the firm, the crux of all decision-making. Weston was indeed powerful and generally had Millburn's ear, but he was acutely aware of his inferior status relative to Peter Kroll. And this rankled. Matters were not helped by the obvious contempt in which he was held by Kroll, who barely made any effort to acknowledge Weston's existence, let alone presence. Kroll's position as Director of Security should have made him junior to Weston, but it was perfectly obvious that the opposite was the case. To make the situation even more humiliating,

Millburn refused to even countenance a discussion with Weston about Kroll. It was a subject that was never to be broached.

Weston both feared and despised Kroll. The man had a brooding malevolence about his pinched, humourless features. Kroll's cold, calculating eyes would stare right through Weston as though he didn't exist.

It wasn't Weston's fault that he had a friendly face, but he always felt that this made him appear weak in Kroll's eyes. He was a large, jovial man who physically dwarfed the wiry frame of Kroll, yet Kroll somehow managed to physically intimidate him, and Weston resented that. He longed for the day that Kroll moved on.

Through the plate glass door and walls of his office, Weston had a commanding view of the huge office. In particular, he had clear line of sight to Kroll's office on the opposite side wall. He could see Kroll's comings and goings quite easily, and he was bothered by his recent observations.

He was convinced that something serious was afoot. Over the past few days, Kroll had spent an inordinate amount of time in Millburn's office, and Weston had also noted the two thugs Trevor and Julian in the office on Friday. Furthermore, Millburn had been incommunicado for much of Friday, refusing to take any calls and only receiving Kroll in his office. Weston had worked through the weekend, and the same had continued: Millburn refused to see him and had spent much of Saturday holed up in his office.

It did not make any sense. Gencor shares were trading at a 50% premium to their closing price the day before the Prime Minister's announcement, and the company was virtually assured of winning the contracts to develop the new nuclear generating programme. There was no other serious contender. So what was wrong with Millburn and Kroll?

On this particular morning, Weston had not arrived in the office until ten. It was a Sunday, after all, and Weston wished to take advantage of a quiet and largely empty office to continue working on the annual reports. He had been astonished to find Millburn and Kroll already in. It was unheard of. Apart from them, the office was mainly deserted except for some of the IT people installing upgrades and servicing the equipment on which all modern offices depend for their survival. Weston had sat down to continue work on the end of year report, due for the forthcoming AGM. But he couldn't concentrate. He was really bothered by Millburn and Kroll, and he resolved to find out what was going on. But he would have to wait for a suitable moment.

As he watched, he saw Kroll stand up inside his office and pick something up from his desk. Kroll then hurried from his office into Millburn's, entering with barely a knock, which was another thing that Weston was unable to do. Folders. He was carrying folders.

Weston maintained a discreet eye on Millburn's office. Kroll was in there for some time, before re-emerging with the folders. Weston watched him return to his office and place the folders back into his desk, which he then presumably locked.

Whatever was going on was contained in those folders. He had to find out what was in them. As Weston looked out through the plate glass walls, the germ of a plan began to form in his mind.

*

In Thames House, Sir Mark Wellesby was in a considerable dilemma. The file that was open on his desk had occupied him all day, since it had arrived from the Central Registry that morning. Wellesby had hoped never to see it again. An electronic version of the file did not exist and, as far as he knew, the pink folder in front of him was the only copy.

He had first learnt of its existence when he had assumed the mantle of Director General. His predecessor had thought it wise that he be informed, just in case. And now, in the twilight of his life, it had come back to haunt him.

He knew that he should tell Jeremy Langham, his designated successor, and the Prime Minister. But the truth was, he didn't want to. He didn't want the awkward questions, the inevitable volcanic rage from the PM, and he did not trust Langham.

There was a name on the front page of the file. The man who had warned them all those years previously. The man whose warning had been quietly brushed under the carpet. In the national interest.

Before he did anything else, Wellesby decided he would contact him, assuming he had not died yet; he must be quite an old man by now.

*

William Terleski was busy typing at his desk when the call came through. He scowled and tried to ignore the phone in order to concentrate and finish the sentence he was working on. But it was no good, he lost his train of thought and snatched up the handset.

'Yes?' he barked, irritated by the unwarranted intrusion.

'Er, Doctor Terleski?'

'Yes. Who is this?'

'My name's Hudson, James Hudson. I'm a friend of Susannah's.'

'Oh. I've never heard of you.'

'We only met recently.'

'I see.' Hudson could hear the disapproval in the old man's voice. 'What can I do for you, James?'

'I'm a journalist for the Preston Advertiser. I'm working on a feature about Susannah's research into the possible link between the Chernobyl fallout and the increased incidence of thyroid cancer in Cumbria…'

'There is no link,' Terleski interrupted. 'I don't know how many times I've told her that.'

'She told me you'd say that.'

'Oh, she did, did she? I'll have to have a word with her,' Terleski replied gruffly, but Hudson could hear the old man mellowing. It was clear that he doted on Susannah.

'I was wondering if I could quote you on that? I understand that you worked for the National Radiological Protection Board?'

'I was in charge of it.'

'Oh, she didn't tell me that bit. Sorry,' Hudson replied, embarrassed. He heard Terleski chuckle softly into the phone. It was obviously Susannah's sense of humour to set him up, but Hudson was thick-skinned. He continued. 'I have to ask this, and please don't take it personally, but is there any reason why the government would seek to play down any link?'

'Plenty of reasons. But they didn't. There is no link.'

'Well, er, hypothetically speaking, what reasons?'

'You're not quoting me on those. You'll have to come up with your own ideas.'

'Um, well, let's just say they wanted people to think that nuclear power was safe, it would be in their interests to play down the effects of the Chernobyl fallout. Not just in Britain, but all governments across Europe would have the same motivation, wouldn't they?'

'Possibly. But it's not true as far as I know.'

'That's good enough for me, Doctor Terleski. Thank you very much for your time. Susannah sends her love, by the way.'

'Send her mine, James. Good luck with the article.'

Terleski put the phone down and stared at it. He *had* been telling the truth to Hudson. The government was not playing down the link between Chernobyl and the increased number of cancer cases. The truth was far worse than that. He sat forward and put his head in his hands. He had to tell the world about Red Dawn.

Determined to do it, he returned to his keyboard and had just got back into the flow when the phone rang again.

'Bloody *hell!*' he cursed softly. As before, he hoped whoever it was would go away. But, when the ringing persisted, he reached over and flicked on the answer machine.

'William? William are you there?' A voice from the past, which stopped Terleski dead in his tracks. A voice he had not heard for a very long time. He felt the hairs rise on his neck.

'William, if you're there, pick up the phone. It's urgent. I have to talk to you.'

Terleski swallowed involuntarily and picked up the phone. His mouth was incredibly dry as he spoke into the handset.

'Yes?'

8

Bernard Motson, or *Doctor* Bernard Motson, as he insisted on, was enjoying his short weekend break in the Snowdonia National Park in North Wales. Disdainful of 'day trippers' as he rather sniffily referred to them, he was staying in a remote farmhouse bed and breakfast, well away from the tourists of Betws-y-Coed. Motson took his walking most seriously, and had invested considerable sums in acquiring the necessary accoutrements and apparel. He wore the instantly recognisable uniform of the dedicated rambler, from the plastic map case dangling around his neck to the latest GPS tracking compass clipped to the front of the left shoulder strap of his rucksack. The look was completed by the peculiar trousers that such people choose to wear. Motson had always been pompous and self-righteous, and being a member of the militant walking community only served to inflate this sense of importance and moral superiority. Woe would betide any errant landowner who failed to maintain his styles and footpaths, if Motson had anything to do with it.

His officiousness had been keenly honed whilst working for the UK Atomic Energy Authority. He was arrogant, vain and fully expected to be held in awe by his junior staff. As far as he was concerned, his professional rank and qualifications should command automatic respect and deference. Over the years he had also acquired membership of various professional academic bodies, further extending the number of letters after his name. If importance was directly proportional to the number of letters after a name, then he was an exceedingly important man. Such importance was irrelevant if nobody knew about it, so he had commissioned personalised stationary, at taxpayers' expense, to illustrate the full panoply of his erudition in all its glory. He was known to be a prolific writer of letters.

In the bed and breakfast that morning, Motson had surfaced at his customary hour of six o'clock, making his presence felt by clunking around his bedroom and bathroom. Although it was a Sunday, he considered it a perfectly reasonable hour to rise, so couldn't understand why others didn't, particularly the young couple in the adjoining room who had thumped loudly on the wall and yelled at him to shut up. Serves them right for staying late in the pub, he thought. A life-long celibate, he had also been incensed by the other sounds emanating from their room until the early hours of the morning.

Whilst waiting for the distinctly inconvenienced landlady to prepare breakfast for seven o'clock, Motson planned his walk for the day. A fully confirmed misanthrope, he preferred routes on which he was likely to encounter a minimal number of other walkers. There were simply too many 'day trippers' on the popular walks, thoroughly spoiling them. This meant that he generally had to opt for the more remote walks, well away from other people. Today, as the cloud cover wasn't too low, he was planning an ascent of Snowdon itself. He was going to make his ascent via the old miner's trail that led up past a series of picturesque lakes. Unfortunately, being a popular route, he would have to put up with other people spoiling his view and getting in the way on the ascent. However, from the summit he was going to make a circular descent via the arête of the Crib Goch ridge. It was a dangerous route, with sheer drops falling hundreds of feet on either side and, as such, was only recommended for experienced walkers and climbers. That suited him perfectly, as it meant that there would not be many other people to ruin it. He liked to feel alone, in personal ownership of the landscape that gave him so much pleasure. From the small car park at the bottom of the miner's trail, it was a potentially gruelling eight miles, so an early start was essential, especially with the shorter days at this time of year. A hearty English breakfast was called for, and he had asked the landlady for the 'full works'.

To his surprise, he was joined at breakfast by two burly outdoor types. Usually, because he was generally up so early, he was able to enjoy breakfast by himself. Fortunately they did not subject him to inane small talk, restricting themselves to a grunted acknowledgement of his presence. That suited him fine. Nothing worse than people who want to chat at breakfast time. He simply could not abide it. After his meal, he gave his landlady a brief précis of his plans for the day and set off in his bottom-of-the-range three series BMW, badge removed in a vain attempt to disguise the fact that it was bottom-of-the-range.

The two burly men, who apparently had also planned a full day of walking, signed out and left soon afterwards. The names and addresses were false, but the landlady would never know this, and would never be asked about them.

It was late evening when the landlady began to become concerned. Dr Motson was an experienced walker, but one mustn't forget that he was in his seventies. It was completely dark outside and a steady rain had begun falling. He really shouldn't be out in this weather.

Her husband agreed and set off to the local pub to see if there had been any sight of him. There hadn't. There was no doubt about this, as the publican said he was glad the miserable old sod hadn't been back, which wasn't terribly helpful in the circumstances.

After waiting another half an hour, the landlady called the Llanberis Mountain Rescue Team. Fortunately, she was able to provide them with a route from the information supplied by Dr Motson before he set off. The landlord accompanied the team, who were all volunteers. They would follow Motson's route to begin with, and call up the Sea King helicopter, if it was required, later on.

They found Dr Motson's BMW in the car park at Pen-y-Pass, the start of his route up the mountain. This did not bode well, as it indicated he was still somewhere on the mountain. They followed the relatively easy path up to the summit, but there was no sign of him. The next part of the route would take them along the treacherous ridge of Crib Goch, a very unpalatable prospect in the dark. They were also aware that Dr Motson would have spent several hours on the mountainside by now, adding to their concerns. To make matters worse, the weather was foul, chilling them to bone, and it was obvious that hypothermia would pose a considerable risk for anyone stranded on the mountain. But it was too dangerous to continue on foot in the conditions. They had no choice but to call in the Sea King.

It was definitely a body. The Sea King rescue helicopter pilot was sure of it. Having arrived in the early hours of the morning, their initial search had been fruitless, the heat seeking equipment failing to detect any sign of life on the mountain. It was only when they resumed the search in daylight that the bright red jacket could be seen contrasted against the grey rockfall.

The pilot positioned the helicopter so that his winch man lowered the third crewman. On the ground, he realised that there was nothing they could do to help. The man had fallen several hundred feet down the steep slope, sustaining dreadful injuries as he bounced off jagged rocks on the way. His skull was shattered, along with all of his limbs, which were contorted at obscene angles. He was little more than a battered pulp.

A wallet found in the clothing confirmed the identity of Dr Bernard Motson. The body was recovered and the Coroner was informed, whilst police attempted to trace relatives to carry out a formal identification. It would be an open and shut case. A tragic case of death by misadventure. The old man had lost his bearings in the dark and slipped while negotiating the tricky route around the mountain, presumably after not allowing enough daylight hours to complete the route. The unforgiving terrain had claimed the life of another naïve and inadequately prepared walker, who should not have been out so late and in such treacherous conditions.

No thought was given to the two men who had quietly checked out of the bed and breakfast the morning before. Only one man in London was interested to hear about their walking trip. He pulled a folder from his desk and drew another red line across a photo. There were now only two unmarked pictures left in the drawer.

9

Monday

Sir Mark Wellesby was granted an audience with the Prime Minister early on Monday morning. He had spent most of Sunday agonising about his decision, but in the end he realised that the Prime Minister had to be informed.

That still did not make the task any easier, nor the fact that Jeremy Langham would be accompanying him. To save repeating himself, he would inform Langham at the same meeting. Langham was aware that something important was afoot and was plainly irritated that Wellesby was not taking him into his confidence beforehand. *Tough*, thought Wellesby. He was still boss for the time being.

They were both ushered through to the PM's office, where a disinterested Giles Devereaux was again lounging on a sofa in a corner. The two men were inseparable, thought Wellesby. It irritated him to think that an unelected PR man could rise to such a powerful position in the country, unaccountable and free from scrutiny.

'You wanted to see me, Mark?' the PM enquired as soon as they were seated.

'Yes, sir. There's something you should know.' Something in his tone caused Devereaux to stop what he was doing and look up.

'Yes, what is it?' asked the PM.

'It's about Gencor Energy. Or, more specifically, Sir Charles Millburn. It's a very serious matter, sir.'

Wellesby opened up the file he had brought along with him and spoke for a few minutes. When he had finished, there was complete silence in the room. Even Devereaux was at a loss for words, and Langham stared at him with incredulity.

'Why didn't you inform me before?' asked Langham, rather inappropriately.

'Because it wasn't your place to know,' snapped Wellesby, aggravating the pain in his chest. The Prime Minister sat back in his chair, the colour drained from his face, as he absorbed the full implications of Wellesby's report.

'Sir, I thought that in light of your statement to the House last Thursday, you should be informed.'

The Prime Minister nodded, his mind racing through the ramifications of what he had just learnt.

'How many people know about this?' he asked finally.

'I'm not entirely sure, sir, but very few.'

'What do you suggest we do?' he asked. There was silence from Wellesby, and the PM glanced at the other two men.

'I suggest we do nothing, sir,' stated Devereaux. 'If this ever got out, it would kill off the nuclear programme for good. As a country, we can't afford that to happen.'

'I agree, sir,' piped up Langham. 'This risks the whole nuclear building programme.'

'Mark?'

'I'm not sure, sir. We have to ask ourselves if it could happen again. That's I why I brought it to your attention.'

'Well, I think that's a risk we have to take. This is a flagship policy and it is vital to our strategic interests. Absolutely vital. We cannot allow anything to stop it. The energy crisis will only get worse, and we have to act now. The future of our economy and our country depends on the nuclear programme.'

'Yes, sir. I understand.'

'I want all trace of this Red Dawn programme to be destroyed, including that file of yours. I never want to hear it mentioned ever again.'

'Yes sir.' It was what Wellesby expected, but at least his own conscience was clear. He gathered his papers and left the room, with Langham trailing behind, fuming at not being given prior notice.

Once they had gone, Devereaux stood up from the sofa and sidled up to the PM's desk.

'What did you think about that?' he asked him.

'Not good, Giles. Not good. We cannot have knowledge of Red Dawn ever reaching the public. It would be a disaster.'

'I agree. Would you like me to get in touch with Charles Millburn?'

'Yes, I think that would be a good idea, don't you? Let's just make sure we're all singing from the same hymn sheet on this.'

As Wellesby left Downing Street for the short journey back to Thames House, he was a very concerned man. He had a finely tuned moral antenna and, whilst he could see the logic in the decision made by the Prime Minister, he noted the complete absence of compassion. The PM's uppermost concerns were his policies and position, not the general well-being of the nation, despite whatever lip service he paid to it. Unfortunately, Wellesby's options were limited and he was tired, nearly too tired for a fight.

Langham sat next to him in the official car, fuming. Good, let him fume, thought Wellesby. He would have his moment in the sun soon. In the meantime, he would show him who was still the boss. As the car approached the entrance for Thames House, Wellesby suddenly had a thought. Perhaps there was a way forward, after all. He was just congratulating himself with it when the pain started. It came so fast he gasped, and even the usually callous Langham was minded to turn to him with a look of concern. Normally, the pain passed after a few moments, but this time it didn't go away and he felt himself struggling for breath. He doubled up in agony, unable to breathe, his vision clouding. Somewhere in the distance he heard Langham shouting at the driver to head for a hospital and felt the powerful car respond urgently. He struggled to hang on to consciousness, feeling Langham's hand on his back in a reassuring gesture, the irony not lost him, but he was unable to resist the blackness which began to envelop him. With his last moments of consciousness he heard the driver shouting that they were two minutes away from the nearest hospital. He thought of his wife and children.

Then it went dark.

10

Hudson waited patiently whilst Donald Winston read through his four-page feature spread. The instrument of torture which occasionally passed as the editor's spare chair was working its usual charm on the blood supply to his legs, but Hudson was too excited about his feature to notice.

Normally, he detested Monday mornings, but this week he had woken up feeling energised. It was the Susannah effect. His work and personal life had been transformed by her, and he had strolled confidently into the office before nine o'clock for the first time in weeks. The sour-faced receptionist had enquired as to his mental health on seeing him arrive so early, but Hudson had ignored her and instead requested an audience with his editor to discuss his feature, which he had spent all day Sunday working on.

It was good. He knew it was good; Donald Winston's silence was testament to that.

'Now this, James, is more like it,' he announced, almost with surprise, when he had finished. 'See what you're capable of when you put your mind to it?'

'Yes, Don. Thanks.'

'It ticks all the boxes,' he nodded approvingly. 'Local interest, health issues, raising legitimate concerns for our readers…plus you've got balance to it. You did well to get an interview with this Dr Terleski. The only thing missing is a patient's perspective.'

'I'll ask my friend Ben if I can feature him. He's suffering from thyroid cancer and grew up around here.'

'Good idea. He's the human victim in all this. Hopefully others will get in touch and we can spin this story out over a couple of weeks. Good work, James.'

'What about the conspiracy angle? Should we push that?'

'Let the readers think what they want to. You don't have to be explicit. The fact that you found a government nuclear scientist to deny any cover up will only make some people be even more convinced that there is a conspiracy.'

He was right: As happened with the death of the Princess of Wales, the more that the authorities denied anything untoward had happened, the more the conspiracy theorists became convinced that something *had* happened.

Privately, Hudson was a bit disappointed by Terleski's almost casual dismissal of Susannah's hunch that the Chernobyl fallout was causing the higher incidence of cancer in the area. It would have been the perfect story. Then again, Susannah may well be proven right in her research findings.

Hudson returned to his desk on a high note. He felt revitalised and, dare he say it, was actually enjoying his job for the first time in months. To enhance his mood further, he was meeting up with Susannah again that evening. He clicked his knuckles and attacked his keyboard with renewed vigour, a broad grin on his face. His colleagues wondered what on earth had got into him.

*

Something had got into William Terleski that Monday morning. It was fear. Pure, abject, all-consuming fear. Since the mysterious phone call the previous day, he had not been able to concentrate on anything else. He had spent the rest of the Sunday in a panic, unable to function properly, unable to eat or sleep. The caller had been a man from the distant past, a voice he had not heard in years. And what he had told Terleski had shaken him to the core. So much so that Terleski had become a man possessed. He had pleaded with the caller not to proceed with his course of action, but the man had been insistent that the matter had already been decided. He was informing Terleski merely out of courtesy.

Finally, after several hours of worry, Terleski had decided on a course of action. On Sunday evening he had rooted out the list of names from amongst the documents he had been using to write up his dossier. Most of the list had a neat letter 'D' annotated next to the name. Over the years, Terleski had kept in discreet contact with some of them, but each year the number of 'D's increased, as time reaped its grim harvest. There were only four names left on the list. It had been one of the reasons he had confessed his crimes to his beloved May; it was obvious that the secret of Red Dawn would soon be taken to the grave.

Terleski began contacting the remaining names on the list, but that was when his fear really set in. At first, he was informed by a very subdued housing warden that Geoffrey Adams had died in a fire at his bungalow the previous Thursday evening. It had been a tragic accident. He must have fallen asleep with a lit cigarette somewhere in the house, and apparently the smoke detectors had all failed. All calls to Mr Adams were now going through to the warden, who had the unenviable task of informing the callers what had happened. Terleski regretted the death, very much. But these things happen.

He thought nothing more of it until he tried to contact Howard Roberts in Chippenham. This time, a tearful housekeeper informed him about Howard's fall on the cobbled path. That had happened sometime on Saturday night, but she had not found the body until the following morning. She sobbed down the phone as she described what she had come across on Sunday morning. Terleski felt his blood begin to run cold. He gave his condolences to the housekeeper and hung up quickly. His heart was pounding as he called the next name on the list. Bernie Motson had always been a bit odd and Terleski had had little to do with him over the years, but now he was fervently hoping to speak to him. But Motson's phone rang and rang. Perhaps there was nobody in. The automatic answer phone kicked in and Terleski left a brief message before he hung up. He studied the next name on the list. Thomas Hancock.

He was just about to pick up the phone again, when it rang, surprising him.

'Hello?'

'Is that William Terleski?' It was an unfamiliar and elderly female voice.

'Yes.'

'You just phoned and left a message. I'm a cousin of Bernard's.'

Terleski felt his chest tighten. He shut his eyes, dreading what was coming. But he already knew.

'Were you a friend of Bernard's?' she asked him quietly, in a low tremulous voice.

'We used to work together,' he replied woodenly.

'I'm very sorry, but I'm afraid I have some bad news...'

Terleski had felt numb. Three surviving members of Red Dawn dead in as many days. It was simply too much of a coincidence. There was only one name left on the list.

Mechanically, he had dialled Thomas Hancock's number. The phone had rang several times and Terleski felt the tears well up in his eyes. *Please*, answer the phone, *please*. But Hancock had not answered. Terleski had tried throughout the night, but there was nobody there. He had never felt so afraid or alone in his entire life. Finally, he fell into a fitful sleep in the armchair in his study.

In the dawn which broke that Monday morning, he woke up with a start, half expecting to find someone in the office next to him. After he had collected himself, he decided to give Hancock another try. The phone rang for several times, as it had before, and he was on the verge of regretfully hanging up when the phone was picked up.

'Hello?' Terleski asked the silent ether. 'Hello? Is anyone there?'

There were some scrabbling noises and a crash. Broken glass. Terleski stiffened. Then a voice muttering. 'Shit, dropped the fucking glass...who's that?'

Hancock was slurring his words.

'Thomas?'

'Yep?' came back the bleary reply.

'Thomas, its William. William Terleski.'

'What? Willy? Willy old boy, how the hell are you?' he slurred.

'Thomas, are you alright?'

'Never been better,' he paused to belch. 'Never! What about you, old son?'

'Thomas, you have to pay attention. Listen to me.'

'What's the matter, old boy?' Hancock sounded very drunk, which he was.

'Listen, Thomas. Please. I think we're in danger. You've got to get out of the house.'

'What's in the house?' he asked blearily, unable to comprehend.

'Just get out of the house, now, and meet me at the fishing lake.'

'Fishing? It's six o'clock in the morning, are you insane?' grumbled Hancock, clearly suffering the effects from the entire bottle of scotch he had waded through the night before.

'Just do it. I'll see you there soon.'

Hancock had collapsed back into the sofa where he had lain comatose all night, oblivious to Terleski's persistent calls. It was only when the alcohol had dissipated enough to allow his senses to register the ringing that he had woken up. After finishing the call with Terleski, he tried to replace the handset, but missed, and it fell to the floor. He could feel himself drifting back to sleep, but there was something about the urgency of Terleski's message that unnerved him enough to stand up, relieve himself in the downstairs toilet, then stagger to the front door and head off towards the public fishing lake that was only a short walk from his 1930s semi-detached house.

Terleski's home was in Henley-in-Arden, whilst Hancock lived just south of Stratford-upon-Avon. Both locations were handy for the M40, as most of their work had been based in or around Oxford. Hancock's home was only a twenty minute drive away. Terleski drove down the A3400, through the centre of Stratford, and out again to the small fishing lake which they had once frequented regularly when they used to work together.

The sun was still low as he pulled into the small car park. A light mist hung over the dewy fields, and the cool air was perfectly still. There was nobody around, and a moment of panic set in when Terleski could see no sign of Hancock, but then he caught sight of a dishevelled figure sitting under the drooping canopy of a willow tree, on a log which had been crudely fashioned into a seat.

Hancock turned to face him on hearing his approach.

'Willy! Good to see you!' he announced, offering a shaky hand. It was obvious he was in a bad way, and this was further confirmed when he took a long swig from a silver hip flask. Hancock attempted to stand up, but swayed dramatically and was forced to sit down quickly, with a bemused expression on his bloated, alcohol-ravaged face. It was a sad decline and his condition contrasted sharply with how Terleski had remembered the once brilliant and handsome scientist. He cut straight to the chase.

'Thomas, you have to listen. I think we're in danger. Geoffrey, Howard and Bernard are all dead. They died over the last three days. Apart from Millburn, we're the only two left, do you understand?'

This finally seemed to register through the alcoholic fumes.

'Dead?' he mumbled.

'Yes, Geoffrey in a house fire, Howard slipped on his pathway and Bernard fell down a mountainside. It's too much of a coincidence. I don't think they were accidents. Someone's got to be behind it.'

Hancock stared into the middle distance and Terleski thought he had lost him again. But then, to his great surprise, Hancock's shoulders began shaking, then tears started rolling down his cheeks.

'Thomas?' asked Terleski, frowning. 'Are you alright?'

'It's all my fault,' he blubbed, holding his head in his hands.

'What are you talking about?' No answer, further sobbing.

'Thomas?' Terleski persisted, worried. There was always something about grown men crying that made him feel very uncomfortable.

'I just needed the money, okay?' Hancock wailed.

'Sorry, I don't understand. What are talking about?'

There was another long silence.

'I made some bad investments; I'm in a lot of debt. My pension just about pays the interest on my loans. I'm probably going to lose my house, everything I've ever worked for.' This prompted another bout of tears. It would have been acutely embarrassing had it not been for Terleski's awful sense of foreboding.

'Why?' asked Terleski, a hard edge to his voice.

'Because I'm a stupid idiot. I started day-trading at home, buying penny shares and over-the-counter securities. I did okay to begin with, and then I heard of a new issue. It sounded great. Some brokerage in Liechtenstein put me on to it, offered me a discount on the shares if I bought through them. They told me that the company was about to win a patent on some new medical discovery; they just needed to raise investment capital to turn it into reality, which is why they were issuing the shares. The patent would guarantee the return; the shares would easily double or triple in value as soon as trading began on the alternative investment market. I took out loans against the house and used up my credit cards. I put two hundred and fifty grand into it.'

'Two and hundred and fifty?' Terleski blinked. 'What happened?'

'The company existed alright, the shares were real. But there was no patent. There was nothing. The registered office was just a post office box in Geneva. The company existed only on paper, that was it, nothing else. My money bought genuine shares, but they're worthless. I simply gave my money to a bunch of crooks. The brokerage in Liechtenstein doesn't exist. It's just a very good website, nothing more.'

'Did you call the police?'

'Of course I did, but there was nothing they could do. Apparently I'm a victim of some sort of sting run from Buenos Aires. A few other stupid idiots like me have been done as well. Whoever's behind it has just closed shop and buggered off. My money's gone.'

'What's this got to do with Red Dawn?'

Hancock took a very deep sigh, followed by another large gulp of the scotch. His nose was dripping with a mixture of tears and mucus.

'It was all I could think of. I had to think of the kids. I couldn't leave them with nothing.'

'What have you done?' Terleski asked sharply, already dreading the answer.

'Blackmailed Charles Millburn.'

'W*hat?*'

'He's a rich bastard and I needed the money.'

Terleski shut his eyes and massaged his temples. It was just too awful. He shook his head. 'Have you any idea what you've done? He's one of the richest, most powerful businessmen in the country,' he quietly pointed out.

'Precisely!' Hancock made a point with his finger, which shook with alcoholic tremors. '*Précisement!* That's why I did it. He's got too much too lose, especially now that Gencor's going to win all those contracts.'

'I can't believe this... I simply can't believe it. How could you be so *stupid?*' he shouted at Hancock, who recoiled.

'I'm desperate, William.'

Terleski continued massaging his forehead, thinking hard. It all made sense now. Millburn was a ruthless bastard, always had been. That's why he had initiated the Red Dawn programme in 1986. It was born of his innate capacity to achieve whatever he set his mind on, at all cost. And now Hancock had threatened him with personal catastrophe.

It had to be Millburn. He was the only common link between Geoffrey, Howard and Bernard. He probably had no idea who was blackmailing him, but knew they must have been part of the Red Dawn programme, so was tidying up all the loose ends, eliminating the risk of it ever being a threat to him again. All because of Hancock's stupidity.

Terleski's thoughts turned to the dossier he was writing: It suddenly occurred to him that it might be the only thing that could save him now. Hancock had provoked Millburn's lethal rage and the clock was already ticking. Terleski knew that he had to get home, retrieve the dossier and finish it as fast as he could, then publicise it. It was his only chance.

Hancock took another swig from his seemingly inexhaustible supply of scotch. His eyes had glazed over with the look of a man who had completely given up on life.

Terleski was both frightened and seething with anger. Hancock's greed and stupidity had cost the lives of three of their colleagues and they must be next on the list.

'We need to hide,' he stated firmly. There was no response. 'Thomas?'

'Hmmm?'

'We need to get away before they come for us. I know someone who could help us.'

But Hancock was too far gone to care anymore. In his own mind, his life was already over. All he could think about was what he had lost.

'Are you coming?' asked Terleski, standing up.

'No, you go. I'll stay here if that's alright with you...' he was slurring heavily by now, his voice drifting away.

'Thomas, I need to go. What are you going to do?'

'Haven't the foggiest, old chap. I think I'll stay here and admire the view.' The slur was heavy by now.

'Fine. Take care of yourself.'

Terleski stood up, wincing at the arthritic twinge in his hip. He hobbled back to the path when Hancock called after him.

'William?'

'Yes?'

'Good luck.'

Terleski said nothing, turned and hurried away as fast as his old body would take him.

Hancock settled back into his chair, the alcohol numbing his senses against the biting cold that crept off the water and up his legs. He was sinking into a pleasurable stupor, time was slowing down and things didn't seem quite so bad after all. He raised the hip flask to his lips and offered a generous toast to a curious duck that was paddling along the muddy bank in front of his feet, looking for shallower water in which to forage. It was out of luck. There was a good depth of water in this part of the shore, at least six feet, where some of the larger fish could be found. He looked out across the water to see how the other anglers were faring, but there were none out there. It was still too early for most. Hancock shrugged his shoulders. Fishing was not a sport for the impatient. He shut his eyes, enjoying the floating sensation induced by the scotch coursing through his veins. After a short while, he opened his eyes again, blinking as they adjusted to the light of the low autumn sun.

Part of him was not surprised that the two men were stood to either side of him. Their approach had been silent, professional. He twisted in his chair to look up. Cold, callous eyes gazed back from a rugged, outdoor face. They were eyes that harboured no mercy or compassion. They were the implacable eyes of a killer.

'Is it because of Red Dawn?' Hancock asked with the weary resignation of a condemned man accepting his fate. At least the alcohol numbed the fear to some extent.

'Yes.' The voice was deep and gravely, the sort that could easily silence a room.

'Will it hurt?' he asked with a shaky voice, slowly awakening to his predicament.

'Not if you cooperate,' he replied. 'Have a drink,' he ordered, unscrewing the top of a fresh bottle of scotch which they had brought along specifically for the purpose.

*

Terleski drove back in a blur. He could remember nothing of the journey. Even worse, he was unsure of what would greet him when he arrived. The driveway was clear and the internal lights were on, as he had left them. With a mounting sense of impending doom, he inserted the key into the front door. It was still locked, thank god. He called out, to see if he could elicit any response and to reassure himself with his own voice. Slowly, he entered the house and advanced down his hallway, clutching his walking stick. He paused to listen out, though any advantage of surprise on his behalf had already been lost. His diminished hearing could pick up nothing but the pounding of his heart. Inching his way forward, he approached his study, the second door on the left. The door was slightly ajar, but he couldn't remember if that was how he had left it. He listened, but there was nothing. Steeling himself and drawing his stick, he gently pushed the door open. As his arc of vision into the room increased, he could feel himself shaking with fear. His mouth was bone dry and his bowels felt loose.

The door swung open, only stopping as the leading bottom edge ran over the corner of the rug and got stuck, as it always did. He checked the crack between the jamb and the door, but there was no one behind it.

The room was empty.

Venturing inside, it still looked like his own carefully orchestrated mess, rather than one created by someone ransacking the place. Everything seemed to be where he had left it. Still shaking, he fumbled for his pouch of tobacco and fuelled his pipe, spilling half the contents over the rug. He could sense the early warning signs of palpitations, so he tried to control his breathing, forcing himself to calm down. Perched on the edge of the dusty chaise longue, he started to recover. Having lit the pipe, the sweet smoke quickly began to have its desired effect and he was able to collect his thoughts once again.

Everything he had on Red Dawn was contained in this room. If they came for him, they would be able to bury the top secret programme forever. With the benefit of hindsight, he could see that he had taken a terrible risk, but the stakes were so much higher now. Now the priority was to finish the dossier and expose the scandal. But first, there was one last avenue he could explore: He needed to speak to someone, someone who could help him.

He dialled the special number he had been given by the man who had called him the day before, but it just rang out. With a mounting sense of betrayal and abandonment, Terleski felt the all-consuming fear enveloping him. He was alone. Utterly alone.

He had no way of knowing that the man he was trying to reach was lying in a London hospital, barely conscious and fighting for every breath, as the tumours in his lungs began to squeeze the life out of him.

11

Monday afternoon

Mike Weston was still no further forward in his quest to find out what was going on. He had waited all day Sunday for an opportunity to present itself, only to be frustrated.

Both Kroll and Millburn were behaving very strangely, and this concerned him. As the Chief Executive, he really needed to know if there was anything wrong. Fed up of waiting, he decided on the direct approach. He left his glass cubicle and strode over towards Millburn's office.

'Is Charles in?' he asked the secretary, marching past her.

'No, no you mustn't disturb him,' she spluttered with alarm. But Weston ignored her and strode straight into Millburn's office. He was on the phone and turned around in his chair at the interruption.

'I'll call you back,' he spoke into the phone before putting it down and glaring at Weston.

'What do want?' he snapped. 'I gave specific instructions not to be disturbed.'

'I want to know what's going on, Charles.'

'What are you talking about?'

'You tell me.'

'I'll tell you only what you need to know, Mike. What's this all about?'

'You and Peter. There's something going on, and as the Chief Executive I should be told.'

'There a problem, Charles?' a voice spoke up behind Weston, making him jump. It was Kroll.

'No, there's no problem, Peter. Mike was just leaving.'

'I'm not leaving until you tell me what's going on. I'm not stupid, Charles. Peter's been in and out of here like a yoyo since Friday morning, and you've refused to speak to me or anyone else since. If Peter knows, then so should I.'

'It's of no concern to you.'

'But I'm Chief Executive!'

'Yes, and I'm the fucking Chairman and you'll do as you're told. *Understood?*' Millburn screamed, his face contorted with rage. 'Now get out!'

You could have heard a pin drop. Weston was completely taken aback by the outburst. He hadn't been spoken to like that for years. Millburn was like a man possessed, breathing hard through flared nostrils, his face bright red in anger. Weston turned around to leave, but found his path was blocked by Kroll, who gave him an unpleasant smirk, and stood his ground. Despite his greater bulk, Weston was forced to sidestep around the smaller man to leave the office.

Outside, it was obvious that other staff had heard the outburst. The office was silent as Weston headed back to his office. As he passed each cluster of desks, eyes were averted and fixed firmly onto computer screens. His humiliation had been played out in front of all these people, who were meant to look up to him and respect him.

Weston reached the sanctuary of his office and pulled the blinds down across the plate glass windows, so that no one could see him. His hands were shaking as he sat down at his desk and tried to make sense of what had just happened. He rubbed his face and tried to calm down, which was easier said than done. Millburn had never addressed him in such terms, especially within earshot of a large section of the office. That was arguably the worst thing about it. The public humiliation. At a stroke, his authority had been undermined. Millburn had also made it patently clear who was who in the pecking order.

As Weston began to collect himself, he thought about Millburn's outburst. It was so out of proportion to Weston's perfectly reasonable request. It could only mean one thing: Millburn really *was* hiding something.

As his shock subsided to be replaced by strong sense of injustice and anger, Weston resolved to find out what Millburn and Kroll were concealing, whether he was meant to or not. Millburn could go and fuck himself.

12

Monday evening

Hudson parked his old Golf outside Susannah's flat, in the Victorian terrace that had largely been converted into student accommodation. He felt a tingle at the prospect of seeing her again, and had been looking forward to it all day. Rather than going out, she had invited him around for dinner, so Hudson had come equipped with a bottle of decent wine and bunch of flowers. Nothing too ostentatious, just an elegant and pretty bunch of mixed amaryllis.

The door to Susannah's flat was opened by an attractive brunette who positioned herself suggestively in the doorway, and raised her eyebrows enquiringly. Hudson could not help but give her a rakish grin.

'Er, hi, is Susannah in?'

'Depends whose asking.'

'Leave him alone, Georgina,' Susannah called out from somewhere behind her. 'Come in, James.'

Georgina moved to one side, forcing Hudson to squeeze past her.

'Just ignore her,' Susannah called again, appearing from the kitchen. 'She's always like this. She's jealous, that's all.'

Georgina pulled a face and flounced back to the sofa, where she hugged a large cushion to herself and turned her attentions back to an American sit-com. Suzannah did the introductions.

'James Hudson, meet Georgina Myers, post-doctoral researcher and professional man-eater.'

'Hi,' she turned, giving him a cheeky smile and waving a hand languidly from the sofa, before turning back to the television.

'Hi, nice to meet you,' replied Hudson to the back of her head, bemused and flattered at the same time.

'Sorry to disappoint you James, but Georgina's going out tonight. Aren't you, Georgina?' she hinted loudly, giving her a pointed look. 'She wanted to check you out,' she whispered as she bustled Hudson through to the kitchen. 'Don't worry, I think you passed the test.'

'Yes, you pass, James,' Georgina called out, making Susannah and Hudson both flush scarlet.

'Like I said, just ignore her. Drink?'

Susannah had gone to considerable effort with the meal, and Hudson was glad he bought a decent bottle with him. Hudson also admired her simple but elegant dress, which showed off her perfect figure, and he was pleased that he had made an effort. Georgina left shortly, and their conversation, which had been stilted and forced in her presence, flowed naturally once more.

He described his phone call with Susannah's uncle. '...but I'm not sure he approved of me!' he finished, which made her laugh.

'Don't worry, that's typical of Uncle William. He's just looking out for me.'

'You don't seem the type that needs to be looked out for!' It was meant as a compliment, but Hudson noted the shadow which suddenly passed across her beautiful face. She looked down at her plate.

'I'm sorry, have I said something…?' Hudson was genuinely worried and confused, but couldn't fathom it.

'Oh, no, no. Don't worry, please. You haven't said anything. It's just that I went out with a total idiot a while ago. He really messed me around, and it took me a while to get over it.'

'You're okay now, though?'

'I'm fine. Thanks.' The smile returned, reassuring Hudson, who took another mouthful of food.

'This is delicious…Oh yes, I've just remembered: Your uncle also said that he thought your work was rubbish!'

This made her laugh again. It turned out that there had long been a disagreement between them concerning her Chernobyl theory. But Susannah was open-minded. If it turned out she was wrong, it wouldn't matter, just as long as she found out what was causing the higher rate of cancer. Once they had done that, it could help in the search for effective treatments. Hudson told her about the newspaper feature, which got her very excited.

Eventually, like all good things, the evening came to an end. Hudson, with considerable reluctance, announced that he had to get back home to Preston. It was a school night, after all.

Susannah looked disappointed, and there was an awkward moment between them, as they stood up. Hudson read the situation and pulled her towards him, leaning down to kiss her. Her full, soft lips responded eagerly to his and she pressed herself hard against him, so that Hudson could feel her firm breasts through the thin fabric of her dress. His arousal was instant and intense, and she felt him pressing urgently against her. She knew she should pull away, but something stopped her and before they knew it they were pulling at each other's clothes. Hudson slipped her dress off, revealing her perfect naked body beneath, his hands running over her firm curves, cupping her breasts and exploring her. She moaned and pressed against him, her hands running up under his shirt, encouraging him. He scooped her up in a muscular embrace and carried her through to her bedroom.

Afterwards, she lay with her head on his chest, gently tracing his muscular torso with her fingers. Hudson stroked the long, soft blond hair which fell in cascades over her tanned shoulders.

'I don't normally do that,' she whispered.

'Neither do I,' replied Hudson with a grin.

'Liar!' she exclaimed and hit him playfully, which provoked another round of passionate love-making, after which they both fell into a deep, satisfying sleep.

*

As they slept contentedly, Mike Weston was doing nothing of the sort. He was determined to find out what Millburn and Kroll were up to, and had stayed late in the Gencor office. He had barely left his room since his humiliation at the hands of Millburn and Kroll, and had simmered in quiet rage all afternoon about it.

The office had emptied steadily throughout the evening, whilst Weston worked on the annual reports in his office. The cleaner came and went, escorted by the security guard who held the keys to the various offices on the external walls of the building. Finally, Weston saw Millburn and Kroll leave, locking their offices behind them.

It was the moment he had been waiting for. He slipped out of his office and headed across the now mainly dark open-plan room. The automatic switches for the energy efficient lighting detected his presence, illuminating a trail for him across the floor. Weston headed downstairs to the floor below, where he found the night security guard escorting the cleaners. They always started on the top floor and worked down the building. If nothing else, it made going home quicker. Weston hurried up to the bored looking man, who was chewing gum in the aimless style of the football managers he so wished to emulate.

'Hi, sorry to bother you, but I need the keys to Mr Millburn's office. I've left some pretty important stuff in there which I need for the reports I'm writing. Do you mind…?' he asked, indicating the various keys hanging from the man's waist band.

The man worked his jaws slowly, chomping the gum with noisy smacking sounds, thinking it over, and relishing this one small moment of power. Strictly speaking, he knew he shouldn't relinquish the keys. But he couldn't really object. Mr Weston was a very important man.

'I can't leave here,' he pointed at the East European cleaners. 'You'll have to borrow them and bring 'em back.'

'No problem. I'll be right back.'

'And don't tell no one, right? Or I'll be in right trouble.'

'Don't worry,' Weston smiled reassuringly.

With a jangle, the guard removed the correct bunch from his belt and handed them over. Feeling his heart skip a beat, Weston headed back upstairs. He checked that the office was empty and headed over towards Kroll's office, cursing the lighting system that revealed his every move. Outside Kroll's door, he felt his nerves beginning to get the better of him, his sweaty fingers slipping over the various keys. He eventually found the key that was numbered to match the lock for the office, inserted it and opened the door. He had not wished to let the security guard know that it was Kroll's office, not Millburn's, that he was really interested in.

As he crept in, the light came on automatically, exposing him to the whole world, and he froze like a rabbit caught in headlights. His heart was pounding and his shirt clung to his sweating skin. He had to act fast. The folders were in Kroll's desk, he was sure.

He strode over to the functional beech-effect desk, so ubiquitous in offices throughout the country. Unlike Millburn, who preferred the finer things in life, Kroll had rather more ascetic tastes. The three drawers were locked, but that did not stop Weston. He had his own key, gambling on the fact that such locks were operated with a generic key, one of which he possessed for his own desk. He fumbled with the key, and inserted it into the top drawer.

To his relief, it worked. Kroll, as Director of Security, had such conceited arrogance that it never occurred to him that someone like

Weston would seek to raid his desk, or that he would require a more substantial lock on it. Such recklessness should have served as a warning to Weston, but he was too excited by the glimpse of the brown folders inside the drawer to give it any more thought.

He noted that there were five folders and he quickly spread them across the desk, opening them up. He frowned at their contents.

Each folder contained several photographs, including a single large picture of an elderly man. Four of the five had red lines drawn over them. There were several pages of documents accompanying each set of photographs, and it was clear to Weston that the documents detailed various addresses and employment histories. They were like detailed job applications. But they couldn't be; the men were all too old and the employment histories indicated that all had retired. There was something else that was distinctly odd, too. In each folder was a list of recent known movements of each of the individuals. Why on earth would Kroll, or Millburn for that matter, want such information? It did not make any sense at all. The other photographs were of buildings, cars and streets. With mounting concern, Weston realised that they were surveillance pictures. But why were these five men under surveillance? It occurred to him that, according to their employment histories, all them had worked in various branches of the British nuclear establishment, which was at least relevant to Gencor Energy. So what was Kroll's specific interest in them?

Weston became conscious of the time and realised he needed to return the key before the guard became suspicious. He needed to photocopy the documents and attempt to establish their significance in his own time.

He hurried out of the office and switched on the nearest photocopier, cursing the time it took to warm up. He glanced at the main office doors, conscious that he was fully illuminated. Surely the security guard would return at any moment? After an agonising wait, the green light came on and Weston copied the documents as quickly as he could, taking care not to disturb the order of the contents in each folder. As soon as the final sheet of paper rolled out of the machine, he bundled up his copies and rushed back to Kroll's office, to replace the folders in his desk, remembering to lock it again.

Job done, he dumped the copies on his own desk and hurried back downstairs, to return the keys to the guard, who grunted his thanks. It was good to see the fat cats running around after him for once.

Panting as he hauled his large frame up the stairs rather than wait for the lift to go one floor, Weston returned to his office. The lights were still on; the automatic timer lasted several minutes before switching them off if they ceased to detect any movement. The blinds on the glass walls were still drawn from earlier on, so that no one could see inside.

He walked in and stopped dead.

'Hello Mike. Find what you were looking for?' asked Millburn quietly from the armchair in the corner, casually flicking through a pile of papers. With horror, Weston realised they were the photocopies he had left on his desk. Speechless, he simply stared at Millburn.

Then the door slammed shut behind him, making him jump. Weston turned to see Kroll standing there, his face grim.

13

Tuesday

Hudson awoke to find Susannah still curled up in his embrace, then had the even greater pleasure of remembering what they had done the night before. He felt himself stirring once more, springing up with an aching intensity. She murmured lazily as he nuzzled her ear, before rolling onto her side to receive him, gasping as he gently entered her again. It was long and slow, their bodies melded together for what seemed an age, coming to a brief but intense end. Afterwards, they lay on their backs and she sighed contentedly.

'Do you have to go to work?' she whispered. Hudson sorely wished he didn't, but he had little choice.

'Sorry, but Donald will have my arse if I don't. I'm still on a warning.'

'Shame. We'll just have to catch up later,' she murmured slyly, leaning over to give him a long, lingering kiss and Hudson found himself aroused yet again. With considerable regret, and not wishing to spoil the moment, he pulled away from her. She pulled a face of mock disappointment, and Hudson was about to relent, then caught sight of the clock.

'Shit! Look at the time! I really will be late!'

Quickly, he threw his clothes on, grateful he had made an effort to be smart for Susannah's benefit, realising he probably only just had time to make it through the rush hour traffic and back to the office in Preston, let alone pop to his flat to get changed. He stole a kiss, paused, then came back for a second one from a bemused Susannah, and ran to his car.

He noticed the damage straight away.

The near side tyre was slashed and someone had taken a key all the way around the paint work. Cursing, Hudson got his hands filthy changing the wheel. Fortunately, only one tyre had been slashed, so he was not completely stranded. Working feverishly, as an anxious and sympathetic Susannah looked on, he changed the wheel in record time and, kissing her goodbye again, raced off for Preston. The last thing he needed was to be late for work, considering his warning the previous week. He doubted whether Winston would be in the mood for any more of his fiendishly inventive excuses, no matter how well his feature article was going.

Hudson nearly made it on time. He strode into the office, making a show of talking purposefully into his mobile. 'Yeah, great, thanks for that – I'll be in touch, bye.'

He caught the eye of the editor, who glanced at the clock. It was five minutes past nine.

'Just had a call from Susannah Harlowe, Don. A bit more info for the feature. Rubbish signal up here, though.' He sauntered nonchalantly to his desk, ignoring the suspicious looks of his colleagues.

'James, a word, if I may?' ordered Winston. *Here we go*, Hudson sighed inwardly. He went over to his boss's cubicle and perched on the uncomfortable plastic chair once more.

'Right, I've gone through your feature. It's fine, just a few minor alterations. But there's more to this paper than fancy features. You've neglected the rest of your work this week.

Hudson sighed. He knew there'd be something wrong.

'I was going to concentrate on that today, Don.'

Winston fixed him with a weary eye.

'Look, James, you've done a good feature. It shows you're capable enough. But you just need to apply yourself to the bread and butter stuff as well. Remember, if you want to change papers, you're going to need a hell of a good reference from me. It's very competitive out there.'

This took Hudson by surprise, and he coloured, unable to think of a quick response.

'I wasn't born yesterday, James. I know this paper isn't what you aspire to, but while you're still here I would appreciate a bit of commitment. Plenty of others would give their left arm for this kind of opportunity, don't forget that.'

'No, sorry. I won't. I'm very grateful for the opportunity,' he gulped, hoping to sound as sincere as possible.

'You did well to come up with story and I liked the bit you did with that patient at the hospital, the friend of yours. I want more journalism like that please, but spread across everything else. Now, bearing in mind you were late, *again*, I might add, please get on with your job.' And with that, he turned back to his computer. Violent images flashed through Hudson's mind as he stared at the back of Winston's head before he turned and headed over to his desk, strewn with papers and post-it notes. Winston was incapable of praise without diluting it with an admonishment of some sort. He sat down and switched the computer on. One of the first things he did every morning was check the Reuters news feed from London, in case there were any national stories which were relevant to the Preston Advertiser. As he scanned the tag lines for each story, one word jumped out. Gencor. The nuclear generator. It was a name that had cropped up in his research into the Chernobyl disaster, so he clicked on the story.

> "Gencor Energy Chief Executive leaps to death from top floor window of Canary Wharf HQ:
>
> [LONDON (Reuters) - Dan Smith] 29 Sept 2009 08:25BST -
>
> Mike Weston, 52, fell from the building just before 10:00pm last night. Initial reports suggest that he had been working late and alone when the tragedy occurred. His death was witnessed by a security guard, who saw the body fall past a window, and is now being treated in hospital for shock. Mr Weston was declared dead at the scene. He leaves no family.
>
> Gencor Chairman Sir Charles Millburn, whose company is the leading contender to win the £35 billion contract to build and operate Britain's new generation of nuclear power stations, has described the incident as a tragedy for the firm. "Mike was a wonderful colleague and friend. The firm owes much of its success to his unstinting effort and hard work. He will be greatly missed by us all, and we are devastated by his death."
>
> Police have indicated that they are not looking for anyone else in connection with the death and it is thought that Mr Weston was suffering from a depressive illness, brought on by stress.

Sir Charles Millburn will become the interim Chief Executive until a permanent replacement can be found. Shares in Gencor dipped slightly when the market opened at 08:00 but have recovered since Sir Charles' statement. Read more"

Hudson shrugged. There was nothing relevant to the Preston Advertiser's usual content, or his Chernobyl feature, so he moved on. After spending another five minutes scanning the news feed, he gave up and moved onto his emails. He always checked those last, as they usually tied him up for some time once he had started reading and replying to them. There was the usual dross from all the aspiring journalists who had ended up as local authority press officers or corporate public relations agents. Rather unsurprisingly, there was nothing terribly exciting. A few of them were worth a couple of paragraphs in the local news section. But it was very uninspiring stuff. Compost collection awards might be a enthralling topic for council officials, but singularly failed to do it for Hudson. This was what he hated about the job. Donald Winston was absolutely right. Hudson lacked any motivation whatsoever when it came to the 'bread and butter stuff', as his boss called it.

Sighing deeply, he scrolled down the list of dreary emails when he stopped and frowned. He wondered what William Terleski wanted. He must have got Hudson's email address from the paper's website. Hudson clicked on it, dreading that Terleski was withdrawing his permission to quote his interview comments.

Later on, thinking back, that was the precise moment that Hudson's world changed forever. 09:27 Tuesday 29th September 2009. If he had deleted the email without reading it, he would have been safe and nothing would have happened to him or Susannah. But hindsight is a wonderful thing.

The email opened up in front of him. He read it once, blinked, and had to go over it again before it registered. *What the hell is this?* he thought, clicking on the attachment. A large word document opened up on his screen. Hudson frowned again and started reading but, as he did, the colour slowly drained from his face and he became oblivious to everything going on around him.

When he had finished reading the document, he sat back, stunned. At first, he did not know what to think or do. What he had just learned was monumental. It couldn't be true. It simply couldn't. He read through the document again, just to make that he had understood it correctly. He had. There was no mistake about it.

He tried to work out what to do next but then, all of a sudden, a smile broke out across his face.

It was a hoax. It had to be. Susannah and her uncle had dreamt up an elaborate scheme to wind him up. They both appeared to share the same Mephistophelian sense of humour. They'd nearly had him, he thought, shaking his head and smiling ruefully. But, he had to hand it to them; they had excelled themselves with this one. Susannah must have put Terleski up to it; only someone with his background as the former head of the National Radiological Protection Board could have deployed such technical terminology.

He fished out his mobile phone and dialled Susannah's number. Irritatingly, she took an age to answer and then the surprising happened. She busied him, sending the call through to her answer phone. A bit put out by this, Hudson did not leave a message, but hung up. She must be in the middle of something, he thought, optimistically.

Five minutes later he tried again. This time she answered on the third ring.

'Ha, ha very funny,' he began, good humouredly.

'What?' she answered curtly, her voice strained.

'Nice try, you two. Set me up a treat didn't you, you and your uncle William?'

'James…' she tried to interrupt.

'…You nearly got me with it; I was just about to see my editor about it.'

'What are you talking about, James?' she insisted angrily, sounding upset, which perplexed him slightly. He adopted a more serious tone.

'The document your uncle sent me. About some ridiculous project called Red Dawn. I received it this morning.'

'I don't know anything about it, James. Uncle William's dead.'

Hudson must have held the phone for an age before speaking. The hair on his neck stood up and he felt a shiver of fear pass through him, as though someone had just walked over his grave.

'Dead?' he asked. A colleague looked up, and he turned away from her.

'They found him this morning.'

'What happened?'

*

William Terleski's gardener was local man, long retired, but who supplemented his meagre pension by helping out two days a week. It might not be excessively well-paid, and Terleski's overgrown jungle would take an army of gardeners to restore it to its original glory, but it was good exercise and Doctor Terleski was a decent chap. Terleski's arthritic hip had put paid to his ability to mow the extensive lawns, so this had become the gardener's principle occupation, in addition to tidying up where physically possible.

The first requirement of the day, an unavoidable obligation, was a cup of tea with the old man himself. That morning, the gardener had arrived at his customary early hour of 7:00 am and hammered on the front door, observing that it really did need a lick of paint. He would mention it; perhaps that could be an extra job for the Spring. Conscious of Terleski's slow movement, the gardener waited a while. After a while, he hammered again. Still no answer. This concerned the gardener. Perhaps Dr Terleski had fallen?

He tried the door, which was unlocked and swung open to reveal the dark hallway. There was no sound apart from the whispering of the draft excluder sliding over the polished tiled floor. Stealing himself, the gardener slowly entered the gloom, fearful of what he might find inside.

*

At that precise moment in London, Peter Kroll was stirring a copious amount of sugar into a cup of coffee. He was sitting opposite Charles Millburn, in Millburn's office. Although it was early, they had had a busy morning already, with Millburn having had to issue a statement to the financial markets, mourning the 'tragic' death of Mike Weston. Kroll had also been busy during the night removing all CCTV footage of the office from the fateful evening before. The police looking into Weston's apparent suicide would be told that, by awful coincidence, the system was down for routine maintenance. Any marks which they had inflicted on Weston's body whilst heaving him, struggling violently, out of the window, would have been obliterated with his impact on the stone paved plaza several hundred feet below.

The speaker on Millburn's telephone, which sat on the desk between them, had been switched on so that they could both hear the conversation. Kroll's assistant, Trevor, was on the line.

'So it was that stupid bastard Hancock trying to blackmail me, then?' Millburn asked rhetorically after listening to Trevor's initial report, relieved that they had identified the culprit.

'Yes, sir.'

'Good. That's that dealt with. What about Terleski?'

'Hancock had told him everything.'

'What happened?' Kroll asked.

'Last night? He put up quite a fight. He knew we were coming and why,' replied Trevor.

*

Inside the dark hallway, the gardener called out Terleski's name, but there was no answer. With mounting trepidation he headed quietly towards the office, that being the most likely place to find him. Pushing the door open carefully, he was confused by the scene.

Part of him was relieved not to find Terleski in there, but he was sure the office wasn't quite right. There was the usual mess, but it seemed less orchestrated than usual. Papers were strewn around and Terleski's idiosyncratic yellow post-it notes were scattered over the paperwork, rather than protruding from stacks of files and documents. It didn't look right. It took him a while to realise that the laptop was missing, but his gardener's eye finally picked out the anomalous patch of clear desk where it had once sat. Perhaps he had gone out, taken the laptop with him and forgotten to lock the house up? That was wishful thinking, and the gardener knew it. Deeply concerned by now, the gardener searched the rest of the house. There was no sign of Dr Terleski anywhere. He decided to search outside, before calling anyone.

*

Trevor's gravely voice chuckled out of the telephone.

'The old bastard caught Julian with his walking stick.'

Kroll did not share the amusement. 'Did you find anything there?' he snapped.

'He had a lot of stuff on Red Dawn. Papers, documents; that sort of stuff. We've collected it all, and his laptop.'

'What was he up to?'

'We couldn't get him to talk much, sir. Not if we wanted it to look like suicide. Julian tried using electric, but we couldn't get much out of him. He was a tough old bastard, I'll give him that.'

'So what did you find?'

'The laptop's encrypted, we need to bring it in.'

*

The gardener ventured outside to the grounds at the rear of the house. The garden was enclosed by a high Victorian wall, matching the brickwork of the house, and topped off with sandstone coping stones. An ornate summerhouse was built into the south-west facing corner. There was no obvious sign of Dr Terleski anywhere, but then the gardener remembered that he quite often frequented the summerhouse. How silly not to have thought of that earlier. He was probably in there, working on his laptop. The summer house was situated such that it could enjoy sunshine for most of the day. The doors were shut, probably to keep the chilly autumn breeze out. Approaching the doors, he called out cheerily.

'Anyone in?'

There was no response, so he opened them just to check.

The sight that greeted him sucked the wind out of his lungs and he staggered backwards, staring in horror. He tripped and fell over, his eyes still riveted to the open doorway. Then he scrambled to his feet and ran to the house as quickly as his old legs would allow him, utterly terrified.

*

'Presumably you didn't think to ask Terleski for the password?'

'It was a bit late by then, sir.'

Kroll shook his head in irritation and glanced up at Millburn, who looked angry.

'It must be important if he went to those lengths,' Millburn observed, acidly.

Kroll nodded in agreement and leant forward to speak into the telephone. 'We need to find out what's on that laptop. Bring it in as soon as possible,' he ordered.

'We're on our way now, boss. We should be there soon.'

Kroll ended the call, and closed the brown folder on the photograph of Terleski's face, after drawing a red line across it.

'Get rid of those, Peter, for god's sake,' muttered Millburn.

Kroll nodded and headed over to the shredder, where he fed the five brown folders in, collecting the waste and placing it in a separate bag for disposal.

'When is this going to end, Peter?' asked Millburn, lighting up a fresh cigarette, his forty-a-day habit now fully restored.

'Don't worry, Charles. Red Dawn is safe now.'

*

The gardener found the telephone in the hallway and, his hands shaking, dialled the emergency services. Breathlessly, he managed to inform them of what he had found, before he collapsed onto the chair next to the telephone, unable to comprehend what had happened. He would wait there until the police and ambulance crew arrived.

Suddenly, the phone rang, making him jump. He ignored it at first, it wasn't his place to answer it and he certainly wasn't up to it anyway. But it rang on persistently. Perhaps it was the police. He picked it up.

'Terleski?'

'No, no he's not here,' he stammered, breathlessly. 'I'm the gardener…I can't speak right now.'

'Has something happened?'

'Yes.'

'Is he dead?'

'Yes.'

The phone went dead, leaving the dial tone. In the distance he could hear sirens approaching. They wailed into the forecourt, and crunched to a halt on the gravel. A police constable was the first to enter and find the gardener sitting by the phone, in shock. Two paramedics followed shortly behind. One of them attended to the gardener whilst the other accompanied the policeman to the summerhouse.

Through the open door, they could see the toe caps of Terleski's brown leather brogues, pointing downwards; his feet were pushed neatly together by the effects of gravity on his legs. The blue nylon rope had dug into his neck cruelly, almost cutting into the skin. It was obvious that there was little they could do. The constable cautioned the paramedic that it may be a crime scene, so they had better leave the body *in situ* until they received permission to remove it. However, a cursory look around the summerhouse indicated that it was unlikely to be sinister. The rope was tied around a roof truss and, as Terleski's feet were only inches from the floor, it seemed clear that he must have stood on one of the benches fixed to the outer wall before leaping or simply stepping to his fate. He would have been unable to reach the benches once he had swung into the middle of the hexagonal room and he would have lacked the strength to haul himself back up the rope. A change of mind wouldn't have mattered once he had committed himself to this course of action. The fall wouldn't have been enough to kill him instantly and the paramedic observed that the neck didn't appear broken. He had been strangled by the noose, probably quite slowly, though there were no signs of scratching around the neck, which would have indicated any frantic struggle to remove or loosen the noose. Trevor and Julian had been careful not to mark him when they held his arms firmly whilst they waited for him to die.

'Poor sod,' muttered the paramedic.

'Must have been desperate,' agreed the policeman, quietly. He had seen corpses before, but it was something he could never get used to.

'Not the most painless way to go either. I've seen far easier ways of doing it,' the paramedic observed matter-of-factly. The policeman merely nodded, not wishing to have a discussion on the subject, but the paramedic continued on blithely.

It had been one of those days, apparently. One of his colleagues had been called to the scene of another death just outside Stratford that morning. An old man had been found floating face-down in a fishing lake, apparently having drunk the best part of a bottle of whisky, which had been found lying on the bank. He had probably fallen in, too inebriated to haul himself from the icy water. The policeman shivered, wishing the paramedic would shut up. He really, really hated this part of the job.

Clearly unable to do anything to help the corpse in the summerhouse, the paramedic left to assist his colleague, whilst the police officer stood guard at the grisly scene, waiting for his colleagues and a doctor to arrive.

*

When Susannah had finished tearfully explaining what had happened to her beloved uncle, Hudson was deeply shocked.

'He hung himself? I can't believe it. I'm really sorry, Susannah. Do you still want me to come over later?'

'Yes, please, I need to see a friendly face,' she sniffed.

It wasn't the time or place to discuss the document he had received from Terleski. He would print it off and take it over with him when he had finished work. In the meantime, he wasn't sure what to do. He wanted to speak to Winston about it, but realised that he would need to discuss it with Susannah first. It directly concerned her uncle, and Hudson wanted her opinion on it. It could still be a hoax of some sort, and he did not wish to embarrass himself with his editor.

But what if it was true? Hudson knew that he had a huge story on his hands, a career-defining moment. He had to make sure he had his facts right before he did anything else. He desperately needed to speak to Terleski. Why had the old man killed himself after sending it? It just didn't make any sense. The email it was attached to suggested that Terleski was very frightened. Hudson read the email again:

```
To: j.hudson@preston_advertiser.co.uk
From: terleskiw@tiscali.co.uk
Sent: 28 September 2009 20:48
Subject: Urgent CONFIDENTIAL
Attachment: Red_Dawn_Project.doc (612kb)

James
    I have attached something I have been working
on of late. You will find it of immense interest.
It is also of immense interest to others who will
wish to stop me divulging this information. I do
not have time to explain. My life may be in danger.
I am not sure, but I suspect that others involved
have been killed. The document is not finished, but
I am not sure I will get the chance to finish it,
so have sent it to you for safekeeping. If anything
happens, you must tell people about the Red Dawn
programme, but be very careful.
    Good luck,
    William.
    Please call me to discuss.
```

The last line jumped out at Hudson. Why ask Hudson to call him if he was intending to commit suicide? The email took on an entirely new significance now that he had learned of Terleski's subsequent death. The fact that Terleski wanted to discuss it with Hudson did not indicate a man about to kill himself, unless it was a very sick joke; one bitter old man's parting shot to the world.

Perhaps that was what it was: A macabre practical joke, to create mayhem in his wake. Hudson knew nothing of Terleski, whether this was the type of stunt he was liable to pull. He decided not to act until he had shown the email and document to Susannah.

It was to prove a regrettable decision.

14

Jeremy Langham was briefing the Prime Minister about Sir Mark Wellesby's condition, trying to put on his most sympathetic and subdued expression, whilst concealing his elation at the prospect of assuming the mantle of Director General.

'Sir Mark will not be returning to work, Prime Minister. The doctors don't think he will leave hospital. It seems that the tumours are encroaching on his pulmonary artery. He doesn't have much time left.' Jeremy Langham was in a suitably sombre mood as he addressed the equally dour man opposite him.

The PM nodded gravely, as he digested this news. He had never had much time for the erstwhile head of the Security Service, but now that the man was clearly gone for good, he could afford to be generous. 'He was a good man, Jeremy. I will see to it that he is afforded every comfort. Now, I imagine that you are to be the Acting Director General until you are confirmed in the post?'

Langham swelled at the thought of it. He was on the cusp of achieving his life's ambition.

'Yes, Prime Minister, if that is what you wish?'

'Of course it is.'

'Thank you, Prime Minister.'

'Wellesby seemed concerned about this Red Dawn thing. I trust that you can be relied on make it quietly go away. We don't want anything to affect the nuclear policy I announced to the house last Thursday, do we?'

From his habitual place on the sofa in the corner, Giles Devereaux nodded his head in agreement, watching Langham closely. The Director of Communications was aware of the immense damage any disclosure would cause. But, to his relief, Langham was 'on-message':

'As you know, Prime Minister, I indicated my views on the matter yesterday. It is in the national interest to put the matter to rest. It happened a long time ago, and we should draw a line under it and move on. Fortunately, no official records exist other than the file held by Sir Mark. I have since destroyed that file.'

'Very good, Jeremy. We're facing an energy crisis. There is simply no alternative to nuclear power. The public now understands that, and we don't want anything to change it.'

The rest of the meeting carried on without a hitch, Langham readily assuming the mantle of Sir Mark Wellesby. As far as the PM was concerned, he found Langham far more amenable to his way of thinking, and the two came to an excellent mutual understanding of one another. The Prime Minister was very satisfied at how things had turned out, especially now that Langham had informed him that all mention of the Red Dawn programme had been expunged from the records. It was, after all, in the national interest.

*

Less satisfied at how things had turned out was Sir Charles Millburn. He was white with rage.

'He did *what?*' he screamed at Kroll, who flinched.

'It appears that Doctor Terleski was in the process of compiling a dossier detailing the Red Dawn programme,' he explained. There was worse to come. 'It also appears that last night he emailed a copy of this dossier to James Hudson, of the Preston Advertiser.'

'The Preston Advertiser?' Millburn was incredulous.

'Yes, Charles. It's a small regional newspaper.'

'And who the *fuck* is James Hudson?' Millburn shouted, spittle flying from his mouth.

'One of their journalists.'

'I don't believe this. I just don't fucking *believe this*!' He stood up and paced around the office, cursing. 'And what the hell has the Preston Advertiser got to do with this anyway? He doesn't email it to the whole of fucking Fleet Street, but to the *Preston Advertiser*? WHY?'

'I don't know.'

'You're paid to know!' Millburn screamed at him.

'Yes, Charles. I'll see what I can find out.'

Millburn turned to Trevor and Julian, who were sitting quietly next to Kroll. 'And then you two will put a stop to it. Understand?'

'Yes, sir,' they chimed.

They had arrived with Terleski's laptop a couple of hours previously, handing it over to Kroll's in-house technical experts. The IT consultants had made short work of circumventing the basic password protection, allowing Kroll to check through Terleski's folders and documents. It had not taken him long to find the dossier, the discovery of which had horrified him. No wonder the old man had resisted interrogation so bravely. Although Thomas Hancock had been behind the original blackmail attempt, it transpired that Terleski posed by far the greatest threat. In fact, had it not been for Hancock's rash attempt to recover his lost fortune, they would never have found out about Terleski until it was too late. In that sense, Hancock had done them a favour. But as it was, it seemed that they may already be too late. It all depended on whether they could find and stop this James Hudson in time.

15

Tuesday evening

Hudson raced down the motorway to Manchester as fast as he could through the rush hour traffic. He had been out of the office as soon as the clock hit five, clutching a print-out of Terleski's email and dossier.

He had been unable to concentrate on his work all day as his mind turned over all the possibilities. Was it a hoax? If so, why him? That was easy enough to answer: His link with Susannah and the story about her research. Was it true? Again, if so, why him? This was precisely why he could not get the idea of a hoax out of his mind, the fact that Terleski had sent it to him. Surely something so monumental should have been sent to one of the national newspapers, or the BBC, or some other national news outfit.

He tried to put himself in Terleski's shoes. The man was suicidal, so was quite mixed up. Hudson must have one of the last people to speak to him. Hudson's feature on Chernobyl was relevant. So, on those grounds, it made sense. But the email hinted of darker forces at work. Others may have been killed. The dossier contained their names and what they had apparently done for the Red Dawn programme. Terleski was frightened and had asked Hudson to discuss the dossier with him.

Would a man frightened of losing his life then go on to take it? Perhaps, if it ended the psychological suffering inflicted by the knowledge of imminent doom, or offered a painless alternative to a certain fate? No. Hudson wasn't convinced. His gut instinct told him that wasn't so.

Which left only one credible alternative: Terleski had been killed. But as soon as Hudson considered it, reality jumped back in. It was all so ludicrous. Britain was a modern, liberal, free society. Such things simply did not, could not, happen. After all, there were plenty of people who were a thorn in the government's side, or who challenged big business interests, yet lived to irritate them another day. An unlucky few found themselves on the unpleasant side of a libel court ruling or antisocial behaviour order, but that was about as far as it went. People weren't *killed*. Surely?

Yet the stark fact remained that Terleski was dead.

And he had written something that could destroy the government's new nuclear programme, and threaten the commercial interests of Gencor Energy PLC.

By the time he arrived at Susannah's flat, Hudson's mind was in turmoil. He didn't know what to think. He was so distracted that he failed to notice the dark, customised BMW pull into a parking space a few cars further on down the street, or the well-built, grim faced man sitting in it who watched him go into Susannah's flat.

Hudson and Susannah sat together on the sofa, nursing mugs of hot tea, whilst Susannah read through the email and dossier. Her eyes were still red, from bursting into tears once more when Hudson had arrived. Not only was she upset at the loss of her beloved uncle, but also by the manner of his passing, to the point that Hudson had thought twice about showing her the dossier.

'This doesn't make sense,' she commented, frowning, after reading the email.

'Wait until you read the dossier,' Hudson replied quietly, keen for Susannah to arrive at her own conclusions.

She turned the page over and started reading.

"In the beloved memory of my late wife, May, I dedicate this work. It was at her behest that I commenced work on this dossier. I have many crimes to confess and atone for, and I wish to dedicate this to the memory of the many that have died as a result of my actions. Their families deserve the truth and I have done my best to find it and present it as such. There are many others who share culpability with me. Their names and the crimes they are responsible for are recorded here. For too long I have carried the burden of my crimes. It is time for me to atone, and time for others to share the blame. I am aware that I am breaking the law in writing this, but that is of little consequence when set in the context of what I have done.

This is a detailed account of the Red Dawn programme, which ran from May 1986 and continues to this day.

On the night of April 26th, 1986, Reactor Number Four at the Chernobyl Nuclear power station was destroyed by two explosions, in very short succession. The explosions were caused by a combination of the criminal negligence of the operators and poor reactor design. The investigation into the disaster revealed that an initial explosion was the result of excessive steam production as the reactor went out of control, whilst a secondary explosion was likely to be the ignition of the graphite moderator, as it came into contact with the atmosphere. The investigators were not completely sure, but this seems the most likely. What is not in doubt is the huge radiation leak that followed, particularly of caesium and iodine isotopes.

For reasons known only by the individuals concerned, the Soviet authorities took three days to acknowledge the disaster, despite radiation monitors across Europe detecting elevated radioactivity in the atmosphere. Even after they had admitted the possibility of an explosion, they sought to understate its true severity.

The radioactive cloud spread across Europe, depositing a trail of radioactive isotopes as it went. In Britain, our particular misfortune was the heavy precipitation which washed through the cloud, with particular repercussions for the high pastureland of Wales and Cumbria. Had there been sufficient warning, it may have been possible to administer drugs to the affected population, certainly to minimise the effects of ingested radioactive iodine. Sadly, as a result of deliberate obfuscation by the Soviet authorities, no such warning was given until it was too late. Besides, little could have been done to ameliorate the effects of Caesium-137, of which huge quantities were released by the explosion. Half of all the iodine and caesium in the reactor escaped into the atmosphere. Both these radioactive isotopes have particular properties, which are salient to this account and have ramifications for what follows.

Caesium-137 is a radioactive isotope of the element caesium. It is created during nuclear weapon detonations and as a by-product of the fission process within nuclear reactors. Along with gallium and mercury, it is the only other metal that is liquid at room temperature. The relevance of this fact will become apparent later on. However, the important consideration here is its effect on human health. External exposure to large amounts of Caesium-137 can cause burns, acute radiation sickness, and even death. The harmful effects are made even worse if it is ingested or inhaled. This allows radioactive material to be distributed throughout the body, where it resides in soft tissue, especially muscle tissue, and causes terrible localised damage to the tissue DNA. Its radioactive half life of 30.17 years means that its radioactivity decreases by half approximately every thirty years. Even after sixty years, its radioactivity will still be a quarter of its original level. For this reason, it is still present in the atmosphere as a result of nuclear weapons testing carried out in the 1950s and 1960s. Therefore it is not only highly radioactive, but will persist in the environment for hundreds of years.

In the environment, Caesium-137 is one of the most dangerous radioisotopes. In addition to its persistence and high radioactivity, it has the further insidious property of being mistaken for potassium by living organisms and taken up as part of the fluid electrolytes. It is not readily secreted, and it is passed on up the food chain, being concentrated in the process. For this reason, livestock controls have to be introduced in contaminated areas to minimise this concentration effect and protect human health.

Radioactive isotopes of iodine are also formed in nuclear reactors and nuclear detonations. Of particular concern are Iodine-129 and Iodine-131. Iodine-129 has a half life of 15 million years, though this means the intensity of its radioactive decay is low. By contrast, Iodine-131 has a much shorter half-life of only eight days, so it persists in the environment for a far shorter timescale. However, the downside to this is that its radioactive decay is much more intense, resulting in a higher radioactive dose. In the human body, Iodine-131 is readily absorbed by the thyroid gland, where its concentration and relatively high radioactivity can cause cancer of the thyroid. Marked increases in the incidence of this particular cancer have been observed in areas polluted by Iodine-131.

As I have mentioned earlier, when we found out about the true nature of the explosion at Chernobyl, it was too late for us to do anything about it. The radioactive material had already blown over the United Kingdom and had been washed onto the ground. Although the Chernobyl facility was over a thousand miles away, the radioactive cloud had not been subjected to rainfall before arriving over the UK. As a result, although some of the material had been lost *en route* through dry deposition, much of it still remained airborne. Over Britain, substantial rain fell from the middle levels of the troposphere, and washed some of this material onto the ground on May 3rd. At the time, we played down the risk to the public. We didn't want to cause panic, especially as there was nothing we could do to reverse what had happened. Nevertheless, we expected a huge increase in cancers, especially amongst children. Quite rightly, the media and environmental groups suspected that this was indeed the case, despite our denials...."

Susannah looked up, ashen-faced. 'My God, James,' she whispered. 'It's true. They did cover up the Chernobyl fallout. Uncle William lied to me.'

Hudson remained impassive. 'Read on,' he instructed. He knew what came next, and it was far worse than anything he had imagined. The next few paragraphs described the ongoing radiation monitoring of soil on farms across Cumbria and Wales, which Terleski had been responsible for in his capacity as head of the National Radiological Protection Board. But it was what Terleski described after that which had made his blood run cold. If it was true. He followed Susannah's reading, waiting for the reaction.

Suddenly, she stopped and put her hand to her mouth, too shocked to speak. She had just discovered the truth behind Red Dawn. She turned to Hudson, her face pale.

'I can't believe this James. I just can't believe it. It's impossible. It has to be. Uncle William could never have done this.'

'That's why I wanted to show you. I don't know if it's all a big joke. I thought that you and your uncle were behind it, to wind me up.'

'No James, I promise. I would never do anything this…this *sick*. Neither would Uncle William.'

'But he sent it to me. It came from his email address, and he wanted me to discuss it with him. He *must* have written it.'

Susannah did not reply. She stood up and walked around the small lounge of the flat.

'It can't be true, it just can't be,' she repeated, over and over.

'Then why did he write this dossier?'

'I don't *know*, James,' she snapped back. 'It doesn't make any sense.' Susannah was clearly very upset by it all. 'And why did he send it to you and not me? He's *my* uncle,' she observed bitterly.

'I suppose it ties up with my feature article,' he offered, embarrassed by the fact that her uncle has chosen him for his last living communication with anyone.

'And *why* did he have to kill himself?' she begged, her bottom lip quivering. Hudson stood up and pulled her head into his shoulder to comfort her, where she sobbed for some time while he stroked her hair. As he waited for her to recover, his mind was spinning.

What if it was true? What if this Red Dawn project really existed?

Eventually, Susannah pulled away and rubbed her eyes. 'Sorry,' she mumbled.

'It's okay,' he replied gently, holding her shoulders. 'Are you alright now?'

She nodded and sniffed. There was a hint of a smile.

'Look, I haven't shown this to anyone else. I thought it best to show you first so, at the moment, no one else knows, okay?' She nodded again and Hudson continued. 'I think we need to look into it. I can check out a couple of the facts, and then we'll know whether it's a joke or not. I won't tell anyone about it until then, agreed?'

She seemed reassured by this. It probably *was* just a stupid joke. Her uncle must have been in a very odd frame of mind but, if he was about to kill himself, that could explain it. But tonight wasn't the time or place for it, so Hudson promised her he would look into it first thing in the morning.

Hudson headed through to the kitchen and rustled up a quick supper for them both whilst Susannah composed herself. Over the meal, Hudson did his best to distract her from what had happened to her uncle, aided with a bottle of wine. Afterwards, she indicated that she wanted an early night, so they went to bed. Hudson wasn't expecting anything but, to his surprise, she forced herself on him with an urgency that nearly caught him off guard. 'I need you,' she breathed in his ear as she slid herself onto him. Gasping as he entered her, he responded just as urgently and they lost themselves in each other's bodies, her momentum increasing until she stiffened and let out a small cry of ecstasy, as Hudson let himself go. She slumped forward onto him and they both fell into the welcome embrace of sleep.

16

*B*ang, bang, bang. Somewhere in the dark recesses of his mind, Hudson heard a noise. *Bang…bang…bang.* Louder this time. Enough to drag him out of his exquisite slumber. He came to.

Bang! Bang!

'James? James? Wake up!' Knocking at the bedroom door. *Bang, bang* again. Georgina's voice.

'Yeah, what is it?' he mumbled groggily.

'Quick! Someone's messing with your car!'

'*What the hell?*' He was out of bed like a shot and threw on his jeans. He rushed out of the room, to be greeted by an anxious Georgina who drew him over to the window.

'Look! Someone's smashing up your car!' she pointed out.

'Shit!' he exclaimed in angry disbelief. He raced out of the flat and onto the street wearing nothing but his jeans.

'What the *hell* are you doing?' he shouted at the man smashing up the old Golf. Too late, Hudson realised the man was equipped with a baseball bat but, in his fury, he carried on regardless.

Hudson was a big man who wasn't afraid to tackle men even bigger than him, but even he went down when the man swung the bat into his torso as hard as he could. Hudson gasped at the pain in his ribs and struggled to stand up again before the next blow. He lunged at the man's legs in a rugby tackle, and they both crashed to the ground, with the bat clattering on the car bonnet. With a flash of fear, Hudson suddenly realised that his assailant was a very powerful man, more than a match for him, but it was too late for any regrets; he was fully committed to the fight now. Before he could release his grip on the man's legs, Hudson felt his head being grabbed and twisted. The man was trying to break his neck. He wriggled free and delivered some frantic punches into his opponent's body and groin, before a heavy fist caught him full in the face, throwing him onto his back. He felt the cartilage in his nose go and his top teeth cut through his upper lip. Dazed, he tried to crawl to his feet, but was caught by a vicious kick in the ribs which knocked him over again. Desperately, Hudson tried repeatedly to get to his feet, but the barrage was unrelenting.

    With mounting fear, Hudson realised he was in trouble. He had to get up before a boot connected with his head, but he couldn't avoid the kicks long enough. With superhuman effort he finally managed to roll away from the onslaught and scramble to his feet. His whole body was racked with pain, but he forced himself up, sensing that if he stayed on the ground, he was a dead man. In the poorly-lit street he saw the heavily built man coming for him again. Hudson may have been a big man, but his assailant was powerful and fast. Hudson went in close, deciding it was the safest option. The two men grappled with each other, exchanging blows. Hudson could feel the man try to bite his ear and he twisted his head out of the way and butted his head into the man's mouth. There was a crunch, an audible grunt of pain and the vice-like grip lessened for a fraction of a second. Hudson tried to take advantage and throw the man to the ground. But the manoeuvre failed and Hudson instead found himself on the ground. His opponent was formidable. Another brutally aimed boot crashed into his unprotected ribs and, in desperation, Hudson grabbed hold of it, trying to pull the man over. In response, his assailant started stamping on his head and neck, and Hudson felt the strength sap from him as his head banged onto the road. He curled up into a foetus position to protect his head from the ferocious onslaught. But it wouldn't be long before a boot found its mark.

'Stop it Alex! Stop it now!' A distant voice. Familiar. Another blow to the head.

'Leave him alone, Alex! I'll call the police!' This time, it was screamed. The blows stopped coming.

'Just go away, Alex! Just leave him alone!' Susannah screamed again.

'You fucking slag!' the man shouted back. 'Didn't take you long did it?' he jeered. 'Shagging this bastard already are you?' He slammed a brutal kick into Hudson again, causing him to groan and curl up in pain.

'Stop it!' Susannah screamed again. Hudson rolled to his hands and knees, gasping, his head spinning and blood trickling from his mouth and nose.

'Bastard!' the man cursed, before knocking Hudson over onto his back, where he lay defenceless. The man swaggered over to pick up his baseball bat, twirled it menacingly, and then beat it against the palm of his hand. Hudson was at his mercy now, his arms raised in submission. There was a tense moment lasting several seconds, then his assailant just spat at him and swaggered off down the road, where he climbed into his customised BMW and roared off.

Susannah ran up to Hudson and helped him to sit up. Georgina rushed over to help, and they helped Hudson rise unsteadily to his feet.

'Are you okay?' she asked.

'Felt better,' Hudson mumbled through split lips. They helped him back into the flat, where Susannah fetched a bowl of warm water and a bottle of Dettol. Tenderly, she cleaned his wounds and bandaged his heavily bruised ribs, whilst Hudson did his best not to wince, already feeling humiliated enough.

'Shall I call the police? Do you want to go to hospital?'

Hudson shook his head. 'Who was that?' he wanted to know instead.

'I'm really sorry, James. I'm so, so sorry,' Susannah looked to be on the verge of tears once more.

'Who is he?' Hudson mumbled once again.

'My ex. Alex Warburton.'

Hudson nodded, as if it all made perfect sense. But it was scant consolation for his injuries.

'I'm really sorry, James,' Susannah continued. 'I never thought I'd see him again.' She was weeping now. 'We split up weeks ago.'

'Can't think why, he seemed such a nice bloke,' he muttered through clenched teeth, wincing at the pain in his chest. Susannah sobbed. 'It wasn't your fault, don't worry,' he continued, trying to reassure her. He knew from experience that he hadn't broken any ribs, but was heavily bruised. His well muscled torso had protected him to some extent. 'I'll be okay,' he smiled, rather unconvincingly. It also occurred to him that Warburton may have been responsible for vandalising his car the night before, a thought which made Susannah shudder, as it meant that he must have been watching them for a while.

'Don't worry,' he promised her. 'He won't get away with it again.' And Hudson meant it. He had been caught unawares this time around. Next time, he would be ready and waiting for Warburton. He had unfinished business to settle.

Bandaged up, and insistent about his desire not to go to hospital – and spend hours and hours waiting on a trolley – Hudson gingerly crept into bed. Dosed up with painkillers and a large shot of vodka, he finally managed to fall into a fitful sleep, with Susannah at his side.

17

Wednesday

The pain was even worse when he woke up. His head throbbed and his chest was tight. As soon as he opened his mouth, his lips split open painfully once more, so that he had to dab at them constantly with a tissue. The prospect of another day in the office was not an enticing one. But, after a cup of tea and another handful of painkillers, he began to feel a bit better. A glance in the mirror revealed a swollen nose and one black eye, with an impressive array of grazes and bruises on his face, arms and upper body.

'You shouldn't go in today. Stay here and I'll look after you,' Susannah ordered. It was a very tempting proposition, but Hudson felt that he couldn't let Don Winston down, the day before publication. It was always the busiest day of the week, and Hudson still had a lot of the 'bread and butter' articles to write up and submit to the editor's electronic basket. He also needed to get the car into a garage. Perhaps he should have called the police after all. At the very least, that would give him a crime reference number to pass onto his insurers and get the car fixed. He decided to phone up and report criminal damage and leave it at that. He didn't want Susannah to suffer any retribution. It was also a matter of personal pride: He didn't particularly wish to admit that he'd been beaten up.

After fighting off both Susannah's and Georgina's protests, Hudson headed off back to Preston. The car had a cracked windscreen and various dents to the body panels but, other than that, it was mechanically functional.

He needed to change before work, so he nipped back to his waterfront flat. It was only a short walk to the office from there anyway. He reached Preston in good time and parked up outside the apartment block next to the docks. Nursing his bruised ribs, he headed through the communal foyer and climbed carefully up the short flight of stairs to the first floor. Usually he bounded up three at a time, but not today.

Outside his door, he fished out his key and pushed it into the lock.

The door swung open before him, the lock useless.

Hudson stopped, feeling his blood run cold.

Slowly, disbelievingly, he stepped into his flat. Broken glass crunched underfoot on the laminate floor. The contents of drawers were strewn about. What had once been carefully filed folders and books were torn and lay haphazardly over the floor. Even his clothes had been tipped out and thrown across the floor. Hudson swallowed deeply, trying to take it all in. And then he realised what was missing.

The laptop. For *fuck's sake*, they'd nicked the laptop.

*

'What did you find?' Kroll demanded.

'Not much, sir. Just a laptop, but there wasn't much on it.'

'Any sign of Hudson?'

'No, sir. We don't know where he is, but we've got the flat and the newspaper under surveillance. He should turn up soon.'

'So we haven't got the proof then?'

'No, sir.'

Kroll sighed deeply into the phone.

'We absolutely must have that proof, Trevor. Do you understand? Then deal with Hudson.'

'Yes sir.'

Kroll hung up and glanced across the desk at Millburn, who was staring out of the window, his jaw muscles flexing in silent rage. It never ceased to amaze him how the simplest of tasks could be complicated by unforeseen events. Especially when the task was given to someone else.

It had been on the third reading of Terleski's dossier that the awful possibility had presented itself. They had missed the detail on the previous readings, for the simple reason that they already knew the entire story. It had been Kroll who had spotted the reference, presumably a slip on Terleski's behalf.

Terleski had incontrovertible evidence which could prove his story to a third party without any doubt.

And they had no idea where it was.

Julian and Trevor had cleared Terleski's study of all papers and documents relating to Red Dawn, and had applied electric shocks to his teeth and genitals to find out all they could. They hadn't gleaned much, not even the password for his laptop, but they had been confident that whatever he hadn't told them was on the laptop, which they had since gained access to. Then they had hung him, having first rendered him unconscious by use of a pressure point in his neck. A pathologist would never suspect anything but suicide.

The problem was, the wily old fox had left something behind and they had absolutely no idea where it could be. The only possible lead they had was Hudson, so the emphasis of their operation had shifted from eliminating Hudson to finding the proof. If Terleski's last communication had been with Hudson, and especially as it had concerned Red Dawn, then it was highly likely that Hudson was in possession of the proof.

*

'What happened to your face, sir?' Constable Simpson asked Hudson after he had taken a statement. It looked more like a domestic incident rather than a burglary. Hudson had touched nothing since calling the police, so the flat was still in the same state he had found it in.

'Oh, nothing much,' Hudson replied nervously, caught off guard.

Simpson gave him a withering look. 'Wasting police time is a very serious matter, sir. It would be better for all of us if you told the truth. If you want my opinion, I'm not so sure that there's been a burglary here.'

'I *am* telling the truth, officer. I came home this morning and found my place like this. The only things missing are my laptop and some CD-Roms.'

'Where were you last night, sir?'

'I don't see why that's important.'

'It is to me. We can continue this down at the station if you prefer?'

Hudson swallowed, feeling like a criminal. This was why he never usually called the police. It must be his journalistic irreverence towards authority, manifesting itself somehow in his manner of speech or attitude. Whatever it was, he always felt distinctly uncomfortable in the presence of the police, somehow feeling guilty for crimes he was not even aware of.

'That's not necessary, officer. I was at my girlfriend's flat in Manchester.'

'Name and address?'

Hudson gave them, feeling he was betraying Susannah.

'Did your injuries happen last night, sir?'

'Er, yes, officer.'

'Care to tell me how? We can always ask your girlfriend, remember.'

Hudson gave in. It must have been his tiredness, or the painkillers, but he simply did not have the stomach to engage in a battle of wits with the constable.

'Those are serious injuries, sir.' At least the constable was more sympathetic towards him now that he seemed to have a credible explanation for Hudson's battered face. 'Are you going to press charges?'

'I'm not sure what that would achieve,' replied Hudson gloomily. 'I don't want any trouble for Susannah.'

'Well, if you make a statement, we can bring him in and caution him. We can also warn him to stay well away from you and your girlfriend.'

Hudson nodded wearily. It seemed a sensible argument and at least he now had his crime reference number to get his car repaired under insurance.

Outside, in a nondescript car, a man adjusted his earpiece and scribbled down the name and address with interest. Their target had a girlfriend, did he? Most interesting, most interesting indeed. He called his colleague, who was watching the offices of the Preston Advertiser.

'Trevor? Our man's shown up. Turns out he has a girlfriend.'

'Worth a look?'

'Might be. I've got her address. I'll find out what Hudson's planning to do, then I'll pop over and have a look around.'

'Good idea, let me know what's happening.'

*

Like many thugs and bullies, Alex Warburton thought that he was above the law, even when a panda car pulled up outside his Manchester gym. The two burly police officers sent to arrest him filled the doorway with their bulk and pulled themselves up to their full height as they walked into the reception area. Warburton straightened up from where he had been demonstrating weight-lifting equipment to a customer on an induction course, gave them a look of contempt and swaggered over to them.

'Yeah, what do you want?' he demanded with a leer, flexing his muscles for their benefit. The two officers stepped towards him.

'Alex Warburton?'

'Depends whose asking.'

'Alex Warburton, you are under arrest on suspicion of assault; you do not…'

'Oh, fuck off!' Warburton sneered and turned to go back to his customer. The two officers looked at each other and grabbed hold of him, which immediately sparked a sustained and violent struggle, during which several pieces of equipment were knocked over and the glass window in reception was smashed.

Warburton was finally subdued with the use of pepper spray and batons, before being led in handcuffs to the panda car, with additional charges of resisting arrest and assaulting a police officer added to the score sheet. Twenty minutes later, he was locked in a police cell, venting his fury at Hudson and Susannah, and the world in general, much to the amusement of the duty sergeant.

18

After the police constable had gone, and he had tidied up his flat, Hudson finally made his way into the office for ten o'clock. Winston was about to vent an hour's worth of pent-up fury on him, but stopped dead as soon as he saw Hudson's battered face.

'What the hell happened to you?' he asked, genuinely worried, as the rest of the staff gathered around Hudson in concern. He didn't like to explain. It's not much fun describing how you were beaten up. It made Hudson feel slightly pathetic, and he didn't particularly wish to dwell on the matter. The only redeeming aspect was that it was quite nice having the women in the office fussing over him for once. Having related his story, with only a couple of minor embellishments and garnering additional sympathy for the break-in at his flat, his colleagues drifted back to their desks. Hudson assured Winston that he was fine to carry on working, noting the relief on his editor's face. It was, after all, the busiest day of the week.

Hudson settled into the routine of the day, with Terleski's dossier tucked away safely in his shoulder bag. It wasn't until lunchtime before he had cleared enough work to begin looking into some of the old man's claims. Either way, it would not affect his feature article, as that had already gone to Winston's electronic basket for editing.

Whilst the rest of the office were disappearing to the sandwich bar below, Hudson stayed at his desk and began flicking through the dossier once more, looking for a good place to start. At this stage, he was only seeking to establish whether it was a hoax or if there was anything, anything at all, to support any of the claims.

Terleski had stated that others had died. His email suggested that they may have been killed to hide what they knew. Hudson decided that it was a good place to start, to see if there was any substance to his claims. He flicked through the dossier, finding an incomplete appendix at the back that listed various names and contact details of the colleagues whom Terleski alleged had been similarly involved in Red Dawn. As Hudson picked up the phone, he felt a cold tingling spread down his spine. *What if? What if?*

He tried the first number, belonging to a Mr Geoffrey Adams. According to the dossier, Adams had been a senior figure in the Nuclear Installations Inspectorate and was a vital member of the Red Dawn programme. Terleski had given a detailed account of the man's alleged role in the affair, and his name had been annotated in the dossier, with a single highlighted word. It read 'dead'.

The phone rang for some time, and Hudson was about to give up and try another number when it was answered breathlessly by someone who sounded as though they had run to the phone. Which they had.

'Hello, Acorns Retirement Village.'

'Geoffrey Adams please.'

There was a long silence.

'Who's calling?'

'A friend.' *Never, ever tell them you're a journalist.*

'Um, I'm afraid I have some very bad news…'

Hudson listened with mounting horror as the warden described the fire in Adams' bungalow, and the discovery of his body by the fire brigade. It looked like he had taken sleeping pills and fallen asleep with a lit cigarette. Extremely tragic, but they had been assured that the smoke would have got to him before the flames. If he was interested in coming, the funeral was to be held at the end of the week. Hudson expressed his deepest condolences and thanked the man.

After hanging up, Hudson sat still for some time. It had to be a coincidence. These things happen.

Next on the list was Howard Roberts. Apparently, he had been a senior official working for the rump state-owned nuclear generating company prior to its privatisation and subsequent reincarnation as Gencor Energy PLC. His retirement had coincided with the company's privatisation, but he too had been an instrumental member of Red Dawn. According to Terleski's account.

Hudson spoke to Mr Roberts' housekeeper, who tearfully informed him of the shocking accident on the pathway the previous weekend. Poor old Howard had slipped and shattered his skull on the hard cobbles. The housekeeper had warned him several times that they were a death trap, but she had been ignored and now look what had happened, she sniffed. Hudson quietly offered his condolences, feeling the icy tendrils of fear creeping up his spine. One death was a coincidence, but two…?

Then there was Dr Bernard Motson, formerly of the UK Atomic Energy Authority and, again, a member of Red Dawn. Dead. A terrible fall in the Snowdonia National Park.

Thomas Hancock, too. The Senior Civil Servant, the Government Technical Advisor, who had worked closely with Terleski at the National Radiological Protection Board, had been found floating in a fishing lake, with a vast quantity of alcohol in his system. It could easily have been an accident. But Hudson had gone way beyond innocent explanations and simple coincidences by now.

As he hung up on Hancock's grieving son, Hudson felt numb. Five surviving members of Terleski's Red Dawn group were dead, in as many days. All the deaths could be explained. Taken by themselves, there was nothing suspicious about them. But the dossier provided a common link: Red Dawn.

Hudson sat back in his chair and let out a deep breath. He tried to take on board what he had just stumbled across. He knew that there could only be one likely explanation. And he knew that he was alone in knowing this.

And he also knew that there was only one man who could be responsible.

Hudson turned back to Terleski's dossier and started reading again:

> "When we found out about the true nature of the explosion at Chernobyl, it was too late for us to do anything about it. The cloud of radioactive particles had already blown over the United Kingdom and had been washed onto the ground. Although the Chernobyl facility was over a thousand miles away, the radioactive cloud had not been subjected to rainfall before arriving over the UK. As a result, although

some of the material had been lost en route by dry deposition, much of it still remained airborne. Over Britain, substantial rain fell from the middle levels of the troposphere, and washed some of this material onto the ground on the 3rd May. At the time, we played down the risk to the public. We didn't want to cause panic, especially as there was nothing we could do to reverse what had happened. However, secretly, we expected a huge increase in cancers, especially amongst children. Quite rightly, the media and environmental groups suspected that this was indeed the case, despite our denials.

The surprising thing is, it seems we were wrong. Scientists across Europe have monitored the incidence of cancer resulting from the Chernobyl explosion, and the level is far below what we were all expecting. It seems that our predictive models were wrong for radioactive exposure at the lower end of the scale. Nevertheless, it is still the case that several farms in the UK remain subject to livestock restrictions due to the radioactivity present in the soil. Across the whole country, more than four hundred farms are still being monitored for the presence of radioactive caesium in the livestock. As I explained before, the caesium in the fallout was absorbed into plants, which were then eaten by sheep on hill farms. As it is not readily excreted, the concentrations build up in the animals, and then in humans who eat those animals.

So far, this is all a matter of public record. That is the beauty of the Red Dawn programme. Sometimes the best place to hide is in the open. The evidence has been all around us for twenty years, yet the programme has still remained a secret. Perhaps the plan was very well executed, or we were incredibly lucky, or both. The fact remains that we got away with it. If you had told me at the time we started that we could pull it off, then I would have thought you were mad. Yet succeed we did.

I had always assumed that the truth would come out one day, releasing me from the burden of guilt that I have carried all these years. Yet, the older I became, the likelihood of the truth emerging seemed to diminish. Many of my colleagues involved have died, taking their secrets to the grave. I can no longer rely on someone else revealing Red Dawn. I must be the one who reveals its secrets, before it is too late. My wife made me realise that.

So, what is Red Dawn?

First, we must consider the facts. As I mentioned, there are over 400 farms in the UK that are still subject to restrictions resulting from radioactive fallout. The principle element being monitored is radioactive Caesium-137. Livestock from these farms is tested for ingestion of radioactive caesium before they can be moved or sold for human consumption. The county of Cumbria is particularly affected. Secondly, there is evidence of an elevated risk of cancer for the inhabitants of areas surrounding these farms, particularly with regards to the incidence of thyroid cancer in Cumbria.

For years, the widely-held assumption has been that the government has deliberately hidden the true effects of the Chernobyl fallout over Britain. This assumption was wrong for two very important reasons.

Firstly, the government never actually deliberately downplayed the consequences; it was simply that there was little that could be done about it at the time.

Secondly, the explosion of Reactor Number 4 at the Chernobyl Nuclear Power Station was not responsible for the long-term quarantining of hill farms in the UK."

When he had first read this section, it had taken Hudson a while for the implication of that last paragraph to sink in. Had he understood it correctly? *The restrictions on certain hill farms in the UK had nothing to do with Chernobyl?*

"My role at the time of the Chernobyl explosion was head of the National Radiological Protection Board. Since April 2005, this has become the Radiation Protection Division of the Health Protection Agency. The original purpose of the Board was to disseminate information concerning the protection of mankind from radiation hazards. Part of our remit was to monitor radiation in the environment, from our facility in Glasgow. We detected elevated background radiation from the Chernobyl explosion two days before the Soviet authorities informed the world. This was over the days immediately following 26th April 1986.

The information that follows has never been revealed to the world. Many of those who could corroborate it are now dead. But it is the truth, as far as I have been able to recollect and from the notes that I have kept over the years.

In the middle of the night of 19th May, 1986 I was busy working in my office at home. Those who know me will testify to my insomnia, without which I doubt I would have been able to cope with the heavy workload I was experiencing after the Chernobyl explosion. At approximately 02:30GMT in the morning of the 20th, I had nearly completed my work for the day, when I was alerted by my colleagues in Glasgow. An elevated radiation reading was being reported from the Cumbria region. At the time I was informed, they were checking the equipment to make sure that there was no malfunction. By 03:00GMT it had been confirmed that background radiation levels in Cumbria were significantly higher than normal. I decided to contact the District Emergency Planning Officer for Cumbria and alert him to the situation. To my surprise, he told me that he was already aware of the problem, but declined to inform me further as he required special authorisation to do so. This was highly irregular, but there was little I could do about it. Local authorities take the lead when responding to any such problem. Later that morning, at about 07:00GMT, I received a phone call from the Department of Trade & Industry in London. I was to attend an urgent COBRA meeting, under the aegis of the Nuclear Emergency Planning Committee. The need for absolute discretion was impressed on me.

The meeting was highly irregular. It was convened behind closed doors in an ancillary office block outside Whitehall, rather than the Nuclear Emergency Briefing Room. Those present included representatives of all the key national agencies relating to the nuclear industry, including the Government Technical Advisor, Dr Thomas Hancock. The meeting was chaired by Charles Millburn, in his capacity as Minister of State for the Department of Trade and Industry, as the Secretary of State, Sir Clive Heathcote, was away, conducting trade negotiations in Brussels. The DTI have ultimate responsibility for nuclear planning and emergencies in the UK. As is his style, Millburn dispensed with the formalities and warned us that what we were about to hear was for our benefit alone and was not to be discussed outside the room under any circumstances. He reminded us of our obligations under the Official Secrets Act. Over the years, I have thought long and hard about this and I am confident that the public interest far outweighs any obligations I may have under the Act. If I am prosecuted, then so be it, but at least my conscience will be clear. What follows is taken from the transcript of that meeting.

We were informed that during the night there had been a catastrophic failure of a storage vessel at the Sellafield

Nuclear Reprocessing Plant in Cumbria. There are a total of twenty one storage vessels in building B215, which contain the highly radioactive liquid waste produced by the reprocessing of nuclear fuel rods. Some of the most hazardous radioisotopes, including caesium-137, are present in this waste. The waste comprises radioactive materials that will remain hazardous for tens of thousands of years. They are stored at the Sellafield site for want of a better alternative.

It is not known what happened precisely, but it seems that an accident with a high-lift platform damaged the main cooling system, along with the emergency back-up systems. This damage was not repaired in sufficient time to prevent Storage Tank 19 from boiling and venting its contents into the atmosphere. The ventilation systems in Building B215 were undergoing essential repairs and equipment upgrades and were unable to cope with the release. The tank boiled for several hours before emergency teams were able to cool it sufficiently, during which time over half of its contents were released into the atmosphere. To compound the problem, there was heavy rainfall in the region, which localised the radioactive fallout.

At first, I assumed that the local emergency plan would be put into effect. That was why I contacted the District Emergency Planning Officer after we had detected the elevated radiation readings for the area.

I was wrong. Charles Millburn obviously had an alternative plan in mind. This was the Red Dawn programme.

The logic was simple. Very few people knew of the disaster. As the cloud had already been washed out over Cumbria, there was little that could be done to protect the populace. We were fairly confident that, as the radioactive fallout was localised, it would not be detected abroad. The final, and fortuitous, piece of the jigsaw was the fact that the radioactive elements released by the leak were similar to those spread by the Chernobyl explosion. Therefore, it would be possible to use the Chernobyl fallout to disguise the Sellafield leak."

At this point, Hudson stopped reading again. It was unbelievable. Had someone told him that European governments had deliberately downplayed the true effect of the Chernobyl disaster in order to bolster support for national nuclear energy programmes, he would have found that hard enough to stomach, but believable. The Red Dawn programme was outrageous. The British Government had deliberately concealed a major leak of highly toxic radioactive materials, warning no one of the dangers.

Hudson was aware of Charles Millburn, now *Sir* Charles, not least because of the high coverage the man had received in the media in recent days. As the Chairman of Gencor Energy PLC, he was one of the key actors in the government's new policy of expanding the nation's nuclear generating capacity. Yet, according to Terleski, he had orchestrated the cover-up of what was arguably one of the worst nuclear disasters ever to befall the UK. As this dawned on Hudson, he had begun to feel a tingling of real fear. In a matter of weeks, Millburn would surely be proudly announcing that his company had secured the £35 billion contracts to build and operate the new generation of power stations. This dossier, if true, could seriously threaten that. If the national press ever got hold of this….

Hudson continued reading.

"Why was there a need for a cover up? The impetus behind this decision was the political context, both national and international. At the national level, the Chernobyl disaster had discredited nuclear power in the eyes of the public, yet it was simply not a credible option for the UK to abandon its nuclear energy programme. Had a Sellafield leak on this scale emerged so soon after Chernobyl, the political commitment to nuclear power would have become unsustainable. There was a general election planned for 1987, and such a disaster would have played directly into the hands of the Labour opposition, who opposed nuclear energy and the nuclear deterrent. Today, it is easy for people to forget that during the 1980s the Soviet Union far outnumbered conventional NATO forces in Europe. The balance of power was achieved only through the fielding of short-range tactical nuclear weapons such as the US-built Pershing II missile system, the deployment of which in Europe was largely complete by late 1985.

The Pershing II system put enormous pressure on the Soviet military planners and, whilst there was a very genuine concern that the Soviet Union may have been provoked into launching a pre-emptive first strike, it was this pressure that was instrumental in bringing President Gorbachev to the Geneva Summit in November 1985, to discuss long-term arms reductions. The United Kingdom was a core supporter of the Pershing II deployment, yet this position would have been threatened by a serious nuclear accident at Sellafield. Millburn made all this clear to us and he was right; a serious accident at Sellafield could have had repercussions that ultimately affected our national security.

Since the early 1980s the European peace movement had grown dramatically, seeking the complete removal of nuclear weapons from European soil. A disaster at Sellafield would have bolstered their cause substantially, helping them influence the Labour opposition and winning political influence for the peace activists. However, that was only ever a hypothetical possibility, not a definite outcome. With hindsight, I believe a cover-up was the wrong decision to make. It is easy for parties in opposition to adopt extreme positions, but once in office they tend to behave with greater sobriety.

At the international level of diplomacy, the Chernobyl disaster was a boon. The Cold War was at its height, and the disaster was a perfect way of discrediting the Soviet Union and its claims of technological superiority. President Reagan had described the Soviet Union as the Evil Empire, and their attempted cover-up only served to confirm the low value they attached to human life. As it turned out, the Chernobyl disaster was the catalyst for President Gorbachev's *glasnost* reforms, which ultimately paved the way for the collapse of the Soviet Union. If it had emerged that we had suffered a similar nuclear catastrophe, we would have lost our claim to moral and technological superiority. As it was, I believe we lost our moral superiority by orchestrating our own cover-up.

Another consideration was the billions of pounds of investment at stake in the THORP reprocessing plant at Sellafield, which had been under construction since 1978. Any major disaster would halt the development, representing an enormous waste of taxpayer funds and jeopardising thousands of jobs. In 1986 the plant was still not completed, so was yet to generate any revenue to offset its enormous construction costs.

The final factor was the fact that there was little that could be done to protect the local population. Mass evacuation was too late, and inconceivable, and the land was already contaminated. The only useful actions we could take were identical to the precautions already in place as a result of the Chernobyl fallout, such as the quarantining of the hill farms in Cumbria.

In sum total, there were a number of compelling reasons to hide the Sellafield leak. The fact that the Chernobyl fallout provided us with a perfect opportunity to cover it up made it an even more attractive proposition. Millburn and his advisors had grasped this immediately, and it wasn't hard for him to persuade us of the necessity. At the time, there was too much at stake. Personally, I considered it to be in the national interest to hide the leak. Today, I recognise that I was wrong, which is why I am writing this.

To begin with, I suspect Millburn's motives had less to do with the national interest and more to do with saving his own political career. He had nothing to lose, as he would have been made the senior scapegoat for any nuclear accident. It was clear that the Secretary of State had either washed his hands of Millburn already, or did not know about the Red Dawn plan. Either way, it was Millburn who was taking responsibility.

Therefore, we all agreed to the Red Dawn project. It made sense at the time, as the plan had already been largely worked out. Red Dawn was the code name for a project devised in response to the major fire at the Windscale reactor in 1957, which later became known as Sellafield. The Windscale facility was at the forefront of Britain's independent nuclear weapons programme, producing plutonium for use in warheads. A fire in the graphite moderator of one its 'piles' resulted in a serious release of radioactive material into the surrounding countryside. Following this, both 'piles' were shut down to prevent the risk of a further incident.

At the time, there were no procedures in place to deal with nuclear emergencies. The British nuclear weapons programme was borne of the extreme urgency to develop an independent deterrent, and achieving success in this took precedence over all other considerations. However, after the Windscale fire, Red Dawn was among the many proposals developed during the subsequent reviews which ultimately led to the formulation of new procedures. Red Dawn was a proposal derived from the very real concerns in the military that further accidents would seriously undermine the country's efforts to be a major nuclear and, therefore, military power. This feeling was especially acute after the 1956 Suez fiasco when global power shifted so firmly towards the United States. Britain was forced into a humiliating withdrawal, along with France and Israel, after the US acted unilaterally to force us to pull out of Egypt, critically weakening our presence in the Middle East and allowing the US to occupy the subsequent politico-military vacuum. Therefore, a strong independent nuclear deterrent was seen as a vital strategic objective to help maintain British global influence. France and Israel came to exactly the same conclusion, which led directly to their bilateral collaboration on independent nuclear programmes, again in the face of US opposition.

Red Dawn was drawn up by the Ministry of Supply to organise a cover up of any future major leak if it was deemed necessary for the protection of our vital national strategic interests. However, the proposal was shelved in 1958 and as a result the code name never received a new alphanumeric designation when the Ministry of Supply was amalgamated into the Ministry of Defence in 1958. It retained its old

Rainbow Code, which identified the various British military research projects during the Second World War. Therefore, as far as the MoD was concerned, no such plan had ever existed, which only served to increase its potential usefulness to us. The details were known only to the very small number of civil servants and military officials who had drawn it up. Charles Millburn must have been advised of the plan by a surviving member of that group, probably his Permanent Secretary at the DTI, Rupert Symonds.

The purpose of the revived Red Dawn programme was to cover up all trace of the leak from the storage facility in building B215 at Sellafield. My own particular role within the programme was to disguise the fact that elevated background radiation had been detected in Cumbria. I altered records and destroyed documents where necessary. This proved to be quite straightforward, as much of the radioactive material had been washed down to the ground by the heavy rain, so there was only a short period of time where its presence was detectable in the atmosphere. Obviously, the background radiation levels at ground level in the affected areas increased, but this was restricted mainly to the same high areas that were affected by the Chernobyl fallout. This time, the high incidence of rainfall in Cumbria was to our benefit, ensuring that the fallout from Sellafield was localised.

To hide the fact that the soil radioactivity had increased, we ensured that we controlled all the monitoring and testing of soil on quarantined farms. This strategy has proved extraordinarily successful over the last twenty years. Some environmental groups have complained that our readings have been too low, but these reports have remained peripheral and have failed to gain currency within the wider media. Again, fortune has favoured us. The last thing the hill farmers want is evidence that the radioactive contamination of their land is worse than already reported. Therefore, they have inadvertently cooperated with us by keeping environmentalists off their properties.

The fact that this story has never emerged is testament to the efficiency of the Red Dawn programme. Over the following pages, I will highlight the roles of specific members of Red Dawn. Unfortunately, much of the documentary evidence has been destroyed. However, a comprehensive reassessment of soil samples should demonstrate higher than reported radioactivity, as well as a contamination ratio different to that produced by the Chernobyl fallout. This is for the simple reason that, although similar, the relative mix of materials, and their chemical signature, released by Sellafield is different to that released by Chernobyl. We have been able to conceal this fact by controlling the formal testing of soil samples. (See Appendix 3(b) for data readings.)

This is a brief summary of Red Dawn. I have set out the details in the rest of this dossier, under each appendix. I have not yet mentioned the cost of Red Dawn, in human terms. We cannot be sure exactly how many additional deaths were caused, but we are certain that the Sellafield B215 leak has resulted in a higher incidence of cancer, especially amongst children. It is likely to number in the hundreds. Their deaths will haunt me for the rest of my life. I do not seek forgiveness; I wish simply to atone for my actions. The truth must be told."

Hudson sat back in his chair and took another deep breath, still trying to digest what he had discovered. Since learning of the deaths of Terleski's colleagues, any lingering scepticism he harboured had been completely dissipated. Hudson was now convinced that Terleski was telling the truth.

The Red Dawn programme really did exist.

And Sir Charles Millburn had the most to lose from it.

The problem was, Hudson was at a loss over what to do next.

19

An enraged Alex Warburton knew exactly what he was going to do next. After being kept in the filthy, stinking cells all morning, he was finally released from custody on police bail, with notice that he would be appearing in court at a later date to face charges of assaulting a police officer. It was ironic really. If he hadn't resisted his arrest, he would have been let off with just a caution for attacking James Hudson. But such considerations were beyond Warburton's limited comprehension. As far as he was concerned, there was only one person responsible for all this, and that person was going to pay for it.

His weary solicitor had engineered his release for a fat fee and it had been as much as he could do to keep Warburton quiet during the interview. He seemed determined to incriminate himself. In the end, though, the cells were full and the police were only too glad to get Warburton out of their sight. His police bail conditions meant that he had to report back to the police station every morning until his court appearance.

As Warburton stormed out of the police station, the solicitor reflected on the fact that sometimes his clients were their own worst enemies but, as long as they paid him, he wasn't overly concerned. Having said that, he was glad to see the back of the oafish Warburton who, he was in no doubt, was guilty as hell of the charges laid against him. Therefore, he would be submitting a plea of not guilty. After all, that's what paid the bills.

*

After considering what to do next for some time, Hudson realised that he had to see Susannah. At first, he had considered going to Winston with his discoveries, but realised that he needed to share them with Susannah first. After all, it was her uncle who had provided him with the dossier, and Hudson was now convinced that his death had a more sinister explanation than suicide. It was only right that Susannah be first to know what he had discovered about her uncle's former colleagues.

Citing great discomfort from his injuries, Hudson received Winston's permission to take the rest of the afternoon. The editor even made it clear that he was grateful for Hudson's efforts that morning, without which the rest of the staff would have had to work late in order to get the newspaper off to the printers by the deadline that evening.

Fortunately, Hudson had not booked his vandalised car into a garage yet, so he was able to collect it from outside his flat and drive down to Manchester. He knew vaguely where Susannah worked, so decided to head there directly. He had been unable to contact her by phone, but that was understandable given that she was working in the laboratory all day, where mobile phones had to be switched off.

Having found a parking place, he ventured into the Cancer Research Institute, where he was able to track down Susannah with the help of a receptionist who, at first, had been wary of Hudson's injuries. He had had to deploy all his charm to win her over.

Susannah, however, was very pleased to see him and gave him a warm embrace, much to the chagrin of the receptionist, whose sensibilities were offended by such public displays. She sniffed loudly with distaste, so Susannah took Hudson into the small common room and bought him a coffee.

'This a nice surprise,' she smiled. 'I needed cheering up, especially after the last couple of days.'

However, her smile faltered when Hudson did not reciprocate and instead concentrated on stirring his coffee.

'What's the matter, James? Is everything alright?' she asked anxiously.

Hudson sighed, not sure how to begin. 'I think I may have found something out. It's not good.'

Susannah was silent, studying him intently.

'I've tried to get in touch with your uncle's colleagues, the ones he mentioned in the dossier.'

'And?' her voice was thin and nervous.

'They're all dead, Susannah.'

She just stared at him, putting her hand to her mouth, her eyes wide with shock.

'Dead? How?' she asked in disbelief.

Hudson explained the series of accidents that had apparently befallen Terleski's four colleagues. 'By themselves, they all seem to be random accidents to random people. It's just that we know they were linked by your uncle's dossier. And they have all died during the last five days.'

'Oh my God, James,' she whispered. 'What's going on?' Her large eyes watered, the fear etched across her face.

'I don't know, but I think we have to accept that your uncle was telling the truth. And I think we have to accept the possibility that these deaths were not accidental.' He paused. 'Or suicides.'

'No!' she gasped, unwilling to accept the enormity of Hudson's implication. Again she put her hand to her mouth in shock, while Hudson explained.

'That's why I needed to see you. I don't think your uncle committed suicide. I think he was killed because of his involvement in the Red Dawn programme.'

It took Susannah a while to compose herself after Hudson's revelations. Suicide was bad enough, but *murder*? She was aghast at the suggestion and couldn't accept it at first. It was something that only happened to people very, very far removed from her everyday life. The possibility that a man she loved deeply had been murdered was almost too much to contemplate. It was a possibility that simply did not exist in her genteel world.

'I don't believe it, James. He can't have been murdered, he just can't,' she shook her head adamantly.

'I'm not sure either, Susannah, but look at the facts. His four colleagues have all died in the last few days. What are the odds of that? The only common link between them is your uncle's dossier. And why would he go to so much effort writing it, then kill himself before he finished it? It doesn't make any sense, unless someone wanted to stop him.'

'But why?' she implored.

'Someone who felt very threatened by their existence and what they knew. Imagine if the dossier became public knowledge, or any of them had spoken about the Red Dawn programme. Who would stand to lose from that?'

'I don't *know*, James,' she insisted, still unwilling to contemplate his argument.

'Sir Charles Millburn. It has to be him, or someone protecting him. According to your uncle, he created Red Dawn. His company is now one of the largest nuclear generators in the world. Can you imagine what would happen if it was revealed he had been behind the cover up of the largest nuclear accident in this country's history?'

Susannah was becoming increasingly agitated. She didn't want to hear any more. 'Stop it, James! Just stop it!' she begged, holding her head in her hands. 'It's not true, it can't be!'

'It has to be! How else do you explain it?' he demanded, his voice rising with frustration. The lady behind the canteen looked up. She didn't like the look of him, not one little bit. Hudson sat back in the chair and sighed in frustration.

They sat in silence for some time, lost in their own thoughts.

'Okay,' she started quietly, after a while, 'assuming you're right, where do we go from here?'

'I'm not sure,' he shrugged. 'We've got no firm evidence other than the dossier and the correlation with the deaths of your uncle's colleagues. It's all circumstantial. We could take this to the police, but what would they do with it? No, somehow we've got to prove the existence of Red Dawn. We need to find some evidence, anything to prove what they did.' Privately, Hudson also did not want to risk losing control of the story at this stage. He knew that if he was right, it would be a career-defining exposé, and there was no way he was going to miss that opportunity. They would go to the police only once they had enough evidence, so that the police could investigate and he could publish.

That decision would soon cost them both dearly.

'I need to get back to the lab,' Susannah announced quietly. 'I need to finish something. I won't be too long.'

'I'll wait. Then I can give you a lift back.'

She smiled her thanks and, with a swish of her medical coat, headed back to work, leaving Hudson to mull over what he had said, alone in the common room.

*

In his office at Canary Wharf, an anxious Kroll took the call at his desk. It was Trevor.

'Yes?'

'It's Trevor, sir...'

'Have you got the proof?' Kroll demanded, interrupting him.

'No sir…there's been a problem.'

Susannah's flatmate, Georgina, sauntered casually up the road of Victorian terraced housing towards their shared accommodation. She had finished her post-doctoral research early for the day and was planning to write up her notes on the computer in the comfort of the flat rather than in the laboratory. She hummed a tune to herself, completely lost in the music playing through her ipod earphones.

'What sort of problem?' Kroll demanded, alerted by the tone of Trevor's voice.

'We've been investigating the girlfriend, Susannah Harlowe…'

'And?' Kroll asked sharply.

'We found out she's Terleski's niece.'

'His niece?'

'Yes sir, that's correct.'

'Then she's the link to Hudson! She has to be. Good work, Trevor.'

'The thing is, I thought it would be a good idea to check out her flat…'

Georgina turned up the music as she approached the peeling red door of the Victorian terraced house, nodding her head with the rhythm. She paused outside the door, searching for her keys. She'd thrown them into her shoulder bag earlier, but couldn't seem to find them now. They must have dropped to the bottom of her bag. Cursing, she crouched down and started removing items and rummaging around to find them, with the music still playing.

'I went down to Manchester to have a look around, whilst Julian stayed up in Preston to keep an eye on the journalist.'

'What about the girl?'

'She was at work. In a cancer institute.'

'Shit. That's all we need. Did you search the flat?'

'Yes. To see if she had the proof.'

'Did you find it?'

'No.'

'So that's the problem?'

'No. Not exactly.'

'What, then?'

Georgina finally located her keys amongst all the clutter in her shoulder bag. She inserted the correct one into the rather inadequate cylinder lock. But, as she pushed the key in, the door simply drifted open. It wasn't locked. She frowned. She could have sworn she had locked it that morning. It certainly wouldn't have been Susannah's fault; she was too fastidious about such things, so it must have been herself. Georgina shrugged, still not unduly perturbed, and stepped inside the hallway, the music still blaring in her ear. She pushed the front door shut and that's when she stopped, her blood running cold. Splintered wood in the doorframe indicated where the latchplate had once sat. She stepped back, fumbling to turn off her ipod.

In the silence, she could feel her heart thudding. The door to the lounge lay slightly ajar. Georgina felt the fear welling up inside her, and her throat went dry. She listened but could hear nothing. She should leave right now, go and find help. But something compelled her to reach out slowly, putting her hand to the door and gently pushing against it. It began to swing open, revealing the room.

Then she put her hands to her mouth in shock.

Since his release from custody, Alex Warburton had a score to settle. Instead of returning to his gym, the scene of his humiliation at the hands of the police, he headed for Susannah's flat. His mind was full with the violent retribution he was going to inflict on her and her stupid bastard of a boyfriend. He would put her in her place, teach her a lesson. He was going to show her who the boss was. Who the hell did the little bitch think she was?

He raced his modified BMW up her street, his rage intensifying by the second. He parked in a hurry, leaving the car at an angle in a space too small for it. Slamming the door hard, he strode towards her front door purposefully. He could still see her smooth, firm body. It had been a long time. Perhaps he'd see it again. Yes, that would teach her, show her what she was missing. His breathing was heavy as the testosterone began to rage inside him. He hammered on her front door.

'I thought no one was there,' Trevor explained to Kroll. 'Her flatmate had gone out, so I thought I had plenty of time.'

Warburton hammered on the front door again. No answer. Then he heard a noise inside. The little bitch was there. She was hiding from him. Something inside his head snapped and he put his shoulder to the door. Three lunges and the softwood frame gave, the door crashing open. Warburton burst inside, wild-eyed. Where was the little bitch? She was going to get it now.

He booted the door to the lounge open, then stopped in his tracks. Something wasn't quite right. Too late, he caught the movement out of the corner of his eye.

'I heard him at the door. Next minute he just came through it. Took the lock clean off the frame. He was built like a shithouse.'

'What happened?' asked Kroll sharply.

The blow caught the unprepared Warburton on the side of the head, but he recovered quickly. He saw his assailant attempt to flee via the front door and lunged for him, bringing him down in the doorway to the hall. Warburton laid into him ferociously, landing blow after blow on the man. Nobody hit him and got away with it lightly. However, he had underestimated his opponent and Trevor managed to get a good hold and throw Warburton off him. He went on the attack, but Warburton jumped up to meet him. They grappled with each other, falling over the small coffee table and crashing onto the dining table, breaking two of the legs off and falling to the floor with it. Trevor stood up and laid some kicks into Warburton before trying to make his escape again, but Warburton was like a machine. Pumped up with rage, he was unstoppable and leapt onto Trevor's back, a powerful arm around his throat. Trevor kicked back at Warburton's shins but couldn't weaken the grip. They careened backwards into a wall, as Trevor desperately tried to dislodge him. Warburton merely grunted at the impact and they clattered into the kitchenette. Trevor found he was gasping for breath, with pinpricks of light in his peripheral vision. He could feel Warburton's hot breath on his ear as Warburton panted with the exertion of crushing his throat.

In desperation, Trevor's hands scrabbled for something to use. His left hand found the knife block and he fished for a handle. Warburton saw what he was doing, but was too slow to prevent it. With a vicious rearward stab, Trevor sank the blade up to the hilt beneath Warburton's ribcage. The vicelike grip on his neck slackened immediately and Trevor twisted out of the embrace. He turned to face Warburton, who had a look of shock on his face. Trevor pulled the knife out and plunged it in again, twisting it up under the sternum. He had chosen well. The eight inch chef's blade was more than enough for the job, but it was a job that shouldn't have needed doing. It was a professional error, which should have been avoided. He twisted the blade further, ensuring it inflicted maximum damage to the organs in the chest cavity. He gritted his teeth with the exertion and looked hard into Warburton's stunned face. Then he pulled the knife out and watched Warburton sink to the floor, bleeding profusely. Cursing at the mess, Trevor dropped the knife into the sink with a clatter and stood back to survey the scene, as the life ebbed out of his victim.

'You killed him?' asked Kroll, the anger clear in his voice.

'I had to sir. I tried to get away, but he gave me no choice.'

'What about the body?'

'I managed to dump it.'

'How did you leave the flat?'

In a state of shock, Georgina surveyed the scene. The burglars had smashed the place up and taken the usual electrical items. They'd even broken the dining table. Stunned, she went through to the kitchenette to find smashed crockery littered across the floor. One of the cupboard doors was hanging precariously from its one remaining hinge. She headed through to her bedroom, which had also been ransacked. Drawers had been emptied, the contents tipped out and scattered over the floor and bed. Underwear and make-up was strewn everywhere. Susannah's bedroom told a similar story. Not content with stealing, the burglars had trashed the place too. Georgina sat down on the sofa and burst into tears.

'I had to make it look like a break-in. I took the video and stereo, plus some CDs, then trashed the place. The police probably won't even visit; it'll be an open and shut burglary case.'

'What about the blood?'

'I did my best. As long as the police aren't looking for it, they won't find any traces.'

Kroll was silent for a moment. The incident could have ended in catastrophe, but it seemed to be entirely unforeseen. He would let Trevor off. This time.

'So, there was no sign of the proof against Millburn?'

'No. I looked everywhere.'

'Then where the hell did he hide it?' Kroll demanded in exasperation.

'Could be anywhere, sir.'

Kroll pondered the problem for a while.

'He would only have left it for someone he trusted. He sent his dossier to the journalist, and the girl's his niece. They are the most likely candidates. Keep watching them for now.'

'Yes sir.'

20

Susannah managed to finish work early, keeping Hudson waiting for less than an hour. As she came out of the laboratory, she checked her mail box next to the reception and removed several envelopes. She was about to go through the mail, when her mobile rang. It was probably her answer phone messaging service. Stuffing the unopened envelopes in her bag, she fished it out of her jacket to check, and smiled when she saw the caller identity.

'It's Georgina,' she announced, rolling her eyes at Hudson. 'Probably wants my advice about her bloke…Hi Georg…what's the matter?…Calm down, calm down.' Hudson looked up, sensing the alarm in Susannah's voice.

'What? Burgled? No way!…What's been taken?'

Susannah listened while Georgina described the scene she had come home to, repeating it out loud for Hudson's benefit. The flat had been trashed. Several DVDs and CDs were missing, along with the stereo system and television. They were both thinking the same thing: It was too much of a coincidence. The police were on their way apparently. Finally, she hung up.

'We need to get over there right now, Georgina's really upset.'

'Sure, my car's outside.'

Traffic was heavy, giving Susannah time to let it sink in as they snaked their way across the city.

'I can't believe we've been burgled,' she sniffed as the realisation dawned. 'This is the first time. We're so careful about locking up and security…Oh god, I hope they haven't taken any of my jewellery…'

She rummaged in her bag for a tissue, pulling the unopened envelopes out to do so. Having found a small handypack, she began putting the letters back in her bag. But then she suddenly stopped. Hudson glanced at her.

'What's the matter?'

'It's Uncle William's handwriting,' she said quietly, swallowing. Hudson looked over to see the handwritten envelope in her hand.

'Oh my god!' she blurted. 'It's postmarked Monday. That's the day he died!'

Hudson pulled onto the side of the road, where he stopped the car. Susannah was staring at the envelope.

'Are you going to open it?'

There was no reply from Susannah, who carried on staring at it.

'Susannah?'

She glanced at him tearfully.

'What if it's his last note, James?' she asked softly, a tear running down her cheek. He nodded in understanding.

'There's only one way of finding out,' he replied gently. She took a deep breath and slit the envelope open with her finger. She extracted a single sheet of white paper, covered with Terleski's black scrawl.

Reluctantly, she began reading and the look of apprehension on her face was replaced with a frown.

'What does it say?'

She turned to look at him, her expression a mixture of fear and confusion.

'He's got proof. Proof that Red Dawn exists.'

*

A patrol car had been in the area at the time Georgina had placed her call to the local police station, so the two officers had called in to look at the scene and take a statement from her. She was lucky; most reported burglaries warranted little more than the standard issuing of an insurance crime reference number and a letter from the Victim Support charity.

Having watched too many crime dramas on television, Georgina had been careful not to disturb any potential forensic evidence and had waited for them from the comfort of the sofa.

Police constables Evans and Harris had arrived shortly and, having seen Georgina, were in no rush to leave. PC Evans had the pleasure of taking a witness statement from her, leaving PC Harris to look around the flat, to his obvious chagrin. He swaggered into the kitchen as purposefully as he could, for Georgina's benefit, who didn't notice, and idly nudged some broken glass with his gleaming toe cap. He made a show of surveying the scene with an expression of detached professionalism on his face. The light bulb flickered, about to burn through its filament.

'Got a new light bulb, love?' he called from the kitchen. 'I'll change it for you.'

'Left hand drawer,' Georgina replied testily, disliking the over familiar term of address and resenting the thinly-veiled chauvinism. She was beginning to regret their presence in the flat.

PC Harris found a new light bulb and reached up to change it. Then he stopped, and frowned. He peered a little closer at the ceiling.

'Dave? Come and have a look at this,' he called to his colleague. Rolling his eyes theatrically, PC Evans pulled himself away from the lovely Georgina and joined Harris in the kitchen.

'What now?' he demanded, to demonstrate to Georgina who was the superior officer.

'Up there, by the light fitting.'

Evans peered at the ceiling, then glanced at Harris with a frown. 'I think we'd better get forensics down here to have a look.'

An hour later, the forensic officer stepped down off his small stool. 'It's blood alright,' he announced to the two officers. 'The thing is, whose is it?'

The three men turned and looked at a very frightened Georgina.

*

'Are you sure about this?' asked Susannah, as they headed south out of Manchester and onto the M6 motorway towards Birmingham.

'We've got to find that proof,' replied a determined Hudson. 'I don't like what's going on and I want to find out, for sure, one way or another, if Red Dawn really does exist or not.'

'But what about Georgina? She needs me right now. And I want to see what's been taken.'

'What if it wasn't a burglary? What if someone was trying to find this letter, or the proof?'

Susannah said nothing.

'What about my flat? They took my laptop, but nothing else. What if that was linked to all this?'

'You're starting to sound paranoid, James.'

'*Paranoid?*' He was incredulous. 'Your uncle and four of his colleagues are dead! All within days of each other. And you call me paranoid?'

Susannah was quiet again. The whole thing seemed crazy to her. At first, she had been swept along by Hudson's infectious conspiracy theories but, privately, even she now thought that her uncle must be playing some sort of game, his parting shot to the world before he killed himself. He had probably scanned the internet for news articles on former civil servants and randomly selected four who had died recently to insert into his wild story. That would explain why there was no obvious link between the men and Uncle William other than his ridiculous dossier. But Hudson was convinced, and even she had to recognise that if they followed her uncle's trail to its logical conclusion, then at least they would know. But she suspected that the 'proof' would merely confirm her own suspicions; her uncle would reveal the ruse and Hudson would be unbearable, having fallen for it. But at least they would know.

She sighed and watched the sun drop behind the western horizon as they roared down the motorway. Life certainly hadn't been dull since she had met James, and she allowed herself a sneaking glance at his craggy face, his chin set in determination. No, life had not been dull.

21

Sometimes Detective Inspector Carl Brannigan craved nothing but a dull life. Twenty years spent investigating brutal murders in and around Manchester had taken its toll. Despite his best attempts, it was impossible to remain completely unaffected by the capacity of human beings to inflict untold pain and suffering on one another. In return, society's punishment for those responsible and apprehended by Brannigan was the denial of their liberty, but in surroundings better than the basic living conditions for the bulk of humanity. It was not ideal, but better than nothing, and Brannigan was zealous when it came to getting his man. So zealous that his marriage and health came a distant second and third on his list of considerations. Both had gone by the wayside a long time ago. He was overweight, lonely, irascible and utterly brilliant at his job. Disliked but respected. By his colleagues and crooks in equal measure.

Brannigan rubbed his eyes to alleviate the tiredness induced by six hours of staring at the computer. A mound of box files sat, menacingly, on the adjoining desk. The unsolved case pile. He glanced at the cheap plastic clock on the wall, the hands creeping slowly towards five o'clock. His shift was due to end at eight, by which time, undoubtedly, the pile of folders was likely to have grown. For all the government's talk of reducing crime, it seemed more rampant than ever. And that wasn't just because of the plethora of new offences brought in to tackle hate crimes and antisocial behaviour. Members of the criminal fraternity who harboured any intelligence had long since calculated that there was little chance of being punished for their crimes. Even if they were caught and successfully prosecuted, the prisons were full to bursting and the judiciary was under pressure to send fewer convicted felons down.

However, murder was a crime still deemed important enough to warrant investigation, and DI Brannigan was adamant that those responsible would be brought to justice.

As he rubbed his weary eyes, the internal mail courier deposited yet another fresh addition to the pile of box folders. Brannigan groaned his thanks to the courier who grinned sheepishly at his contribution to Brannigan's obvious backlog of work. He casually opened up the folder, to giving it a cursory glance. Known drug dealer found beaten to death on wasteland. He sighed wearily and tossed it onto the heap of folders. It was never ending.

*

As the sun began to set, the well-to-do lady parked her immaculate people carrier in one of the car parks that served the sprawling grounds and woodland of Cuerden Valley Park, just south of Preston, close to the motorway that linked the town to Manchester. It wasn't her usual parking area, but for some reason the one she normally frequented had been full today, so she was forced to find an alternative, much to her annoyance. The change in routine also meant that she would have to follow an unfamiliar path, which really wasn't on, as her poor little dog would probably get confused, or lost or succumb to some other awful calamity. She hated her routine being altered in any way. She tutted and cursed, then made a fuss of positioning an expensive ramp at the boot of her vehicle to allow her rotund Labrador to descend at his own leisure. The fat hound crawled out the warm boot, where he had been quite cosy, and reluctantly padded down the ramp, sniffing the cool evening air with dismay. His mistress fussed about him a bit more and made a palaver of putting the ramp back inside the car, taking great care not to scratch the gleaming paintwork. She tutted again as she struggled to change out of her driving plimsolls and into heavy duty walking boots. There was considerable risk that her socks might come into contact with dirt during the delicately executed change of apparel. Such an awful possibility did not bear thinking about: The car had only been valeted the previous day.

After consulting her wristwatch and noting the rapidly diminishing sunlight, she tutted yet again. The detour had ensured that they were a full twenty minutes late commencing their regular evening callisthenics, and poor Bergerac would have his business to attend to at any moment. As far as poor Bergerac was concerned, the only business he really wanted to attend to involved wolfing down the biscuits he had seen his owner secrete in her pocket before they left the house. But he would have to wait. They were always his reward after an energetic walk, the only problem being that they invariably contained more calories than those he had recently expended.

His mistress found the single path that led away from the car park and into the undergrowth, and she set off purposefully. Bergerac lolloped along behind her, rather reluctantly, but mindful of the biscuits in her pocket. However, he soon realised that this was not the usual dreary walk and, finding a vigour that surprised him, crashed off into the undergrowth. His owner marched on, aware of the rustling noises around her as Bergerac tore through the bracken and undergrowth. She sighed, thinking of the mess he would make of the car. Their usual route was far cleaner, winding as it did through one of the more actively maintained areas of the 650 acre park. This route, on the other hand, was most distasteful, with muddy puddles and excessive foliage. They would have to make a point of arriving earlier at the usual parking place.

For his part, Bergerac was having a rather grand time. The new walk was throwing up all sorts of interesting new aromas from the virgin territory. There was one aroma in particular that caught his attention and he homed in on it. It had a sweet, metallic note, which reminded him of the contents of the white bags his mistress sometimes brought back from her trips to the shops. Bergerac hauled his sweating bulk through a coppice of young silver birch, then into a dense thicket of bracken. And then he stopped, casting his nose about him.

His owner was aware that the racket coming from the undergrowth had ceased, and she also stopped.

'Bergerac? Berrrrr-ger-aaac!' she called. No response. Perhaps he was finally attending to his business, so she gave him a couple of moments. No good rushing him, that wasn't fair on the poor thing. She headed into the undergrowth, roughly in the direction from whence she had last heard him. She called out again, but to no avail. Her concern growing, she plunged further into the tall, cloying bracken, feeling nervous as it enveloped her. She stopped to get her bearings, and then she heard a noise, a low growling. *Bergerac!* She headed confidently towards the noise.

'Come here Bergerac, you naughty boy!' she chided indulgently as she homed in on the errant hound. The black Labrador was having none of it, though. She found him in an area of flattened bracken, wrestling furiously with something in a burst of energy not known since he was a puppy.

'Bergerac! What have you got there? Come on, leave it alone, you naughty little doggy.' The dog was oblivious to her.

'Bergerac! I'm going to get cross with you now if you don't come right away!'

Not fully conversant with the nuances of the English language, the hound decided to chance his luck and carried on as before. His owner strode up and grabbed him by the collar. She looked down to see what Bergerac had been playing with.

And screamed.

*

The sun had set when Hudson and Susannah reached Henley-in-Arden. The motorway around Birmingham had been less congested than usual and they had made good time. Susannah had spoken to Georgina on the phone, but had not revealed where they were going, despite Georgina's pleas. Susannah had been worried to learn of the police interest in the speckles of blood on the ceiling, which was apparently fresh, but calmed Georgina down by assuring her that, if the burglars had cut themselves, at least the police would be more likely to investigate and hopefully get a match from the DNA database. Susannah promised her that they would be back later that evening.

They cruised down the pretty, gentrified high street, before turning off for the country lane that headed towards Terleski's house, with Hudson following Susannah's instructions.

Terleski had bought at the right time. Although he had found it difficult enough to finance his purchase in the 1980s, property prices for the popular village would have been completely beyond him now.

Hudson was certainly impressed as they followed a long brick wall and turned into a gravel driveway. In front of them, the wrought iron gates had been shut, so Susannah climbed out to open them. The cars headlights played over the house and grounds which, although they were in a state of genteel decay, had the effect of enhancing the property, rather than detracting from it. The double-fronted bay windows needed a lick of paint, the ivy was threatening to spread its tendrils over the panes and the garden in front of them could be politely termed a nature reserve. Despite the slightly tatty appearance, it was all very pleasant.

However, Hudson felt a chill when he thought about what had recently happened here, and the dark ramshackle property suddenly took on an eerie perspective.

Susannah walked back to the car.

'They're chained. I can't open them. We'll have to climb in.'

'Great,' muttered Hudson under his breath, as he switched off the engine, plunging them into darkness.

Both of them failed to spot the headlights further down the lane, which also suddenly vanished.

*

The forensic officers spent some time at the scene in the parkland, photographing the exhumation in minute detail. A tent had been erected over the site in order to preserve any evidence. The lady who owned Bergerac had been taken away by a police counsellor for comforting. A brief statement was required, but it was clear she was merely in the wrong place at the wrong time and had stumbled across an appalling discovery.

Putrefaction had yet to begin, but it would have only been a matter of time before a combination of relatively warm and damp conditions took their course. The victim had died very recently. A narrow minor road ran past the copse and the killer must have thought he was dumping the body somewhere where it was most unlikely to be discovered. He or she, though it was assumed it was a he, had not realised that the huge parkland site was criss-crossed with narrow and, in some cases, poorly defined footpaths. In a further indication of the hurried nature of the disposal, the body was not properly buried, merely concealed beneath scrub and bracken, and was fully clothed. A wallet was found in a jacket pocket, providing them with a preliminary identification.

A cursory examination of the corpse revealed massive wounding to the chest and stomach, presumably with a sharp instrument. Death had been accompanied by a huge loss of blood, and the body was heavily bloodstained, giving rise to the scent which had attracted the dog.

Presumably, the killer must have been heavily bloodstained too. It did not require the services of a forensic expert to make the assessment that the death was suspicious. The body was released to the care of the pathologist who would be carrying out an urgent post-mortem for what was quite clearly a murder investigation.

Detective Inspector Carl Brannigan had been notified of the discovery of the body within minutes, even though technically it was outside his patch. The reality was that his murder squad had the expertise to mount a suitable investigation, where the local constabulary would have been out of their depth. Although he had a backlog of cases to investigate, this particular one was already showing considerable promise.

The deceased, identified as Mr Alex Warburton, was known to the police, having been bailed that very morning on a charge of assaulting a police officer. Most interesting. Even more revealing, the database revealed that he was also involved in an assault on a Mr James Hudson the evening before, outside the address of a Miss Susannah Harlowe. Hudson had not wished to press charges, but the database revealed that the same James Hudson had reported a break in and theft from his flat in Preston that very morning. The officers in attendance had noted facial injuries to Hudson, which had led to the complaint of assault, and revealed that Warburton and Harlowe had been in a relationship previously.

The police make use of geographical information systems which can link seemingly disparate information very quickly and easily, hence Brannigan's rapid assessment of the situation. The system revealed that police officers had been called to Susannah Harlowe's flat that afternoon by her housemate, Georgina Myers. Officers had attended the scene and had discovered fresh blood in the kitchen, which had been confirmed by forensics. Furthermore, a detailed examination of the kitchen under ultraviolet light revealed spray patterns that were not visible to the naked eye. Samples had been taken, as they were suspected of belonging to the burglar or burglars, but Brannigan was already forming other ideas.

He checked Hudson's address: A waterfront apartment in Preston. Then he pulled out a local road map. The body of Alex Warburton had been found in Cuerden Valley Park. He consulted the map. It was just off the junction of the M6 and M65. Very convenient for someone travelling back to Preston.

Brannigan picked up the phone.

22

Hudson and Susannah stood in the darkness of Terleski's driveway, waiting for their eyes to adjust and listening for any noises. The dark shadow of the empty house loomed in front of them. Hudson was about to approach the locked gates when he suddenly tensed.

'Shh! What's that?' he hissed. They both froze to the spot. Nothing.

'What is it?' Susannah whispered.

'I thought I heard a car,' Hudson whispered back.

'I can't hear anything,' she replied.

They stood in silence for a while longer, but Hudson must have been mistaken. Besides, it was a free country and there was nothing to stop anyone wanting to drive down this lane if they so wished. It was just his nerves getting to him.

'Do you still want to go in?' Susannah whispered.

'We have to,' Hudson murmured back, drawing confidence from the sound of his own voice. He stepped up to the tall wrought iron gates, just as the moon peered out from beneath a scudding cloud, bathing the garden in its milky glow. The gates were ornamental, their function clearly losing out to form, and would be easy enough to surmount, with the bars far enough apart to place feet into the gaps and onto the cross-pieces. Hudson was first to scramble up and over the gates, but caught the hem of his jeans on one of the spikes and fell awkwardly to the ground, grunting loudly as he did so. Susannah clambered over after him, with Hudson making sure she didn't snag herself in similar fashion. Helping her to the ground, he pulled her into the undergrowth.

Fearful of the noise they had made, they hid in the shadows of the undergrowth next to the wall, to see if they had alerted anyone to their presence. Susannah clung to him and Hudson could feel his heart racing. They waited for some time, until they were convinced it was safe to continue. As the adrenalin rush subsided he became painfully aware that his hands were badly grazed; he could feel grit from the driveway stuck into his palms. In the darkness, Hudson rubbed his hands together to dislodge the imbedded grit and then pinched his hands between his knees until the resulting soreness subsided.

Cautiously, they left the sanctuary of the shadows and approached the house. The gravel crunched beneath their feet with terrible loudness so they stepped onto the grass verges of the driveway, where progress was quieter. Following Susannah's directions, they crept around the side of the imposing bulk of the old Victorian building, and headed towards the rear, out of sight of the road.

Hudson inspected the solid French windows that overlooked the gardens to the rear. The old fashioned mortise lock would be impossible to force without causing serious damage and noise, especially as the old doors were likely to be made of oak. Instead, he checked the low bay windows to either side, with their sash casements. He was in luck. Looking through the glass, he could see that one of the old latch locks was broken. In addition, there were no signs that the house was alarmed. He pushed his sore palms against the top of the bottom casement and exerted gentle pressure. The sash slid upwards, the castors squealing as the weighted sash cord ran over them. Hudson winced at the noise and they waited for seemed an age, listening for the slightest indication that they had been heard. When they were sure they were still safe to continue, he clambered over the low sandstone sill and into the dark room, beckoning Susannah to follow. Once inside what must have been the old drawing room, he turned to Susannah.

'It's up to you now,' he whispered. 'Have you got the letter?'

'I can't see what I'm doing; I need a light.'

'Here, use this.' He handed her the tiny pen torch from his key fob, which only emitted a faint glow. But it was adequate for their purpose. Susannah pulled the letter out and unfolded it.

Woodfield House

Henley-in-Arden

Warwickshire

WV12 1LX

Monday 28th September 2009

Dearest Susannah

I am forced to send you this letter to safeguard some information which is of immense value. If something should happen to me, you must retrieve it before it falls into the hands of those who wish to suppress it. It is in relation to the dossier I have already sent to your friend James, and he will find it of great interest should he have any doubts about the veracity of what I have told him. The evidence has already been carefully secreted, as I do not think I will have time to make alternative arrangements with it.

As an extra precaution, should this letter fall into the wrong hands, you must use your intuition to find the location. Only you can do this.

Yours ever,

William

Remember how May liked hunting in the main, especially when the season was right?

'We need to find Auntie May's book collection. I think it's in Uncle William's study,' Susannah whispered.

'Lead the way.'

Susannah nodded nervously in the glow of the faint torchlight, and headed out of the room, into the hallway. With trepidation, they approached Terleski's study. Inside, though they weren't to know it, his papers had been tidied into neat piles by the relatives who had been sorting out his estate. It was certainly far tidier than Susannah's recollections of it. Susannah played the feeble torch beam around the room, until it fell on a large bookcase against the back wall. May Terleski had been an English teacher, with a strong interest in American literature and poetry. This had been the basis of her master's degree, which she had undertaken on her retirement. After long years teaching bored and disinterested pupils at a variety of local comprehensives, she had craved one last chance to exercise the grey matter. As soon as she retired she had embarked on a communication course, loving every minute of it. Susannah remembered the pride she had shared with Uncle William when she had been awarded the MA. The certificate still hung on the wall.

Susannah murmured the last line of the letter to herself:

Remember how May liked hunting in the main, especially when the season was right.

It was obviously a clue, but one that only someone with Susannah's intimate personal knowledge could solve. She approached the bookcase and played the torchlight over the book spines.

In the main. A reference to the University of Maine.

Hunting. Constance Hunting, Professor of English at the University of Maine. That part of the clue had dawned on her immediately, but that was as far as she had got with it. The only way they could pursue Terleski's trail was to visit the house, where Auntie May's beloved book collection was kept. Auntie May had waxed lyrical about Maine and the poetry of Constance Hunting, which had been the basis of her MA thesis. She had once mused about enrolling on a creative writing course over there, but that was just idle fancy. She entertained many such thoughts. Sometimes she would enthuse to Susannah about the great wide world that lay out there, encouraging her to see some of it before it was too late. It was already too late for Auntie May.

The torchlight picked up the collection of works by Constance Hunting.

'Here it is, I've found it,' she whispered.

*

DI Brannigan put the phone down. He was on to something. He could feel it in his bones. The chase was on.

There was no sign of either Susannah Harlowe or James Hudson, at home or their places or work.

Forensics had been in touch with an update. An examination by ultraviolet light had revealed blood spatters all over the kitchen at Susannah's flat, invisible to the naked eye, but still there nevertheless. The pathologist had spoken to him on the phone to state that, subject to further examination, the cause of death was massive trauma inflicted by a large bladed weapon, such as a kitchen knife. Forensics had found a large kitchen knife with traces of blood. In Susannah Harlowe's kitchen. They were now checking to see if the blood samples matched those of Alex Warburton. Brannigan was prepared to stake his house that they would.

Brannigan could already see what must have happened. Warburton had left custody at lunchtime. That fact had already been confirmed with the station. Warburton then decided to pay Susannah a visit. Again, that fact was incontrovertible, as officers at the flat had confirmed that the thug's distinctively customised BMW was parked on the street outside. However, Warburton hadn't bargained on Hudson being there. Or perhaps he had, and wanted to finish off whatever business he had started the night before. There was a fight, it went a bit too far and, for whatever reason, deliberate or not, Warburton was stabbed to death. Could have been self-defence, could have been deliberate. Or perhaps Susannah was by herself, acted in self-defence, then asked Hudson for help in hiding the body. Cuerden Valley Park was on the way to Preston, so Hudson would have known about it. Either way, he was convinced they were responsible. If it was self-defence, the courts could be reasonable. But hiding the body and running away? It didn't look good, not good at all. Both were looking at substantial custodial sentences.

The fact that the body was found so quickly pointed to a panicky disposal. The murder had not been planned, or if it had, it had not been planned very well. Hudson had stuck to the area he knew, knew the quiet spots to dump a body in a hurry. He had found that little side road off the motorway, saw the trees and thought, yes, that's a good place. As good as any. Trouble was, he didn't know there would be dog walkers. How could he? In a panic, he picked the wrong place. Presumably it would all come out in court, when the defence lawyers would push for a charge of manslaughter on the grounds of provocation or self-defence, rather than murder.

But that was a matter for the courts. In the meantime, Brannigan still had to find them, and arrest them both for murder.

*

With mounting excitement, Susannah removed the books from the bookcase and passed them to Hudson, who flicked through them eagerly. Slowly, their faces turned to disappointment.

Nothing.

'There's nothing here,' hissed Hudson. 'Are you sure this is right?'

'Absolutely. Unless you can think of anything better,' she challenged him. Ignoring this, Hudson peered into the space on the bookshelf vacated by the books. There was nothing there either.

'Okay, I think you're on to something, but it's not as obvious as we would like it to be. Realistically, would he have left the proof right here in his office? No. Especially if he knew someone might find it. Either that, or someone's already been here and found it.'

'So where is it then?' asked Susannah, ignoring the last possibility.

'The books must be a clue as well.'

They spread the books and poem pamphlets out across the desk, desperately searching for inspiration. The onus was on Susannah, who had led them to this point. Hudson sighed and began reading the titles out aloud.

'Cimmerian and Other Poems; After the Stravinsky Concert and Other Poems; Beyond the Summerhouse….Hang on, that's where they found him, wasn't it? In the summerhouse?'

Susannah nodded, her eyes welling up at the thought of it. Hudson was silent for a while, before the awful irony began to dawn on him.

'Do you think that's what he meant?'

'What?'

'Perhaps your uncle meant the summerhouse. It's the only title that makes any sense. To me anyway.'

'I don't know.'

'Well, it's worth a look, isn't it? Unless you can think of something better,' he said, throwing her earlier comment back at her.

She didn't reply, merely shrugged. There was little else to go on.

After creeping outside, Hudson and Susannah cautiously approached the small hexagonal brick structure in the corner of the garden. There was nothing to indicate what had happened there three days earlier, but Hudson felt a cold lump of fear rise in his throat as they paused outside the scene of Terleski's horrific demise.

'The poem was titled *Beyond the Summerhouse*,' he whispered to Susannah. 'It must be near by.' Hudson wished to procrastinate on entering the small building, which suited Susannah too, and they both scanned the surrounding wall and overgrown flower beds in the moonlight. But, after a few minutes of searching, they had found nothing.

'We'll have to check inside,' he quietly informed Susannah, who nodded reluctantly.

Hudson steeled himself and pulled the door open. He shone his pencil torch around the inside before stepping in. His eyes could not help but flick up to the beam from where Terleski must have hung. Taking another deep breath, he entered the dark, forbidding shadows, noting that Susannah hovered outside the doorway, unwilling to go any further. Hudson felt his skin crawl at the thought of Terleski dangling from the beam, motionless, his unseeing eyes wide open with the terror of his final moments. The feeble glow of the pen torch provided little comfort, and Hudson felt an overwhelming urge to abandon the summerhouse to its ghosts. But that would be doing Terleski a disservice, his professional voice told him. Focus on the story. Focus on the story.

He played the torchlight over the walls. The place was cold and damp, and the brickwork lower down the walls was discoloured by green algae, sustained by the rising damp and relative shade inside the building. Oak benches were built into the walls, supported by wooden lintels that spanned the obtuse angles of the internal corners of the hexagonal building. Other than the benches, there was nothing else in the way of fixtures or fittings. The walls were of plain, exposed brickwork, with two openings for south facing windows. The quarry-tiled floor was in shabby condition. But that was it. There was nothing there. Perhaps the police had removed the contents for examination? Perhaps they had found the proof hidden by Terleski?

Hudson sighed and turned to leave. But as he spun on his heel, he was aware of a slight movement beneath his foot, and he felt the edge of his heel catch on a tile. He shone the torch down instinctively. The tiles of the poorly maintained floor seemed quite loose, which was hardly surprising considering their condition. Hudson thought nothing of it and stepped out of the summerhouse, joining Susannah.

'Nothing,' he reported, the disappointment obvious in his voice.

'What shall we do now?'

'I don't know. Search for more clues?' Hudson paced backwards and forwards in frustration. 'Why did he have to make it so bloody cryptic?' he asked no one in particular. 'Why be so vague? *Beyond* the summerhouse could be anywhere. Why couldn't he be more specific? Like, on *top* of the summerhouse, or *beneath* the summerhouse?'

'Perhaps he didn't mean the summerhouse at all? That's only our interpretation of the clue. It could be completely wrong.'

'Could be. It's just that it seems to make sense. Think of the clue. *Remember how May liked hunting in the main, especially when the season was right.* It's got to be that book. It's the only one that refers to a season. So, it's got to be something to do with the summerhouse. But *what?*'

'I don't know, James.'

They stood in silence for a while, mulling it over.

'I'm going to have another look. In case I missed something.' Hudson stepped back into the summerhouse. He flashed the torchlight up to the timbers in the roof, examining them carefully. He stood on a bench and ran his fingers along the top course of brickwork, following the wallplate around the base of the roof. Nothing. Cursing softly, he jumped down off the bench. There was a clatter.

'Shit!' he muttered, looking down at the floor. His heel had landed on the edge of one of the loose tiles, flipping it over and exposing the sharp sand on which they were embedded. He placed the tile back, but had messed up the sand, so that the tile did not sit flat. He stamped on it with his heel to knock it flush.

And that's when he noticed it. *Whump, whump.* He moved his heel over to the right and stamped down. Good solid *thwack*. He stamped on the tile he had just replaced. *Whump.*

He got down onto his hands and knees and tapped the tiles with his knuckles. Four of the nine-inch tiles, including the one he had dislodged, had a hollow sound.

'Susannah!' he hissed, insistently. 'Come here! I think I've found something!'

She crept cautiously into the building, whilst Hudson scrabbled at the tiles. He removed the dislodged tile again. The tiles had been bedded directly onto compacted sand, with no mortar, hence their deterioration over a century of use. It also meant they were easy to remove. With mounting excitement, he pulled at the edges of the other three tiles. They came free with little effort, exposing the smooth, compacted damp sand in an eighteen-inch-square hole in the floor. With his fingers, Hudson gently probed and loosened the sand, drawing it back to the edges of the exposed square. After reaching a depth of a couple of inches, his fingertips felt a smooth hard surface beneath the sand.

'There's something here!' he announced excitedly to Susannah, who held the torch above him. He scooped sand clear of the hole, while Susannah crouched down and shone the torch closer.

Quickly, he exposed a black, metallic surface with a handle folded down flat against it. He brushed the sand right to the edges of the hole and found that the smooth surface also had edges, which just fitted the square formed by the excavated tiles. It was clearly a box of some sort. He pulled on the handle, and tried to lift the box, but experienced considerable resistance. The sand had been packed tightly around the sides and, having absorbed moisture from the surrounding earth, was clinging to the box. Bracing himself directly above the box, he tried again, lifting it as perpendicular to the hole as he could. Finally, the friction and resistance was overcome and the box slid clear of its resting place.

With mounting excitement, Hudson found the simple catches on the sides and released the lid: The box had not been locked, presumably because Terleski had realised it was probably a waste of time. There was a waterproof seal running around the edge, protecting the contents from damp. Unable to contain himself any further, he shone the torch inside and inspected the contents.

'Bloody hell!' he exclaimed. 'It's true. It's all true.'

Hudson pulled out a waterproof bag with a black object inside. He opened the seal on the bag and pulled out the object.

'It's an old Dictaphone,' he breathed excitedly. He pulled out another package. It was a thick bundle of papers, also in a waterproof bag. The title on the front page was easily visible through the plastic.

TRANSCRIPT OF MEETINGS, RED DAWN PROGRAMME

Hudson opened the package and pulled out the papers, which were held together in sheaves with treasury tags. Numbers had been scrawled on the top left corner of each sheaf, in red pen. Hudson glanced at the other package, which contained a series of small tape cassettes. Those were also numbered in red pen. He selected cassette number one, and sheaf number one. Fumbling with the unfamiliar device, he inserted the tape into the Dictaphone and pressed the play button. He was amazed to see that the old device still worked. It must have had fresh batteries quite recently.

The tape crackled and hissed. There was a lot of background noise and the sound seemed muffled. Hudson turned up the volume to its maximum setting and they strained their ears to listen. A hubbub of voices became audible, but then a strong, authoritative voice cut through and silenced the proceedings.

'…..so, you see gentlemen, we have a choice. The accident at building two one five can become public knowledge, in which case some of us lose our jobs, our nuclear industry is jeopardised and we suffer a major setback in the Cold War. This would play right into the hands of those who seek to scrap our nuclear deterrent and the special relationship with the United States.' Long pause. 'But there is an alternative - The fallout can be attributed to the Chernobyl explosion and the public need never know. As far as the public is concerned, there is little we can do anyway. The radioactive cloud has already blown over them. Alerting them now would only create unnecessary panic. The risk is not much more than that already posed by the fallout from Chernobyl and, fortunately for us, the chemical composition is roughly similar. If we all cooperate, we can do this. I believe that it is in the national interest to do so…..'

The hair on Hudson's neck stood up. According to the numbered transcript in his other hand, these were the words of Charles Millburn. Now Sir Charles Millburn, Chairman of Gencor Energy PLC. And they'd got him on tape, addressing a meeting and asking those present to cover up the accident at Sellafield. The tape went on:

'….Thank you for your support gentlemen. I think we can all agree that this is the right decision to take. I probably don't have to reiterate this, but I must impress on you all the need for absolute secrecy. This is not to be mentioned in any official correspondence. As I explained earlier, the code name for this project is Red Dawn but that is not to be repeated or mentioned outside this room. Officially, this project was scrapped in 1958. It does not exist. Understand? Good. We will meet on a weekly basis until all necessary arrangements have been made. Thank you.'

There was the sound of chairs scraping and papers being shuffled, along with low, inaudible mutterings, then there was a click as the recording was stopped. Hudson was about to stop the tape, when he heard another click a few seconds later, with fresh noises.

'Gentlemen, it has been a week since our last meeting. What progress have we made?...'

'Bloody hell,' whispered Hudson after listening for a few more minutes. 'It's all here. Your uncle taped all the Red Dawn meetings. Look at all the tapes.' He lifted the freezer bag up to show Susannah.

'I can't understand why he didn't mention it in the letter or the dossier?'

'He did. I've just remembered. He referred to a transcript at least once. It just didn't occur to me before. The only way a transcript could exist would be if he committed the meetings to paper from memory, or from sort of recording. These tapes will finish Millburn, and your uncle knew it. Can you imagine what would happen if they found out about these?' he asked, breathless with excitement. 'I can't believe he's got this on *tape*. It's unbelievable.' Hudson was stunned. Until this moment, all they had to go on was Terleski's dossier and the five seemingly unrelated deaths of the former civil servants. And Hudson's paranoia, especially in view of the burglaries they had both experienced.

But this proved beyond any doubt that Terleski was telling the truth. Red Dawn did exist. And they knew who was behind it. Hudson looked up at Susannah, her face lit in eerie relief by the dim torchlight reflecting off the transcripts.

'Susannah?' he asked quietly, seriously.

'I know. You don't have to say it.' Her bottom lip quivered.

'Your uncle…'

'I know,' she nodded, trying to control herself.

'He didn't kill himself, did he?'

She shut her eyes, squeezing out a tear drop which ran down her cheek and shook her head. It was too awful. Simply too awful.

'We need to get out of here, go somewhere safe and work out what to do next.'

Hudson was suddenly acutely aware of the need to get away from Terleski's house. They stuffed the transcripts and the Dictaphone machine back into the metal box as fast as they could.

'What about the hole?' asked Susannah, referring to the excavated tiles.

'Leave it. We don't have time. Come on, we need to go,' Hudson urged. He grabbed Susannah's hand and, carrying the document box in the other, ran with her across the lawns, their way lit by the bright moonlight. They skirted around the imposing house and down the driveway towards the wrought iron gates. At the gates, Hudson lifted Susannah up and over. She dropped down the other side, landing softly on the gravel. Hudson climbed up his side of the gate, hauling the box with him. He heaved it over the top of the gate and into Susannah's outstretched arms.

Suddenly, an arm reached around Susannah's throat and Hudson caught the glint of a knife. Susannah screamed and, startled, Hudson fell backwards from the top of the gate, landing heavily on his back.

'Run, James! Run!' screamed Susannah before her voice was suddenly cut off. In blind panic, Hudson scrambled to his feet and stumbled away.

The edge of the driveway saved his life. In his desperate scramble, he didn't see it and tripped just as the gun shot rang out. As he fell, he felt a searing pain in his left side, and he tumbled forward. Momentum kept him on his feet as he staggered into the dark shadows offered by Terleski's overgrown garden. Another shot rang out and Hudson caught the flash of the muzzle a split second before he heard, or rather felt, the bullet zing past him. Terrified, he stumbled on into the undergrowth, before coming up against the high garden wall. Trapped, he had no choice but to climb over and, gasping from the intense pain in his side, he hauled himself up using the branches of a neglected plum tree. He scrabbled over the top of the wall and fell down into the field on the other side, spraining his ankle as he landed awkwardly. At least there was now a solid wall protecting him. He put his hand to his side, which was wet. His fingers felt tacky and he realised he was bleeding, which wasn't surprising given the intense pain. With shock and disbelief, he realised he must have been shot.

But all he could think of was Susannah. What had happened to her? Was she still alive or had they cut her throat? The flash of the knife had been unmistakeable. He had to find out, try to help her.

Hudson set off along the wall, following it around towards the road. The sprain to his ankle was mild and rapidly eased off, in stark contrast to the pain in his side, which was becoming ever more intense. Gritting his teeth, Hudson ploughed on. Up ahead, he heard a car door slam. Through the hedgerow, he caught a glimpse of an interior light. He hurried forward. The car was in the road.

And then he heard the muffled whimper. *Susannah!*

Galvanised by the sound of her voice, Hudson ran towards the hedgerow, completely disregarding his own safety. The hedge was poorly maintained with large gaps, as the landowner used the land for arable only. Through the gap ahead, Hudson could see a man forcing a hooded Susannah into the car. Another man sat in the driver's seat.

Susannah was struggling violently, and her assailant was cursing. Hudson was yards away. The man struck Susannah hard, causing her to cry out, and something snapped in Hudson's head. His hands seized a discarded piece of fence rail and he leapt through the hedge, bringing the timber down as hard as he could onto the man. Hudson hit him so hard the timber snapped and the man crashed forward onto the car, before sliding down to his knees. Hudson swung the remaining shaft into his face, knocking him to the road. Without hesitating, he reached into the car and grabbed Susannah, hauling her out. Out of the corner of his eye, he spotted the document box on the back seat and lunged for it.

In what seemed slow motion, he dragged her up the road towards his parked car, having to release her to fish for his car keys, his other hand carrying the box. The man in the driver's seat behind him began to react and Hudson heard the car door open.

'Come on Susannah, come on!' he shouted, pulling her along as fast as he could, the box swinging in his other hand. Out of the gloom, Hudson's battered Golf emerged. There was a shout behind them and Hudson cringed, waiting for the bullet. Another shout, sounds of running feet.

'Come on!' he shouted again.

The car was unlocked and he bundled Susannah in, throwing the box into the back. He raced around to the driver's side. The footsteps were pounding up the lane towards them. Hudson leapt in, frantically trying to insert the keys into the ignition. *Come on! Come on!*

A shadow outside the car. The engine roared and Hudson slammed his foot to the floor, swinging the car into the road in reverse.

Glimpse of a man outside. Hudson found the headlight switch. The man lit up in front of them, levelling a pistol at the windscreen. Hudson instinctively ducked and slammed the car into first, the wheels spinning and engine racing. There was a bang, the windscreen shattered, then a muffled thump as they hit the man. He bounced up the bonnet and rolled off to the side as Hudson's tyres squealed on the road. Hudson mashed the gears into second, smelling the burnt tyre rubber and clutch. They careered up the lane, Hudson barely able to see through the shattered windscreen.

'Are you okay?' he shouted at Susannah, who had managed to pull the hood off. She didn't answer, utterly terrified by the ordeal, just merely nodded. Hudson's legs felt like jelly and, unable to stop himself, he retched, spitting the bile down between his legs. Up ahead, the lights of Henley-in-Arden appeared out of the darkness. He raced down the long high street and out southbound, towards Stratford-upon-Avon, checking his mirror for signs they were being pursued.

The pain in his side was becoming unbearable, feeling like a red hot poker had been run over the skin. He groaned with the pain.

'I thought they'd killed you,' sobbed Susannah. 'I didn't know what they were going to do to me...'

'I think I've been shot,' Hudson grunted tersely through clenched teeth, interrupting her. This focused Susannah's attention.

'What? Where?'

'My side. I'm bleeding.'

Susannah reached out and put her hand on the wound, to staunch the blood. His clothes were sodden with it.

'We need to get to a hospital,' she announced, fearful for him.

Hudson nodded, accepting the inevitability of it. There would be a hospital close by, surely.

As they headed towards Stratford, the red H-signs appeared on road signs. *Town centre*. Hudson struggled to concentrate on his driving, feeling increasingly light headed. Almost driving automatically, he followed the hospital signs into the town centre. Accident and Emergency appeared in front. He brought the battered car to a halt close to the entrance, and Susannah jumped out to help him. An orderly spotted Hudson's bloodstained clothes and called for assistance. Within seconds, he was being whisked into the hospital on a stretcher, leaving Susannah in his wake. His last words were: 'The box! Don't leave the box!'

She returned to the car and retrieved the box. On her return, she was informed that Hudson had been admitted straight to the emergency unit. She was told to wait.

23

Millburn was incandescent. Kroll had not seen him this angry for a long while and, this time, he was on the receiving end of it.

'So you're telling me they had the proof?' he shouted, incredulously.

'Yes, Charles. They followed them to Terleski's house. It was there the whole time, buried in his summerhouse.'

'And Trevor had it in his car?'

'Yes, er, that's right, Charles.'

'And he went and fucking well lost it?' he screamed, his face contorted with rage.

Kroll blinked, realising how disastrous it looked. Trevor and Julian had followed Hudson and the girl down to Henley. They knew that Terleski must have made recordings of the meetings, from mention of transcripts in his dossier. He could only possess transcripts, if he or someone else had secretly recorded the meetings. There had never been a stenographer at any of the meetings, as Millburn had wanted no record. Terleski had made no mention of it, even under torture and they had found nothing amongst the removed files and documents. They had not even been looking for it until Kroll had spotted the reference to the transcripts in the dossier that they had found on the old man's computer.

Worse, the journalist and his girlfriend had found the transcripts *and* the tapes, which Trevor and Julian had then seized, but they had grossly underestimated Hudson. Somehow, incredibly, Hudson had got away from them. Then, to compound matters, had retrieved the box containing the evidence and rescued the girl. It was nothing less than an unmitigated disaster.

'Charles?' Kroll interrupted his line of thought.

'What?' Millburn snapped back, barely able to contain his fury as he paced up and down the carpet behind his desk.

'There's something else you should know…'

Millburn stopped pacing and fixed a baleful eye on Kroll, who swallowed hard and explained.

'They've WHAT?' he bellowed at Kroll when he had finished. 'You told me they'd hidden the body properly, you fucking moron!'

'I'm sorry, Charles, but Trevor made a mistake.' Experience had taught him to be candid with Millburn. Millburn placed his hands on the glass topped desk, and leant forward, his powerful broad shoulders hunched aggressively. Kroll could hear his laboured breathing and felt a little shiver of fear pass through him as Millburn's intense gaze bored into him. His boss was not a man accustomed to suffering fools or mistakes.

'The police have issued a warrant for the arrest of the journalist and the girl. On suspicion of murder.' Kroll swallowed, and Millburn stared at him without blinking. For the first time in his life, Kroll felt frightened of Millburn. The silence lasted for an age and Kroll could feel his mouth going dry as Millburn continued to stare at him with his unflinching gaze.

'Could you repeat that?' Millburn whispered. The voice was barely audible. A classic warning sign.

'Er, it appears that the police wish to speak to them about the death of Alex Warburton.' There was another long silence.

'And what happens now?' Millburn asked eventually, his voice barely a murmur.

'I don't know, Charles.' Kroll could feel his heart thudding. Wrong answer.

Millburn exploded. He grabbed the monitor off the table and hurled it past Kroll, who couldn't help but flinch as it just missed him. He forced himself to remain standing where he was as the monitor smashed on the floor behind him.

'You don't *KNOW?*' he shouted. 'What the hell am I paying you for? We've got two people out there, one of whom is a *journalist*, a fucking *journalist* for Christ's sake, with information that could destroy us, and you don't *KNOW?*' Kroll blinked and swallowed as Millburn tried to control his breathing, which was coming in ragged snorts. 'I'll tell you what I know, Peter,' he continued in his dangerously quiet voice again. 'You are going to find those tapes and destroy them before they destroy us, am I clear?'

'Yes, Charles,' replied Kroll, swallowing involuntarily, aware that a quiver had crept into his voice.

'Those tapes are out there somewhere and these two must be the only two people alive who know about them. They were the only people Terleski trusted with his evidence.' He let this sink in for a while. 'At the moment, no one else knows. You've got to find them before they can tell anyone else.'

'Yes, Charles.'

'We've got to find them before the police do, do you understand?'

Kroll nodded. Then, suddenly, the path to redemption opened up before him. A smile flickered over his lips.

'That's the answer, Charles.'

'What is?'

'The police. We use them to find Hudson and the girl for us.'

'How?'

'I've still got some contacts.'

Millburn thought about it and nodded. It was very risky, but would have to do in the circumstances. They would have to silence Hudson and Susannah before they had a chance to speak or share their discovery about Red Dawn.

'Okay, do it. But don't fail me this time.'

*

DI Brannigan was working late, in anticipation of news on the two prime suspects in the Warburton murder case. It would only be a matter of time, surely. The national number plate recognition system was checking all major trunk routes for Hudson's missing Golf, whilst both their bank accounts were being monitored for any use.

In the end, though, they had been found from a surprising source.

'How interesting,' Brannigan murmured when the notification was emailed to him. Hudson had been admitted to the main hospital in Stratford-upon-Avon with what appeared to be a gunshot wound, although he had lied about his identity. His car had been clamped and removed from outside the main accident and emergency entrance. As a result his numberplate had been flagged up on the police system. Subsequent enquiries had revealed a young man matching his description being admitted to the hospital. Brannigan accessed the CCTV network for the hospital and examined recorded footage of Hudson's arrival.

'Bingo,' he muttered, again to no one in particular. He picked up the phone and rang the local police station in Stratford. After the preliminary introductions, he cut to the chase.

'We have a positive ID on a male IC1, name of James Hudson, wanted in connection with the murder of Alex Warburton, currently receiving treatment at your local hospital. I want him under arrest as soon as possible. He is believed to be with a suspected accomplice, one Susannah Harlowe, female IC1. I want her arrested too, please…many thanks…keep me posted.'

He turned to his colleagues. 'Right, lads. We've got them.'

Kroll took the phone call at his desk.

'Stratford hospital? You're quite sure?...Gunshot wound...what about the girl? She's with him... I see...Excellent.'

He hung up and immediately dialled another number.

'Trevor? Get your useless arse over to Stratford hospital. It seems you got lucky. Hudson's there, having surgery for a gunshot wound. The girl's with him too. Make sure you finish the job off this time. The police are on the way to arrest them. They mustn't, I repeat mustn't, be allowed to speak to them. Understand?'

'Yes sir. I understand.'

'Then get on with it.'

Kroll slammed the phone down and looked at the door leading to Millburn's office. He decided he would speak to him once it was over. There was no point in antagonising the man further.

24

Susannah waited anxiously for news of Hudson's condition but, after an hour in the waiting room, a grim-faced doctor came through to speak to her. Susannah felt sick.

'Are you a relative?' he demanded, sternly.

'No, a friend. His girlfriend,' she replied, fearful of what she would hear.

'Well, the good news is that it was just a superficial flesh wound. We've cleaned it up, given him some stitches, antibiotics and a tetanus booster. He's in recovery now. You're boyfriend seems reluctant to discuss his injury but if I'm not mistaken it looks very much like a gunshot wound.' He gave her a brief matter-of-fact smile. 'I trained in South Africa,' he explained, before continuing. 'That's what I've recorded on his notes. He also appears to be the victim of a serious assault, judging by his facial injuries. It's none of my business, but if you two are in some kind of trouble, then I recommend you call the police, or at least speak to someone who can help you.'

Susannah nodded, unsure of what to say, extremely conscious of the black box sitting between her feet on the floor.

'Okay, you can go and see him now.'

Susannah followed the doctor through to the recovery room, where Hudson was sitting up on a trolley, wearing a hospital gown. There was nobody else in the room. He smiled weakly when he saw her, still recovering from the effects of the anaesthetic.

'If you think I look bad, you should have seen the other guy,' Hudson murmured drowsily.

'Oh, James, I'm so relieved,' Susannah rushed over, kissing him.

'Ow,' Hudson winced. 'I'm quite sore.'

'The doctor said it was a minor flesh wound.'

'The bullet just clipped my side. I never thought it could be so painful. I'd hate to think what it would have felt like to have been hit properly.'

That brought it all back home. They had been shot at, Susannah had nearly been kidnapped. Someone had been following them, presumably to retrieve the document box they had found in the summerhouse.

'Oh, God, James. What are we going to do?' pleaded Susannah.

'We need to get out of here, go somewhere safe and find someone to help us. We need to tell someone about Red Dawn, but we've got to be really careful who we choose. I can't think straight at the moment. My brain isn't working.' Hudson shut his eyes again, exhausted by the anaesthetic.

'James? James? Wake up. What about your editor? Can he help?'

Hudson struggled to open his eyes.

'Don? No. This is too big. We wouldn't stand a chance.'

'Then who?'

'I don't know, I can't think…I'm so tired…' He drifted away.

'I think we should call the police.'

That woke Hudson up. 'No,' he stated firmly. 'This is a massive government cover-up. The police might be part of it.'

Susannah said nothing, her eyes watering, as Hudson lay back again.

'I'm frightened, James,' she whispered. Hudson reached out and squeezed her hand. After a while, he opened his eyes.

'I'm thirsty, Susannah. Can you get me a drink please? Something fizzy.'

Susannah left him and headed off to find a drinks dispenser, having first checked the board above his pillow to see if he was prohibited from drinking or eating anything. She headed down the corridor, past the nurses' station and into the public waiting room for minor accidents. The drinks dispenser was just around the corner from the reception, and Susannah stood in line whilst a couple of teenagers took their time deciding what to buy.

She noticed two police officers walk in and approach the reception area, their faces set with grim determination.

'Can I help?' Susannah heard the receptionist ask them.

'We understand you have a James Hudson here? Receiving treatment for a suspected gunshot wound?'

Susannah froze to the spot, and turned her face away.

'Let me have a look for you,' the receptionist replied. A keyboard rattled noisily. 'Um, I'm sorry, but we don't have a James Hudson on the system.'

'We think he was booked in under a false name. Try John Harris.'

'Ah yes. He's out of surgery. Probably in the recovery room. Down there at the end of the corridor, through the doors, then along the next corridor. It's a sterile area, so you need to be accompanied by a nurse. I'll ask for you.'

'Thank you. He hasn't been a problem?'

'Er, no. I haven't heard anything. Why?'

'I'm not at liberty to say. Do you know if he was accompanied by anyone? We're also looking for his girlfriend, a Miss Susannah Harlowe.'

'I'm not entirely sure. I think there was someone; a tall blond girl, if that helps.'

'Thank you. We'll look into it.'

Susannah heard them head off up the corridor, and risked a glance around the corner. The two officers were swaggering purposefully up the corridor, accompanied by a nurse. When a sufficient gap had opened up, Susannah left the relative sanctuary of the drinks machine and followed them cautiously up the corridor. She saw them disappear into the recovery room and she crept up outside. What she heard chilled her to the bone.

'James Hudson, I am arresting you on suspicion of involvement in the murder of Alex Warburton. You do not have to say anything…'

Susannah couldn't believe what she was hearing. Alex was *dead*? It couldn't be true. There had to be some kind of mistake. She felt her legs going weak and the nausea rise. The shock of discovering her former boyfriend had been killed was almost overwhelming. And they had arrested James for it. Recovering herself, she peered through the window to see Hudson being handcuffed to one of the bed rails, a look of fear, anger and surprise on his face. Then their eyes met across the room.

'We're looking for Susannah Harlowe. Where is she?' one of the officers demanded.

'I don't know what you're talking about,' Hudson whispered, staring at Susannah, imploring her to escape.

'You know you can get done for obstruction of justice, and aiding and abetting? Where is she?'

Susannah made her mind up. She had to help James. Quickly, she hurried away from the recovery room, her mind racing. *Think, Susannah, think!*

*

Trevor and Julian walked into the hospital reception. They knew they were exposing themselves to the CCTV network, but Kroll's orders were clear. He had assured them that all the recorded images would be destroyed. There would be no trace of their presence. All they had to do was kill Hudson and the girl, recover the box, and escape. Right under the noses of hospital staff and, possibly, the police. It was a tall order, but Kroll had been insistent. They had to make amends for their earlier errors. He had already advised them of Sir Charles' displeasure over the matter, and the veiled threat was more than enough to focus their attention on the task at hand. No more mistakes. Just results. Or else.

They walked past reception, not wishing to draw any attention to themselves and headed towards emergency admissions. Kroll's information had been detailed. In the last update, Hudson had emerged from surgery and was in recovery. They had him at their mercy, a brief window of opportunity to get the job done.

Hudson opened his eyes, to find the concerned face of Mr Matheson, the consultant surgeon, looking down at him and pointedly ignoring the presence of the two police officers in the room.

'How are you feeling, James?'

'Sore. And I ache all over.'

'The aching could be the muscle relaxant. Part of the anaesthetic. It will go soon. I can't do much about the soreness, I'm afraid. You will have to wait for the injury to heal.'

Hudson nodded and lifted his hand to scratch his face, only to find it firmly attached to the trolley. The handcuff.

'This man is not to leave the hospital until I give my permission, is that clear?' Matheson snapped at the two police officers, outraged by Hudson's treatment. 'And I want you to wait outside. He's hardly likely to go anywhere is he?' They glowered at him, but there was little they could do but comply with his request. After completing his checks, Matheson left the room, leaving Hudson alone.

Shackled to the trolley and completely helpless.

Trevor and Julian headed down a corridor towards the Recovery Room. It was a busy part of the hospital, even at this time of night, and the corridor milled with patients, doctors, nurses and anxious relatives. No one took any notice of them.

'It must be up there, through those double doors,' murmured Trevor. A nurse pushed a trolley of blood-taking equipment towards them. At the last moment, Trevor bumped into it. There was a crash as all the contents rattled. He grabbed hold of it to steady himself.

'Sorry,' he muttered, stepping past it and carrying on. The nurse scowled, checked the trolley was okay, and continued.

Trevor secreted the syringe in the palm of his hand; the nurse had not seen him take it. Surreptitiously, he removed the protective cap and withdrew the plunger, filling it with air. If Hudson had just been in surgery, he would already have a cannula inserted in a vein in his arm. It would take seconds for Trevor to insert the needle and inject the air. Then there would be no saving Hudson. The air bubbles would course through his bloodstream, passing through the right atrium of the heart, before congregating in the small capillaries of the lungs. His fate would be sealed. No amount of medical intervention would save him. The air bubbles would form a pulmonary embolism and the blood in his body would cease to flow, unable to pass through the airlock. Starved of oxygen, his brain would respond by stimulating his respiratory nerves, causing him to gasp for air. The pain would be excruciating, but he would be unable to cry out. Simple, quick, effective. Painful. Trevor gripped the prepared syringe in his hand and approached the secure double doors with Julian right behind him. They were just yards away from their target.

A police officer burst through the double doors, coming towards them. Trevor froze, but realised that the police officer had his head down, counting some loose change. He was headed for the drinks machine. Beyond him, Trevor saw another police officer, standing outside a door.

The door was marked Recovery Room.

The door swung open and a wheelchair emerged. The police officer stood to one side to let it pass. A blonde doctor emerged, pushing the chair and obscuring the occupant.

Trevor and Julian slowed.

The trio in front headed away from them towards the lift at the end of the corridor.

Trevor walked to the door of the Recovery Room.

The trio were by the lift.

Trevor glanced into the room.

The lift pinged as the doors opened.

The room was empty.

Trevor glanced up at the trio by the lift. The doctor had pushed the wheelchair inside, turning it around so they both faced him. The police officer shouted something.

The lift doors began to close. The police officer shouted again and fell backwards, clutching his groin. And just as the doors shut on the doctor and her patient, their eyes met with Trevor's, and the recognition dawned.

Then the doors shut.

'He was the car driver!' Hudson shouted at Susannah, as the lift went up. Hudson had seen him clearly inside the car when he had rescued Susannah earlier.

'But *how* have they found us?' wailed Susannah.

'It's the police. It's got to be. I told you!'

'Oh my god,' breathed Susannah. It all depended on her now. Hudson could not walk, he was still too weak from the anaesthetic, though he had just enough strength to kick the police officer in the groin to stop him coming into the lift.

Susannah had stolen a doctor's tunic and strode into the Recovery Room, drawing on all her medical experience to give her a suitable air of authority. She had demanded that Hudson's handcuff be removed in order for him to attend a post-operative X-ray examination, to make sure they had removed all the particles from his wound. The handcuff would interfere with the X-ray, and the medically ignorant police officer was in no position to argue with her. He insisted on accompanying them to the X-Ray room, though. Susannah replied that only one of them could come, thus eliminating one of the officers. He went off to fetch a cup of coffee. Susannah helped Hudson into a wheelchair and marched them brusquely out of the Recovery Room. The officer thought nothing about the black box she handed to Hudson, assuming it was medical records or equipment of some sort. It was only when they entered the lift and he had stood outside the door whilst Susannah manoeuvred the wheelchair that his doubts surfaced. The door began to shut, the lift access blocked by the wheelchair. He shouted a warning, realising too late what was happening, but then Hudson kicked him in the groin, and the door had shut.

But not before they caught sight of the two men racing towards them up the corridor.

'You're sure it was him?' Susannah asked.

'Definitely.'

The lift stopped and Susannah pushed them out onto the second floor. They raced down corridors, people jumping out of their way.

'Find another lift,' ordered Hudson. 'We need to get out of here.' He felt so helpless and vulnerable, completely reliant on Susannah to get them to safety. They careered down some more corridors, with people standing aside to let the rushing doctor and patient past, and found another set of lifts. Hudson jabbed at the buttons. There were three lift shafts, but none of them were available.

'Come on, come on,' he prayed, jabbing at the buttons again. Finally, after what seemed an age, there was a ping. 'Lift going down,' the recorded voice intoned. Into the lift. Wait for doors to shut. *Ping.* 'Lift going down. Please select floor.' More jabbing of buttons, select ground floor.

Ping. 'Doors opening. First floor.'

Shit. Hudson's heart was in his mouth as the doors slid open, expecting to see their attackers waiting on the other side.

The old lady shuffled in, with agonising slowness, smiling her thanks to them, oblivious to their predicament. Hudson and Susannah held their breath as the lift doors finally shut again and they continued to the ground floor.

Ping. 'Doors opening. Ground floor.'

The doors slid apart and Hudson could see that they had emerged near to the maternity wards of the hospital. Susannah headed for the exit, through a largely deserted seating area. The League of Friends cafeteria had long since shut for the evening, and there were few visitors milling around. This meant that they really stood out. As quickly as she could, Susannah pushed the wheelchair through the doors and outside into the night. A lone taxi had just dropped someone off and Susannah flagged him down. He stopped and opened the passenger window a crack.

'Sorry love, I only take bookings,' he announced gruffly through the small gap.

'Please, this man has been discharged. He needs to go home tonight.' She gave him her most dazzling smile.

'Hang on,' he sighed. 'I'll check with base.'

Some call signs were exchanged over the radio and the taxi driver made the request. Hudson shivered in his hospital gown, looking around nervously while they waited for the response.

'Alright, get in,' he muttered. Susannah smiled her gratitude, and helped Hudson into the back seat, then climbed in afterwards, much to the driver's surprise. *Lucky patient*, was all he could think. 'Where too, love?'

Susannah was almost caught out, but thought quickly. There was really only one place they could go. The taxi driver nodded at her request and they set off. Hudson sank back into the seat and allowed sleep to overcome him; he was physically and mentally exhausted. Susannah removed her doctor's tunic and tenderly spread it over him, to keep him warm. Again, the taxi driver thought it most odd, but said nothing. He'd seen far stranger things in his lifetime of picking up dodgy fares. In the mirror, he saw the girl wipe a tear away, and thought it best not to pry. The young man must be very ill.

It fell to Trevor to ring Kroll. He took a deep sigh, thought about the secret bank account he held in the Cayman Islands and whether he should drive straight to the nearest airport instead, and placed the call.

'Sir, we've lost them.'

25

Detective Inspector Brannigan was furious when he arrived at the hospital. He found the two police officers who had been responsible for making the arrest and gave them a thorough dressing-down in front of the colleagues who had been sent to lend assistance.

'What happened?' he demanded.

'Er, the girl was dressed up like a doctor, sir. We didn't realise. We didn't have a photograph of her.'

'And you didn't think it was the slightest bit odd that she asked you to remove the handcuff?'

'No sir, it was so they could go to X-ray.'

'X-ray? You need your fucking head X-raying, to see if there's anything in it,' snapped Brannigan.

'And then he assaulted me before getting into the lift.' Constable Evans explained what had happened, hoping that it would earn him some sympathy. It didn't.

'He kicked you in the bollocks,' Brannigan stated with slow deliberation, unable to believe what he was hearing. 'The man could barely walk, yet he managed to kick you in the bollocks. Pathetic. Utterly pathetic. And where was Roberts?'

'Um, he'd gone to fetch a coffee, sir.' Evans squirmed.

Brannigan shook his head, incredulous. He had heard enough. If he had anything to do with it, these two idiots were going to be form-filling for a very long time. He would have a word with their superior officer. In the meantime, though, the priority was to track down Hudson and the girl.

'Right, well the first thing we need to do is look at the CCTV.'

'Er, sir, there's a problem with that. It seems that all the footage from this evening is missing. Some sort of software glitch apparently. The IT people can't understand it.'

Brannigan shook his head again. It had been a very long day. He had identified two very likely suspects for the murder of Alex Warburton who had now got away; he had driven all the way down from Manchester for an arrest that had not materialised; the idiots in front of him were an affront to Darwin's theories about evolution; it was now very late at night; and he'd had enough.

'Bunch of useless idiots,' he muttered, audibly enough for them to hear, and stomped off back to his car to converse with his colleagues from Manchester. The problem for Brannigan was that he was now operating outside his own police force's turf. It was only with the permission of the Chief Superintendent of the Warwickshire Constabulary that he had been allowed to come down at all. But he had had enough of the diplomatic niceties. The fact of the matter was that they had allowed the two suspects to escape which, as far as he was concerned, only served to demonstrate their guilty part in the murder. Now he would have to wait for them to appear on the radar again.

Fed up and exhausted, Brannigan sent his colleagues back to Manchester, whilst he booked into a cheap motel for the night, in the vain hope that something may have cropped up by morning.

*

Susannah paid off the taxi driver, using the last of her cash. She helped Hudson out of the car, and up the driveway

'You must be joking,' Hudson spluttered, when he realised the difficulty posed by her choice.

'It's the only place I could think of. It's the last place they'd look. We've no choice, James. We don't have any money to pay for a hotel, and they're probably watching our bank cards. They'd find us straight away.'

'I'm not sure I can climb those again,' Hudson announced flatly, looking up at Terleski's wrought iron gates. He shivered in his hospital gown. His clothes had been abandoned at the hospital when they had fled.

'You'll have to try,' Susannah announced. 'I'll help you.'

Stung by the perceived insult to his masculinity, Hudson limped up to the gates, his cold bare feet picking up sharp gravel. Summoning every bit of strength in his body, he began to haul himself up. His limbs were still weak and he felt himself falling back, when he received a firm push from Susannah. He didn't complain.

The effort was agonising, but finally he was over the top once again. He climbed down clumsily on the other side and waited for Susannah to join him. He felt useless.

They entered the house through the window they had used before. Susannah left him, whilst she hunted for a torch or candles in the kitchen, not wishing to attract attention to their presence in the house by switching on the lights. It turned out that Terleski kept a prepared candleholder for power cuts, and Susannah returned, the flickering candle lending an eerie atmosphere.

'Come on, let's get you sorted out,' she instructed. Hudson was too cold and tired to argue.

The central heating timer was still switched on, so Susannah ran a bath. It was the most luxurious bath Hudson had ever enjoyed. A hot bath after playing rugby on a freezing cold pitch in driving rain was always pleasurable, but this was in a higher league altogether. Taking care not to splash the stitches across the ribs on his left side, Susannah tenderly washed him, whilst Hudson felt the warmth returning to his limbs. Once he was wrapped in a warm, dry towel, she went off to find him some clothes. Unfortunately, all she could find was a shirt, trousers and jumper, all too small. But better than nothing. Hudson baulked at the offer of Terleski's underwear, and accepted only the socks, which were also too small. It was all a small price to pay for being out of the emasculating hospital gown.

The bath had refreshed him, and he felt much better. Now though, the full impact of what they had experienced hit him. They were in a living nightmare. It had come as a complete shock to hear of

Warburton's murder. Although Hudson still bore the bruises from Warburton's assault only a day earlier, he didn't wish such an outcome on anyone. But even more shocking was the revelation that the police considered them to be the main suspects. On top of that, Hudson had to come to terms with the fact that Red Dawn existed, they had the proof, and someone had most definitely tried to kill him. It was almost too much to comprehend, and he felt a hopeless fear spreading through his body. Susannah was clearly thinking the same, her eyes had gone distant. Hudson realised how much he owed her. In his hour of need, she had come up trumps. Now it was his turn. He had to pull himself together, for her sake as well as his.

'We've got to stop these people. We've got to tell someone about Red Dawn and stop them.' There was a determined glint in his tired, red eyes. He looked up at Susannah and smiled to reassure her. He patted the black document box. 'I've got an idea.'

He outlined his plan to her. 'What do you think?'

'It's the only choice we've got. If they're the only people who can help us, we'll have to.'

'You'll have to lend me your phone. Mine's still at the hospital.'

Hudson took the phone. Having lost his mobile phone, he had also lost his list of contact numbers, but he was betting that the man he was trying to call had his voicebox redirected to his mobile outside office hours. After the operator put him through to the office number, Hudson's hunch was proved correct. The call was rerouted.

Hudson held his breath.

'Hello?' a bleary voice asked.

*

Brannigan had slept for barely an hour on the uncomfortable motel bed before he was rudely awoken by his mobile phone.

'DI Brannigan,' he mumbled, barely awake.

'Sir, it's PC Evans. From the hospital, sir.'

'What do you want?' snapped Brannigan, waking up. Evans was not on his Christmas card list after the monumental cock-up earlier on. But he was about to make amends for that.

'Sir, I thought you should know: A taxi driver has come forward. He picked up two people matching Hudson and the girl's descriptions.'

Brannigan sat up, wide awake. 'Where did he take them?'

'A house in Henley, sir. About twenty minutes up the road.'

'Are you picking them up?'

'Cars are on the way now, sir.'

'I'll be right there. What's the address?'

PC Evans gave him the address. 'Sir, the funny thing is, it's already on our database. The owner, a Doctor Terleski, was found dead there two days ago, Tuesday morning. He'd hung himself.'

This was almost too much for Brannigan. 'I'm on my way,' he announced, leaping out of bed and pulling his crumpled suit on.

*

Hudson was on the phone for quite a while before he hung up. Susannah looked at him expectantly.

'We're on. He's coming to pick us up. He'll be here within two hours.'

The relief swept over Susannah. Just two hours to wait until they were safe. She nearly wept as a way out of the living nightmare opened up for them. Hudson was similarly affected. All they had to do was stay put for a short while, then they would be out of there, away from danger. It was almost too much to believe.

'I asked him to bring me a change of clothes, too,' he smiled. 'Not that there's anything wrong with these, of course.' He could afford to joke. The nightmare was nearly over.

'Well, I didn't want to say anything…'

'But…?'

Susannah smiled for the first time in ages. She too could sense that they had finally turned a corner. They could begin to put their awful experience behind them, clear their name with the police with the help of Hudson's contact, and move on with their lives. Those responsible could be brought to justice. And Red Dawn could be exposed.

Hudson walked over to Susannah and carefully put an arm around her shoulders, mindful of his stitches, leaning in to give her a small kiss on the neck.

'Thank you. You were brilliant,' he whispered. She reached up and squeezed his hand. They stood like that for some time, staring out into the darkness, both absorbed in their thoughts.

Hudson thought nothing of it at first. The blue lights flickering on the horizon were probably headed out to another motorway accident. He carried on gazing out of the window. It must be quite an incident. There were several sets of lights. The odd thing was that they appeared to be getting closer. The motorway was in the opposite direction.

'Susannah?' he murmured.

'Hmmm?'

'Look. Over there.'

'They're coming this way?'

'*Shit!*'

26

They stumbled over the rough ground of the field behind the house. It could have been worse. The farmer had yet to plough the stubble in; it was what remained from a late wheat harvest. But in the pitch darkness, the earlier bright moonlight having been obscured by cloud, they could not see their footing. The hedgerows which had once divided the land had long been ripped up for more efficient farming, and the field was vast. Hudson was acutely conscious that a helicopter using thermal imaging would pick them up instantly. It was imperative that they find cover before one arrived.

'Up there,' he gasped to Susannah, as behind them, the police cars roared down the lane and pulled up outside Terleski's house. Looming out of the darkness ahead of them was a woodland. Holding hands, they crashed through the overgrown set-aside strip which bordered the field and into a barbed wire fence.

Hudson scrambled over the fence, which was only waist height and consisted of just three strands of rusty wire, and pushed it down for Susannah. She climbed over, snagging her jeans.

'I'm stuck!'

With mounting panic, Hudson tried to hook her off the wire. Across the field, they could see lights swarming around Terleksi's big house.

'Ow, it's scratching me!'

'Hold on,' he instructed. She balanced herself on his shoulders, holding the document box, whilst he felt along the wire, locating the barb which had pierced her jeans. His fingers fumbling with panic, he finally managed to free her.

'Come on!' he hissed, grabbing the document box off her and heading into the forbidding gloom of the trees. Susannah needed no encouragement and, holding on to the back of his shirt, they headed into the wood. Although most of the trees had shed their leaves, there was no moonlight to penetrate the canopy and they could barely see a thing. Branches and briars whipped and clawed at their faces, but they were oblivious to the pain, entirely focused on their desperate bid to escape.

When they had gone a few hundred metres, Hudson stopped. In contrast to the crashing of their headlong charge into the trees, the silence was palpable. The only sound was their breathing, hard and ragged from the exertion. And from fear. On Hudson's whispered command, they both stood completely and waited, listening out for the sound of a pursuit.

They didn't have to wait long. Across the still night air, they heard shouting from the direction they had come. Their presence in the house must have been detected and the hunt was now on. Torches flashed in the distance, and with a sickening realisation, it occurred to Hudson that they had probably left a trail in the soft, damp soil of the field. Worse, what if the police had brought a dog handling unit with them? Also, if a helicopter was not already on the way, then it would surely be a matter of time before one was called to assist. Then it would be over.

'Come on, we need to keep moving,' he whispered, ignoring the rapidly growing pain in his side. The borrowed shirt was sticking to his side, wet. He clenched his teeth and ploughed on into the undergrowth, leading Susannah behind him. He had no sense of where they were headed, just a vague notion that they were travelling in a straight line away from Terleski's house, putting the maximum distance between them and their pursuers. The hunt was surely on by now, and Hudson was expecting to hear dogs barking behind them at any moment, or the ominous thudding of helicopter rotors above.

Suddenly, after forcing their way through thick undergrowth, they burst through the treeline and onto a poorly maintained track of some sort. It wasn't a proper road, but wide enough for a vehicle. Hudson, acting on instinct, turned left, pulling Susannah along behind him. He felt exhausted and the pain in his side was steadily getting worse. They needed to find shelter. As if reading his mind, the heavens opened above them and it started to rain.

They stumbled forward blindly, but then, out of the gloom, a small shack appeared. Slightly further up, there was a small cottage set in a clearing, and the smell of wood smoke lingered in the air. As they approached, it was clear that the shack was a small open-sided log store. They huddled beneath the rusty corrugated tin roof as the rain came pelting down around them. As the raindrops hammered into the metal roof, Susannah clung to the exhausted Hudson. They seemed out of options.

*

Samuel Gregory, 'Grease' to his friends and colleagues, blinked and yawned, trying to focus on the empty M40 motorway ahead. He pressed his foot down on the throttle, the speed edging up to ninety, forcing him to concentrate. What the hell was he doing? It was three o'clock in the morning! James Hudson better have a good story for him, or else.

But this is what you had to do to get the story. It was part of the job, the job that he had fought so hard to win, had beaten so many other candidates, including Hudson, to secure. Since then, the shine had started to wear off, and the job was not quite living up to its promised glory. It involved long hours and was badly paid, certainly in comparison to other graduate professions, but then again there were thousands of others who would love the opportunity for a place on The Guardian newspaper group's graduate trainee journalist programme. It was certainly better than the dreary fallback options of sales or accountancy. Gregory was pretty sure there weren't many accountants racing up the M40 at three in the morning.

He had reached an impasse in his career. He rarely got near a major story and any contributions he made were always amalgamated into the work of the journalist he was work-shadowing. He just needed a break, and perhaps this was it. The chance to break a major story. Something to impress his sub-editor with.

'Grease' was an apt moniker, if slightly unfair. His rich black hair, worn slightly on the long side, always looked brilliantined, though it wasn't. His mother was of south Mediterranean stock and he had inherited the same swarthy looks. Grease or not, the women rarely complained. The nickname had stuck with him through university and he had found himself unable to shake it off in the world of work, when an injudiciously circulated email from an old friend had enlightened his new colleagues, much to their amusement.

He yawned and ran his hand through his thick hair and readjusted himself in the seat of his Audi. He had been watching a late night film at home, a room in a shared apartment in West Ham, when the call had come through. He had just lit his last cigarette of the day and was savouring the fine, sweet smoke of the light Virginia tobacco. It was a bad habit, acquired from his mother. Smoking was mandatory in the south of Italy, and for some reason it didn't seem to kill people as effectively as it did in the north of Europe. Diet, lifestyle, genes. Whatever. He should stop, plus it was rapidly becoming a no-no with the ladies. If ever there was a motivating factor, that was it. But not right now, at one o'clock in the morning after a crap and unproductive day in the office. He had just taken another deeply satisfying drag on the cigarette when his mobile had rang. The unbelievably irritating jingle had been downloaded onto his phone by the last woman he had slept with 'to remind him of her'. It certainly did that. Resolving to change it and never see her again, he had noticed that the number was his office redirected.

'Hello?' he had answered cautiously.

'Grease?'

'Er, yeah? Who is this?'

'Grease, it's me, James Hudson.'

'James! How are you? Got a real job yet, you slacker?'

'Sorry Grease, this isn't a social call. I don't have much time to explain.' The seriousness of Hudson's tone caught his immediate attention.

'What's the matter?'

'I'm in the shit. Badly. I'm caught up in something I don't know how to get out of.'

'How can I help?'

'Have you heard of Sir Charles Millburn?'

'Of course I have. My newspaper loves Gencor and anything nuclear. James, he's a wanker, but what's that got to do with it?'

'This isn't funny, Grease. I've found something out about him. It could end the government's new nuclear programme.'

'Sounds promising. What is it?'

'We need your help, first. Look, Grease, I'm not joking. I'm really in the shit. I think we're being targeted for what we know. I've got taped recordings of meetings. They prove what Millburn's done, and I think he's trying to stop us.'

'What do you mean?'

'I was shot at earlier. Someone tried to kidnap Susannah.'

'*Shot at?*' Gregory was incredulous.

'That's right. I'm not joking. We're in hiding and I need you to come and get us. Your paper can protect us as witnesses.'

'Woah. You're not bullshitting me on this?'

'Trust me, Grease. This will be your biggest story. I'm not even interested in the credit anymore. I just want to get out of here alive.'

'You mentioned Susannah. Who's she?'

'My girlfriend. She's part of this.'

'Okay, I'll see what I can do.'

'Grease?'

'Yeah?'

'There's something else you should know. We're wanted by the police.'

'The police? What for?'

'Murder.'

Gregory played the conversation over in his mind and took a deep breath, hoping he was doing the right thing as he pulled off the dark, empty motorway and headed towards Henley-in-Arden. Just then, his phone rang again.

*

Kroll snatched up the phone urgently.

'Yes?...you've tracked the signal...and the GPS reference?...Got it.' He scribbled on a pad, hung up and dialled a new number.

'Trevor, we've got a trace on her mobile. Middle of nowhere, but hasn't moved for a few minutes. They must be hiding somewhere. Find them…What?…I don't give a shit about the police, just *find* them!' he shouted and slammed the phone down.

*

Hudson left Susannah's mobile switched on after he finished his call, so that Gregory could call them back.

'Hopefully Grease can find us. We're close to the lane that runs past your uncle's house. He thinks he knows where this cottage is on his sat nav. If we follow the track back to the road, he'll meet us there.'

'When?'

'He's about fifteen minutes away. We need to go now.'

The rain was beating down hard, droplets bouncing off the tin roof of the log shack. Hudson shivered in the sodden shirt borrowed from Terleski, grimacing at the pain from the stitched wound in his side. The lure of the warm, dry sanctuary of Gregory's car was irresitible. Hudson peered into the darkness around them, but could see no sign of any approach. The noise of the rain on the roof made it impossible to hear anything. They had to chance it. Grasping hold of the document box with his strong side, he took Susannah's hand and led her out into the full onslaught of the rain. The track was already muddy and slippery under foot, and it took all of their concentration not to fall over. The cold rain beat off Hudson's head and ran in rivulets down his neck, chilling him further. Their route took them away from the relative safety of the smoky cottage but Hudson knew that they were just moments away from safety. It was worth the risk.

As they stumbled down the unlit track, Hudson could make out the sound of the motor vehicle approaching. He tensed, then relaxed. It was heading towards them. *Grease*!

'Come on Susannah, he's come to pick us up,' he cajoled her, dragging her along faster. Through the teeming downpour, they picked out the glow of headlights coming up the track towards them. Hudson felt the relief wash over him. Their ordeal would soon be over. The bright lights picked them out, dazzling Hudson who put an arm up to shield his eyes. He heard the engine revving as Grease struggled to find a purchase on the slippery surface of the rough track. The car approached them quickly, its wheels spinning. It got closer and closer. Hudson frowned. Why wasn't he slowing down? Hadn't he seen them?

The sickening realisation dawned on Hudson at the last moment. With his last remaining strength, he pushed Susannah to one side as hard as he could, as the car charged forward relentlessly. The car just missed her and Hudson barely had time to stand up before it hit him. He crashed over the bonnet and into the windscreen, his back shattering the toughened glass. That was what saved him, the windscreen absorbing the energy of the impact.

The car slewed to a stop and Hudson rolled off the bonnet, falling onto the muddy ground, stunned. He heard Susannah scream; then a shouted command from the car.

'You get the girl!'

Cars doors opened in a hurry and Hudson heard a pair of feet splashing towards him. Recovering himself quickly, he scrambled to his feet as a shadow loomed out the darkness. Miraculously, he was still holding the document box. He swung it wildly at the form in the rain, feeling it connect with something. There was a muffled grunt, and Hudson stumbled into the darkness, sensing the slim opportunity to escape. He splashed blindly down the muddy track, hearing Susannah cry out somewhere in front of him. He carried on oblivious, his eyesight still rendered useless by the dazzling of the car's headlights.

Suddenly, he crashed into a large obstacle in the track and fell heavily to the ground. There was an audible grunt and another scream. Susannah! He had run into her assailant, knocking them both over. He sensed Susannah close by and grabbed hold of her. A hand grasped hold of Hudson's leg, and he lashed out with his foot, hearing a cry of pain as it connected with something solid. Hudson staggered to his feet, hauling up Susannah with him. Behind them, the red taillights of the car glowed softly through the rain. They had to run in the opposite direction. Hudson dragged Susannah along with him, but she slipped on the sodden ground. In panic, he pulled her up again and they stumbled into the darkness towards the road.

Behind him, Hudson heard shouting and the car door slam. The engine roared and he heard the wheels spinning in the mud and gravel. *Come on, Susannah!* With renewed vigour, he gripped her firmly under her arm and pulled her along. He had no idea how far they were from the road. Behind him, the car was thrown into a frantically executed three point turn. Any minute now and it would come racing after them. Hudson felt the fear spreading through him, turning his legs to jelly. He heard gears crunching and high engine revs, then the arc of the headlights swept over them, lighting up the track ahead. There was no escape.

Hudson heard the engine roaring behind them, the headlights bearing down on them mercilessly. It was only a matter of seconds now. Either side of the track was fenced with barbed wire. There was no way they could flee into the relative safety of the woods.

Suddenly, a solid hedgerow appeared in front of them. With mounting terror, Hudson realised that their way was blocked. He stumbled forward as the muddy track gave way to a hard surface, desperately looking for an escape.

Before he could think, there was a loud screeching of tyres and he was aware of bright lights bearing down on them from the left. He barely had time to react before the car came to a stuttering halt, centimetres away from his legs. He looked up into the terrified face of the driver hunched over the steering wheel, his features illuminated by the soft glow of the dashboard.

Samuel Gregory stared back in horror at the apparition he had nearly run over.

Without a moment's hesitation, Hudson stepped around the car grabbed a rear door and bundled Susannah inside.

'Drive! Drive!' he screamed at Gregory as he leapt in after Susannah. Gregory reacted instantly, just as the other car careered down the track and into the road, narrowly avoiding clipping the rear of his car. The engine of Gregory's Audi growled as he floored the accelerator, and the tyres bit into the tarmac with a squeal. They roared up the lane, with

Hudson in the back seat watching their pursuers, whilst Susannah hunched down. Gregory was clearly terrified, but sensed the danger and urgency, and responded well to it.

'They're coming!' shouted Hudson, with desperate urgency. Gregory changed down, revved the engine and felt the turbo kick in. The extra power surged them forward and they sped recklessly up the narrow lane, Gregory throwing the car into blind corners. If they met anyone coming the other way, they wouldn't stand a chance. The pursuing headlights began to fall back as the extra power of Gregory's Audi began to tell.

A T-junction appeared in front of them and Gregory made the snap decision to go left. Without even looking he threw the car into a tight left turn, screeching onto the B-road, the tyres barely gripping the wet tarmac. Fortunately there was nothing coming, but he lost control of the car on the slippery surface and they slewed across the carriageway as he grappled with the steering. Hudson held his breath as the car snaked from one side of the road to the other, the tyres squealing, but Gregory managed to hold it and correct the oversteer. They straightened up and Gregory mashed through the gears, building up speed again. They were doing over eighty on an unfamiliar road, in the dark and in pouring rain, but Gregory was infected with the need to get away, gripping the steering wheel tightly, his eyes wide with fear.

The TomTom glowed on the dashboard and Hudson leaned forward between the two front seats and glanced at it.

'Take the next right,' he ordered. Gregory complied, braked heavily and they found themselves charging down another narrow country lane. There was a distant glint of headlights behind them. Hudson ordered a few more turns in the warren of country lanes, before leading Gregory back to a main road. He peered anxiously into the gloom behind them; the headlights were a long behind them now. They seemed to have lost their pursuers.

But Hudson had forgotten about the mobile phone in his pocket.

'I think we've done it,' he gasped, turning away from the rear window and grimacing at the pain in his side. 'Thanks, Grease.'

Gregory glanced at him in the mirror, he face pale and tense. 'Are you going to tell me what the *hell* is going on?'

*

Brannigan arrived at Terleski's house soon after the first panda cars had turned up. It was a chaotic scene as officers spread out across the field behind the house to search for the two missing suspects. A dog handling unit and surveillance helicopter had been called up, but neither would arrive for several minutes yet. Brannigan was curtly informed by an embarrassed Detective Inspector from the Warwickshire force that his assistance was not required in the search, but he was free to inspect the house should he choose to, as long as he did not disturb any evidence.

As the police officers conducted their search across the fields behind the house, Brannigan walked towards the big old house. The front door had been forced open with the same lack of finesse that had dispatched the padlocked chain on the driveway gates. He was aware that the owner of the house had committed suicide, or at least had been found dead, two days earlier. The fact that Hudson and Susannah were linked to Doctor Terleski was cause enough for concern.

Brannigan stepped into the deserted hallway. Despite the flickering of the blue lights from the panda cars parked outside, he began to feel strangely unnerved, as though his sixth sense was trying to warn him about something. He realised that the other police officers were spreading out across the field, and he was alone in the house. He shivered involuntarily, then caught himself. Ghosts did not exist. Pulling himself together, he cursed the unsubtle tactics of his colleagues. They may as well have telephoned in advance. Muttering to himself, he switched on the lights and began to look around.

It did not take him long to find the open sash window in the drawing room. This must have been their point of escape as well as entry. In the light from the window, Brannigan could make out their tracks in the wet grass, heading towards the fields at the back. Part of him could not help but admire their resourcefulness and determination in avoiding arrest. But their bid for freedom would end soon. Their arrest was inevitable, despite the general incompetence his colleagues had displayed to date. As soon as the dog teams and the helicopter arrived, there would be little chance of escape. Brannigan smiled grimly to himself. He always got his suspects in the end.

Leaving the drawing room, he noticed that a light was already on upstairs. They must have left it on in their rush to flee. Puffing with the exertion, he hauled his large bulk up the staircase. He noticed the humidity at the top of the stairs and correctly guessed that they must have used the bathroom. He was right. A candle resting on the toilet cistern guttered in the draft created by the open drawing room window downstairs, illuminating the bathroom in a soft glow. The bath was still half full of lukewarm water, and a pile of used surgical wipes lay on the floor, next to a hospital gown. The journalist had been shot, according to the doctors at the hospital. A large calibre bullet had ploughed a furrow across the skin and flesh of his left dorsal muscle. A flesh wound, but a nasty one at that. He would be in considerable discomfort. More importantly, Brannigan dearly wished to talk to him about the injury. Hudson was clearly involved in serious crime of some sort. Either that, or Alex Warburton had shot him before Hudson killed him. That was more likely, and now the journalist was running scared, afraid of the charges against him. Brannigan sighed. He would get to the bottom of it one or another. There was nothing else of interest upstairs, so he plodded down again and walked into what must have been Doctor Terleski's study.

From what he had gathered, Brannigan understood that Terleski was a doctor of physics, not medicine. Being a bit old fashioned, Brannigan was of the firm belief that only those involved in the treatment and care of the sick should use the title on a daily basis, especially as every second person seemed to hold a doctorate these days. Brannigan approved of Terleski's office, though. The dark wood panelling lent it a gravitas appropriate to intellectual endeavour, whilst the piles of documents and books spoke of industry. The solid desk in the centre of the room caught his attention. He thought it vaguely odd that the man did not seem to have a computer. Brannigan glanced around. The paraphernalia of a modern office was there; the laser printer, the cables, fax machine. But no computer. It was no longer vaguely odd; it was patently obvious that the computer was missing.

Brannigan scanned Terleski's bookshelves. There were several tomes on nuclear physics and the nuclear industry, regulatory pamphlets and whole host of scientific journals. Another bookcase contained more literary works, and he noted large gap on one of the shelves. That must be the pile of books on the desk. Constance Hunting. *Never heard of her*, he shrugged.

Out of the corner of his eye, he noticed a red light, winking at him. He turned to look and spotted the telephone. It sat on a pile of books within easy reach of whoever sat at the desk. The red light flashed slowly at him, beckoning him over. Curious, Brannigan shuffled over, squeezing his large form between piles of books, holding his overcoat in to prevent it snagging on anything. He bent over the telephone. The answerphone warning light was flashing.

One new message.

With the tip of his pen, Brannigan pressed the play button and stooped down to listen.

'William? William are you there?....William, if you're there, pick up the phone. It's urgent. I have to talk to you.' The caller sounded very tired, and short of breath.

There was a noise as someone, presumably Terleski, picked up the phone. He sounded hoarse and nervous.

'Yes?'

'It's Mark,' the caller breathed. 'Mark Wellesby.'

'I know. How are you Mark?'

Brannigan froze to the spot. *Mark Wellesby?* No, it couldn't be. Why the hell would the head of MI5 be phoning an elderly retired scientist in Henley-in-Arden?

'Not so good, William. I've got the big C. I can't last much longer, looks like Langham will be taking over soon.'

Langham? Jeremy Langham? It *was* Sir Mark Wellesby on the phone. Brannigan remained rooted to the spot. According to the papers, Wellesby was now critically ill in a London hospital and Langham had been appointed Acting Director General. The inadvertently recorded conversation continued. Terleski had not picked up the phone in time to prevent the answer phone recording the call.

'I'm sorry to hear that, Mark.'

'There's not much I can do about it, I'm afraid. Look, William, this isn't a social call. Something's come up I think you should know about. It concerns Red Dawn.'

There was a pause as Wellesby waited for a response from Terleski, but none was forthcoming, and Brannigan got the sense that Terleski was shocked to hear the phrase. *Red Dawn?* What the hell was *that?* Wellesby continued, and Brannigan noted that he was unable to complete sentences without pausing for breath. The man sounded in pain, and his speech was laboured.

'The Prime Minister needs to know about Red Dawn. I have to inform him as part of a security review of the nuclear sector. Thought it best, what with the new generation of plants being considered. If news of Red Dawn ever got out, the whole programme would be in jeopardy. The PM needs to understand that. I suspect that his sentiments will be to bury the whole thing for good. I think that is the wisest course of action as well, but thought it best that you heard the news from me first. Based on the information you gave us all those years ago, I thought it was the least I could do. What you did was very brave.'

'I gave you that information in confidence, and for you to do something with, not sit on it for over twenty years.' There was a long silence, then Terleski continued. 'Who else will know about my involvement?'

'Apart from the PM, just Jeremy Langham and Giles Devereaux.'

'Who?'

'Devereaux? The PM's Director of Communications. The PM doesn't fart without his permission.'

'After everything I did, you buried the whole thing, let Charles Millburn get away with it. I risked everything for nothing. And now you want to tell others about it, so they can tell you to bury it, is that what you're saying, Mark? Ease your conscience will it, get someone else to make the difficult decisions for you?'

Charles Millburn? Brannigan racked his brains. The name seemed familiar, but he couldn't quite place it.

'It's the big picture, William. This country *needs* nuclear power. It's the only viable option we have, and Gencor is the only British company capable of building and operating the plants. We can't let the Japs or the French in. It's a strategic industry. Can you imagine what would happen if the public found out about Red Dawn? The whole programme would be called off, and we would have a full-blown energy crisis.'

Gencor. That was it. Sir Charles Millburn was the Chairman of Gencor Energy PLC. Brannigan was riveted. *What the hell was this all about?*

'You can't let Millburn get away with it!' Terleski was forceful. 'And I don't want you tell anyone about my involvement.'

'I'm sorry, William. I knew you'd be upset, that's why I called.'

'But if the PM knows what I did, and Devereaux, what's to stop it becoming wider knowledge? What if Millburn finds out? He'd kill me!'

'Don't worry, William. I'll make sure, if the PM orders it, that all the information we hold, including your report, is to be destroyed. There will be no trace of Red Dawn.'

'Except what I know. And the others. You'll have to trust them to keep quiet.'

Wellesby chuckled softly. 'It's been kept secret for two decades. I hardly think it's going to come out now, do you?'

'You should have done something when I told you. Then the safeguards could have been put in place so that a leak like that never happens again. You let Millburn orchestrate the cover-up to suit your own ends.'

Brannigan frowned. A *leak*?

'Politics, my dear fellow. Nasty old business. If anything had gone wrong, we could have blamed Millburn and locked him for a very long time. But we needed the leak kept secret, it's as simple as that I'm afraid.'

'What's going to happen to me?'

'Nothing. Just keep quiet, that's all. Get rid of anything you have on Red Dawn. Look, I'm just paying you a courtesy by letting you know.'

'No you're not, you're warning me. You're threatening me.'

'No, I'm not, William. I can assure you. You're perfectly safe. And the others too.'

'I have your word on that?'

'You have my word.'

Brannigan blinked. He hunched over the telephone, trying to make sense of what he had just heard. The date and time stamp placed the call on Sunday morning. Terleski's body had been discovered on Tuesday morning, nearly two days ago now. The pathologist's preliminary assessment had placed the time of death on Monday night. Judging by what he had heard on the tape, Terleski was a very worried man. How many people receive a direct phone call from the head of their country's security service? Whatever Terleski was involved in, this Red Dawn business, was serious. Very serious indeed. According to the recording, there had been some sort of leak which had been covered up. Terleski was obviously an informant to the security service, which had failed to act on his information, thereby becoming complicit in the cover-up of the leak. And the DG was trying to cover his own arse and absolve himself of any responsibility by informing the Prime Minister under the guise of a security review into the nuclear industry. Clearly the burden had weighed heavily on his conscience over the years, but if the PM ordered that the information be destroyed, that got Wellesby off the hook. The man was dying. He wanted to clear his conscience of at least one of the morally dubious acts he had committed over the years. That was perfectly understandable.

Brannigan shook his head ruefully. He had stumbled on something of major importance, a completely unexpected twist. He decided that he wanted to listen again and reached down to press play.

'I think we've heard quite enough of that, haven't we?' the voice spoke out quietly from behind him. Brannigan jumped, spinning around in surprise. There was a metallic click.

The man who stood before him was of slight build, in slightly careworn clothes, with a tired-looking expression. His face betrayed no emotion and was unremarkable to look at except for curiously thin lips which lent him an utterly humourless demeanour. The cold eyes, rimmed with dark smudges of fatigue, were dispassionate. The gaze seemed to pass right through Brannigan as though he was of no consequence whatsoever. But what really attracted Brannigan's attention was the pistol that had just been cocked and was now levelled at his stomach.

It wouldn't be until later on that morning that he was reported missing.

27

Thursday morning

Donald Winston snatched up the handset of his phone within two rings. 'Yes?'

'Don, it's James.'

'Thank god,' breathed the relieved editor. 'Where the hell are you? The police have been looking for you.'

'I know. I think I've been set up. Susannah's ex-boyfriend has been murdered.'

'Way ahead of you. I've had the details since last night. Did you do it?'

'Of course I bloody didn't!' Hudson snapped, incredulous.

'Okay, I believe you. Why are you hiding?'

'You're not going to believe it.'

'Try me.'

Hudson took a breath and ploughed into an explanation of the dossier he had been emailed by Doctor Terleski, how he had initially thought it was a joke but then Terleski had been found dead. Hudson explained how he had phoned the list of colleagues provided in Terleski's account, to discover that they had all died within days of each other. Then Susannah had found a letter sent to her describing the existence of proof. They had followed the trail to Terleski's house, where they had discovered the document box containing the taped recordings of the meetings which had set up the Red Dawn programme. It took Hudson a while to explain the Red Dawn programme, and he could hear Winston furiously scribbling notes. Hudson explained how two men had then attacked them, shooting him and attempting to kidnap Susannah along with the document box. They had narrowly escaped, only to encounter them again in hospital. Finally, they had fled back to Terleski's house to hide, on the grounds that it was the only place they could go to as Hudson had lost his clothes, wallet, everything in hospital.

'You were *shot?*' asked Winston incredulously.

'I was nicked. Just a flesh wound, nothing too serious but it hurts like hell.'

'Where are you now?'

'A friend's place.'

'Where?'

'I'd rather not say, if that's alright with you.'

'You don't trust me?'

'Can I trust you?'

'Of course you can, James.'

'After what we've been through, you'll have to excuse me for being a bit wary.'

'I understand, James. But you need to come in, see what we can do with this story.'

'It's too big, Don. You can't protect us. We need to go to one of the nationals. They'll know what to do.'

There was a long silence. Winston did not reply.

'Don?'

'Yes?'

'I'm sorry, Don, but put yourself in our shoes. Our *lives* are at risk. We can't afford to make a mistake. Don't worry, the paper will be properly credited. It was part of the deal.'

'Deal? You've made a deal?'

'Yes. Sorry, but I had to.'

'Who with?'

Hudson paused.

'Oh, come on James. You can at least tell me that.'

'Guardian,' Hudson replied after some thought. Winston snorted into the phone.

'Alan will have a field day with this. I've known him for years,' he commented, reflecting on Alan Dunscombe, the editor. 'Or, at least, I know *of* him,' Winston corrected. 'You could do worse, I suppose. This sort of thing's right up his street.'

'We need his help with the police investigation, too,' confessed Hudson. 'We're innocent, Don. I swear. We had nothing to do with it.'

'What's he said about that?'

'Nothing. We haven't spoken to him yet. We're meeting him soon.'

'Get him to call me if you like. I'll vouch for you.'

'Thanks Don. I appreciate it. Like I said, I'll make sure the paper's properly credited.'

'Good luck, James.'

Winston replaced the handset in its cradle. His hand still in place, he looked up at the thin-lipped, humourless man sitting opposite. The man gazed back at him impassively, but Winston wasn't that easily intimidated.

'Happy with that?' he asked sarcastically.

The thin lipped man did not reply, but turned his head away and stared out of the window, deep in thought. It was an interesting development, not entirely unforeseen. He stood up and smoothed the creases from his rumpled suit.

'Keep me notified,' he ordered. 'And not a word of this to anyone. Understand?'

Winston nodded reluctantly and the thin-lipped man left the office as quietly as he had arrived.

*

After a few hours sleep at Gregory's London flat, Hudson and Susannah accompanied Gregory to the Farringdon Road headquarters of the Guardian newspaper.

Waking up had been a painful experience for Hudson. Although Susannah had dressed his stitches and they had enjoyed a warm shower before collapsing on Gregory's sofa bed, the wound throbbed painfully when he woke. The flesh around the stitching was inflamed, the skin tight, warning of possible infection. His ribs, badly bruised from the impact with the windscreen several hours earlier, ached with every breath. He swallowed some painkillers and eased out of bed, feeling worse than when he had arrived at Gregory's flat. Susannah applied antiseptic ointment from Gregory's medical kit to the wound while Hudson gritted his teeth at the pain. She insisted that he needed antibiotics to fight any infection, but those had been left behind in the hospital and Hudson did not want the delay or further risk of visiting a doctor to obtain a fresh prescription. A heated argument ensued, the situation not helped by the incredible stress both had been subjected to over the previous forty eight hours.

To break the impasse, Gregory promised him treatment at the newpaper's offices, appeasing them both. Hudson was in no fit condition to endure the rigours of tube travel, so Gregory laid on the luxury of a black cab. Their journey through the heavy traffic had passed largely in silence and as they approached the newspaper offices, the tension became increasingly palpable.

On the journey down the motorway a few hours earlier, Hudson had explained everything to Gregory, who had listened in amazement. At the time, swept along with the excitement of the car chase and their seemingly narrow escape from the men pursuing Hudson and Susannah, the whole story had seemed entirely plausible. But in the cool light of day, it now seemed rather fantastical. Gregory was in no doubt that his old college friend was in deep trouble, but whether this was down to a secret government programme called Red Dawn remained to be seen, and Gregory began to wonder what his notoriously volcanic boss would have to say on the matter. He would soon find out.

As they pulled up outside the Guardian offices, the driver glanced at them warily in the mirror. His attempts at small talk had been met with silence, and he didn't care much for Hudson's battered appearance, though he had to concede that the girl was quite a looker. He doubted he would receive a tip from this fare, a suspicion confirmed when the suited one with the slicked back hair leaned forward and asked for a receipt.

Susannah and Hudson climbed out together, while Gregory dealt with the receipt from the surly driver. She sought his hand and squeezed it tightly, for reassurance.

'Are you okay?' Hudson asked gently. She had been through a lot, but had held herself together. But her beautiful almond eyes were dulled with fatigue, both nervous and physical. She was reaching the limit of her endurance.

'I just want it to be over,' she whispered.

'Don't worry, it will be soon. Once we've shown all this to Grease's boss, the paper will look after us.'

'What if they don't believe us?'

'They will. They have to. We've got the proof here.' He gripped the handle of the document box tightly, as Gregory thanked the driver, who muttered something rude and roared off.

Hudson took a deep breath and looked up at the building.

'Here goes,' he muttered, and they all stepped forward.

*

It was just after half past eight in the morning when they entered the building. On the northern news channels, there was extensive coverage of the murder in Cuerden Valley Park. The gruesome details of Alex Warburton's demise were relayed with relish on the breakfast programmes. The television channels carried pictures, issued by Manchester police, of the two main suspects wanted in connection with the crime. Suitably suspicious and unflattering images of Hudson and Susannah had been obtained and were broadcast into homes across the northwest, though journalists were unable to secure an interview with the investigating officer, Detective Inspector Carl Brannigan. Brannigan's colleagues thought it odd that he did not show up at work but, then again, he'd been up for most of the night according to those colleagues who had travelled with him down to Stratford for the embarrassing non-arrest. Perhaps their boss was sleeping it off. He'd be in later, they were sure of that.

In the meantime, the story would gather momentum, soon gaining the attention of the larger networks and other media outlets. The ghoulish pleasure of the journalists was heightened by the fact that one of their own was the chief suspect in the murder enquiry.

28

Inside the atrium of the Guardian's headquarters, Hudson checked his watch nervously while they waited to be signed in by Gregory. It was quarter to nine on what would turn out to be the longest day of his life, though he didn't know that yet. A feeling of nausea washed over him, making his limbs feel weak. What if they didn't believe him? What if they weren't offered protection? Hudson recalled the fate of Mordechai Vanunu, the Israeli nuclear scientist who had betrayed his country's secrets to The Sunday Times, revealing Israel's nuclear capability to an astonished world. It was a spectacular coup for the newspaper. As part of the deal, the paper was meant to be looking after him, protecting him from an understandably vengeful Mossad. But the operation had been amateurish from the outset. Mossad agents set up a honey trap, lured Vanunu to Italy from under the noses of his newspaper minders, and then kidnapped him to face Israeli justice. About the only positive outcome to the whole episode was that they didn't kill him. But Hudson was no spy or traitor. He simply knew the truth about the worst nuclear accident ever to have hit the UK. And someone clearly didn't wish him to know, or tell anyone else.

Gregory returned from the reception with the obligatory visitor passes and led them into the elevator. Hudson felt his nervousness increasing. As the lift swished silently upwards, they seemed so far removed from their experiences a few hours earlier. What if no one believed them? Even Hudson was wondering if he had imagined it until the painful throbbing in his side reminded him. He had been shot. *Shot.*

The lift doors opened and they entered another lobby. Gregory led them to a meeting room, furnished with the standard corporate issue beech-effect table and chairs, palm plant in the corner.

'Wait here. I need to speak to the editor. Help yourself to tea, coffee.'

Gregory left them and Hudson poured them both a coffee, which Susannah received gratefully, nursing the cup in both hands. The room overlooked the busy street below, full of people going about their everyday, ordinary lives. Hudson looked down wistfully, wondering how he had found himself in this situation. The black document box sat on the table, a malevolent presence in the room. They had played the taped recording to Gregory back at his flat. It was the clincher. Hudson suspected that without the hard evidence to back up his story, then Gregory would not have arranged to meet his editor.

Gregory left the reception lobby and entered the large open plan office that housed the main journalistic hub of the paper. He headed past the workstations for each section of the paper and proceeded towards his Chief Political Editor's desk.

Terry Gallimore looked up from his computer and raised an enquiring eyebrow.

'What's up, Grease?'

'I've got a story. A big one.'

*

'Run that past me again, will you,' asked Gallimore quietly, frowning, once Gregory had finished explaining. 'Sounds like he's pulling your plonker.'

'James Hudson's an old friend of mine from journalism college. I don't think this is a wind-up, Terry. It's not his style. He was always pretty straight down the line. What I *do* know is that I picked them up in the middle of a field last night and someone was chasing after us. I managed to lose them.'

'You're not imagining anything?'

'No, Terry. I was shitting myself, if you must know.'

'What did you say you've got?'

'Tapes. The girl's uncle taped the meetings. It's Sir Charles Millburn, clear as a bell.'

'You're absolutely sure?'

'Absolutely.'

'Okay, we'd better have a word with them, then.'

Gallimore accompanied Gregory back to the meeting room in the lobby. After the preliminary introductions, Gallimore asked Hudson to explain what had happened, mentally cross-referencing the story with Gregory's account. Hudson handed him a copy of the dossier which Terleski had written and emailed to him, the start of the whole affair. He led Gallimore through the events of the past three days, culminating in the discovery of the tapes and the shooting.

Gallimore rubbed his face when Hudson had finished playing the tapes, and glanced at Gregory. They were both thinking the same thing.

They would have to speak to Alan Dunscombe, the notoriously fiery Editor-in-Chief.

'We need to take this higher, James,' Gallimore advised. Gregory nodded at Hudson. 'Who else knows about this, that you know of?'

'Outside this room, no one apart from Don Winston, my editor,' replied Hudson. 'He knows I'm here.'

Gallimore nodded. 'Okay, let's go and see Alan.'

They followed Gallimore back into the large office and over to the enclosed glass cubicle that sat in one corner. Dunscombe was on the phone and angrily gesticulated for him to wait when Gallimore knocked on the door. Gallimore sighed and shrugged his shoulders.

'Fantastic mood again, I see,' he muttered to the assembled party. Then the editor's personal secretary spotted them and hurried back from the water dispenser to interrogate them.

'What do you want?'

'I need to see Alan.'

'What about?'

'A story.'

'Why can't anyone else help you?'

'Because they can't.'

'Do you have an appointment?'

'No. I don't need one.'

'He's not free until this afternoon.'

'I can't wait until then.'

'There's nothing I can do, I'm sorry. You'll have to come back at....'

'What the hell's going on?' barked Alan Dunscombe as he swung the door open, which banged as it collided with a waste bin behind it. 'What do you want?' he snapped at Gallimore. Dunscombe's eyes were heavily bloodshot; it was rumoured that he was struggling to win his legendary battle with Jameson's Malt.

'Gregory's on to a story, Alan. A big one. I think you need to read this.' He proffered the dossier to his boss.

'I haven't got time to read this,' he snapped, his fierce eyes swivelling and acquiring a fix on Gregory. 'You're the new boy aren't you? Come in. You've got two minutes to sell it to me.' He turned abruptly and marched back to his desk. The party traipsed in after him whilst the secretary scowled, sulking resentfully at Dunscombe's effective skewering of any authority she may have once possessed.

Gregory took a deep breath and, as best he could, gave a summary of the dossier. The two minutes turned into five.

'Do you think this is authentic?' Dunscombe enquired, a dangerous glint in his eye.

'I knew James at college. I don't think he's making this up.' They were talking about Hudson as if he didn't exist.

'On your head be it.' His eyes turned to Hudson, briefly and uncomfortably appraised him, then lingered rather longer than necessary on Susannah. Then he turned his attention to the dossier and began reading, leaving them all standing and unsure what to do with themselves.

Dunscombe placed a pair of horn-rimmed glasses on his swollen, red nose, the capillaries long burst from alcoholic over-indulgence. The folds of skin around his eyes and pock-marked skin all attested to an alcohol consumption that made mockery of any government health guidelines, whilst his untidy mound of grey hair lent to the overall generally shambolic impression. However, his mind was anything but shambolic, even when inebriated, and he read the dossier quickly, grunting every now and again. They stood awkwardly, waiting for him to finish.

Finally, he leant back in his expensive custom-made leather chair, placed the dossier on his desk and drummed his fingers on it.

'Interesting. You wrote this?' he fired at Hudson, catching him unawares.

'Er, no. It was sent to me…'

'Who sent it to you?'

'Dr William Terleski, Susannah's uncle.'

'Why isn't he here?'

'He's dead.'

'Dead?'

'Yes.'

'How?'

'Suicide. Apparently.'

'I see.'

There was silence while Dunscombe thought, still drumming his fingers. 'You have tapes that can verify this dossier. Is that true?'

'We think so.'

'You think so or you know so?' he snapped, his eyes flashing.

'Er, we think so,' Hudson replied, standing his ground.

'That's not good enough, sonny. You can't come in here, throwing accusations like this around on a whim. Who the hell do you think you are?'

Hudson didn't know what to say. It wasn't the reception he had expected, whilst the pain of the injury and overwhelming tiredness had sapped him of his intellectual vigour.

'Alan, listen to the tape. James, play it to him,' intervened Gregory, rescuing Hudson.

Hudson stepped forward and placed the tape machine on the large oak-topped desk, and inserted the first tape, the one he had played to Gallimore a few minutes earlier. He pressed play and stood back. After the initial hissing and background noise had died down, a clear, strong voice spoke out from twenty years earlier. The drumming of fingers slowly came to a halt as Dunscombe digested what he was hearing. When the tape came to an end, he fixed an eye on Hudson.

'Who's that?'

'Charles Millburn.'

'You're sure?'

'Absolutely. You can hear the other delegates calling him.'

'Okay. We can get a voice match on that, just to make sure…Well, sonny,' he nodded approvingly. 'You might just be on to something with this. What else have you got?' he demanded.

Outside, the secretary had a look of consternation on her face. They had been in there for nearly half an hour already. *Half an hour*! Without an appointment. It was practically unheard of. She had already been forced to postpone two telephone calls that had been clearly appointed in his diary. The sheer impertinence of it all. And undermining her authority. If she ever left the firm, they'd be sorry. They'd soon realise how indispensable she was. In a huff, she clicked onto a recruitment website to see what was out there.

Hudson played extracts from other tapes and pulled out the data sheets, along with Terleski's notes. He explained what he thought they were. Dunscombe examined them carefully.

'I see. It does seem to be two competing sets of data….Right then, what does all this mean?'

'This is the proof for the existence of Red Dawn. When he was the Trade and Industry Minister in the last Tory government, he orchestrated the cover up for a major leak from the Sellafield storage tanks. Millburn is directly responsible.'

'Yes, yes, I can *see* that, sonny. But you've got to see it from the point of law. What proof does this constitute? Will this stand up in court, or could it be an elaborate hoax? Perhaps this Terleski chap had a personal grievance. All this paperwork could have been put together on any home computer. The tape could have been forged using voice analysis software. I'm not going to go one step further with this unless I can be absolutely sure that it can stand up in court. Millburn could destroy this newspaper if we're wrong. Just think of the libel payment for a start.'

'But this is all we've got.'

'It's not enough.'

'Then why have the other members of the project been killed? Why did someone try to kill us?'

'What?' Dunscombe looked up sharply. 'What are you talking about?'

'I tried to contact Terleski's old colleagues, four of them. They're listed in the dossier. All of them have died in the last few days. Think that's a coincidence? The Prime Minister announced the new nuclear generating programme last week, and Gencor Energy PLC is almost guaranteed to win the contracts. The only thing that could stop it is Red Dawn being made public. If it was disclosed that the worst nuclear accident in British history was covered up by the same person heading Gencor Energy, it would kill off the programme. Public opinion would make a revival of nuclear power impossible. Gencor would lose billions, Millburn would be finished. They're burying Red Dawn for ever by getting rid of anyone who could expose it.'

'That's a very neat theory.'

'Theory?' Hudson was incredulous. 'You try being shot at! I'm telling you, they want this covered up for good. It's a miracle we got this far!'

'Presumably, therefore,' continued Dunscombe, ignoring Hudson's outburst, 'anyone who could have corroborated the existence of Red Dawn is rather conveniently dead, except for Millburn who, I think we can reliably assume, will be a little reluctant to discuss it.' Dunscombe sighed. 'Can you see how this looks? You have no witnesses to back up your story. Whatever evidence you have here could be dismissed by a trainee solicitor. You're a couple of lovers on the run.... Can you see where this is going?'

'After all we've been through to get this story out, you're just going to ignore it?' Susannah protested, making herself heard for the first time.

The editor shrugged and wove his fingers together behind his head, leaning back in his chair with a yawn.

'I thought you lot hated Millburn and Gencor?' accused Hudson.

'I do. He's an evil money-grabbing little shit. I'm not surprised in the least to hear a story like this. But that's all it is at the moment. A story. I need cast-iron proof. I need witnesses that aren't dead or missing. I am not letting the slightest whiff of this get out until I can be surer than sure that it's not going to blow up in my face.'

Gallimore intervened at this point. 'Isn't it worth checking with legal? They could have a look at this and see what we need to go further.'

'Okay. But I can tell you now that there will be absolutely no mention of any murders, understood? At this stage we're just looking at the cover up of a radioactive leak, nothing else. Got that?'

Gallimore nodded and turned to leave the office when Gregory spoke up.

'There's something else you should know first.' He looked uncomfortable and Hudson glanced at him nervously.

'Yes?'

'James and Susannah are wanted by the police.'

'Why?'

'For the murder of Susannah's former boyfriend.'

Gregory hurried from the office to find the newspaper's legal advisor. Like many major newspapers, the Guardian had long found it expeditious and cost effective to employ their own dedicated lawyer to advise on any contentious stories. It saved a lot of hassle and expense further down the line.

Amarjit Chohan was immersed in a dauntingly thick book of case studies when Gregory found him. He was only too glad for the excuse to put the book down for a moment. They walked back into Dunscombe's office to find him pacing up and down behind his desk, a savage expression on his face. He fixed a cold gaze on Hudson and Susannah, who were painfully aware of how bad the situation looked.

'It would appear that we have more than one use for your advice, Amarjit,' he announced gravely, and spun his laptop around for them all to see.

The Reuter's feed was not subtle. The two mugshots of Hudson and Susannah stared out from the screen under the lurid headline of 'Missing Lovers Sought in Manchester Murder Enquiry'. Hudson and Susannah were shocked by the brazen image.

'Now that Amarjit's here, care to explain?' Dunscombe invited acidly.

'Alex was her ex-boyfriend. He was found dead yesterday.'

'Why do the police want to speak to you about it?'

'We, um, we had a fight. A couple of nights ago. He was vandalising my car and I went out to stop him.' He indicated his bruised face. 'But he, er, he got the better of me…'

Hudson's voice trailed off. He knew it looked bad.

'And he turns up dead, so the police put two and two together?'

Hudson nodded, looking down.

'Did you do it?'

'No! Of course not!' Hudson protested. 'It was nothing to do with us.'

'That's right,' joined in Susannah, her eyes watering.

'The prisons are full of people who didn't do it,' observed Dunscombe, turning to address her. 'If you didn't do it, why did you run away?'

'Because we were frightened. My housemate said the police found blood. At first I thought the burglars had cut themselves…'

'Burglars?'

'Our flat was burgled; my housemate came home to find it wrecked. I thought that they must have cut themselves. The first we knew about Alex was when James was arrested in hospital. The police told James that the blood in the flat probably matched Alex's.'

'But why did you run? Why not tell the police what you've told me?'

'We don't know who to trust,' said Hudson. 'There are people after us. They want to kill us. They were at the hospital. We don't know if the police are involved. When we went back to Susannah's uncle's house...'

'Terleski?' Dunscombe interrupted.

'Yes. When we went back to his house after we got away from the hospital, the police came looking for us, but the same men found us again. They seem to know everything the police are doing. If it wasn't for Grease, er Samuel, I don't know what would have happened.' Hudson felt an involuntary shiver pass through him, and he nearly lost his composure.

'We need your help. Please,' whispered Susannah, her eyes pleading. 'Please help us. We've got nowhere to go.'

Dunscombe fixed a steely gaze on them both, weighing up his conflicting emotions. After what seemed an eternity he made his mind up.

'This certainly changes the situation. Amarjit? Are we obliged to cooperate with the police on this one?'

'Sorry Alan, we can't protect people wanted by the police, especially if a warrant is out for their arrest.'

'What? You can't do that!' protested Hudson.

'We have to, it's the law. Otherwise we would be perverting the course of justice,' replied the solicitor earnestly.

'That's ridiculous. What about Red Dawn and Millburn?'

'We can't touch it now, can we?' snapped Dunscombe.

'I think I need to be appraised of everything,' the solicitor interjected, quite forcibly for such a mild mannered man.

They went through the details of their story again with Chohan, which also allowed Dunscombe to gain a better appreciation of events. Chohan was genuinely shocked by the revelations, especially when he heard the tapes. His shock turned to alarm when Hudson narrated the shooting and their subsequent escapes, first from their would-be abductors and killers, then from the police, twice.

'So, you think the police are part of it?'

'I'm not sure. They could be, or there is a leak. Red Dawn may have gone wider than Terleski realised. Either way, I don't trust the police.'

'Yes, but the problem remains that you are wanted in connection with a murder investigation. If we fail to act, we could be guilty of obstructing that investigation.'

'So you want to hand us over to the police? I thought you tried to stick up for people,' Hudson stated with disgust. 'You obviously don't. You're pathetic, more worried about saving your own arses.'

Dunscombe blinked. Chohan raised his eyebrows. The explosion was imminent. No one spoke to Dunscombe like that and survived to tell the tale. There was silence in the room for several moments and then Susannah started sobbing, distracting them all from Hudson's comment. She was tired, exhausted and overcome by their predicament.

'You guys are in serious trouble, aren't you?' stated Chohan quietly.

'We need help,' Hudson replied, his voice cracking. 'We don't where to go or who to turn to. Please help us. Please.'

Dunscombe exchanged glances with the solicitor and the two journalists. He cleared his throat. When he spoke, his voice was surprisingly gentle.

'The problem we have is that you've been in this building. If the police find out you were here and we did nothing, we could be in serious trouble.'

'Hang on,' interrupted Gregory. 'I just signed them in as my visitors, under my name. There's no record of their names. No one will know they've ever been here.'

'Ah,' murmured Chohan, with a flicker of a smile. 'That makes life considerably easier. For us, anyway.'

'They can stay at my place, too,' offered Gregory.

'That's on your shoulders. It's nothing to do with us whatsoever and if you get into trouble, that's your lookout,' warned Dunscombe.

'Fine.'

'Right. That's that sorted. Amarjit, I take it that if we print any of these allegations about Millburn and Red Dawn as they are, then Millburn's team will have us for breakfast.'

'Probably, though the tapes are good. But ideally we need a witness who can testify under oath that these events occurred, or at least corroborate some of them.'

'If you were in my shoes, would you print without such a witness?'

'No.'

'And they all seem to be dead.' He sighed. 'Right then, let's go through all this and see what we can come up with.'

An hour later, Dunscombe had an idea. He ran it past them all, and they agreed it was their best chance. Time was of the essence, especially in view of the threat to Hudson and Susannah.

29

'Where are they?' Millburn demanded in a dangerously low voice.

'At this precise moment, we're not sure.'

There was a long pause as Millburn considered Kroll's reply.

'Why not?'

'We've lost their phone signals. The phones are switched off. As soon as they activate them, we'll have them,' Kroll stated, confidently.

'Put a stop to it, Peter. I'm starting to get fed up of all this.'

'Yes, Charles. They seem to have proved more resourceful than we expected. And lucky.'

'Who picked them up?'

'Trevor and Julian are working on that.'

'So, you don't know that either?'

'No, Charles.'

Millburn absorbed this information quietly, nodding his head sagely as though it was the answer he had expected. Which it was. He was so angry he didn't know where to start.

'Sometimes I wish you would disappear too, Peter,' he sighed. 'This doesn't bode well for the future, does it?'

'Charles, we, er, we simply don't have the resources. This is a black operation and I only have two operatives out in the field. I can't do any better than I am.'

'Peter. I'm fed up with excuses. I thought you had contacts in the police?'

'The police can't find them either.'

'Well perhaps you should consider working for them instead,' snapped Millburn, glaring at him. 'You obviously have a lot in common.'

Kroll swallowed, not keen on the direction Millburn was following. He was saved by the buzzer on Millburn's desk. Millburn snatched the receiver of his intercom up rather than allow Kroll overhear.

'Yes?...What?...I see. Show him in.' He sat back in chair and gazed coolly at Kroll. 'Looks like it's your lucky day. The fucking cavalry have arrived.'

The door opened and a small, weasel-featured man walked in with a confident swagger, his suit sharply cut. Kroll had never met him before, but recognised him from the numerous images in the press. Giles Devereaux, the Prime Minister's Director of Communications. He stood up to leave, but Devereaux waved him back into his seat.

'Peter isn't it?' Devereaux stated in a nasal whine. 'I think you should stay. It does concern you after all.'

Kroll glanced at Millburn, who gave an imperceptible shrug. Devereaux hoisted his briefcase onto Millburn's glass-topped designer desk, the metal studs making an audible click on the surface. Millburn glanced at it in irritation.

'To what, or whom, do we owe the pleasure?' asked Millburn, glaring at the briefcase standing in front of him, imagining the deep scratches the studs were inflicting. Devereaux lay the case on its side and flicked the catches up, rummaging inside. He produced a pink folder. Millburn and Kroll stared at it.

'I think you are already acquainted with this, Charles.' Not *Sir* Charles. Just Charles. He slid it across the desk to Millburn, who blanched. The words *Red Dawn* were clearly legible beneath the *Top Secret* annotation. Millburn said nothing, but glanced up.

'Courtesy of Jeremy Langham,' Devereaux continued by way of explanation. 'It seems that we have a mutual problem.'

Langham? Kroll was confused. He knew the Acting Director General of the Security Service from way back. Langham had been assisting with his search for Hudson and the girl, providing the mobile phone traces. The bastard had promised total secrecy. Even Millburn didn't know that Langham was involved.

'Poor Jeremy is clearly worried that he will be left holding his dick in his hand,' explained Devereaux. 'I suppose this is his insurance policy. What you're doing *is* rather naughty, after all.'

Millburn and Kroll said nothing.

'The Prime Minister has been fully appraised. Call that *my* insurance policy if you will. We're all in this together. The Prime Minister has made it perfectly clear that his new nuclear generation policy is at the centre of his government's energy strategy. It is of the utmost strategic importance. We need to regain national energy independence. We can't be at the mercy of Russian gas or French electricity supplies. Take it from me, Gencor Energy will be awarded the contracts for the new nuclear programme.' He paused and glanced at them both. Now for the price. 'We just need something in return.'

Millburn shifted in his seat. The contracts were his. Guaranteed. No doubt whatsoever. Devereaux continued. 'We understand that you have been ensuring that Red Dawn is, how shall I put it, no longer a problem? Jeremy has explained that you have nearly achieved that objective, but have been experiencing a little difficulty with the finishing touches, that's right?'

Millburn said nothing.

'Our requirement is simple: Red Dawn must be closed down. Permanently. Jeremy will assist you in that, but only as far as providing information. You must act on it. You will be completely responsible. There is to be no trace back to me or the Prime Minister, do I make myself clear? We wouldn't want any more loose ends to tie up, would we now?'

The thinly-veiled threat was enough to stir a response from Millburn. 'What guarantees do we have that you won't do that anyway?'

'Simple. We need Gencor Energy at the heart of our energy policy, with you at the helm. As you know, Red Dawn not only threatens you and your company, it could derail out entire energy policy. There is no alternative to nuclear power, certainly not in the foreseeable future. We have a mutual interest in ensuring that Red Dawn no longer poses a threat.'

There was a long silence while Millburn and Kroll digested Devereaux's offer.

'We can't find the journalist or the girl,' Millburn stated finally, by way of accepting Devereaux's proposal. Devereaux smiled.

'Don't worry. Jeremy's got it covered. He just thought it prudent for us to speak to you first before we, or rather you, could act on it.'

'So you know where they are?' asked Kroll, with evident relief.

'Of course. But you need to move quickly. There isn't much time.'

*

In his office, Detective Sergeant Willcox was becoming increasingly concerned by the absence of DI Brannigan, his superior. It was way past ten o'clock and it was extremely unusual for Brannigan, an avowed workaholic, to pull a sickie in the middle of a critical investigation, especially one that was so fast moving. He tried Brannigan's mobile phone again, but it was switched off. He left a message and returned to the case notes in front of him.

Warwickshire Constabulary had made a royal hash of things last night, allowing Hudson and Susannah to escape from Terleski's house, from right under their noses. However, he had to concede that there was something very odd about that. The police helicopter had found no trace of the two fugitives, even with thermal imaging equipment on board, and the dog handlers had lost the trail too. Willcox was beginning to wonder whether the two suspects had an accomplice, who had helped them escape. Brannigan? No, too convenient. And ridiculous.

Willcox had turned his attention to the house. The owner, Doctor William Terleski, had been found dead on Tuesday morning, two days previously. Suicide was strongly suspected, yet Hudson and

Terleski's niece, Susannah, were wanted in connection with a murder. The girl was linked to two deaths in as many days. Perhaps they had been busier than first suspected?

After making a few phone calls, he located the pathologist who had carried out the autopsy on Terleski.

'Yes?' spoke a clipped, well-educated voice in Warwick.

'Good morning. I'm Detective Sergeant Willcox, Homicide Section, Manchester CID.'

'Yes?'

'I'm looking into the circumstances of Dr William Terleski's death as part of another investigation…'

'Hold on,' the pathologist interrupted.

Willcox could hear rummaging noises and the tapping of keys on a keyboard. He looked up at the ceiling while he waited, clicking his pen impatiently.

'Right, I've got my report here. How can I help?'

'Could you email the report to me so that I can have a look? Would it be okay to call you later with a few questions?'

'Yes, fine.'

'Oh, just quickly before I go – was there anything suspicious at all about his death?'

'Not really. There was no note, but that isn't uncommon. There was bruising under his armpits, and on his forearms, but I imagine those were caused by leaning over the beam in his summerhouse to fix the rope.'

'He was quite old; wouldn't that have been tricky to do?'

'Exactly, hence the bruising. Mind you, he was quite fit for his age, despite his lungs being full of tar. Heavy pipe smoker. Early signs of oral cancer.'

'So, there was nothing untoward about his death?'

'If there was any foul play, I would have expected to find marks on his wrists from being bound up, or tissue under the finger nails. There was neither. The forensic scene of crime officer didn't find anything either. Why do you ask?'

'There are a number of strange circumstances in relation to another murder enquiry. I'm just trying to get to the bottom of it all.'

'Well, I can assure you that my investigation was thorough and by the book.' He was quite indignant and on the defensive.

'Oh, I'm not implying anything like that. I just needed to check. Just doing my job.'

'Just a word of advice, Detective. In my experience of suicides, the family quite often find it impossible to accept that their loved one has killed themselves. They are desperate to find an external factor. I realise that you are just doing your job, but I think you're wasting your time. And mine, for that matter.'

'Sorry to have bothered you. I'm sure that nothing will come of it.' Willcox sighed and hung up, not entirely convinced. This investigation was becoming more complicated, and stranger, by the moment. *And where the hell was Brannigan?*

'Coffee, Jase?' a colleague asked on the way to the kitchenette.

'Cheers, Dave. I'll join you over there. I could do with stretching my legs.'

They leant up against the cheap units, sipping their drinks, making idle small talk. An array of officious signs warned them against making a mess, ordered them not to leave tea bags on the sink, implored them to put mugs back when finished and, most importantly of all, not to help themselves to other colleagues' biscuits.

'Any sign of the DI?' asked Dave, munching on some chocolate digestives he had found hidden in one of the cupboards.

'Nope. I'm starting to get a bit worried.'

'Have you phoned him?'

'No answer. And he never checked out of the hotel in Stratford.'

They polished off the biscuits, taking care to put the empty wrapper back where they found it, and returned to Willcox's desk. A yellow internal message note had been placed on his keyboard. Willcox picked it up and made a face.

'That settles that one, no need to panic. He's got the 'flu. Great. We're meant to run this investigation without him.'

30

Hudson winced as the doctor inspected and dressed his wound. Dunscombe had arranged for the private medic as soon as he realised that Hudson was in pain and in need of treatment. In an empty meeting room, Hudson was sitting shirtless on the corner of a desk, his arm raised in the air.

'I won't ask how you got this,' murmured the doctor, applying a gauze dressing, 'but I would suggest you have several days of rest and a course of antibiotics. The stitches will be due out in a week to ten days.'

Hudson had nodded through gritted teeth, not looking forward to that.

'I imagine you will ignore that advice, so just remember that a serious infection could lead to septicaemia. You need to look after yourself a bit better.'

'Thanks. I'll try.'

The doctor gave him a stern glance over the top of his half-moon spectacles, then packed his things and left. Hudson replaced his shirt with a clean one obtained by Dunscombe's grumbling secretary, who then left to purchase the antibiotics for him.

Inside Dunscombe's office, Dunscombe, Gallimore and Chohan had thrashed over the story, building up a clear picture of the events of the previous week. Any apparent inconsistencies had been run to ground, with Susannah helping to fill the gaps. Samuel Gregory remained as a largely silent observer, listening with incredulity. Given a task to perform,

Susannah had come out of her shell, proving to be a very calm, concise interviewee. The details were related succinctly and without embellishment. It was an astonishing catalogue of events.

For his part, Dunscombe realised beyond any doubt that his paper had a story that would shake the government to its core. It was vital that such a story was handled properly. On the advice of Amarjit Chohan, the in-house solicitor, it was imperative that they were able to provide evidence that would, at the very least, defend them from a civil suit filed against them by Millburn's lawyers. This was evident to Dunscombe, who would be facing an early retirement should he be mistaken in any way. Despite this, he was convinced that Hudson and Susannah had brought him one of the biggest stories of his career.

Dunscombe regarded the exhausted couple with a mixture of respect and concern. Although she was responding well to the questioning, she appeared to be close to the limits of nervous endurance. Her blond hair was matted and tangled, the eyes sunken and dull. The young man was just about holding himself together, seemingly for her sake. There was no question: These were two very frightened people. They had stumbled into something not of their making, innocents far out of their depth in a highly dangerous situation. Quite how dangerous that game was had been revealed by the deaths of the four civil servants who had worked with Terleski on Red Dawn. Dunscombe shared their suspicion that their deaths were not coincidental and that there was a very real possibility that Terleski had also been murdered rather than committing suicide. The fact that Hudson had been shot only served to confirm this, especially when the story was reinforced by Gregory's account of their car chase.

'How are you feeling?' he asked Hudson, who sat down gingerly.

'Much better, thanks. He did a good job of patching me up.'

'Good. We've nearly finished here. Gregory and Terry will be leaving soon, while we find somewhere safe for you to stay and get some rest. Gregory's said you can use his flat for the time being.'

'No. I want to come.'

'That's not a good idea, James. You're in no fit condition. Also, think of the risks. The police are looking for you, as well as the people you have described to us. So, the answer is no.'

'I'm coming whether you like it or not. This is my story and I want to see it through to the end. I want to stop those bastards.'

Dunscombe realised that Hudson was not going to be persuaded otherwise. He chewed on the end of his pen for a few seconds.

'Right. It's probably best that Terry stays here and works on the story with me and Amarjit.' He pointed the wet end of the pen at Hudson. 'You can accompany Gregory. I hate to say it, but you're in a far better position to speak to them about it anyway. Just take care and make sure nothing happens. I want you back here as soon as possible.'

'I'm not staying here by myself,' insisted Susannah.

'Oh, for God's sake!' cried Dunscombe. 'This isn't a bloody family outing! You came here for your own safety and now you want to go back out there again? You need your heads looking at. I'm not allowing it.'

Hudson glanced at Susannah. 'You don't have to come. I'd rather you stayed here, too.'

'I'm coming with you.'

Dunscombe rubbed his forehead in exasperation and thought of the bottle in his bottom drawer. *What was the matter with some people?*

'Right!' he snapped. 'You can both go. It's your funeral. But you're entirely responsible for your own safety and Gregory's. All the proof stays here.'

'We'll need a copy of the tapes and the dossier, otherwise they won't listen to us.'

'Okay. I'll get IT onto it now,' sighed Dunscombe. He knew when he was beaten but, privately, even he could see it was the best way for his plan to work. Without Hudson and Susannah's direct input, it would be far less likely that he could obtain the additional proof he required in order to publish. For a story of this magnitude, he had little choice, and it opened up the best possibility of finding a witness who could corroborate Red Dawn.

*

Charles Millburn could scent victory. He knew that he had won. With the help of the government, there was nothing to stop him now. Their mutual interests were too closely aligned to make failure a possibility. Devereaux had guaranteed the nuclear building programme contracts would be awarded to Gencor Energy. There was nothing written down – there didn't have to be. Millburn knew too much to be double-crossed or cheated out of his destiny, a destiny in which immense wealth featured highly prominently.

Gencor shares were already trading high, with the market anticipating the company winning the contracts. But when that was actually confirmed, they would reach new heights. Millburn decided it was too good an opportunity to miss. His holding was already worth £200million, but he could see a way to multiply that.

Insider dealing was a crime punishable by imprisonment and unlimited fines, but men like Millburn knew how to get around that. The rewards were simply too great not to try. If you had information that you knew with absolute certainty would have an impact on share prices, you would be mad not to act on it. That was certainly the view that Millburn held on the matter.

He picked up the phone.

Simon Goldstein received the call in his expensively appointed offices. He was a man who ran a very small business organisation, but it was an extremely lucrative one. So lucrative in fact, that it negated all need for him to advertise his services. Those who needed to know what he did, knew. He ran what appeared to be a boutique broker, catering for the needs of extremely wealthy clients who wished to execute market trades. And that was how he had started, simply carrying out the investment instructions of his clients and charging a small commission on the transaction. Simple really, and he made money whatever happened to the investment.

That was until he had been approached one day by a client with an interesting proposition. The client had certain information about a certain company, but was unable to act on it. It would raise too many suspicions. However, there was nothing to stop Goldstein acting on a 'rumour' which subsequently proved to be fortuitously accurate.

Goldstein set up a complicated system of off-shore companies into which the client transferred substantial sums which were then 'lent' to companies controlled by Goldstein, and use to purchase shares. The 'loans' were repaid at dizzying interest rates from the profits on the extraordinarily successful investments, but leaving Goldstein with a figure of around 20% of the value of the original loan, his 'commission' as he called it. It became an extremely lucrative operation, with a tiny handful of investors aware of its existence. As a result, Goldstein was an extremely wealthy man, discreet and highly trusted.

'Charles, how are you?' he answered in his quiet, cultured voice.

'Very well, Simon. Very well indeed.'

'I'm glad to hear it. How may I help?'

Millburn explained, and the figures made Goldstein's head spin. Millburn wanted to use his entire £200million as leverage for a future option. He wished to purchase an option to acquire £1billion worth of Gencor shares, at a price 5% higher than the current trading price. Whoever bought the option from him would be obliged to sell the shares to him, at a pre-arranged date and time, at that higher price. If the share price did not move, or fell, the purchaser of the option would acquire them at the market price and sell them on to Millburn at 5% more than the original price quoted in the option. Millburn would make a loss, as the shares he had been forced to purchase were worth less than what he had been obliged to pay for them. His losses would be magnified, as he had leveraged his purchase and did not own 80% of the shares he had acquired, and would have to return them at the price agreed in the option, thus realising the loss instantly.

However, if the shares rose above the price agreed in the option, then Millburn would have the right to purchase them at the lower price and sell them at the higher market price, thus realising a huge profit. If the price rose by 10%, his profit on the option would be 5%, on £1billion worth of shares. A cool £50 million. And he believed the shares would easily rise by another 15-20% once the market had confirmation that Gencor Energy PLC had won the contracts for a massive publicly-funded nuclear building programme. He could make £200million, in cash, doubling his fortune in a matter of days. It was enough to make anyone giddy.

Goldstein could see the potential instantly and calculated his share of the proceeds, which would find their way safely into bank accounts in Cyprus, well away from the clutches of the tax man. It was enough to make him drool. He was being offered the chance to make £40 million, virtually risk-free when Millburn explained the guaranteed contracts for Gencor. All he had to do was make a few phone calls and place the order on Millburn's behalf. He would split it between several of his front companies, so as not to attract the attention of the authorities. Millburn simply had to lend all of his shares to one of the companies in Goldstein's complicated network in order to start the ball rolling, but it was nothing more than an electronic exercise, achieved in moments.

By the time their conversation had finished, both Millburn and Goldstein were very happy men, and Millburn felt the occasion warranted an expensive cigar. He selected a Ramon y Allones from his humidor, and warmed it expertly with his platinum Ronson. Lighting it, he drew deeply on the sweet, fragrant smoke; a moment to savour.

Another £200million. It was unreal. Exhaling languidly towards the ceiling, he reclined in his chair, his features breaking into a smile.

He had won.

*

Finally, Dunscombe and his team had put the finishing touches to Hudson and Susannah's story. Through careful cross examination, Dunscombe was convinced that they were telling the truth. It was incredible. For the first time in his professional career he realised that he held both the government and a major multinational corporation by the balls. An intoxicating moment: He was already salivating over the headlines.

Usually, the Guardian had a reputation for sober headlines, with a notable absence of sensationalist prose. For this story, he would be hard pressed to make it anything but sensational. Dunscombe had already decided to focus on the revelations of the nuclear accident and the subsequent cover-up, but omitting Millburn's involvement for the time being. That would come later, to reinforce the sense of outrage. The deaths of the five retired Civil Servants would be alluded to, but left at that for now. For a start, Dunscombe had no evidence that they were sinister. It was merely coincidental at this stage. The newspaper's readership could make up its own mind.

Already the front page was taking shape. But the problem remained of obtaining enough proof to protect them from any legal retribution. Dunscombe had outlined his plan earlier on in the morning and it was the only credible option they had left to pursue, especially given the almost impossibly short time frame. Realistically, they estimated that they had less than forty eight hours to find enough tangible proof to allow them to run the story, and begin the difficult process of clearing Hudson and Susannah's names. In the meantime, they also had to contend with the fact that the police were searching for Hudson and Susannah, which placed Dunscombe and his staff in an extremely awkward position. Dunscombe had decided that the public interest came first, and Amarjit Chohan had eventually concurred with this, though with his usual list of reservations. The paper had the resources to defend its actions in court should the need arise, if they were accused of perverting the course of justice.

For a moment, Dunscombe was so excited that he nearly forgot about the bottle of Jameson's hidden in his desk. Thanking Hudson and Susannah for their cooperation, he despatched them, accompanied by Gregory Samuel. Then he set to work with his Chief Political Editor, Terry Gallimore, and Chohan.

31

The tears mingled with the light drizzle as they trickled down the man's stubbled cheeks. His haggard, weathered features, aged before their time, were contorted with grief. The little teddy bear was already sodden from the rain as he touched it to his lips then laid it with the greatest care on the small plinth in front of the headstone.

'Happy birthday, my little one,' he whispered, choking on the words. Leaning forward, he pressed his forehead against the cold granite, desperate to feel a physical connection with her. The stone mason had done a meticulous job of etching a copy of a treasured photograph onto the front of the headstone, and the smile of a very pretty ten year old girl beamed out. The epitaph, which had also been meticulously inlaid by a man who regretted every tragedy encapsulated in the words he carved, proclaimed that the angels had taken her back to Jesus on the 10th August 1992, with whom she now lay in peace. Her tiny frail body had been unable to ward off the predations of the acute myeloid leukaemia that had been diagnosed a year before. In the end, she died of an infection contracted after a bone marrow transplant. Despite the best efforts of the doctors, she was simply too weak to fight it off. Her low blood count, ravaged by the chemotherapy, offered no defence. Vincent Markham had cradled the fragile body of his daughter as her little heart finally lost its brave battle and the life force ebbed gently out of her. He held her until she went cold in his arms, rocking her to sleep for the last time. Finally the nurses and doctors, weeping quietly, had gently removed her from his embrace.

The memory was raw, the pain undiminished by time. The sensation of her soft skin on his lips as he kissed her for the last time would remain with him always. The grief only really began the day he and his estranged wife had buried her. Then the abyss had opened, revealing a depth of despair and emptiness that seemed to know no limit. His former wife had a new family, other children, helping her absorb the abject desolation of losing a child. But he had no one. He was utterly alone in his grief, and it poisoned his soul.

Drink didn't solve the problem, but it offered a few hours of respite each day, before the pain began again. His lowest point was reached two years after her death, when he was found unconscious by the side of a road, on the verge of death from a combination of hypothermia and alcohol poisoning.

The following day, he realised what it felt like to have a friend in one's darkest hour of need. In the hospital, he found a community of support, people who understood and could help him. For the first time in years he no longer felt alone. The healing had begun. Making his mind up that day, he vowed that alcohol would no longer play a part in his life. There was also the new career to consider: he would work to help others in his situation.

He forsook his previous career as an engineer and retrained as a bereavement counsellor. He could relate to his patients, or 'clients' as he called them, because he had been there himself. The pitfalls and the agonies that lay ahead would test the strongest of people, but he would be there to help guide them through it. Despite this, he wasn't immune from days filled with despair, but at least he could now recognise that grief was part of the healing process. But birthdays, Christmas and, of course, the anniversary of her passing were still unbearably difficult.

Today would have been Charlotte's twenty sixth birthday. The little girl would be a fully fledged young woman, with the world at her feet. Perhaps she would already be married, with children of her own, making him a grandfather, an experience he would never know. He was quick to remind himself not to wallow in self pity, but sometimes it was hard, so very hard. Why hadn't God taken him instead?

As he pressed his forehead against the cold, wet stone he felt close to her, drawing comfort from the thought. After wishing her sweet dreams and kissing her good night, he sat down beside the headstone, watching over her for an hour. The Cumbria drizzle turned into steady rain, falling from the grey sky with a gentle hiss. The big oak trees that looked over the cemetery, guarding the souls that lay there, were steadfast in the downpour, not distracted from their eternal duty. Beyond them stretched an achingly beautiful view of the dales of the northern Lake District, shrouded in low cloud. Vincent Markham had already paid for a plot next to her, and part of him still yearned for the day when he could join her. But not yet. There was something he had to do.

On the day that Vincent had woken up in hospital to a colossal hangover, he had resolved not only to turn his life around, but to find the man he held responsible for her death. For years, the desperate need for vengeance had consumed him, sustaining him through his darkest days. The problem was that a plan or opportunity had yet to present itself.

As he sat in his increasingly sodden clothes, his mind returned to the problem. Assassinating the man entailed numerous practical problems. There was the method to choose, the timing and the place. With his engineering background, Vincent could easily construct a lethal explosive device from everyday household items. The problem with that was that it was too quick in its delivery. He wanted the man to know why he was dying, and that wasn't possible if he was blown up in an instant, with no warning. Vincent's need for vengeance required that the man both suffered and understood what he had done. Shooting him was difficult, as Vincent did not own a gun and did not know how to obtain one, even on the black market. Ideally, he would like to have the man to himself, both of them alone in a room together, preferably with the man tied to a chair. Then Vincent could bring along his tool box, perhaps a couple of power tools as well, and they could have their little chat. The last thing the man would see would be a picture of little Charlotte and he would understand why his fate had to be thus. Jesus had preached forgiveness, but Vincent was beyond that. He had been abandoned by Jesus and God.

Vincent sighed. Perhaps he would never get to fulfil his desire for vengeance. Playing out the violent imagery in his mind was the closest he would get, and sometimes that was cathartic enough. He also worried what Charlotte would think of him, but another part of him felt that he owed it to her. He knew that she would be sickened by the thoughts he entertained, but Vincent knew that he wouldn't be able to rest unless the man he identified as culpable had paid for what he had done. The doctors had said that it was simply awful bad luck, but Vincent knew better. He knew of the radioactive poisons in the air and soil, and he knew who had put them there.

And that someone, somewhere, was going to pay for killing his little girl.

*

The speedometer was nudging a hundred miles an hour as Gregory sped up the M1 motorway.

'Careful, we don't want to get stopped,' warned Hudson.

'We haven't got long to get there,' came the grunted reply, as he flashed a car out of the way, the engine of the Audi growling as he surged past. All of them were infected with the same sense of desperate urgency that came from knowing that they did not have long to find the evidence they needed to publish the story. Gregory's career would be in tatters if they did not find the proof sought by Dunscombe. He was harbouring suspects in a murder enquiry, would possibly face a jail sentence if they failed to find enough evidence to force the police to change the focus of their investigations. But it was a small risk compared to what Hudson and Susannah had gone through.

'I might phone Don, my editor,' Hudson had suggested earlier.

'No. You'd be implicating him for a start, and they might be monitoring his calls. They'd be expecting you contact him. He'd have to cooperate with the police, he'd have no choice.'

And Gregory was right. They could not do anything that might bring them into contact with the police. Including reckless driving.

'Come on, Grease. Slow down. You'll stuff it up for us if you're not careful. You're the one who warned us about attracting the police.'

Without receiving a response, Hudson noted that the speed eased off a margin, and they slotted into the flow of the traffic.

In the back seat, Susannah was ashen-faced, her eyes fixed firmly ahead on the road. North of Luton, the traffic dissipated and the average speed crept up, but they kept with the flow. They had three hundred miles to cover, but at this speed they would do it in less than three hours, barring no hold ups. Gregory matched the speed of the car in front, taking his cue for overtaking, using him as a marker. He glanced in his rearview mirror. The blue Mondeo behind was obviously doing the same thing with Gregory's Audi, having stuck with them since they had left London. The driver maintained a safe breaking distance and was of no concern to Gregory, so he didn't mention it. He was more concerned with Susannah's welfare, her pale face and tired eyes reflecting the enormous strain of her recent experiences.

'I was sorry to hear about your old boyfriend,' Gregory offered, unable to restrain his journalistic inquisitiveness. Hudson glanced at him. It wasn't the time or place.

'He wasn't a very nice person,' she replied quietly. 'I'm sorry that he's been killed, no one deserves that, but I won't be shedding too many tears.' Hudson stayed silent. He had his own views on the matter, thinking of the beating he had suffered at Warburton's hands.

'It must have been a shock, though?'

'Yes…' she paused. 'But perhaps not. He was mixed up in lots of dodgy stuff; drugs, protection, that sort of thing. He probably had a lot of enemies. But the police seem to think we did it.' She looked out of the window at the countryside flashing past, her expression a mixture of hurt and regret.

'You don't think it could be linked?'

'To what?' asked Hudson. 'Red Dawn?'

'Yes.'

'I don't know. I can't understand why they found his blood in Susannah's flat. That's what the arresting officer told me in the hospital. I thought they were making it up, though, see how I'd react. You know, like a bluff, to trick someone into admitting a crime.'

'It was mentioned in the web reports, so perhaps they're not making it up. He might have been killed there.'

'We had nothing to do with it, okay?' replied Hudson angrily.

'I know, I know,' insisted Gregory, soothing him. 'That's why we've got to find a good reason why he might have been killed there by someone else. We need this for you as much as we do for the paper.'

Hudson nodded. They had to find out who had killed Warburton, and instinct told him that it was all linked together, even before Gregory had suggested it, whatever Susannah might think. It must be the same people who were after them. Warburton must have disturbed them at Susannah's flat, looking for Terleski's tapes.

They continued in silence and the constant, steady hum of the car finally took its toll on the exhausted Susannah. Hudson turned to find her slumped in the corner of the back seat, fast asleep. For the first time in days, he felt a relative degree of safety. Having Gregory with them helped but that was incomparable to the feeling of relief that he felt at being taken seriously by the newspaper. Dunscombe's plan was simple. In order to publish, he needed witnesses to corroborate the details in the dossier. They needed to find someone alive who had been on the periphery of Red Dawn, who could confirm a particular aspect of it. Only the original Red Dawn committee members would have had a complete overview of the conspiracy, but there should be many others lower down who played their own discreet role. Dunscombe was after those people. The more he could get to speak publicly about their involvement, the better.

Contained within the document box retrieved by Hudson from Terleski's summerhouse was a list of all the individuals identified by Red Dawn as being crucial to its successful implementation. They would have been unaware of the full scale of the cover-up, and their discretion in the matter would have been ensured through the rigorous application of the Official Secrets Act.

*

It was precisely this piece of legislation that formed the basis of the heated discussion between Amarjit Chohan and Alan Dunscombe in London.

'Fuck the Official Secrets Act, Amarjit!' Dunscombe snarled, daring the solicitor to contradict him. Chohan stood his ground. Despite his apparently mild manner, he was unflinching when it came to matters of the law. That was precisely why he had been appointed by the Board of Directors. As far as he was concerned, he worked for the Board and shareholders, not Dunscombe. If the paper got into hot water because of a legal oversight, it would be his neck on the line.

'Oh, yes, Alan. That will impress the judges in court. *Fuck the Official Secrets Act*. We can't fail to win with a defence like that,' he replied sarcastically. Dunscombe had always displayed a healthy disrespect for authority, especially where he felt it curtailed freedom of speech, but it was Chohan's job to steer him back to reality.

'It's in the public interest!' Dunscombe shouted, slapping the desk to emphasise the point. 'Charlie Millburn's irradiated half the Lake District and covered it up, and you're telling me that it's *not* in the public interest to reveal that? You're taking the piss, Amarjit!'

'Alan, Charles Millburn didn't irradiate the Lakes,' Chohan pointed out. 'Certainly not personally. But he was part of the cover-up, I'll grant you that.'

'What do you mean; he was *part* of the cover-up? He instigated the whole fucking thing!' bellowed an incredulous Dunscombe.

'Yes, I've listened to the tapes as well. I'm not deaf, you'll be pleased to know, so there's no need to shout either. The problem is, those tapes are illegal. They are an illicit recording of a Civil Service meeting that was subject to the highest level of secrecy.'

'Well, what a fucking surprise,' muttered Dunscombe. 'Tell me something I don't know.'

'Just listen to me for one moment, *please*!' Chohan pleaded, exasperated. He was letting Dunscombe get the better of him and he ran a hand through his hair in frustration, his cheeks flushed with anger.

Dunscombe sat back in his chair, equally exasperated, while Chohan carefully patted down his immaculate hair, taking a deep breath before he continued.

'The Official Secrets Act is very clear about what constitutes breaches. I would say that several of them apply to us. Section five covers any information protected against disclosure that comes into our possession. Subsection one, part a, covers information disclosed…let me see…yes, here we are *disclosed (whether to him or another) by a Crown servant or government contractor without lawful authority.* That covers the tapes and all the data sheets, as well as the dossier.'

Dunscombe scowled and rubbed his eyes. The bottle in the drawer beckoned.

'Subsection two goes on to mention - are you listening to this? - that any person possessing information that they believe is of a restricted nature and who then discloses it will be committing an offence. This certainly applies where disclosure is likely to be damaging. I think we can safely say that that would be the case here.'

Dunscombe sighed and looked out of the window, so Chohan continued. 'If you still don't believe me, then subsection six sums it up nicely: *A person is guilty of an offence if without lawful authority he discloses any information, document or article, which he knows, or has reasonable cause to believe, to have come into his possession as a result of a contravention of Section One of the Official Secrets Act.*'

'Shit.'

'My sentiments exactly, Alan.'

Dunscombe's resolve broke and he yanked the bottom drawer open and extracted the bottle of Jameson's. He waved it at Chohan, who shook his head but gestured for Dunscombe to carry on. Chohan knew what was on his mind. Dunscombe was agonising over a very dark hour in the paper's history. In 1983 a Foreign Office clerk, Sarah Tisdall, had passed secret documents to the paper. These documents concerned what were then top secret proposals to station US cruise missiles in Britain. The newspaper had eventually buckled under legal pressure and complied with a court order demanding the return of the papers to the Government, a process which eventually culminated in a six month prison sentence for Tisdall. Dunscombe certainly did not want a repeat of that.

After refreshing himself with a thirsty gulp, Dunscombe topped up his tumbler and reclined in his chair. The hot Irish spirit burnt its way down his gullet, slaking his alcoholic thirst. He felt better right away. Chohan wasn't abstemious but only touched booze when the working day was over. Unlike Dunscombe, he found it impossible to concentrate after drinking.

'So, you're telling me that we will be committing an offence if we publish anything to do with the dossier, the tapes or the data?'

'Yes.'

'Oh, for Christ's sake, Amarjit! Why the *hell* doesn't this count as a public interest matter?'

'Public interest is not a valid defence. It's inherently subjective, so you could get any Tom, Dick or Harry blowing the whistle on national secrets for the sake of public interest, but only as they interpret it. *You* might think this is in the public interest, but others might passionately disagree with your evaluation.'

'It *is* in the fucking public interest! Look, Amarjit, if I was breathing in a cloud of radioactive fallout, I'd say that I might just have ever such a slight interest in knowing about it!' He finished off the whisky in one gulp and slammed the tumbler down. Picking up the bottle for further replenishment, he thought the better of it and put it back in the drawer, much to Chohan's relief. It was vital that Dunscombe retained a degree of clarity. The Chief Political Editor, a pasty looking Terry Gallimore, finally piped up from somewhere in the enormous sofa that graced the corner of the Editor's office, having remained out of the conversation until now.

'Can't we approach this from another angle?'

'Such as?' demanded Dunscombe

'Well, if we can't publish anything derived from these documents, then we'll have to find our own story.'

'And your suggestion is?'

'Well, what about the Civil Servants, the ones who died recently? I know you wanted to avoid it for now, but if we ran a story about how odd it was for five former colleagues to die so close together, it could draw Millburn out?'

Dunscombe massaged his forehead in exasperation. His greasy, lank hair was out of place and manifestly failed to cover the ever increasing circumference of his bald spot. He looked up, his yellowed and bloodshot eyes glaring out from beneath hooded eyelids, puffy from years of determined alcohol abuse. Dunscombe had long perfected the art of the terrifying stare, and Gallimore was treated to a particularly fine display. As the malevolent gaze settled on him, he knew he was in trouble.

'And how, precisely, do we know they were colleagues?'

Gallimore saw the flaw in his suggestion, but it was too late. 'Um, the dossier, I suppose.'

'The dossier,' he repeated matter-of-factly in a low voice, nodding his head in understanding. Chohan, keeping his head down, winced on Gallimore's behalf.

'And WHAT have we just been talking about?' Dunscombe shouted. 'For the last half hour I've been arguing the toss with Amarjit about whether we can mention anything to do with the fucking dossier. Are you DEAF?'

'No, Alan. Sorry. I didn't think.'

'Then what the *hell* am I paying you for?' he bawled, flecking him with spittle. 'You're paid to think, to have the answers!'

'It was just a suggestion, Alan. And you're quite right,' replied Gallimore, who had the hind of a rhinoceros. He needed it; otherwise he would have left years ago. In fact, Dunscombe's legendary temper was a source of great anecdotal amusement in the pub, though it could be quite an uncomfortable experience for anyone subjected to it.

Dunscombe recovered his composure, and took a deep breath. 'May I suggest, seeing how we have such a short window of opportunity, we stick with the plan?'

'Yes, Alan.'

'Those two kids in here this morning were terrified. It wasn't an act. Whatever they've stumbled on has scared the shit out of them. For what it's worth, I don't think they're guilty of murder or capable of it. I don't trust the police on this. As you know, I generally wouldn't trust them as far as I could spit, but this whole thing stinks. There's a good probability that someone has leaned on the police to help contain this story. We need to help those kids. We need one, just one, witness to corroborate anything in this dossier, on that tape or in that box, then we print, okay?'

Chohan sighed and rubbed his temples. 'Alan, I want my advice put on the record.'

'Don't worry Amarjit, I'll staple it to your arse if that helps cover it.'

'You shouldn't have let them go with Grease.'

'I don't think I had much choice, do you? Look, besides, if Grease went by himself, he wouldn't get anywhere. They need to tell the story to persuade anyone to speak up. Remember, we're asking witnesses to break the law for us.'

'Grease isn't experienced enough for this,' muttered Gallimore.

'Yeah, and who bought this story in? The kid's got potential; he just hasn't had a chance to show it yet. Perhaps if you'd pulled your finger out a bit more to help him, then he'd have the experience by now.'

'I still think you should have sent me,' he replied, ignoring the rebuke.

'Right, enough of this. I need you here to write the story, get the front page set up ready to go. Everyone on Terleski's list will be subject to the Official Secrets Act. As Amarjit has pointed out how naughty it is to go and breach it, we're going to have to persuade them to speak with that in mind. No offence Terry, but you're not exactly famous for your ability to charm. However, you're still a bloody good writer, so let's leave it at that shall we?'

'Okay, Alan, point taken. I just hope Grease doesn't cock it up.'

'He won't, trust me, but talking of cock-ups, Amarjit, how much trouble will I be in if we print this?'

'I don't want to think about it, Alan. Potentially, you're looking at a custodial sentence. Let's see now…here we are…if you went to court under an indictment and were convicted, you'd be looking at up to two years or a fine, or both.'

'Two years? I could do with a break.'

'Come on, Alan, this is serious. They'll go after you for this.'

'I am being serious. It's a point of principle, Amarjit. We can't have the government hiding things like this behind the Official Secrets Act, even if they thought they were doing the right thing at the time. The Official Secrets Act is meant to work in the interests of the country, not the government. I won't be bullied into submission by a bunch of faceless bureaucrats trying to save their arses, and I certainly won't be bullied by Charles Millburn. We have to take a stand on this, and risk the consequences, otherwise we no longer live in a free and just society.'

'Fine sentiments aside, Alan, I have to advise you that you should also inform the police of the whereabouts of James and Susannah.'

'Now you're the one who's joking. I don't believe that is in our interests, and it certainly isn't in theirs. As far as I am concerned, they are a source that requires protection. And besides, we don't know their precise location at this moment, so I can't tell the police, can I?' This was said with a smug grin. 'They're out of this building, so it's not our problem.'

Chohan nodded. He had suspected this would be Dunscombe's response, but at least he had aired his misgivings. Now the task would shift to one of damage limitation. Mentally, he began preparing the defence.

'What if they seek an injunction?' asked Gallimore.

'We need to make sure they don't have the slightest inkling we've got the story and are to about to print,' stated Dunscombe.

'So we're not going to give Millburn a chance to respond to the accusations?'

'Not if we can find someone to corroborate them independently. We won't be printing without that anyway, but the less time Millburn has to respond, the better. The stakes are too high for him to do nothing.'

'What about the risk to us? Personally, I mean?'

'There are plenty of nut cases and lunatics out there already. A couple more won't hurt.'

'Yes, but we could be up against the government with this. What if they want the Red Dawn cover-up to continue, especially with the new nuclear energy strategy?'

Dunscombe snorted. His politics had been forged in the crucible of 1970s industrial strife, during the yawning ideological gulf between the political factions of Left and Right. As a young trade unionist fighting to preserve the restrictive practices that were endemic in the print industry, he had come to the attentions of an increasingly paranoid Security

Service. In those days, the very existence of MI5 was not even acknowledged officially by the government, though it was a badly kept secret. The agency was worried over the growing threat posed by the expansionist Soviet Union and there were fears over the loyalties of British citizens on the far Left, particularly in the influential trade union movement, which was increasingly prepared to exert its direct power over the economy, and through its bankrolling of the Parliamentary Labour Party.

Much to his amusement, Dunscombe suspected that he had been placed under surveillance for a brief period, thus greatly enhancing his romantic self-image as an important revolutionary character. However, such romantic notions were unpleasantly quelled when he received a distinctly unromantic visit from an earnest young officer of the Security Service. It had been a sobering experience.

It all seemed so ludicrous now. The world had moved on and Dunscombe had risen in it. It was fairly clear to all but the most unreconstructed Marxists that their struggle had been futile. Indeed, the print industry had probably been saved by the reforms that eventually broke the union stranglehold, though that was a hard sell for all those made redundant by the process. *Oh, the idealism of youth*, thought Dunscombe, though a part of him still hankered with dewy-eyed sentimentalism for the hubris of the barricades and picket lines. His last taste of revolutionary fervour had been during the Poll Tax riot in 1990, though he was just a bystander reporting from the sidelines, under strict instructions from his boss not to get himself 'nicked' in the process. He was fully aware of the irony of his current position. Now a fully signed-up member of the petty bourgeoisie. The Establishment had co-opted him, buying him off with patronage whilst he left the toiling proletariat behind. Well, that's what he would have thought thirty years ago. Now he was more concerned with paying off his mortgage and setting the kids up.

The world was such a different place now, the Cold War a distant memory, replaced by the drearily interminable 'War on Terror', or 'War to Justify the Existence of Our Armed Forces' as he termed it in moments of political relapse. It chimed neatly with the Marxist theories he had once eulogised: Capitalism always needed a war to distract attention from its inherent contradictions and maintain the status quo in favour of the owners of the means of production. Some of the creakier university departments in the country were probably still preaching such crap to their young, impressionable and largely bourgeois students. That in itself was irony which was probably lost on them.

Nevertheless, the Cold War may be over, but its legacy lived on. Charles Millburn had been part of an institutional cover up that beggared belief. Dunscombe could see the cold, dispassionate logic behind the decision, but that did not excuse its moral ambivalence, to say the least. As the nuclear deterrent was the only thing that allowed NATO to maintain any semblance of military balance with the overwhelming conventional forces fielded by the Soviet Union, it was vital that no nuclear disasters befell the United Kingdom. Such a calamity would have played into the hands of the Campaign for Nuclear Disarmament and its allies in the Labour Party. Dunscombe could see why the Establishment was so horrified by the accident at the storage facility at Sellafield, as it raised the possibility of a public backlash and the risk of a Labour victory at the forthcoming general election. The Labour Party Manifesto for the

1987 General Election included a commitment to decommission the Polaris nuclear missile system, scrap the forthcoming Trident programme, and work to remove all nuclear weapons from European soil. Anything that discredited the nuclear industry would play straight into their hands, and he could see why Millburn and other senior members of government had felt that they had no choice but to conceal the accident at Sellafield: The Chernobyl fallout over Cumbria provided them with the perfect cover.

But just because he could follow their logic didn't mean that he agreed with it. As far as he was concerned it made the UK government no better than the one they were fighting in Moscow. Like many Soviet apologists on the British Left, Dunscombe had been horrified and personally embarrassed to learn of the appalling abuses committed by the Soviet regime against its own people. The failure of the regime to safeguard the most basic of human rights, combined with its manifest economic failure, only served to hasten the disillusionment with an ideal he had passionately believed in since he was a teenager.

Millburn was no better than the Soviet *apparatchiks* who had initially covered up the Chernobyl explosion, condemning hundreds of thousands of citizens to massive doses of radiation because they were not evacuated out of the danger zone, simply in order to save the careers of bureaucrats far away in Moscow.

Dunscombe seethed with anger when he considered the similar atrocity committed in the name of British national security. This anger was exacerbated by the plight of the two terrified people who had visited him that morning. They were innocent pawns, being targeted simply because they had stumbled across information that indicted not just

Millburn, but the whole Establishment. Their only mistake was being in the wrong place at the wrong time, but they were being made to pay dearly for that. Dunscombe was convinced that Millburn was behind the attacks, probably with the assistance of others high up in government: An awful lot of people would have a vested interest in keeping Red Dawn secret.

Dunscombe decided that he would make a stand and suffer the consequences himself. He remembered Harold Wilson's shock resignation when he appeared to be the height of his powers, and this only served to confirm what many suspected: Elements of the security services took an active role in subverting the democratic process. Harking back to his youthful idealism, Dunscombe still regarded himself a defender of the democratic process. The people had a right to learn of Dr Terleski's dossier and the Red Dawn conspiracy, Official Secrets Act or not.

He just had to corroborate the dossier. Just one witness would do it. Dr Terleski had duly obliged by furnishing a detailed list of all the minor players in the cover up. They would not have known about Red Dawn, but they would know of discreet elements of the plan. If any of them could be found and persuaded to speak up, then he could publish. If enough of them could be found, the whole edifice constructed by Charles Millburn would come crashing down.

'Prepare yourself for a rocky ride, you two. I'm going ahead with this as a matter of principle,' he addressed Gallimore and Chohan. 'I know I'm asking a lot, but are you on board?'

'That goes without saying, Alan,' responded Gallimore, whilst Chohan smiled wryly.

'The board will probably sack me, but yes, Alan, you can count on me too.'

'Good, let's get to work then.'

32

Susannah awoke just as Gregory pulled into the service station north of Birmingham.

'How are you feeling?' asked Hudson

'A bit better for the sleep, thanks. How much further is it?'

'We're halfway there.'

'Have you phoned him?'

'Yes, he's expecting us.'

'Did you tell him why?'

'No, we thought it best to wait until we're there. Didn't want to spook him.'

'What if he doesn't want to speak about it?'

'We'll have to go down the list and try others.'

'I just want this to be over.'

'Me too.' He reached behind his seat and took her hand, which she squeezed and held between her knees as if reluctant to let go of him again. Gregory found a parking space near to the main building.

'Right, quick pit stop for whoever needs it. Grab something to eat in the car, so we don't waste any time. I need to fill up as well.'

They headed into the building, and Hudson found himself standing next to Gregory at the urinals.

'Nice girl,' offered Gregory.

'Yes,' sighed Hudson. 'I just hope she's alright. We've been through so much in the last few days. I don't know if she'll want to continue it after all this is over. We don't seem to have had any normal time together. It's been a nightmare.'

'What, you mean finding the tape and everything?'

'And the rest,' replied Hudson wearily. 'First, her ex beat me up outside her place. Then my flat was burgled, then hers, then her uncle dies, then her ex turns up dead, then we get shot at, then the police are after us, then we get chased again. And now this. The whole thing is too much for her. And me, to be honest. I just don't understand how we got involved in all this.'

'Come on, chin up. We're nearly there now. It will be over soon, and you two can start again.'

'I hope so. I really hope so.'

They finished their business in silence and, after stocking up on refreshments for the rest of the journey, headed back outside to Gregory's Audi. They didn't notice the man walking casually away from the car, towards an innocuous Ford Mondeo parked a few cars away. Just another anonymous sales rep.

Sat inside, they waited for Susannah, who came along a few minutes later. She seemed much fresher, having washed her face and reapplied her makeup.

'Ready?' asked Gregory, inserting the car keys into the ignition. He was about to turn them, when Susannah distracted him from starting the engine.

'Hang on; I can't get this stupid seat belt on,'

'You're putting in the wrong buckle, try the other one,' suggested Gregory.

'That's it, thanks,' as it clicked into place.

'Ready now?' he asked, when she had finally got herself sorted out.

'Come on, let's go,' she replied positively, refreshed from the break. Gregory engaged the ignition and, for a split second, a stab of fear ran through Hudson. His sixth sense was warning him about something. Gregory turned the key, just as Hudson looked at him. It was too late to stop him.

The engine burst into life. Hudson flinched, then felt the relief wash over him. It was nothing; his frayed nerves were clearly getting the better of him. He settled back into the seat, trying to relax as the car trundled towards the fuel pumps, but something was still niggling away at the back of his mind. He couldn't place it, but there was something odd. After filling up, they headed back out onto the motorway. Hudson decided not to voice his concerns, as they were completely unfounded, based on nothing more than a feeling.

Behind them, the man in the Mondeo checked the electronic device fitted to his dashboard, his thin lips twitching with satisfaction when he saw it was working properly. It was a satellite navigation system, but one with a difference. This particular model also picked up the signal from the powerful tracking device he had fitted behind the fibreglass rear spoiler of the Audi. It had taken seconds to fit, whilst he had pretended to tie his shoelace next to the car. It would make his job considerably easier. Since they'd left London, he had been forced to rely on visual contact alone. Now he could follow them at leisure, as the device had a GPS capability, locating the car to an accuracy of one metre. He needed something to make his task easier: He had barely arrived in London by helicopter from Preston, when he was back on the road again, in pursuit of his quarry. He was extremely tired, but he had no option but to follow the Audi.

Yawning, and rubbing a hand over his gaunt features, he eased out of the car park and pursued them up the motorway, keeping just within visual contact.

*

After sitting next to his daughter's gravestone for over an hour, Vincent Markham reluctantly stood up. The persistent rain had penetrated his thick coat, and his jeans were soaked. He needed to get back home and into a warm shower before he caught a chill. Besides, he had received a phone call just before he left to visit the cemetery. The meeting he had arranged would be in half an hour's time, so he needed to freshen up for that. He bent down to give the headstone one last kiss, and then headed off home.

Not wishing to be too far from his daughter, his home was a mile or so down the road, a small but attractive stone cottage that had been the sole dividend from his failed marriage. The big family home they had bought when his wife had been expecting Charlotte had been sold, the proceeds split between them. He had just enough funds, topped up with a mortgage, to buy the cottage for Charlotte and himself. His engineer's salary meant that they were moderately comfortable, and he was able to spoil her on occasions. Part of that was a desire to compensate her for the loss of her mother who, since meeting a new man and starting a family, didn't take much interest in her. The new husband was jealous, as far as Vincent could make out. There were times when he seethed with rage about that. It was one thing to walk out on a husband, an entirely different one to walk out on a child.

Over time, the wound of the divorce had healed and Vincent had some blissfully happy years watching his daughter grow up. That had been until she came home from school feeling poorly one day. A few days passed and she had still not shaken off the malady that had originally been dismissed as just one of those viruses that kids pick up. The first consultation with the local GP had not revealed anything. Perhaps it was glandular fever? Have some rest for a while and we'll see how it goes.

It was the nosebleed in the end. Unable to staunch the flow of blood, Markham had driven his daughter straight to the local casualty department. The look of concern on the doctor's face should have prepared him. The bleed was finally brought under control but some tests were conducted and it was advised that Charlotte should remain in hospital overnight for observation. The test results would be available in the morning, after which she should be able to go home. It was her first time in hospital and, because she was afraid, Vincent had spent the night with her, perched awkwardly on a chair next to her bed. Neither slept well, with all the clanking, talking and the generally alien environment.

In the morning, at half past nine to be precise, Mr Adams came to speak with Vincent. Mr Adams was the Consultant Haematologist. His face was grave, an all too often practised method of preparing people for whatever bad news he had to impart. He usually had bad news. Vincent felt a knot in his stomach as Mr Adams quietly explained that Charlotte's blood test results were not normal. He was extremely sorry, but the tests indicated that she was suffering from acute myeloid leukaemia. Cancer of the blood.

Vincent's world fell apart at that moment, although Mr Adams assured him that children generally responded well to the treatment. With great sensitivity, Mr Adams explained to Charlotte the details of her illness and the treatment they would administer to fight it.

Both men choked when she asked if she was going to die. Vincent was unable to speak as he fought back his tears, and it was all Mr Adams could do to explain that, yes, there was a small chance. They would do all they could to prevent that and it was important to remain positive.

The treatment began that week and seemed to go well. The cancer was being fought into remission, a stage where it becomes manageable. The problem is that the chemotherapy is not only toxic to cancer cells, but also to healthy ones, just marginally less so. The idea is to kill as many cancer cells as possible, then allow the healthy ones to recover before commencing another course of treatment. After each course, Charlotte's white blood cell count dropped off, making her susceptible to infection. That was the danger period.

Then came even worse news. She would need a bone marrow transplant to repair her body's ability to produce blood cells. To Vincent's despair, he was incompatible. So was her mother. There was an agonising wait whilst a suitable donor was found but then, one day, they had the call, a call that promised the chance of life. He remembered the day they had headed to the hospital and Charlotte had left her bedroom for the last time.

She never made it home again.

There wasn't a day that passed without him thinking of her, but none more so than her birthday. He tore himself away from the grave and headed home, not really wishing to see anyone. But after showering and changing, he was ready for his meeting. He didn't know what to expect, as the person who had called him had been quite vague.

*

Dunscombe was in his office with Chohan and Gallimore when the call came through. It was only a few minutes after Gregory had left with Hudson and Susannah. Although his secretary was under strict instructions not put any calls through unless it was Gregory, this call had bypassed her. It was Dunscombe's closely guarded direct line.

'Yes?' he snapped, supremely irritated. 'What do you wa…' But he was rudely interrupted by the caller. As he listened, his mouth went dry and he found himself fumbling for the whisky bottle with his spare hand.

'Who the hell is this?' he demanded, but it was obvious that the caller ignored him. There was a slight pause as Dunscombe listened intently.

'You wouldn't dare,' he hissed into the mouthpiece. 'They couldn't prove it.'

'We've got your credit card details, Alan,' the caller advised him laconically. 'It seems that your card has been used to make some very illegal and unpleasant purchases from a website in Thailand. Tut tut, little boys your preference are they? Dear me, they'll lock you up for years. You'll be lucky to survive a year. Apparently, they don't like paedophiles over there. We don't like them here, either. I'm sure the UK authorities will oblige when the extradition request comes through. It always seems to be dirty old men of a certain age. Bit like you, don't you think, hmm?'

'What do you want, you bastard?'

'I think we both know what that is.'

'Enlighten me,' he snapped.

'It would appear that you are in possession of certain documents of a - how shall we put it? - of a delicate nature.'

'Oh, really? And what might they be?'

'Don't insult my intelligence. You know full well I'm talking about Red Dawn.'

'Never heard of it.'

'I see. What does your wife do, Alan?'

'You tell me.'

'Okay, just hypothetically, let's assume that she works for a number of charities including, let's see, the NSPCC, Barnardo's. Am I close?'

Dunscombe was silent, so the caller continued in his languid drawl.

'It wouldn't look very good for her, would it? And think of the shame. Not just hers, but the kids as well. Your eldest – thinking of a PhD at Oxford, I understand? Amazing how a quiet word in the right ear can affect one's prospects. Needless to say, I've got several acquaintances up there. I would hate to have to speak to them about this unfortunate little matter.'

'Leave the family out of it, you bastard,' Dunscombe growled into the receiver.

'The choice is up to you, Alan. Desperate times call for desperate measures, you see. Very sorry to lean on you like this, old boy, but you must understand the dilemma. I can't have these little stories about nuclear accidents floating around the media. It's all so unnecessary, don't you think, this sort of scaremongering? There are enough things to worry about in the world already. Plus I hardly need add that you would be in breach of the Official Secrets Act.'

'The public have a right to know. People have died because of Red Dawn and Charles Millburn.'

'We all have tough choices to make. That's what happens when you run a country, I'm afraid. Charles Millburn is one of the last true patriots. He can see the bigger picture and is prepared to make these brave and difficult decisions. If a few sacrifices have to be made to protect the nation, then so be it. It's unpleasant, I agree, but necessary.'

'What favours are you getting from Millburn?'

'You do have an overactive imagination, Alan. I suppose that's quite useful for you creative types? But let's just put that imagination back in its box for the time being and get back to reality. If I don't receive those documents within the hour and have an assurance from you that this little story of yours has been forgotten, then the Thai authorities will find your credit card details on that website I mentioned. If, on the other hand, you see common sense, then this little problem will go away. Like it never happened.'

'What's to stop you doing it anyway?'

'Nothing, I suppose. I think it best if we have a mutually beneficial relationship from now on Alan. You've always had it in for us, quite frankly, but I'm extending the hand of generosity. Call it an act of magnanimity if you will. I'd like you to work with us in future. That way, I can guarantee that you won't experience any difficulties with the internet. Sound reasonable?'

'How can I work with you when I don't know who you are?'

'Oh, don't worry about that, Alan. We know who you are, and that's what matters. We would prefer it if you steered away from provocative stories in future, that's all, and everyone's happy.'

'I'll have to see. After all, I'm only the editor of a national newspaper.' The sarcasm was thick and heavy.

'One hour, Alan.'

The line went dead.

'Shit.'

'Who was that?' asked Chohan.

'I don't know,' replied Dunscombe thoughtfully, 'but it seems that certain people would rather we did not publish this story.'

'What did they say?'

'We have to return all the documents within the hour.'

'To whom?'

'Don't know. Presumably they'll send someone.'

'What if we don't?'

'For a start, I get stitched up on a porn charge in Thailand, of all places. They threatened my family, too. Nobody does that and gets away with it.'

'What are you going to do?'

'I need to see someone. Hold the fort, will you?'

'Where are you going?'

'To see an old friend.'

'Who?'

'Rather not say. You wouldn't like it.'

'What if it doesn't work?'

'Trust me. It will.'

Dunscombe gathered his coat and bag and hurried out of the door, leaving a bemused Chohan and Gallimore staring after him. He rushed down to the street and climbed into a waiting cab.

'Where to, guv?'

Dunscombe leant forward and gave directions to the driver, who nodded and headed off, leaving him gazing thoughtfully out of the window. Despite his assurances to Chohan and Gallimore, he had no idea if it would work, whether his old friend could help or not, or even if he was in any fit condition to.

Giles Devereaux placed the phone back in the cradle and glanced up at Jeremy Langham.

'Think that will do the trick?'

'I don't know,' replied the Acting Director-General of the Security Service. 'Dunscombe's old school. He might not be so easily persuaded. You'll have to be prepared to pull the gloves off.'

'Can't you arrange something?' asked the Number 10 Director of Communications.

'Well, if it comes to that, we might have to. But only as a last resort. He's too high profile, but there are plenty of other things we can do in the meantime. We can put pressure on the board, too. They won't allow publication once we've dug the dirt on them. There must be plenty of skeletons in cupboards there.'

'We'll know within the hour. See if Dunscombe's got a brain left, first.' Devereaux sighed. It was such an unnecessary distraction. 'What about Millburn and Kroll?'

'They have a team in place. We're following the target for them.'

'Can't you use that as leverage to persuade Dunscombe?'

'No. It has to be done separately. We can't afford for Hudson and the girl to remain at large. They won't stop until they've exposed Red Dawn; they know too much.'

'What about Dunscombe's reaction to that?'

'As I said, something might have to be done with him, but only as a last resort. He could prove very useful to us, as a tame editor. He would never dare step out of line again. I would rather we waited to see what happens.'

'Speaking of which, any news about Wellesby yet?'

'No, the old duffer's still clinging on. You'd think he would have done the decent thing by now, so I can get on with my job properly.'

'Yes, quite. Rather rude of him, really.'

They both smiled. It would be a simple matter of time before Langham was confirmed in the role. His old boss wouldn't last for much longer, according to the hospital, leaving Langham to impose his vision on the Service. The new arrangement with Devereaux was already yielding dividends, with the Prime Minister becoming highly receptive to Langham's draconian proposals on the surveillance and detention of suspected terrorists and criminals, along with a hefty increase in his budget. Within days, he had already achieved far more than that old fart Wellesby had managed throughout his entire tenure..

33

Gregory powered the Audi up the M6 motorway, through Lancashire and into Cumbria. Once they had left the motorway south of Kendal, they proceeded West along the A595 towards the coast. The heavy motorway traffic gave way to slower tourists, holding them up as they admired the scenery. But Hudson and Susannah weren't interested in the scenery. As they neared their destination, they all grew tense. There was no way they could predict how the meeting would go. Realistically, the chances were that it would go badly, but none of them wanted to dwell on that possibility too much. Dunscombe was probably correct in his assessment that their chances of persuading someone to break the Official Secrets Act would be increased if Hudson and Susannah went in person to explain their story. Dunscombe was also making a shrewd bet that if he could bring others on board it would reduce the chances of his own prosecution. When Gregory had phoned the man they were about to meet, he had been careful not to reveal too much. The pretext had been a government-backed university study involving current or former employees of the Sellafield facility. This study project was merely at the consultation stage, to identify those prepared to help. It would be far easier to meet up and discuss the various aspects of the project on a face-to-face basis.

They had brought a copy of Terleski's dossier, and all the information in the document box they had retrieved, including a recording of the first tape on CD, prepared by the newspaper's senior IT consultant. Dunscombe had retained the original tape recordings of the

Red Dawn meetings for safekeeping; a sensible precaution considering their enormous value to the story. The man they were meeting would not be aware of the full scope of Red Dawn but, according to Terleski's information, he had played an indirect role in the cover up. He would be able to confirm his part in the conspiracy, thus lending credibility to the newspaper's story. The more witnesses they could find, the greater the plausibility of their story would be, and the less likely that they would be prosecuted under the Official Secrets Act. Only those at the very top of Red Dawn had a full appraisal of the programme and almost all of them were now dead. But it would have been impossible to implement without the assistance and complicity of others lower down. Those people were simply given specific tasks to undertake, with no questions asked. All would have been automatically subject to the Official Secrets Act, though reminding them of that fact would have been unnecessary. Employees were selected for their reliability and instances of indiscretion were rare. This emphasised how vital it was to make a good pitch in order for Dunscombe's plan to work. They had to persuade someone to talk.

As they approached the small coastal town of Seascale, the Sellafield plant loomed large on the horizon, dominating the skyline. The site itself was vast, the size of a small town, and employed thousands. It was easily one of the largest employers in the relatively impoverished region, another factor that ensured loyalty. The plant sat on the coastline like a malevolent parasite and they were silent as they contemplated its secrets. They drove past, mesmerised by its sheer scale, before turning right just before the next town of Egremont. Grease found his way to the address up the narrow lane that led to a small hamlet of cottages.

Hopefully, the list of names and addresses provided in Terleski's document box was accurate.

They found the small hamlet quickly, spotting the cottage nestling among a handful of houses. With trepidation and a mounting feeling of dread, they parked up and approached the front door, which opened before they even had a chance to knock.

'Mr Buckley?'

'Yes?'

*

Vincent Markham found that he was distracted after his visit to the cemetery. He should have arranged for the meeting the following day instead, but the poor gentleman sat in front of him was clearly in despair. He had been given Vincent's number by another one of his patients. Having been vague on the phone, it transpired that he had just lost his parents in a car accident and needed to talk to someone who could help him come to terms with the loss. That was Vincent's job after all, though most of his time was spent simply listening, as people unburdened themselves of the awful weight of their grief. The unburdening was a catharsis, a necessary first stage in process of recovery. However, Vincent was struggling to listen; he certainly wasn't concentrating. His mind kept coming back to Charlotte. He should have refused the meeting, taken the whole day off, so that he could give his new patient his full and proper attention another time. But after an hour or so, the man had finished talking. Vincent spoke to him briefly and gently, before asking to come back for another appointment soon. The man thanked him and left, leaving Vincent to his own devices once more.

He sank into a well-worn armchair and made a half-hearted attempt at a crossword puzzle before giving up, unable to concentrate. He needed to do something physical rather than cerebral; something constructive, tangible. Fortunately, the rain had eased off, so he ventured into the garden at the rear of the cottage and did some tidying up. Exercise was always therapeutic and as he piled brush and fallen leaves into a heap ready for a bonfire, he began to feel better. The desperate desire for vengeance that had consumed him at the cemetery earlier began to subside. It would never go away entirely, but he had to control it and prevent it from becoming an obsession. But there was one problem with that, and it lay with the media. The man he held responsible for his daughter's illness and death was all over the television and newspapers. Vincent couldn't get away from him. It also confirmed how futile any attempt at retribution would be, which partly relieved him of the obligation, but only served to reinforce his frustrated impotence.

*

The meeting was not going well. Paul Buckley was incredibly suspicious, especially after discovering that they had gained entry to his house on a pretext. Or deception, as he accused them.

'You're a journalist, then?' he glared at Gregory.

'Yes, we both are,' Gregory indicated Hudson. 'I'm sorry for misleading you, but we couldn't discuss this over the phone.'

'I'm not discussing anything with you. I know your type. You're all lying scum!'

'Please could you listen to what we've got to say,' interrupted Susannah. 'I haven't come all this way for nothing.' She put on her most winning, pleading expression.

'I'm not sure I want to,' he replied gruffly, but his tone was already less hostile. He had always had a weakness for beautiful women and Susannah was no exception.

'Just give me five minutes. That's all I'm asking.' Her eyes were wide, imploring.

'Alright,' he muttered. He sniffed loudly, wiped his nose with the back of his hand and nodded for her to carry on.

'My uncle, Doctor William Terleski, was a scientist with the National Radiological Protection Board. In fact, he ended up being in charge. Have you heard his name before?'

'No.'

'He was in charge during 1986. Does that mean anything to you?'

'No.' But it was clear that Buckley was becoming nervous. He shifted on his feet and was now listening intently, his body stiff.

'My uncle died very recently. He left something behind. A dossier.'

Buckley was rigid.

'We have a copy with us.' Hudson rummaged in the shoulder bag he was carrying and Buckley's eyes flitted between it and Susannah, who carried on. 'In the dossier, he described a series of events that apparently took place at the Sellafield plant in 1986. These events were kept secret under a programme known as Red Dawn.'

Buckley blinked.

'Never heard of it,' he croaked, taking hold of the dossier from Hudson, and glancing at the cover. He made no attempt to read it.

'Are you sure?'

'Absolutely.'

'Uncle William also left a box of information that contained a list of people who helped implement Red Dawn. Your name is mentioned on that list.'

'It can't be.' He swallowed. 'There must be a mistake.'

Susannah said nothing. She opened a folder, took out a sheet of paper and passed it to Buckley. He read it and paled visibly.

'That sheet of paper was amongst the records kept by my uncle. It lists your activities on the night of the 19th May 1986 and over subsequent days.'

'This is nonsense!' he protested.

'You were a technician at the plant. Your job was to carry out maintenance in Building B215, where the most hazardous liquid waste was stored.'

'Yes, I was a technician, but I don't know what you're talking about!' he protested loudly, insistently.

'If you're worried about the Official Secrets Act, don't be. With your testimony, the government wouldn't dare launch a prosecution,' stated Gregory. He didn't actually know whether that would be the case, but he was desperate for Buckley to talk.

'There's something else you should know,' Susannah continued in a quiet voice. 'I don't want to frighten you, but we think that there is a strong possibility that my uncle was murdered to keep Red Dawn secret.'

'What?'

'My uncle was an original member of the Red Dawn programme. He was one of the few people to know of the accident in B215, and its cover up. He was found dead a few days ago. Several of his former colleagues have died recently. My uncle was killed because he knew too much, and that was an unacceptable risk for the man who set up the Red Dawn programme.'

Buckley was silent, so Susannah continued. 'Charles Millburn instigated the cover up whilst he was Minister of State at the Department for Trade and Industry. Now he's head of Gencor Energy, and it doesn't take much to work out what would happen if news of Red Dawn came out now. It could undermine the whole nuclear building programme.'

Again, Buckley remained silent.

'We have recordings of the meetings, including the one in which he set up Red Dawn. There is no doubt that Charles Millburn is responsible for the cover up. We're not sure if his boss even knew about it. However, we do know that you were responsible for replacing the equipment damaged by the leak.'

'I don't know what you're talking about. I want you to leave.'

'Oh, come on, Peter! You must have realised the scale of the leak. A *whole* tank boiling off its contents into the atmosphere. You must have known how serious it was. And what about your friends and family? Weren't you worried about them? This whole area was contaminated!'

'Right, can you leave now? I don't want you in my house anymore. Get out.'

'Please, Peter. Help us expose this. The truth needs to be told.'

'Get out.'

'If you tell us, my paper can pay you,' offered Grease, in desperation.

'*Get out!*' he shouted.

'Okay, okay, we're going,' Hudson intervened, trying to calm matters.

Buckley herded them out of his house and slammed the door behind them. They trudged back to the Audi and climbed in.

'That went well,' observed Gregory. Susannah began crying and Hudson climbed into the back to comfort her.

'We're never going to get out of this mess, are we?' she sobbed. 'No one's going to believe us and you're not going to print the story, are you?'

Avoiding the question, Gregory attempted to put a positive spin on the situation. 'There are others on the list we can try. We might have better luck with someone else.'

'We're running out of time,' warned Hudson. 'We need this story out as soon as possible, before they find us.'

Gregory nodded in understanding and pulled his mobile phone out. 'I'll try the next one on the list. Same story?'

Hudson nodded, lacking the energy to think up anything new.

As Gregory made the call, Buckley watched them from behind his lace curtain. He was deeply shaken by the visit. The events of that night, long ago in 1986, had been carefully placed at the back of his mind. Now they came racing back with full clarity.

The irony of the situation at the time was that, since the Chernobyl explosion in April of that year, the United Kingdom's nuclear facilities had come under media scrutiny, and the last thing they needed was an accident. The bloody media were always trying to find fault with nuclear power, thought Buckley. As a result of the scrutiny, a quiet word had gone out to the managers of the facilities throughout the country advising them to avoid mistakes and accidents at all costs. A discrete amendment had been made to the nuclear accident reporting procedure, to control the flow of information should, heaven forbid, an accident occur. The managers had also been quietly advised that any known problems should be rectified as a matter of urgency. This was where Buckley came in. His brief had been to instigate the recommendations of the engineer in charge of the ventilation equipment in storage building B215. Various items of equipment were to be replaced. Previous inspections suggested that they were ageing more rapidly than the manufacturers had originally predicted and, due to their critical function, it was deemed prudent to replace or upgrade some of the items, especially the electrostatic 'scrubbers' and filters that cleaned the air that was expelled from the building.

Unfortunately, this meant relying on the old and inadequate system whilst the work was carried out. In itself, this should have been perfectly safe. The chances of a problem occurring within the building were extremely low.

On the morning of 19th May 1986 the primary ventilation system was shut down and the back-up was activated. Initially, everything was going well. The technicians moved in and began the upgrade.

Under normal safety procedures, heavy lifting equipment was prohibited inside Building B215. However, because of the equipment replacement programme, special dispensation had been given for a mobile lift platform to operate inside, to allow technicians to reach the parts of the ventilation system inside the roof space, and provide them with a safe working platform. The platform operator was a long-serving employee of the plant, someone who knew the risks and could be trusted to act in as safe a manner as possible.

The nuclear reprocessing waste was stored in huge stainless steel tanks, twenty one in all. The older tanks, of which there were eight, were huge horizontal cylinders with dished convex ends. Each tank was ten metres long and three metres across. These were housed in pairs within steel-lined concrete cells that were designed to contain any leaks. The newer tanks were vertical cylinders, six metres tall and six metres in diameter, and they were housed in individual concrete cells. To increase safety, one tank in every three was kept empty, to facilitate the transfer of liquid radioactive waste should another tank be compromised in any way. Should a leak occur, the liquid would be contained within the concrete cells, the walls of which were up to two and a half metres thick.

Heat had always been recognised as the main problem and the cooling systems had been designed to allow a large margin between their maximum capacity and the heat actually produced by the waste. Without cooling, the heat produced by the radioactive decay within the liquid waste would eventually be enough to boil the waste, causing it to evaporate into the atmosphere. The older eight tanks had quite rudimentary cooling systems, the first four possessing only a single cooling coil per tank. The next four, tanks five to eight, were more advanced, with two additional cooling coils. However, as these contained the oldest waste, the heat produced, and therefore the risk of boiling, was quite low. The newer tanks were equipped with more advanced systems, each containing seven cooling coils. Nevertheless, the principle was the same: Water was forced around the system by a series of pumps based in two cooling towers. There were three high pressure circuits in total: A primary, secondary and back-up, which fed the cooling coils within the tanks.

The newer tanks contained more recently produced waste, with a higher level of radioactivity, and therefore more heat. Subsequently, the cooling requirement for Tanks Nine to Twenty One was of greater necessity, though the cooling capacity of the newer tanks greatly exceeded the heat produced.

By 1986, the storage of highly radioactive liquid waste in Building B215 was reaching its peak. No one, anywhere in the world, had yet worked out a solution for storing nuclear waste safely for the tens of thousands of years it would take to fully decay, so it was left in the tanks until such a solution presented itself. Nuclear waste had been accumulating in the tanks since 1955 and no better storage or disposal alternative had yet been found. In the meantime, Britain had been setting itself up as the world's premier reprocessor of nuclear waste, whilst the burgeoning international nuclear industry churned out ever more waste each year, with nowhere to put it. Other than Building B215. It was one of the most lethally toxic depositaries on the entire planet.

Like many of his colleagues, Buckley tried not to think too much about the enormous waste tanks, instead placing his faith in the complex and detailed safety procedures that had been established over years of practice.

The problem with established procedures is that they are not very good at handling unforeseen eventualities. Whilst there was a written procedure for changing pumps that broke down, it did not envisage a full scale upgrade and replacement programme on the grounds of political necessity. Therefore, the safety supervisors and engineers had to devise a hurried procedure to undertake the work. Nevertheless, the technicians and operatives were fully briefed beforehand.

At first, the work had proceeded with great caution, but as the programme progressed, familiarity with the task speeded up the pace of work. Actions that had been carefully considered each time they were performed at an early stage now came automatically. Careless is too strong a word, but *unthinking* may be appropriate. When driving a car, one does not always consider each and every gear change consciously; it happens naturally. However, every now and again, for no discernible reason, one makes a tiny error, the gear is missed or the wrong one is selected. Likewise, the platform lift operator who had been given special dispensation to use his machine inside B215.

Normally, the strict operating procedure for a mobile lift platform is that it should never be moved whilst the platform is raised. The reason is simple: With the platform up, the machine's centre of gravity is raised and the risk of it falling over is greater. This risk is magnified by the introduction of lateral movement to the base; in other words, if it is moved. However, the technicians and operator were becoming exasperated by the laborious procedure. To ensure that the platform was in its correct location, it had to be raised with a technician on board. If it wasn't quite right, the platform had to be lowered, the technician alighted, the stabilisers were raised, the platform moved, and the stabilisers were put down again before the technician went back up. The operator had obviously cut a corner, or made a mistake. Nobody knew. Perhaps he forgot to reposition the stabilisers properly. Whatever it was, it proved to be a catastrophic error. Something caused an angular momentum in the raised platform, the centre of gravity shifted beyond the vertical and the outcome was inevitable. With balletic grace, the whole machine toppled over, smashing into the main cooling pipes and hurling the technician onto the floor, where he slammed into the hard concrete.

Buckley remembered first the shock, then the terror as a pool of coolant spread rapidly across the painted concrete floor. For a moment, no one had reacted, catatonic with horror at what they had just witnessed.

Then the warning alarms began as a pressure monitor detected the loss of coolant pressure to the storage vessels, and the realisation sank in.

Panicking, they had dragged the injured man clear of the leaking water and into a corridor outside the main hall, whilst the building was evacuated. He had screamed with agony as broken bones grated together, but the priority was to get him into a safe area. His hard hat had protected his head from the impact with the floor, undoubtedly saving his life, but not spared him the broken limbs he had sustained. But

Buckley and his colleagues were merciless in their dash to escape the building. None of them needed any encouragement to get out.

Outside, the shaken men gathered around their injured colleague, whilst first aid was administered. The platform operator was ashen-faced, feeling the full weight of responsibility on his shoulders. An emergency containment crew arrived on the scene, alerted by the automatic alarm system. Donning protective suits, they headed into the building to assess the damage for themselves.

The leader of the team felt his skin crawl at the sight that greeted him. The fountain of water erupting from the shattered cooling pipes was being sustained by the pumps in the external cooling towers as the electronic management system demanded more water to maintain pressure. A large pool of water had already formed on the floor between the rows of enormous tanks. With a feeling of relief, he realised it was the cooling system and not the tanks that had been compromised. *Thank god.* The liquid coming out was just water and not radioactive waste. Thinking quickly, his first command was to switch the cooling pumps off and stem the flow of water pouring into the building. Their ears were also being assaulted by a cacophony of noise from the various warning alarms. These were deactivated, simply so that they could hear themselves think. As the fountain of water subsided with the switching off of the pumps, they edged towards the damaged pipe work, sweat pouring off them inside the protection suits. The damage did not require particular expertise to assess. All three cooling circuits were damaged, the pipes crushed and ripped open by the falling platform.

'Shit,' the crew leader muttered to his colleague. 'This could be bad.'

Through the misty visor of his protective suit, his colleague merely blinked, his eyes conveying far more than words ever could. They paused to look at the enormous storage tanks, now bereft of all means of cooling. As the enormity of the problem sank in, both experienced a terrible feeling of foreboding.

'We need to call Vincent about this,' muttered the second man to his superior.

Vincent Markham was the site engineer responsible for the cooling system. As the system had been catastrophically damaged, he would be in the best position to effect emergency repairs and assess the risks and timescale.

Vincent was summoned and arrived on the scene in a matter of minutes. The General Manager for the Sellafield site was also informed and an immediate information blanket was placed on the scene. All those present and aware of the accident were reminded of the need to maintain the utmost discretion.

When Vincent entered the building, he was appalled by what he saw. A quick check of the tank thermostats revealed that, so far, the temperatures had not risen by much. But they had risen, nevertheless. Vincent knew that the contents of tanks holding the most radioactive waste would boil after approximately fourteen hours without cooling, but significant evaporation of their contents would occur within about twelve and a half hours, according to the hypothetical calculations performed for the safety assessments. There would be few people willing to hang around once that started to happen. Therefore, realistically, they had a window of twelve hours to restore the cooling circuits, probably less as they had to take into account the time lag before the cooling took effect in the tanks. Then he learnt something from Buckley that made his blood run cold: The ventilation system was out of action due to the repairs being conducted. Buckley recalled the exchange outside the building, when Vincent had gone to appraise the General Manager of the situation.

'What's your assessment?' the General Manager demanded.

'It's bad. All three high pressure cooling circuits, including the back up are compromised.'

'How long have we got?'

'Twelve hours at most. We need to raise a civil emergency alert, evacuate the local population, and leave a skeleton staff on site here.'

'Sorry. Out of the question for the time being.'

'*What?*'

'The tanks aren't compromised, there's plenty of time to repair the pipes, and in the meantime we can cool the tanks directly with fire hoses. We've had a minor accident, no need to make a fuss.'

'There's a risk that one or more of the tanks could *boil*. We can't take that risk. The ventilation system is out of action, the gases would go straight into the atmosphere!'

'Yes, it is a risk, I'll grant you that, but on balance I don't think it's likely to happen, do you?'

'It's remote at the moment, yes, but if we can't fix those pipes then it becomes a bloody certainty!'

'Look, this is one of the largest nuclear waste sites in the world. Can you imagine what would happen if news of this got out? There would be pandemonium. What if an evacuation was not justified? We would risk national outrage for nothing. I'm not prepared to take that risk on the remote chance of a leak. We've had leaks here before, but we didn't panic. We won't panic this time either. Now, I suggest you get on with those repairs.' With that, the General Manager had left to make an initial report to his superiors, leaving a visibly angry Vincent to handle the situation.

Buckley shared Vincent's concern, but accepted the need to get on with the task at hand. But Vincent had a point: Thousands of innocent people living and working in the vicinity of the building were completely oblivious to the imminent danger within B215.

The older tanks, which contained waste dating back to the 1950's, posed less of a risk. Heat generation was greatest during the first three years of storage and, after that, it diminished exponentially. Vincent was, however, extremely worried about Tanks 18 and 19. These were the ones most recently filled and therefore producing the most heat, and the thermostats reflected that. A quick check provided unequivocal evidence: The temperatures on Tanks 18 and 19 were already rising. The increments were small, but they were definitely there. The one hundred and forty five cubic metres of highly radioactive liquid waste held within both tanks was slowly and inexorably becoming warmer.

The following hours had passed in a blur, as they raced frantically to restore the cooling system. A separate team rigged up fire hoses to the River Calder and began hosing the tanks down inside their concrete cells, manually regulating the temperatures. It worked for all the tanks, except 18 and 19, where the temperature remained stubbornly high, still creeping upwards. It was vital to restore the main cooling system before they lost control of the temperatures in both tanks. Dousing the exterior of the tanks was only providing a temporary respite, an inefficient way of extracting heat from the enormous tanks. It would only delay the inevitable if they couldn't repair the pipe work. The water pumping operation was also making working conditions impossible for the technicians repairing the pipes, hampering their work.

The repair work was extremely difficult, as it necessitated replacing entire sections of pipe, the problem being that large-section stainless steel pipe is not an off-the-shelf product. It is made to order, at great expense, by a very select group of manufacturers operating at the cutting edge of foundry technology. To further compound problems, as such orders are usually bespoke, it would be very difficult to find sections of pipe handily lying around that were of the exact dimensions, with flanges to match. In short, they were in trouble.

Vincent Markham was informed of the growing problem but, after racking his brains for a while, came up with a solution. There was major construction work going on at the Thorpe reprocessing facility. They should be able to find stainless steel pipe that was a close enough match to make temporary repairs. Proper repairs could be done at a later date by fixing each cooling circuit one at a time. But for now the priority was to reinstate the cooling system, however rudimentary it may be. This meant that they would concentrate on fixing just the primary circuit, leaving the remaining circuits for later.

It was over two hours before they managed to obtain a suitable length of pipe from the Thorpe site. To the inexperienced eye, the task now seemed straightforward enough: Cut out the damaged section on the primary cooling circuit, cut a length of replacement pipe and then weld it into place. However, the section of replacement pipe wasn't an exact match, meaning that the welding bead would have to be much thicker than normal. Usually, such pipe work is joined together in pre-formed lengths that have flanges at either end which allow bolt-through fixings: A high-pressure seal is achieved by means of a special gasket inserted between the flanges. That wasn't possible in this case, and the pipes would have to be joined by means of a thick bead of molten metal, applied by hand rather than robot. It would have to be built up slowly in layers and there were two joints to be made. The task was further complicated by the close proximity of the pipes to one another. It was difficult to gain clear access to all sides of the pipe. What seemed at first glance to be a simple task was in fact fraught with difficulties. More difficulties meant more time. And that was the one thing they didn't have.

All of them felt the pressure mounting as Vincent supervised the cutting away of the damaged pipe. But he didn't want to push the technicians any more than was necessary; they were all aware of the urgency, and Vincent didn't want any mistakes to be made.

By seven o'clock that evening, the heavy lift platform had been removed and the damaged sections of pipe work cut away. But the closely monitored temperatures of Tanks 18 and 19 were on an upward trajectory that was clearly accelerating, the increments becoming larger each time the temperatures were checked. The other tanks had also warmed up slightly, but were well within safety levels. The focus of concern remained fully on Tanks 18 and 19. According to the theoretical calculations made when the tanks were designed, they still had eight hours left in which to complete the repairs, fill the cooling circuit with water, remove any airlocks and commence pumping. Buckley shared Vincent's hopes that the calculations were on the pessimistic side, and he remembered Vincent remonstrating once more with the General Manager.

Vincent was still of the opinion that a local evacuation should be undertaken, just to be on the safe side, but the General Manager was adamant that no such thing should happen. As long as just one cooling circuit could be restored, the plant would be perfectly safe. He even congratulated Vincent on his plan, which should mean that cooling was restored in less time than originally envisaged. But Vincent had seen no cause to celebrate and returned to the building, seething.

Whilst Vincent and the technicians were working frantically to restore cooling to the tanks, a subtle cordon had been established outside the building. It was clear that measures were being taken to suppress details of the earlier accident, which had been played down to a simple machinery failure resulting in the injury of two technicians. There was no radiation leak, so the Nuclear Installations Inspectorate was not informed. Only a tiny number of site workers were aware of the drama unfolding in B215, and they were under no illusions about the imperative to maintain absolute secrecy.

Once careful measurements had been made, a section of pipe was cut from the replacement piece. It was still too heavy to lift by hand, so a rope hoist was wheeled in. They manoeuvred the section into place, which had been cut to make as tight a fit as possible. It was too tight, so it had to be removed and filed down. The need for haste, and the awkward location, militated against the use of precision equipment, so a heavy duty angle grinder was brought to bear on the piece of pipe. After another half an hour of adjustments, the pipe finally slotted into the gap. However, it is difficult to cut large section pipe accurately whilst *in situ*, especially where it is not possible to deploy precision equipment. The small errors made when cutting the damaged pipe away had caused the subsequent difficulties, but at least the replacement piece was in place now.

The technician charged with the welding task shook his head at the undertaking that now presented itself. It was clear that the new section did not align very well with the original pipe. He was going to have to spend a long time building up the weld bead to fill the gaps. The first task was to spot-weld the pipe into place, to hold it firmly whilst he worked on the beads. Fire hoses snaked across the floor around him, the water cascading down the sides of the steel storage vessels to cool the contents. With no time to waste, the technician took a deep breath and set to work on the pipe.

An hour later, the first joint was done. The technician, who had previously worked in naval construction, was not terribly satisfied, but he had done the best he could in a bad situation. Buckley remembered the acrid stench of welding fumes in the air as they stood around the pipe, examining the joint.

'Not a bad job?' Vincent had asked, optimistic.

'This side's alright, but the other's shit,' the technician shook his head. 'I can't reach it properly to do a decent job.'

'Will it hold under pressure?'

'Your guess is as good as mine, guv. I wouldn't stake my life on it.'

'We'll just have to hope, then. Let's get on with the other joint.'

They were all acutely aware of the rapidly warming tanks 18 and 19.

'How long have we got?'

'Just over four hours.'

'Shit. How're the tanks?'

'Number nineteen's heating up faster than eighteen. I'm worried.'

The technician nodded and, by way of reply, simply flicked his protective visor down and started welding the joint at the other end of the inserted section of pipe. Unable to help, Vincent sought out the General Manager again, this time accompanied by Buckley.

'We need to talk. It's going to be close. You really should consider declaring a civil emergency.'

'I can't.' The General Manager seemed agitated and distracted. 'The decision has been taken out of my hands.'

'*What?*

'There are those who believe that it is of vital national importance that public confidence in this storage facility is maintained.'

'Who?'

'I can't say.'

'Can't say or won't say?'

'I can't say.' The General Manager had a hunted look about him, his features drawn and strained. 'There's nowhere else we can store this waste. It is the only place in the whole country. We can't afford to provoke public outrage and mass panic.'

'Your words or theirs?' sneered Vincent, barely able to contain his rage.

The General Manager averted his eyes, confirming Vincent's suspicions, and continued rather unconvincingly. 'Can you imagine the damage to our industry if we called a civil emergency, even if it turned out to be a false alarm?'

'But there's a bloody good chance it *won't* be a false alarm! We've got two tanks in there which could *boil*. What then? The air can't be filtered; it'll go straight into the atmosphere!'

'You'll have to fix the problem before that happens. You have no choice,' the manager mumbled. 'You have to succeed.'

'But what if we can't? It's bloody *lunacy* not to take precautions!'

'I can't do anything about it!' he snapped. 'We cannot risk damaging public confidence in this facility. I have been given very, very clear instructions.'

'By whom? Who is telling you that we can't protect the public? Because that's what it is, isn't it? Basically you're saying that we can't take reasonable steps to protect the public if a leak occurs?'

'I've got orders from high up,' he replied quietly. 'They're long-standing orders if you must know, but they've just been reaffirmed. Minor leaks from this building are not to be reported to the public, for the reasons I've just given. Now, if the whole thing was about to go up, that's a different story. But it isn't. Okay, we've got no cooling at the moment, but you're sorting that out. You've only got to fix a piece of pipework, haven't you?'

'I don't believe this. It's *criminal.*'

The General Manager made a dismissive gesture with is hands. 'Nothing I can do about it,' he muttered. With that he walked off, running his hands through his hair, clearly agitated and distracted, leaving Buckley and Vincent staring after him in amazement.

They both returned to the scene of the pipe damage. The technicians were gathered around watching their colleague proceed with the welding of the second and final pipe joint, shielding their eyes from the bright flame of the oxyacetylene torch. The mood was one of nervous impatience.

'How's he getting on?' shouted Vincent over the roar of the flame. The air was thick with the acrid fumes from the welding gear.

'He's getting there,' one of them answered with a shrug. There was little else he could say.

Vincent went off to speak to the technician monitoring the tank temperatures. Number 19 was giving most cause for concern. The rest were still well within safe limits, though Number 18 was also beginning to warrant a closer look. Vincent checked his watch; they had less than three hours in theory, but judging by the condition of Tank Number 19, even this was beginning to look optimistic. He hurried back to the site of the welding, where the technician was cursing, emitting a stream of coarse profanities.

'Fucking pipe! *Come on*! Just fucking *reach*!' he was shouting at the inanimate object in front of him. The tension and stress was beginning to overwhelm him and he was yanking at the gas pipes feeding his welding torch, trying to manoeuvre the head into a better position to seal the join on the rear underside of the pipe.

'Calm down, calm down,' implored Vincent quietly, placing a restraining hand on his arm. 'We don't need you losing it right now.'

The technician extricated himself from his awkward position and straightened up. When he flipped his visor up, the sweat was streaming from his face. He looked exhausted and close to tears, the frustration etched on his features.

'I don't know if this is going to work,' he shook his head despondently. 'I can't get a good bead down that far side.'

'Just do your best.'

'We haven't got long, have we?'

'No. Not really. But you're nearly there. As soon as you're happy with the joint, give me a shout and we'll start filling this circuit.'

The welder nodded.

'You're feeling okay now?'

'I'm fine, guv.' The visor came down and he crawled back under the pipe to finish the weld joint.

Twenty minutes later, he manoeuvred out of his tight position and announced that he had finished. There was palpable sense of relief amongst the anxious workers. They had a fixed cooling circuit. They were back in business, and not a moment too soon: The temperature increases in Tank 19 were accelerating.

At the control console, Vincent programmed the pumps in the cooling tower and began the process of filling the repaired circuit with water. This normally didn't take too long, as the high pressure pumps could shift thousands of litres a minute. Nevertheless, it seemed to take an age. The tension in the room grew as the technician monitoring the temperature of Tank 19 began shouting out each degree rise in temperature. It was obvious to everyone that the time lag between each interval was getting shorter and shorter. Already, evaporation from the increasingly warm liquid waste would be occurring inside the tank. It wouldn't be long before this would overwhelm the filters built into the head of each tank and radioactive vapour would begin escaping into the building. With only the old and completely inadequate ventilation system to handle it, there was little to prevent it escaping into the wider atmosphere.

The high pressure circuit seemed to fill up with water with agonising slowness. The cavernous hall of the storage facility was completely silent except for the sound of water pouring over the tanks from the fire hoses. But now there was a new, more welcome sound: The water sloshing through the repaired pipe. However, this was tempered by the shouts of the technician reading off the temperature in Tank 19.

Some of the other technicians in the vicinity of the tank began edging away from it. None of them wanted to fail in their duty, but all were thinking the same thing: *Let's get out of this building and as far away as possible. Right now.*

'Okay, the primary circuit is full,' announced Vincent finally, after what seemed an age. 'Venting circuit for airlocks.'

A series of automatic bleed valves released any air trapped in the circuit, a vital precaution before the pumps began pumping at high pressure. As the air was released, more water flowed in to fill the displaced volume. Once all the air was expunged from the system, the water pressure crept up to its operating level. All eyes were on the repaired section of pipe, especially those of the former naval shipyard worker. His expert eye would soon detect any possible failure in his handiwork. As the water pressure increased, the section of pipe began creaking as the metal flexed. They all knew that the replacement section was not of the same proof as the original piping – the metal being thinner, it would have a lower maximum operating pressure and would demonstrate greater expansion in comparison to the original. This discrepancy would put extra pressure on the stiff, unyielding weld joints, which are always weaker than the metal they are connecting. As the creaking continued, they all watched with bated breath.

Deep inside the joint, around the area where the technician had had the most trouble reaching, a hairline fault was developing. Slowly at first, the molecules began tearing apart from one another within the weld. As the seconds passed, the joint grew weaker and weaker, the tearing accelerating. Suddenly, a point was reached when the joint could not withstand the pressure anymore. There was an audible crack, and a thin jet of highly pressurised water squirted out behind the pipe, hissing noisily.

'SHIT! The joint's failed!' the welder shouted to Vincent, who immediately reduced the pressure in the system. They all experienced a sense of despair. There wasn't time to drain the system and carry out another repair. They were in trouble. Ashen faced, Vincent quickly considered the options available.

'Is the joint still holding?' he shouted at the technician, as the pressure in the system subsided. There was a delay as the man cast his eye over the joint on either side of the fracture.

'It doesn't seem to be getting any worse.'

'We'll have to run the system at low pressure, then. We haven't got a choice.'

The technicians exchanged worried glances. At lower pressure, the rate of heat extraction would be reduced. The cooling capacity of the circuit would be diminished, especially as the system first had to stabilise the already high temperatures in the tanks before it could even begin reversing them. The risk was that the rate of heat extraction from Tank 19 would be less than the rate it was producing heat, and the tank would continue to get hotter and hotter, despite the cooling circuit being back in operation. But they had no choice.

As the pumps pushed water around the system at a lower pressure, the technicians monitored the temperatures in the tanks. Automatic warning lights were flashing for most of the tanks, though the alarms had since been switched off for the sake of their hearing, and sanity. As the minutes ticked slowly by, they all strained to spot the first signs of evidence that the tanks were beginning to cool, or had at least stabilised. If only they could increase the flow rate in the pipes, but that would mean the pressure would rise, risking a catastrophic failure of the leaking joint.

According to the safety procedure, they should have around two hours before the contents of Tank 19 reached a temperature at which a hazardous level of evaporation would occur. According to the technician monitoring it, the tank was already only five degrees below this point. Clearly, they didn't have two hours. Buckley remembered the feeling of fear, the cold sweat as the awful realisation dawned that perhaps they wouldn't be able to stabilise Tank 19.

The older tanks, 1–8, were not posing as much concern as their contents had decayed enough not to produce enough heat to cause them to boil. Their collective focus was on the temperature readings for the newer tanks, 9–21.

'Tank 18 has stabilised!' called the technician monitoring it. A cheer went up.

'What about Tank 19?' Vincent enquired, brusquely cutting across any premature celebration that the partially restored cooling system was working. The technician scrutinised the dial and shook his head.

'It's, er, it's still rising,' he replied, an edge of nervousness in his voice. 'Shit! We've just gone up another degree!' They were now just four degrees away from the critical evaporation point.

'Are you sure?'

'Yes!'

'Is the rate of increase slowing?'

'A bit. The interval was longer that time.'

'Keep an eye on it,' he instructed, rather unnecessarily. All eyes in the room were already fixed firmly on it. As they waited, they could hear the gentle sound of water flowing through the cooling system, accompanied by the sound of water from the fire hoses sluicing over the tanks. Those near to the pipe could also hear the unmistakeable hissing from the crack in the repaired joint.

'It's just gone up another degree!' the technician announced, unable to control the panic evident in his voice.

Vincent could feel his legs turn to jelly as fear coursed through him once more. Suddenly a new sound became audible. Tank 19 began groaning and creaking as the heat caused the thick stainless steel skin to expand. It sounded like a giant central heating system had been switched on for the first time.

'Okay, gentlemen,' Vincent announced quietly. 'Any of you who are not essential here should find your way to somewhere safe.' The invitation was not lost on the frightened men, who immediately began walking towards the exits.

'I'll stay here, if you need me,' offered Buckley. He knew he was the only one without family.

Vincent nodded his appreciation. 'Thank you, Pete. The rest of you should leave now.' They didn't need any encouragement and, in moments, Vincent and Buckley were the only two remaining inside the building. Buckley had never felt so afraid in his life.

'Do you want to increase the pressure?' he asked Vincent. 'That might do the trick.'

'No. We can't risk the pipe failing. We're just going to have to pray.'

Buckley nodded and cautiously approached the tank, which squatted malevolently in its concrete cell. The creaking and groaning was getting worse, and Buckley found the noise terrifying, though he tried not to show it. He checked the thermometer. As he watched, it edged up another degree before his very eyes.

It had finally reached a critical point.

Buckley edged away from the tank, walking backwards, unable to tear his eyes away from it. He suddenly felt incredibly small, insignificant. He was five metres away when a blood-curdling alarm shrieked through the building, freezing him to the spot. The alarm was unmistakeable, the most terrifying sound for anyone working at a nuclear facility:

There was a radiation leak in the building.

'Get out!' shouted Vincent, and this time, Buckley found his legs. They lumbered to the exit, grateful now for the cumbersome protection suits that had hampered them throughout the day. It felt as though they were wading through treacle as they headed towards the nearest exit. In his panic, Vincent fumbled with the electronic key pad. Buckley cursed him *Come on, hurry up!* His back, facing the huge tank, felt extremely vulnerable. Impatient to escape, he barged Vincent to one side and jabbed at the keypad. The lock clicked as the solenoid engaged, and Buckley kicked the door open, dragging Vincent through with him. Breathing hard in his suit, Vincent followed Buckley down the corridor, his heavy boots pounding on the concrete floor. The radiation alarm reverberated through the building. They passed through some more double doors which led to the final exit of the building. Moving as fast as he could, Vincent was now breathing in ragged gasps, trying to keep up with Buckley. Finally, they reached the final door to the outside and burst through it. After a moment's disorientation, Vincent found his bearings and sought out the General Manager. He found him standing a good distance away from the building, his face ashen. The radiation alarm was clearly audible to those outside.

'Tank 19's venting fumes now,' gasped Vincent. 'It's only a matter of time before it boils. There's no ventilation scrubbing or filtering in place. We need to declare an emergency.'

'I don't have authorisation for that,' he mumbled, staring at the building.

'What? The fallout could spread for miles. We've got to do something!'

'I *can't*. London was adamant, absolutely adamant, that if only one tank leaks then we do *not* call a civil emergency!' he shouted back.

'How the fuck can they do that? Have they any idea what's in those tanks?'

'Of course they do! They've analysed the risk scenarios.'

'Then why the hell won't they do anything?' Vincent demanded.

The General Manager sighed and shook his head, as if disagreeing with what he was about to say. 'If it's just one tank the dose per person will be tolerable; the radiation will be widely dispersed. Take a look at the weather.'

'This is *criminal*!' Vincent shouted. 'You have to do something.'

'I can't do anything. I'm sorry. We cannot allow public confidence in this facility to be compromised in any way, especially after Chernobyl. Those are my orders.' He was unable to look Vincent in the eye; the man was clearly under immense personal strain and it was clear that people in much higher authority had leant heavily on him.

Unknown to Vincent or Buckley, it had been quietly decided that a single tank compromise would be acceptable. Any more than that, then a public emergency would have to be declared, but if it was just one, then they could live with the consequences. In London, an elderly Civil Servant was studying the pink folder he had first put together in 1958, wondering whether the plan it outlined would be feasible.

Red Dawn was being resurrected.

The media would be hysterical if a leak was reported at Sellafield just a couple of months after the Chernobyl. The pressure to shut down the nuclear industry would be irresistible, but that wouldn't solve the waste problem. It was vital that the public, or the media, did not find out about the accident. The General Manager had already been instructed to impose a complete information embargo on the site, and a discreet but effective cordon had been put in place around the facility.

Whilst Tank 19 was venting its lethally poisonous contents into the atmosphere, Building B215 was quietly sealed off. All those who had been involved with the accident were identified and quietly spoken to. They were left in no doubt as to their obligations not to discuss the incident with anyone, including each other. The result was that only a handful of people on the site knew about the ongoing radiation leak.

Throughout the night, Tank 19 boiled off its highly radioactive liquid waste, the surrounding world oblivious to the toxic cocktail being carried on the strong westerly breeze over the Cumbria highlands. The same breeze shepherded an Atlantic weather system into the area, where the moist clouds met the cold air sitting above the mountain and precipitated heavy rainfall, washing the radioactive mix to the ground.

By morning, over half the tank had boiled off which meant that the damaged cooling system finally had enough capacity to withdraw heat from the tank's residual contents. The boiling subsided, then the liquid waste began to cool down. By eight o'clock the tank had stopped venting radioactive gases. The building was flushed with clean air and technicians in protective gear went in to assess any damage and to start repairing the other cooling circuits.

They didn't know it, but Red Dawn had begun.

Buckley stood in his small living room, watching the Audi containing Hudson, Susannah and Gregory pull away. It may have happened over twenty years ago, but the events of that fateful night were still very fresh in his mind. He knew that Vincent Markham had taken it badly, but had still toed the line. Perhaps counter-intuitively, the workers of the Sellafield plant are fiercely loyal to their employer. A rigorous vetting process weeds out anyone who is unlikely to conform in the first place. In area of high unemployment and low wages, Buckley was grateful for his well-paid job and was intensely hostile towards anyone who even hinted that nuclear power may be a "bad idea". He knew there had been a cover-up, most likely orchestrated at the highest political level. The fact that no mention of the incident had ever been made was testament to that. Only once, inadvertently, had he even come across the name of Red Dawn, guessing correctly that it was linked in some way to the accident.

But Buckley was not overly concerned by the cover-up, despite living in the area. As far as he was concerned, the cover-up was perfectly understandable. There was no alternative to the storage of highly radioactive liquid waste, so it was best to maintain public confidence in the only facility available, however lacking it may be. And although he lived in the vicinity of the leak, he trusted the carefully explained assessment given to him by an anonymous expert from London that the risk was minimal; the weather conditions that night had dispersed the pollution far and wide and he had nothing to worry about. He was assured that he was at greater risk from over-exposure to the sun.

Therefore, it was all fine, as far as he was concerned. There had been plenty of other little leaks and accidents in the past that had been discreetly dealt with, no harm done. This was just another in what was, presumably, a long line of incidents. Yes, it was all fine.

But what wasn't fine was the fact that a journalist – a *journalist*, for Christ's sake – was sniffing around the story. Having written down the details of the Audi, he picked the phone up and called a special number that had been given to him by the expert from London in anticipation of precisely such an event.

34

'So, who's this Vincent Markham?' asked Gregory from the driver's seat. Although he had made the call, he had only been given the barest of details by Hudson.

'According to Dr Terleski's notes, he was the cooling system engineer on shift the night of the leak. Apparently, he prevented a much greater catastrophe, as he got the system up and running before more tanks went critical. The notes indicate that he kept on working at the plant for another six years. He left in early 1992, no reason given. Says here that his last known job was some sort of counsellor.'

A vital element of the Red Dawn programme had been information restriction, to identify and control all those involved with the cover up, to ensure that any potential breaches of security could be prevented. The additional notes left by Terleski in the document box contained a break-down of the technicians and engineers who had been at B215 on the day of the accident. None of those people knew about Red Dawn, or the mechanics of the cover up, but between them they would be able to piece together the events of the accident itself. Even if only one of them was prepared to corroborate the description provided by Terleski, then that would be enough grounds for the newspaper to publish its story. They needed just one person. They were that close.

*

Details of the phone call were passed to Kroll within twenty minutes of Buckley placing it. The original call had been received by a very discreet call centre operator in London who had requested a code. The code was linked to a file which would identify the intended case officer, allowing the operator to affirm that the call was genuine and to place it through to the correct extension. However, the code was linked to a file which flagged up Sir Mark Wellesby's name, placing the operator in a quandary, as Sir Mark was currently lying in hospital, close to death. A quick check of protocol indicated that the call be referred to the Acting Director General, Jeremy Langham, instead. Langham had assumed responsibility for Sir Mark's caseload.

Langham had been most concerned by the call and, after ascertaining the key facts, passed the information on to Peter Kroll at his office in Gencor's headquarters.

'Peter, it's Jeremy. We seem to have yet another problem...' Langham explained the visit to Buckley.

'Okay, my men have got it covered,' replied Kroll. 'They're quite close to them already, so it shouldn't be long for them to get there.'

'We don't know where they're going next, yet.'

'But you're tracking them aren't you?'

'The signal's been intermittent. But we should have them pinpointed quite soon, though. I'll let you know.'

'Good. Thank you.'

'There's something else, Peter.'

'What?'

'That bastard Dunscombe's lied to us. He didn't give us everything.'

'I thought you'd had a word with him?'

'Devereaux did. We sent a courier to pick up all the evidence.'

'So what was missing?'

'We don't know entirely, but Buckley said that they girl told him they had a recording of the meeting setting up Red Dawn.'

'A *recording?*'

'I'm afraid so. Not good, is it?'

'No. What about Charles?'

'He was on the recording apparently. Buckley never listened to it, though.'

'So they might be bluffing?'

'I doubt it. He didn't think so.'

'Shit.'

'Yes.'

'How did they know about Buckley?'

'Your guess is as good as mine. Terleski must have left a list of some sort.'

'You mean all the engineers and technicians?'

'Possibly.'

'If Dunscombe gets them to talk…'

'Yes. I know.'

There was a long pause.

'What are we going to do about it?'

'Continue as planned. We need to neutralise the two journalists, Hudson in particular, and the girl. Get rid of anyone who agrees to speak to them as well. Then we can deal with Dunscombe. We need to destroy his credibility, then destroy him, so that no one believes a thing he says. He'll be finished.'

After concluding the call with Kroll, Langham took a moment to gather his thoughts. He shut his eyes and took a deep breath. All these loose ends that had to be tied up. The pressure was getting to him and he would be glad for the whole affair to be over. A file was open on his computer. Another loose end. Loose *cannon* was more appropriate. The file had first been compiled in 1974, and had been left largely untouched since 1989. On the front cover, below the security tag, there was a name:

Alan Dunscombe.

'Hello Alan. I think it's about time we had another little chat,' he murmured softly to himself.

*

At his cottage, Vincent Markham awaited his guests with a mixture of curiosity and anxiety. The phone call had been a surprise and he was, to put it mildly, highly suspicious. He had been tempted to decline, on account of his melancholic mood, but recognised that social contact can prove to be the best antidote to despondency. He would have plenty of time later on that night to indulge his grief, when vivid memories of his daughter came flooding back in the lonely darkness of sleepless nights.

The caller had indicated that they were only a short drive away, so he was expecting them at any time. For want of something to do while he waited, he put the kettle on.

Shortly, he heard the tyres of a car crunch onto the gravel in front of the low stone wall that constituted the boundary of the small garden in front of the cottage. He watched from inside the dark cottage, the glass of the small windows impenetrable from the outside. It was a smart Audi. The sort of car driven by outsiders and second-homeowners. This served only to heighten his suspicions. The driver climbed out: Tall, dark-haired and handsome; foreign looking. He was followed by another tall and well-built man, more rugged in appearance. Then a beautiful blonde young woman climbed out. Vincent was reassured by her presence; it made the men seem less intimidating. Dunscombe had been right in that respect: Susannah's presence would help persuade people to talk.

Whoever had called him earlier, presumably one of the two men, had told him that they were conducting preliminary enquiries of potential participants in a government-backed university study on present and former employees of the Sellafield complex. Vincent was of the opinion that this was nonsense, as normal practice would have been to go through official channels at Sellafield, and to inform him in writing first. Nevertheless, like Buckley before him, he was intrigued. He wanted to find out the ulterior motive behind it.

He opened the door before they had a chance to knock, catching them off guard.

'Mr Markham?' asked the foreign-looking one, when he recovered himself.

'Yes?'

'I spoke to you a short while ago. My name is Samuel Gregory, and these are my colleagues, James Hudson and Susannah Harlowe. May we come in?'

'Do you have any identification?'

This stumped Gregory, who only had his press card, and was loath to show that right away. Fortunately, Susannah saved the day.

'Yes, Mr Markham. This is my university staff card.' She handed it over, while Hudson patted himself down, as if looking for it. He did not want to show a press card yet. Gregory caught on and made a meal of trying to find his non-existent student identity, but fortunately Markham was satisfied with Susannah's. The story seemed to tally so far, so he opened the door wider to let them in. Perhaps their research into Sellafield employees was genuine after all, though this failed to answer the question as to how they had obtained his contact details. Gregory soon put him out of his ignorance.

'Mr Markham, I'm afraid I have to confess that we're here on a pretext.' He swallowed nervously as Vincent fixed him with an unblinking gaze. Gregory ploughed on, expecting another explosive reaction akin to Buckley's.

'I'm a journalist, not a student. I work for the Guardian newspaper.'

Vincent took a deep breath. He harboured an instinctive mistrust of journalists, a mistrust entirely justified by the subterfuge he had just experienced.

'What do you want?' he demanded.

'We're here because of my uncle, Mr Markham,' Susannah explained. 'He died recently and left a document which included your name.' It was best that she took over proceedings, as it was obvious he was less hostile towards her than the two young men. Vincent was genuinely alarmed by now.

'What sort of document?'

'A dossier. My uncle claimed that he was involved in something that started many years ago and still continues to this day. The document was his description of the events that took place.' She let this sink in, watching Vincent carefully for his reaction. He had gone very still and quite pale.

'Go on,' he managed, his voice weak.

'Have you heard of something called Red Dawn?'

'No.' He hadn't, it was the absolute truth. Hudson could feel the disappointment rising within him.

'My uncle claims that you were involved in Red Dawn.'

'I've never heard of it.'

Trying to hide her disappointment, Susannah continued.

'Do you have any recollection of events on the nineteenth of May, nineteen eighty six?' She may as well as have hit Vincent with a brick. His reaction was instant and angry. Defensive.

'What the hell is this?' he demanded, his darting between them nervously.

'My uncle said that you were the engineer with responsibility for the cooling system in Building B215, the store for highly radioactive liquid waste. On that day, an accident seriously damaged the cooling system. You were unable to repair it in time to prevent Tank 19 from boiling off most of its contents. By awful coincidence, the ventilation system was in the process of being upgraded and couldn't cope with the discharge. You weren't able to prevent radioactive waste leaving the building and reaching the atmosphere. As a result, a large area of Cumbria was polluted.'

There was a long silence. Vincent blinked several times, his features pale.

'Who is your uncle?' he asked after several moments had passed.

'Dr William Terleski, head of the National Radiological Protection Board. According to information he left behind, he was part of a secret programme called Red Dawn. The programme was the official cover up of the accident. Were you involved as my uncle described?'

'Why are you here?' he stalled, his mind racing.

'My uncle is dead. We think he was murdered, along with other members of the programme, to keep it secret. We know that he and four of his former colleagues all died within a week of each other. We think our own lives are in danger. The man who set up the Red Dawn programme has a lot to lose if the public finds out about it. We think he is trying to stop us. We need someone to corroborate my uncle's account, so the story can be published in the newspaper. That should help protect us.'

'Who is behind this? Who are you afraid of?'

'Charles Millburn.'

Vincent shut his eyes. He had been right all along. Years earlier, he had deduced that the order not to declare a civil emergency must have emanated from Millburn's office. He held Millburn directly responsible for his daughter's illness, rightly or wrongly. His bitterness had poisoned his soul, creating a dark hatred that required a focal point, and Millburn had long occupied that spot.

Up to this point, Vincent had been impotent in his desire for retribution. Out of the blue, not only had his suspicion been confirmed, but new possibilities had suddenly opened up.

'Mr Markham?'

Vincent opened his eyes. 'I've never heard of Red Dawn.' He paused. 'But I was the engineer in charge of the cooling system for B215. We could've evacuated the area before the leak. We had hours to do it, but the powers-that-be didn't want to shake public confidence in the facility. Remember, for years and years they had been telling the public it was all perfectly safe. Okay, it was a freak accident, but you can't afford to have any accidents at all when you're storing that stuff, and especially when it's the only facility in Western Europe.'

'Why didn't you leave the area, if you knew about the leak?'

'They said the radiation wasn't as bad as they thought it would be. They told us it was dispersed by the storm that night. An expert from London came to talk to us. I guess that's where your uncle comes in. I assume that they manipulated the radiation readings? Yes, that makes sense. So, we didn't know how bad it really was. Also, you've got to remember, it was a bloody good job to have. Not many places you can earn that sort of money around here.'

'So, you wanted an evacuation of the area?'

'Yes, we could see it was going to be close with Tank 19. You see, although we had all three separate cooling circuits, the pipes still ran alongside each other, so they weren't really independent from one another. The accident damaged all of them at once, so it was always going to be a tough job to restore the cooling system. We pumped water using fire hoses and cooled the exterior of the tanks, but it wasn't enough for Tank 19. The waste was too recent, still very hot. Plus, it was just sod's law that the accident was caused by the upgrade work on the ventilation system. If the new ventilation system was in place, we probably could have contained the leak…And my little girl would still be alive.' He looked wistfully out of the window at the garden. Susannah paused. *Little girl?*

'I'm sorry, I don't understand.'

'She was only ten. God knows what she was breathing and eating for all those years. But they told us the risk was minimal.'

'She was ill?' whispered Susannah, feeling her heart melt. Vincent merely nodded, unable to speak. His eyes watered.

'Your warnings were ignored, then?' asked Hudson quietly, steering the conversation back. Vincent cleared his throat and swallowed.

'Yes. It was decided at a level above the General Manager's that the national interest was better served by keeping the accident quiet. We were forbidden to mention it to anyone.'

'So why are you talking to us now?'

'I've had enough of lying. I've got nothing left to lose. If they want to prosecute me, then fine. At least the truth will come out then.'

'Will you help us with the story?'

Vincent considered this for some time.

'I can only help you with the things I was involved in. I knew there had been a cover up, but I didn't know it was called Red Dawn or who was involved in that. Secondly, I don't want any money. The only way that I'll do this is out of conscience. If you insist on payment, then it must go charity. Thirdly, if it will bring Charles Millburn down, then I'm definitely in.'

*

Trevor and Julian approached the house cautiously. They had received constant updates on the location of Sam Gregory's mobile phone from Kroll's office in London. The signal was weak, the cell coverage poor, and they had lost track of it several times. But they had a signal now, and it wasn't moving. It hadn't moved for several minutes, indicating they had stopped somewhere. The coordinates were cross-referenced to a geographical information system to reveal that it was highly likely that the phone was in an address belonging to a certain Vincent Markham. A quick search of this name revealed that he had previously been security-vetted to work at the Sellafield nuclear facility. Further probing revealed that, to Kroll's horror, he had been the engineer responsible for the cooling system in B215. Presumably, he would know all about the accident, though little of the cover-up, and probably nothing at all about Red Dawn. Nevertheless, he could still prove to be a highly dangerous individual if he could be persuaded to talk to the journalists.

Kroll's orders were simple: Neutralise the threat to Gencor Energy PLC and retrieve any and all classified information. This time, there'd be no messing about. Billions of pounds were at stake.

*

Vincent Markham described his time at the Sellafield plant. There were lots of minor accidents, which was normal for such a huge and complex site employing thousands of people. The laws of statistical probability suggested that in a site the size of a small town there were bound to be human errors resulting in accidents. In fact, Vincent was proud of the safety record, which indicated far fewer accidents than statistics would predict. This seemed a strange opinion for him to hold in light of what had happened in the storage facility. Nevertheless, all the employees knew that the general public expected there to be no accidents at all, hence the culture of secrecy that had developed at the plant. The employees were incredibly loyal to what was arguably one of the best employers in the area: It was certainly the largest. All had a vested interest in protecting the reputation of the facility. This was one of the reasons they all harboured an instinctive loathing of the press which, in their view, was only interested in discrediting the facility, with a view to closing it down.

He began questioning his loyalties after the cover-up was ordered. It was no minor leak that would cause alarm rather than injury. The leak from Tank 19 released huge quantities of highly radioactive waste into the atmosphere. There was an overriding public safety imperative that was completely and deliberately ignored. His concerns were only allayed by the insistence of the management that the radiation readings in the surrounding area were nowhere near as high as they had predicted, which justified their decision to cover up the leak: They would have caused public panic and disruption for little justification.

Vincent was horrified when Hudson and Susannah informed him about Terleski's own role in altering the radiation readings. He looked over the documents they had brought along, which included two sets of records for the recorded radiation levels across the United Kingdom. One set comprised the original and accurate readings, the other was Terleski's adulterated ones. Vincent was outraged.

'We've been living amongst this for twenty years? And those bastards in London knew about this all along?' He was shaking. 'My little girl died because of this! Your uncle helped to kill her!' Markham's voice broke with the emotion and he choked back tears.

The accusation stung bitterly and Susannah felt the shame overwhelm her. She felt tainted by association, and hung her head.

'It's not her fault,' Hudson intervened gently. 'She's trying to get this exposed, remember.'

'Speaking of which, we need to get back to London,' interrupted Gregory.

Vincent took a deep breath. 'I'm sorry to snap at you like that,' he apologised to Susannah. 'This is all a bit sudden…You mentioned that you think your lives are at risk? What about me?' Vincent asked Hudson, bringing the conversation back to his own immediate concerns.

'The paper will protect you,' intervened Gregory. 'And once we've published, no one will dare touch you. Our safety depends on publishing this story as soon as possible.'

'But how much of a risk is there? I just want to know what to expect.'

Hudson exchanged looks with Susannah.

'I was shot at yesterday. The bullet just clipped me, nothing major. Just a cut. But they were trying to kill me.'

Vincent swallowed, clearly frightened. 'They *shot* you?'

Hudson nodded, regretting mentioning it now.

'Look, I'm not sure about this.'

'But we need your help, Mr Markham. You're our only chance. And this is your chance to get at Millburn. He's responsible for all this, for everything that happened…for your daughter…'

'We can't let them get away with it,' begged Susannah. 'Please help us.'

Vincent took another deep breath and ran a hand through his hair. It was a big decision to take, the stakes seemed so much higher than before. He caught sight of a picture of Charlotte on the mantelpiece and that made his mind up. Yes, he owed it to her. He had to be strong for her. He had to make Millburn pay, whatever the risk to himself.

'Okay. I'll do it.'

'We need to get back to London, right now. Can you come with us?'

Vincent nodded. He had nothing else scheduled, but his mind was in a whirl from the pace of events.

'We should get out of here as soon as we can,' Gregory continued. 'Are we all set to go?'

'Where are we going in London?' asked Vincent, pale and frightened.

'Straight to the newspaper. They're ready to run the story, we just need to include a short interview with you.'

'Do I need to bring anything?'

'Don't worry about anything, the paper will sort you out.'

Vincent still looked worried and thought about it for a few moments. 'Can you just give me five minutes to sort myself out? I need to cancel a couple of appointments for tomorrow.'

'Try to be quick,' Gregory advised. 'I'll give my boss a call; tell him you've agreed to help us. He'll be very pleased.'

He pulled out his mobile, unaware that it was silently broadcasting their exact location. He dialled Dunscombe's direct line, only to receive a persistent beeping. The display on the phone indicated that no service was available. Cursing, he tried again, but the result was the same. *Bloody phone*. Must be the surrounding hills blocking the signal.

'Have you got a phone?' he asked Hudson and Susannah.

'James lost his and the battery's gone on mine. We haven't had a chance to charge it up.'

'Mr Markham? Could I borrow your phone, please?'

'Of course, no problem.'

'Thanks. I won't be long.'

Gregory found the phone in the kitchen and punched the number in, copying it from his mobile, and held the receiver to his ear while he waited for it to go through. He frowned and pressed redial.

Nothing. He pressed the button a couple of times and listened.

There was no dial tone. Nothing.

'Is your phone okay, Mr Markham?'

'Yes, it's fine. That's the one you called me on earlier.'

'It doesn't seem to be working now.'

'What? Hang on, let me have a look.' He came through into the kitchen and tried for himself. 'I don't understand. It was absolutely fine earlier.'

Hudson came in to have a look as well. 'What's the problem?'

'Phone's out,' replied Gregory. 'I can't get hold of the office.'

Hudson felt the hairs on his neck rise. 'This isn't right. Something's not right about this.'

'What do you mean?' asked Vincent quietly.

Hudson said nothing, feeling a growing sense of unease. His sixth sense telling him that something was very, very wrong.

'We need to get out of here,' urged Hudson. 'Now!'

Vincent and Gregory barely had time to register this when a loud knocking at the front door startled them. They froze to the spot, staring at the door.

'Shh,' cautioned Hudson. He crept past a frightened-looking Susannah and tried to get a view from the sitting room window. He could just make out a well-built man on the front step, wearing outdoor clothing.

'Mr Markham! Open up please, sir. It's the police!'

Hudson shook his head at the now terrified Vincent, and motioned for them to head towards the rear of the house.

'Mr Markham! Open the door or we will have to make a forced entry.'

Vincent closed his eyes. This wasn't happening, *couldn't* be happening. Hudson edged along the window to get a better look at the man on the doorstep, and felt a jolt of fear as he recognised him. The man in the hospital!

'Quick, we need to get out of here,' hissed Hudson. 'Out the back door, now.' They hurried towards the back door and had just stepped outside into the garden, when a burly man vaulted over the stone wall that constituted the boundary of Vincent's property, stopping when he saw them, as surprised as they were.

Hudson briefly considered making a run for it, but was unable to get beyond thinking about how to get Susannah into safety with him. His train of thought was brought to a swift conclusion as the man pulled out a semi-automatic pistol.

'Back in the house,' the man ordered in a gravely voice that brooked no dissent, gesticulating with the pistol.

In terror, they all filed silently back into Vincent's house.

'On the floor, hands on your heads,' the man instructed. When they were in position, he kept them covered with his pistol and opened the front door with his spare hand, letting his accomplice in. The accomplice grunted with satisfaction when he saw them. He fished in his pocket and produced four nylon wrist restraints, similar to the nylon ties used to secure bundles of electrical cables.

'Hands behind your backs,' he ordered. Hudson felt his bowels loosen involuntarily. With no choice, he put his hands behind him. The man slipped the loop over them and pulled tightly, causing Hudson to wince as the sharp plastic cut into his flesh. Once done up, the bindings could not be loosened. They could only be removed with a knife. The tough plastic could not be broken by force alone, especially in the position they had been tied. They were all entirely helpless. For some reason, their feet had not been bound, but the reason for this would soon become apparent.

One of the men signalled for his accomplice to follow him into the kitchen, where they held a brief conference in hushed tones. Hudson strained to listen, but could hear little. The other three captives were ashen-faced and Hudson realised that he was only one capable of thinking beyond their immediate predicament. The shock and fear had had a paralysing effect on the rest of them. Thinking fast, Hudson considered the options. With his legs free, he could make a run for the front door, but he would struggle to open it before they caught him. With a sinking feeling, he realised that he should have run when he had the chance to in the garden. He cursed himself. Could that have been a fatal error, with no second chance? He had never been in a position where his life potentially hung on such a seemingly banal choice: run or stand still. The gravity of the situation had not even sunk in fully until his hands had been bound. Is this how the Jews felt when they were herded into the gas chambers? All those opportunities to escape that had been squandered; fooling themselves that it couldn't happen to them; that the appalling rumours couldn't possibly be true; that if they cooperated then nothing bad would happen.

His grandfather, who had served in one of the war crimes investigation units at the end of the Second World War, had told him how lines of people, stripped naked, had queud to be machine-gunned in the ravines of Babi Yar. They knew what was coming, could see and hear it, yet they had stood still, meekly awaiting their turn, hoping against hope that some miracle would intervene to save them; perhaps if they cooperated they would be spared. Tens of thousands had let themselves be methodically shot in the open air by a handful of SS soldiers. Until now, Hudson had found it incredulous that people could willingly submit themselves to such a fate. If certain death awaited you, then why not at least run or try to overpower your captors? What have you got to lose? But now, he recognised the paralysing fear, which dulled the senses, prevented all circumspection and instead focused the brain on the immediate source of the terror. Survival depended on breaking that paralysing fear, considering the options of escape. And then seizing the opportunity. At Babi Yar a pitiful few had survived, either by jumping into the pits before the machine-gun bullets hit them, or leaping from the transport lorries carrying them from the holding centres in the surrounding Ukrainian towns. Hudson thought about this intensely and vowed to seize the first opportunity that presented itself.

After their brief conference in the kitchen, the more senior of the men took a mobile phone out of his pocket and headed into the garden. Hudson could hear him talking, but again could not make out any of the conversation. Susannah began shaking with fear and he rubbed his knee against hers to reassure her. Gregory was doing his best to look tough, but his fear was plainly obvious too. Vincent was grey and withdrawn.

Hudson stole a glance at the man watching guard over them. He looked every inch a thug. Closely-cropped salt and pepper hair, a brutish face. The man was well-built and clearly very fit, judging by his agility in vaulting the garden wall. However, what really caught the attention were his eyes. They were sunken, dark, devoid of humour and utterly dispassionate. The eyes of a killer. Then an awful realisation dawned on Hudson. The two men had made no attempt to hide their faces from their prisoners. That could only mean one thing:

They were all going to die.

35

In London, Kroll received Trevor's phone call with jubilation. At last, they had them. It was all going to be fine. He gave his instructions to Trevor, who hung up to carry them out. Kroll clapped his hands together and picked the phone up, dialling Millburn's mobile.

'Charles? It's Peter. I thought you should be first to know: We've got them!'

'Excellent news, Peter. Excellent.' Millburn's relief was evident. 'I knew you'd get them in the end.' Mending bridges now. It had only been a couple of days earlier when he was threatening Kroll. 'Now that Red Dawn is safe, we can move on. There will be a substantial bonus in this for you, Peter.'

'Thank you, Charles. It's appreciated.'

'Not at all, Peter. Good work should always be rewarded….Just one little thing. What about our mutual friends in the north?'

'As I said, Trevor and Julian are dealing with them right now.'

'It was Trevor and Julian I had in mind.'

'Ah, yes. I see. Don't worry. There will be no trace leading back to us, I'll make sure of it. Red Dawn is safe.'

'As it should be, dear fellow, as it should be. Good bye, Peter.'

Millburn placed his mobile back in his pocket and settled back into the soft leather seat of the Bentley, a smile across his urbane face.

He was going to make it. Perhaps he had been a bit rash placing his options on the stock market through Simon Goldstein, his special broker, before he knew for certain that the journalists had been dealt with. But it didn't matter now. He had got a better price before the rumour mill had kicked in and started edging up the share price. If all went to plan and the government confirmed Gencor Energy PLC as favoured bidder for the nuclear contracts, he would stand to collect as much as £200million on the options. Perhaps more. Kroll could have a slice of that. Let bygones be bygones.

His chauffeur was ferrying him to his country estate in Surrey, an impressive pile with a hundred acres of land. Not enough. Millburn thought a thousand acres was more appropriate, but every penny of his wealth was currently tied up in the stock options. As soon as he had it back, with a vast profit, he would set about buying up the surrounding farms, making offers the owners could not possibly refuse. He felt as though he owned them already. It was a good feeling. Very good indeed.

*

Trevor glanced around Vincent's kitchen, and his eyes fell on the knife block. He selected a wicked-looking filleting knife and stood in the doorway to the sitting room, sharpening it with a butcher's steel. He mulled over Kroll's instructions. *Make sure you find out what evidence they have, all of it, before you finish things off.* To save time, Trevor was going to have to be brutal. It tended to yield effective results in a short time. He weighed up the cowed huddle on the floor. Yes, the lad. He seemed the strongest and in control at the moment. And he was in love with the girl. Weaken him first, then start on her. Trevor whispered to Julian, who pulled a chair up behind Hudson, sat down and grabbed him by the hair, pulling his head back, holding it tightly between his knees. Trevor swaggered up to him, and examined the knife, turning the blade in front of Hudson's now terrified eyes. Hudson tried to struggle, but Julian gripped his head with a vice-like grip. Trevor reached forward and, with his left hand, stretched Hudson's right eye-lid open. He pressed the tip of the knife into the soft flesh under the eye ball and exerted gentle pressure.

'What information have you got and where is it?' Trevor asked quietly.

'I don't know,' stammered Hudson, as bravely as he could. The knife went in a bit deeper and Hudson cried out in pain and terror.

'Yes you do. Tell me.'

'Fuck off,' Hudson gasped, recklessly. 'You're going to kill us anyway.' Vincent shut his eyes, to avoid seeing what was coming next. Hudson braced himself for the onslaught of pain, but Trevor simply made a grim smile and pulled the knife away. As an afterthought, he kicked Hudson viciously in the side, on the stitched up bullet wound. Hudson cried out with the excruciating pain as the stitches tore open and warm blood flowed down his side.

'Don't worry. We won't miss you next time,' promised Trevor with a leer as Julian released him. Hudson slumped to the floor, gasping in agony. Any doubts that the hostages harboured about the intentions of their captors had been brutally dispelled: They were going to be shot.

Julian then grabbed hold of Susannah, holding her head back in a similar fashion with her long blond hair.

'No! Leave her alone!' pleaded Hudson from the floor.

Trevor smiled sadistically and placed the knife under her ear and began slowing slicing upwards. Susannah screamed with the burning pain as the knife began cutting into her.

'Stop it! Please stop it!' begged Hudson. 'I'll tell you whatever you want, just leave her alone, please!'

'See? That wasn't so difficult was it?' commented Trevor. 'Shame. I was enjoying myself. Perhaps I'll have some more fun with her in a minute. You can watch, if you like. We won't mind.' He winked at Julian, who chuckled unpleasantly. Trevor always did have a way with women.

'Don't touch her!' protested Hudson. Susannah was shaking uncontrollably, going into shock, while Vincent and Gregory looked on, aghast. A thin trickle of blood ran down Susannah's neck, staining her top.

Hudson told them everything. The dossier, the document box, the taped meetings, the datasheets. He explained about the meeting with Vincent, and the plan to publish the story in the Guardian, with Gregory's help. Trevor laughed at that.

'There isn't going to be a story. Do you honestly think we're going to let that happen?'

'Bastards,' muttered Gregory.

'Yeah? What are you going to do about it, pal?'

'What are you going to do to us?' asked Vincent quietly.

'Shut up. All of you.'

It soon became clear to Trevor and Julian that all the information they sought was in Gregory's car. The newspaper just needed Vincent's corroboration of the details of the accident before they could publish. When he was satisfied, Trevor went outside to call Kroll, to brief him on what they had discovered. Satisfied with what he heard, Kroll gave him the go-ahead to proceed. The four were too much of a threat to be left alive. The time had come to bring the matter to an end. Then they could concentrate on Dunscombe and prevent the paper from publishing anything.

Hudson sensed the change in mood as soon as Trevor returned. He conferred quietly in the corner with Julian, who nodded grimly.

'Get up!' barked Trevor, gesticulating with his gun. They complied meekly, struggling to their feet, their legs like jelly. They were all terrified.

'Right, you two in front of me, now!' Trevor ordered Hudson and Susannah. Hudson felt numb. Was this it? A bullet in the back of the head? Julian opened the front door, checked outside to make sure they weren't being observed, and nodded. Trevor poked the gun into Hudson's back.

'Move! To the road and turn left, get into the car. Quickly!'

This was why their feet had not been bound. It was part of the plan. They were hurried down the short pathway and bundled into the car in which Trevor and Julian had arrived. It was just around the corner, explaining why they hadn't heard it. Behind them, Vincent and Gregory were taken to the Audi and similarly bundled into the back. With their hands bound tightly behind their backs, there was little any of them could do to resist.

Susannah leaned into Hudson in the back seat of the Ford saloon as Trevor drove them in silence. Hudson glanced at her, trying to be strong for her sake. He could feel her shaking though the thin material of her top.

The car headed up towards the Northern Lakes, along busy roads full of tourists; a different world outside the vehicle. Finally, they turned off onto a small and deserted minor road. The car threaded its way through fields enclosed with dilapidated stone walls, past sheep sauntering casually by the roadside. The beauty of the scenery contrasted horribly with their predicament. At this moment, Hudson would give anything to have the chance to walk through those fields, hand in hand with Susannah. He thought furiously, desperately trying to conjure an escape plan from somewhere, but nothing would present itself. Hudson began to experience the onset of despair, knowing that time must be running short.

After another twenty minutes, the road climbed steeply into the bleak, desolate mountains. The slopes surrounding them were scarred by the vast spoil heaps that had been tipped down the mountainsides. Mining country.

They continued up the poorly maintained road, their ears popping with the increase in altitude. Eventually, Trevor pulled off the road and onto a rough track that lead towards more spoil heaps. Apart from a couple of scruffy sheep, there was no one else in sight. In fact, they had only passed one other car on the road. They were well away from the tourist trail.

Hudson could feel the fear well up inside him. He had no doubt that these were the last minutes he was going to spend alive. It was a crushing realisation and he fought the urge to let it overwhelm him. Is what it felt like to be condemned? Taking the last steps from the cell to the scaffold? Hudson legs felt the nausea spread from the pit of his stomach through his body. Suddenly his bowels felt incredibly loose and he clenched hard to prevent soiling himself. That would be the final indignity. He struggled discreetly against the restraints, but the tough, sharp nylon cut cruelly into his wrists. There was nothing he could do to free himself. With mounting terror, he realised that only a miracle was going to save them now.

The car bounced on the uneven track and disappeared out of view of the road behind the spoil heaps, coming to a stop in a small rubble-strewn clearing, which must have been the centre of operations in the old mining days. Glimpses of heavily rusted railway tracks peeped through the rubble and thin vegetation. The old tracks made their way up to some equally rusty corrugated iron sheeting that presumably concealed a disused mine entrance.

Shit, this is it, thought Hudson, looking around wildly for an escape route. As the car came to a halt, Gregory's commandeered Audi pulled up alongside with Julian at the wheel. In the back seat, Vincent and Gregory were pale-faced, having come to the same conclusion as Hudson. Trevor climbed out to speak with Julian. Again, the captives could not hear the conversation.

An image flashed through Hudson's mind, terrorising him. It was from video footage taken in Bosnia-Herzegovina by Serb paramilitaries. The Serbs had captured and beaten some young Bosnian men, barely adults, then driven them to their execution in an orchard. The bloodied and bound men were filmed climbing down from the lorry and made to lie against a grass verge. They must have known what fate awaited them as the laughing Serbs fired shots into the ground next to their victims, taunting them cruelly for no other reason but to amuse themselves. Again Hudson had wondered why they didn't run or fight. Instead, they barely flinched as the bullets slapped into the earth inches from their heads. It seemed inexplicable, not to at least try to resist, escape. But now he understood. Fear, all consuming fear, sapped the will to resist. It paralysed the brain and body. For those who knew their ultimate, inevitable fate, the final shot would end the mental torment, so some victims welcomed it. The only chance of survival came with overcoming that fear, channelling it into action, extroverting rather than introverting it. If you accepted you were going to die, you *would* die.

With huge effort, Hudson found reserves of willpower that he didn't realise he possessed. He wasn't going to be a victim. If the opportunity arose, he would fight to live.

It was Susannah's turn first. The car door on her side was opened and strong hands reached in, grabbing hold of her. She was hauled out of the car, sobbing hysterically. Then they dragged her roughly towards the boot of the neighbouring Audi and unceremoniously dumped her in it, slamming the lid down on her.

Then they came back for Hudson. He struggled against the strong hands that grabbed him, and lashed out with his feet, managing to land a blow on Trevor's stomach before he was punched hard in the groin. Doubled up in pain, he found he could not resist for any longer. They dragged him out of the car and Julian grabbed him firmly around the ankles to prevent any further kicking. The two killers carried him around to the boot of the Mondeo and dropped him hard. Hudson gasped in pain as he landed on protruding edge of the spare wheel kit. The lid slammed down and he was in pitch blackness.

Outside, he heard the doors of the Audi open.

'Get out,' ordered a voice that clearly belonged to Trevor.

'No, please no! I don't want to die, please no!' begged Gregory, sobbing.

'Shut up and get out!'

'Please don't kill me! I won't tell anyone if you let me go, please don't kill me, please, no, no no!' There was the sound of a slap, as metal connected with flesh. Gregory cried out in pain.

'I told you to shut up. Now, get out! Both of you!'

Hudson heard noises followed by the car doors slamming shut. In the darkness of the boot, he could see the Bosnians climbing down from the truck, white faced and bloodied.

'Walk!'

The Bosnians were taking their last ever steps, knowing they were going to their deaths, but accepting it. Some were shaking, but still they did as they were told. Docile, compliant. Unresisting.

'Walk!' shouted Trevor again.

Hudson heard Gregory and Vincent stumble away on the rough ground, the noise growing fainter. They were must be taking them to the disused mine, thought Hudson. Presumably, they wanted to deal with them first, and needed to ensure that Hudson and Susannah were safely locked up in the meantime. It wouldn't be long before it was their turn.

This was his last chance. He had nothing to lose.

Hudson's back was against the rear seats of the Mondeo. He tried kicking at the bootlid, but to no avail. There wasn't enough room for him to get any force into it. In the pitch black, he felt his panic rising. *He had to succeed, he had to live.* He kicked hard again, hurting his knee on the underside of the boot lid. He wanted to live, so much. There was so much left to do with his life. He kicked and kicked, but still nothing. In desperation, he contorted himself and tried to push the boot open with his feet, his back braced firmly against the seats. Suddenly, he realised the *seat* was *moving*. He pushed again. Yes! The back of the seat was flexing. That was it! He pushed again, as hard as he could, but the seat just flexed. It wouldn't pop out of its restraining catches. *Think! Just think!*

Then he had it.

He kicked upwards and managed to dislodge the parcel shelf. For the first time, he saw light. A chink of beautiful light, a sight to lift the soul. With his feet, he pushed and kicked the narrow parcel shelf out of the way. *If only his hands were free.* He managed to get onto his knees and slide his head and shoulders up between the back window and the rear seats. He needed to find the seat release catch, to allow the seats to push forward. There was a catch on either side of the seats but, try as he might, he couldn't move the catch. He needed his hands. He tried to do it with his chin, wincing in pain as the cut on his lip inflicted by Alex Warburton tore open once more. He tasted blood, but carried on trying, desperate.

Time was ticking. They would be returning from the mine at any moment. These were his last precious seconds alive. He had to make every single one of them count. Lying on his back in the boot, he kicked up at the toughened glass of the rear window. *Kick, kick, kick!* Nothing. *Kick, kick, KICK!* It started to move. Yes! The seals were going. Then another kick managed to shatter it, further loosening the seals holding in place. With one final kick, the window broke free and the glass fell out in one shattered piece. He wriggled around and stood up in the boot space, pushing himself up through the open back window. There was no one in sight.

Time stood still, every second an eternity.

Two shots rang out, in quick succession. They came from the mine. With horror he realised that Vincent and Gregory were dead and it was his turn next.

He had run out of time.

36

Alan Dunscombe was an extremely worried man. He knew he was playing a dangerous game fooling the man who had demanded the return of the Red Dawn evidence. But he had no intention of allowing himself to be bullied by such people. The old friend he had visited for advice had been horrified by the situation but had suggested the stalling tactic. It would buy time until Gregory found a witness, allowing them to publish.

Dunscombe had no idea who had threatened him and his family but, whilst he had been out of the office visiting his old friend, his IT people had prepared a copy of the recorded phone call onto a flash drive. The tiny electronic stick protruded from Dunscombe laptop and he listed to the call again. All calls to Dunscombe's private line were recorded as a matter of routine. It helped with recalling the facts, especially if he'd had another hard night in the company of Mr Jameson.

Amarjit Chohan frowned as he listened to the conversation being replayed. Although the sound reproduction through the laptop was a bit tinny, the message was clear. The mild mannered lawyer did not take kindly to such bullying tactics.

'It's one thing threatening you, but your family? It's despicable.'

'Tell me about it,' muttered Dunscombe, feeling a huge weight of responsibility towards his wife and children.

'Perhaps it's just me, but doesn't that voice sound familiar to you?'

'Yes…I know what you mean. But I can't place it. Terry?'

Terry Gallimore, the Chief Political Editor, looked up. 'Yeah, I'm sure I've heard it somewhere before, too. But don't ask me who.'

'Could we do a voice analysis?'

'No, unless we compare it to voices we already suspect. IT could do that for us, I suppose, but we don't have enough time or computing power to trawl the internet looking for a match.'

Dunscombe shook his head in irritation. 'And where the hell is Gregory?' he demanded angrily of no one in particular. 'He should have called in by now. We need to get this story on the road before any one realises what we've got here.'

Chohan and Gallimore both shrugged. There was nothing they could do.

The phone on Dunscombe's desk rang. His direct line. *Gregory!*

'Gregory? What have you got?' Dunscombe breathed excitedly into the phone. Then his manner changed. '…What?…Look, who is this? If you think you can threa…'

He listened quietly, the colour draining from his face. It was a different man who put the phone down.

'They know,' he stated woodenly.

'What?' asked Chohan.

'They know about the Red Dawn tapes. And the list of people Gregory's got.'

'*How?*' exclaimed Gallimore, incredulous.

Dunscombe was pale. His hand visibly shaking, he reached for the bottle in his desk and pulled out a packet of cigarettes. He rarely smoked, but certain occasions warranted it. This was one of them.

'I'm not sure, but this doesn't look good,' he muttered quietly, draining the glass and drawing heavily on the cigarette, thinking furiously.

'Who did you go to see before?' asked Chohan suspiciously. Dunscombe caught the direction of his question.

'No, it wasn't him. Definitely.'

'But who was it?' asked Gallimore.

'I can't tell you. But he's on our side.'

'Well, in that case, can he help?'

'He already is. But this changes everything. It might be too late.' He sighed and rubbed his face, the worry very evident. 'Where the *fuck* is Gregory? Try and call him, will you?'

With urgency, Gallimore dialled Gregory's number but shook his head.

'The phone's switched off,' he reported.

Dunscombe became more agitated. 'The only way they could know about the tapes and the list is if something's happened to Gregory and the other two.'

'Who was on the phone? Was it the same person as before?'

'No. It was different.' Dunscombe ran a shaking hand over his thinning grey hair. 'But they said they would do whatever it took to protect Red Dawn.'

'Gencor?'

'No. He knew something about me that only one organisation could know.'

'What?'

'I'd rather not mention it, but let's just say that I'm known to the authorities. It looks like Millburn and Gencor really do have friends in high places. It explains why they knew so much about my family before.'

'Five?'

Dunscombe nodded. 'Looks like that. Either way, we've got to return everything this time, and they mean everything.'

'Shit. If MI5 are involved, we're fucked.'

Dunscombe took a deep breath. 'Perhaps.' He took a long drag on the cigarette, his mind churning over the options. 'But there might just be a way out of this…' He explained what had been discussed with his old friend earlier, to an astonished Chohan and Gallimore.

*

Jeremy Langham reflected on the phone call with Dunscombe. He knew he had frightened him. It was a satisfying feeling. Some of these newspaper editors thought they were a law unto themselves; it was about time they were put in their place. Minutes earlier, Kroll had called him with the news that the journalists had been intercepted, along with a former Sellafield engineer who had agreed to talk. The instructions had been simple, brutal: Get rid of them. They were far too dangerous to be left alive.

Without a witness, Dunscombe had nothing. Just wild rumours, the rantings of a suicidal mad man leaving a dossier and a forged tape recording as his parting shot to the world. Langham would destroy Dunscombe once all this was over. He would end his career in the gutter. It was vital for the country. Yes, the new nuclear generation programme was vital for the country. Gencor Energy PLC and Charles Millburn were also vital for the country. People like Dunscombe were not. People who built entire careers out of undermining the country. It was treachery, and a true patriot like Langham would ensure that he paid the price. By now, the two journalists and the girl would have paid the price. Along with that fucking traitor of an engineer.

Langham closed the folder on his desk. Soon the entire episode would be closed.

37

On hearing the shots from inside the disused mine, Hudson felt fear grip him like never before. Time seemed to slow down and he felt as though he was living in a dream. His movements seemed painfully slow and sluggish. Standing up through the rear window opening, his feet on the boot floor of the Mondeo, he was constrained by the fact that his hands were bound behind his back.

He had to get out of the car. Now.

He managed to extricate one foot from the boot space and onto the boot lid, but then he lost his balance in the rush to escape. Feeling himself falling sideways, he had no option but to jump. As hard as he could, he launched himself out of the car, doing his best to make sure his other foot cleared the edge of the rear window. He nearly made it, but his toe just caught under the inside of the boot lid. He toppled over the side of the car, landing heavily on his shoulder. His cheek slammed into the ground, and he felt bones crunch. But the adrenalin was pumping hard and the pain barely registered, the whole side of his face just felt numb.

He was determined to live.

Rolling onto his knees, he staggered to his feet and lurched drunkenly towards the Audi. Surely the two killers would come at any moment now. Turning his bound wrists to the car, he tried to find the boot catch with his fingers, but he was unfamiliar with the car. In frantic desperation, his fingers scrabbled for a boot catch but, as he was working blind, the task was nearly impossible. Tears of frustration ran down his face. He couldn't let Susannah down. He just couldn't. Time dragged on and it seemed like he'd already spent an eternity trying to open the boot and free Susannah. Surely the two killers were coming; by now they must have emerged from the mine opening and seen what he was doing.

Come on, open up, he prayed. Suddenly, as he was about to give up and concede defeat, he felt movement. *Yes!* He pushed the button with his fingers, and heard the magic sound of the boot pop open. They hadn't locked it!

He turned around to face the boot and stared in at Susannah's crumpled form. At first she couldn't believe her eyes, her face contorted in terror at expectation of her turn to be executed.

'James?' she whispered in disbelief at the apparition leaning over her.

'Quick! Get out! We haven't got long!'

In a daze she scrambled into a crouching position and, with no other option, had to roll out head first. Hudson cushioned the fall as much as he could, but she still banged her head on the rough ground, cutting her forehead open. He bullied her onto her feet and they ran as fast as they could away from the clearing. They had only gone twenty metres when Susannah tripped and fell, crashing to the ground again. Hudson doubled back, feeling his panic rise. He coaxed her to her feet again and stole a glance at the mine entrance. To his horror a figure emerged.

'RUN!' shouted Hudson.

'Hey!' a voice shouted behind them. Suddenly the whole of Hudson's back felt like an enormous target. His skin crawled in anticipation of the bullet hitting him. They ran for their lives along a rough track covered in shale.

'I can't go any further,' sobbed Susannah, stumbling again. 'I can't!'

With mounting desperation, Hudson scanned around for cover. He could just make out an opening to his right, near to a ruined winding house.

'In there! Quick!'

They scrambled over rocks and into the pitch black gloom of the opening. Behind them, they could hear the killer scrambling over the rocks behind them. The other one wouldn't be far behind. They felt their way further into the impenetrable darkness, their own bodies blocking out light from the opening. Behind them the light in the entrance seemed brilliant by contrast to the pitch black in front of them. They were in a trap of their own making. They had no choice but to continue further into the old tunnel.

Hudson felt his way forward with his feet, but the uneven and rubble-strewn floor of the tunnel was treacherous. Susannah kept bumping into him as she tried not to lose him in the darkness. He took another step forward and *bang!* The blow to his head was agonising, causing pinpricks to his peripheral vision, making him stagger and cry out. He had walked into a rocky outcrop to the side of the tunnel roof. They had been too close to the side, where the tunnel roof curved back down into the walls. Progress ground to a snail's pace, as they were reduced to feeling their way forward with hands and feet. The killers would find them in no time. They were trapped. Susannah leaned into him and sobbed gently, realising this was their last tender moment together before oblivion.

A noise from the entrance. They turned to face the bright light of the tunnel opening. There was a shadow, then a human form appeared, silhouetted in black against the backdrop of the brilliant light. He seemed to fill the entire entrance and Hudson could not fail to recognise the object in his hand. The semi-automatic pistol was being held almost casually, such was the killer's confidence that his prey was well and truly cornered. A torch light came on and Hudson knew that this was it. The end. It would only be a matter of seconds before the man found them.

Then it would be over.

*

At the Guardian Newspaper offices, Dunscombe was almost beside himself with worry about Gregory. His plan *had* to work. Gregory would obtain the witness they needed to corroborate their story.

Dunscombe glanced at his Phillipe Patek. They had only an hour at most before they would be forced to hand over the rest of the evidence to another anonymous courier. Gregory had to call soon, or the story would be dead. He was placing his faith in the plan he had discussed with Chohan and Gallimore. But waiting was the toughest part of it and he found himself wrestling with the urge to reach for the bottle.

Although he was oblivious to the fate that had befallen Gregory, Dunscombe recognised that he was playing a dangerous game. His opponent, Gencor Energy, was powerful and resourceful, with the agencies of the state behind it, but Dunscombe had a lifetime of journalistic wiles to fall back on. He wasn't going to concede defeat readily and would take the brinkmanship to the wire.

But he was worried about Gregory. The omens were not good, and each passing minute without news made them worse. What the *hell* had happened?

*

The torch beam played on the damp, rough hewn tunnel walls, advancing towards them, the harbinger of death. Hudson positioned himself in front of Susannah to shield her, and they crouched down, leaning as tightly as they could into the wall. If only Hudson could get his hands free, he could fight, they would have a chance. There were large, sharp stones on the ground, but they were useless unless he could free his hands.

The light came closer, and Hudson tried to shrink against the wall. His heart pounded in his chest and he held his breath. Part of him recognised the euthanasic desire for the torment to be over. His mind was racing, a kaleidoscope of images flashing through his mind. His parents, his childhood.

And then the light fell on them.

Hudson braced himself for the bullet, winced, but was then consumed with a sudden madness. He hurled himself at the torchbearer. There was no thought to it, just the last desperate act of a man about to die. Somehow, he reached the torch before the gun was fired and collided heavily with the figure. He didn't know which one of their two captors it was.

The impact caught the man by surprise and he dropped the torch, which clattered against the wall and went out. There was a loud bang and a flash. The gun had gone off. Hudson didn't know if he was hit or not but lashed out savagely with his head, butting the man as hard as he could, connecting painfully with his skull. The man groaned and they both fell to the ground.

Hudson soon lost his advantage. With his wrists bound behind him, it was always going to be an unequal contest. In the darkness, the killer rolled away from Hudson, and Hudson heard him scrabbling in the dark for his weapon.

This was it. At least he had tried. Hudson shut his eyes, prepared for death. In the darkness, he could hear the man panting with the exertion of the fight. He found the torch. The light came on.

This was it now, surely.

The light shone on Hudson's face, blinding him. He was helpless, waiting for the shot.

'James?'

What?

'James Hudson? You're safe. Don't worry, I'm not going to hurt you.'

38

It took a while for it to sink in. The man had to repeat it before it registered. He turned the torch and shone it on his own face. The face did not belong to one of the two killers. It was a humourless face, pinched and undernourished, with thin emotionless lips. It was a face that did not instil much confidence or human warmth. Hudson still did not move, unable to believe the apparent change in circumstance.

The thin-lipped man turned the torch back and asked Hudson to sit up. Reluctantly, and with extreme wariness, Hudson slowly complied. There was the flash of a knife and Hudson felt his hands released from the tight nylon restraints. The man turned his attention to a terrified Susannah, who cowered against the wall of the tunnel. He made quick work of cutting her restraints, and she fell into Hudson's arms, clinging onto him tightly.

'Come on, follow me.'

'What?'

'We need to get you out of here, quickly.'

'But they're out there,' protested Hudson.

'Trust me. It's okay.'

Hudson took Susannah's hand and followed the man out of the tunnel, into the bright sunlight. He paused on the threshold, reluctant to go any further, but the man turned back to them and made a poor attempt at a reassuring smile. Hudson could see that his headbutt had struck home, as blood trickled from the man's hairline. He glanced at Susannah; she was pale, with blood stains on her collar from her cut ear. Her blond hair was matted with blood, and she had a small cut to her forehead from where she had banged her head whilst escaping from the car boot. She was trembling visibly, not wishing to venture any further, distrustful of the man who had apparently rescued them.

'It's okay. It's safe,' the man reassured them.

'I'm not moving until you tell me what's going on, and what about the others?' asked Hudson quietly.

The man started from the beginning before answering.

'I've been following you for some time. I work for the British Security Service. Name's Scott, by the way. My boss put me onto this case when he realised something was happening to former Civil Servants involved in the Red Dawn programme. It didn't take us long to realise that someone, probably Charles Millburn, was trying to get rid of anyone who could expose it.'

'So why the hell didn't you stop all this sooner?' Hudson demanded angrily.

'I couldn't. My boss was taken ill, and his replacement is helping Millburn cover it up. I found myself alone on this investigation. I couldn't risk using any of my colleagues. I wasn't sure who I could trust on this, and I needed concrete evidence against Millburn before we could move against him.'

'But the Security Service was involved with Red Dawn?'

'Yes. Needs must, I'm afraid. At the time, the decision was the right one. The world has changed since then, and we've changed with it. That's life.'

Hudson shook his head in disgust. Journalistic idealism was getting the better of him.

'It doesn't look like it, does it? If you're acting alone? It's quite obvious to me that you, or your organisation, haven't changed.'

'As I explained, my boss had his concerns, but there are those who wish to keep things as they were. It is your misfortune as well as mine that he was taken ill.'

'And what now?'

'We have enough evidence to charge Millburn. But it might not stop there. This could go right to the top.'

'What do you mean?'

'There is a strong possibility that members of the Cabinet Office knew about the operation to keep Red Dawn quiet, and sanctioned it. An awful lot is riding on the new nuclear generation programme. Millburn has friends in high places.'

'Oh my God,' whispered Hudson. 'You mean all the way to the top, the Prime Minister?'

'Possibly, yes.'

'Shit.'

Hudson felt the fear return with a vengeance. 'So we're not safe yet?'

'No. Sorry.'

Hudson ran a hand over his face and shook his head. The nightmare was never ending. 'You still haven't told me about the others. Are they alright?'

Scott explained how he had followed the car out of London, and attached a satellite tracking device when they stopped at the motorway service station. Having lost track of them overnight, he did not want to take any more chances. He had followed them to their abortive meeting with Peter Buckley, and guessed correctly that the former technician had been uncooperative.

'How did you know we were meeting him?' interrupted Hudson.

'I'll get to that in a minute…'

When the group had driven to Vincent Markham's house, that was when the problems started. Scott had seen the nondescript Mondeo, similar to his own, drive slowly past the house and park up around the corner. He saw two burly men climb out, one of them skirting around the back of the property whilst the other went to the front door.

'It was obvious that they weren't on a social visit, but there was nothing I could do…'

Scott's worst fears were confirmed when he saw the group being led out of the house. He realised that they were now in considerable danger, but had to wait for an opportunity to intervene to present itself.

'I managed to follow you up here at a distance, but I couldn't get too close, in case they saw me and panicked. That wouldn't have been good for you. I had to park down the road and run up here. By the tim I got here, I saw them taking the other two into the mine. I didn't realise you were still in the cars. For all I knew, you were already in there, about to face the music. I just got up there as quickly as I could…'

Upon reaching the mine entrance, Scott could hear Trevor and Julian taunting their victims as they forced them deeper into the tunnel. Taking care not to silhouette himself in the mine entrance, Scott slipped inside after them. Peering forward into the gloom, as his eyes adjusted to the darkness, he could see Gregory in the soft glow of torchlight shining on his back. He was pleading for his life, while Vincent remained deathly silent as they shoved both of them forward roughly. With their attention focused entirely on the task at hand, they failed to spot Scott slip in through the entrance behind them, and the noise of his feet scuffing the detritus-littered tunnel floor was muffled by the commotion being made by Gregory. The two killers were thoroughly absorbed with what they were about to do.

'Shut up!' Trevor snarled at Gregory and pistol whipped him across the back of the head. Gregory cried out in pain and Trevor kicked him hard in the back of the legs. Gregory was catapulted forward, landing hard on the ground, on his hands and knees.

'Please don't kill me, please!' he begged.

'Kneel! Both of you!' snapped Julian. Vincent hesitated, and Julian hit him on the back of the head with the pistol, then grabbed his hair and forced him down to his knees, next to Gregory. Eking out the last precious moments of his life, Gregory slowly raised himself onto his knees. Trevor and Julian were savouring the moment; the visceral thrill of taking a life. This hiatus gave Scott enough time to creep closer.

'Now gentlemen, where would you like it? Back of the head, between the shoulders? We aim to please, don't we Trevor?' Julian snorted. Tears streamed down Gregory's face and he was visibly shaking, unable to control his terror. By contrast, Vincent seemed outwardly calm, resigned to his fate. Internally, though, his main emotion one of bitterness that he had not taken the chance to exact his revenge on the man he held culpable for his daughter's death. In his last moments alive, he thought of her, praying that he was now going to see her again.

'You first, Trevor.'

'No, be my guest, I insist.'

Holding the torch in left hand, Julian lifted his semi-automatic pistol, cocked the hammer and slipped off the safety catch. A round was already chambered, so he didn't have to load it first. He pressed the muzzle against the back of Vincent's head, who felt the cold, sharp metal and tensed in anticipation of the bullet tearing through his skull. Next to him, Gregory closed his eyes, shaking uncontrollably.

This was it. His parents, first love, family Christmases, childhood trips; all flashed through his mind. Oh God, this was it.

There was an ear-splitting bang, with a bright flash of light, and Gregory felt Vincent's body being thrown forward onto the ground next to him. His whole body convulsed in terror. It was his turn now. A spilt second later, a second loud gunshot rang out. This was it. This was death.

Gregory was dead.

But he was still kneeling.

Perhaps that was death. Your spirit trapped in its last mortal position for eternity. Perhaps the loss of consciousness is not instant when you are shot in the head. He felt no pain. This was heaven surely. Then he felt the trickle of urine down his leg.

And then he felt a hand on his shoulder.

'It's okay, you're safe.'

Gregory slowly opened his eyes, trembling. In the faint light cast by a torch lying on the ground, its beam pointing at the side of the tunnel, he could make out a body lying on the ground in front of him, face down and arms spread out. There was a sticky, dark, shiny mess at the back of his head. Gregory glanced to his right. Vincent was still kneeling next to him, also shaking.

Vincent was still alive!

Turning slowly, Gregory couldn't make out the face behind him. But he saw Trevor's body was crumpled in a heap behind him, slumped at a funny angle against the side of the tunnel.

'Where are the other two?' asked the disembodied voice urgently, insistently.

It took Gregory and Vincent a long time to answer and, for a horrible moment, Scott thought he was too late.

'Where are James and Susannah?' he persisted, fearing the worse.

Vincent found his voice first.

'In the cars. They put them in the boots. They were going to do us first and come back for them.'

Scott cut the nylon wrist restraints and gave them the torch dropped by Julian. He kept the other one for himself and made his way out. 'I'll go and get them. Just take it easy - you've been through quite an ordeal.'

Scott headed out of the mine entrance just in time to see Hudson and Susannah making a run for it, their hands bound behind their backs. How the hell they'd escaped was beyond him.

'Hey!' he shouted out, but they ignored him and carried on. He began running towards them, impeded by the treacherous ground, wary of turning an ankle. They saw him coming and, clearly mistaking him for someone else, dived into another old tunnel dug into the mountain. Realising their state of fear and confusion, he approached the tunnel cautiously, not wishing to frighten them further. Unfortunately, in his haste he had not holstered his weapon, giving Hudson and Susannah genuine good reason to be frightened.

Finally, using the retrieved torch, he had come across Hudson and Susannah huddled in the tunnel. He was about to tell them it was all going to be fine, when Hudson had leapt at him, a desperate last stand, the actions of a cornered man.

Pinching his bleeding nose ruefully, he congratulated Hudson on his efforts. The gun had gone off when it was jolted against a rock, but fortunately the bullet didn't hit or ricochet into anyone, a miracle considering the confined space they were in.

And here they all were.

Emerging into the sunlight, Hudson and Susannah looked towards the parked cars and couldn't believe their eyes. Vincent and

Gregory were sitting on the bonnet of the Mondeo, rubbing their wrists to restore the circulation now that their nylon wrist cuffs had been removed. There was a large, overweight man talking to them and Hudson turned to Scott, a quizzical look on his face.

Before Scott could explain, Hudson and Susannah found themselves part of a group embrace. It was clear that they were all severely shaken by their experience, and there was no need for words to express the feeling of relief they felt at seeing each other alive.

When they had finished hugging each other, they were all silent, unsure of what to do next.

'May I introduce Detective Inspector Clive Brannigan, Manchester CID. He has been assisting me.'

Brannigan shook hands with them.

'You two were very resourceful. I've been after you in connection with Alex Warburton's murder.'

Hudson's spirits sank. 'We didn't do it, I swear!' he shouted, but Brannigan held his hands up.

'I know, I know,' he said defensively. 'Scott here has briefed me fully. I think I can safely say that the culprits are lying back there in that tunnel. Forensics should be able to confirm it. I know all about Red Dawn, and what your uncle did,' he continued, addressing Susannah.

'So the police are on our side?' asked Hudson.

'Not officially yet. I have been working undercover with Scott. Let's just say he was quite persuasive at first. But now I can help with your case.'

'So what happens next?' asked Hudson.

'We're dealing with powerful and dangerous people. We can't go and arrest them just like that. We will need protection,' replied Scott.

'*You* can't protect us?' exclaimed Hudson, incredulous.

'It's not as easy as that. I'm regarded as a rogue officer at the moment; Langham will see that I'm silenced.'

'Langham?'

'The new Director General. He is strongly of the opinion that Red Dawn be kept secret, and he has close links with Devereaux at the Cabinet Office. They will see that any investigation is quashed before it gets off the ground. You'd be surprised at what gets covered up.'

'What about you?' asked Hudson, turning to Brannigan.

'Scott believes that my superiors will pull the case under pressure from London. But I am willing to help you.'

'What the hell does that mean?' Hudson demanded. 'First you say you can't help us, and then you say you can.'

'I have an idea,' replied Scott on Brannigan's behalf.

'What?'

'Simple. Stick with your original plan.'

'What, you mean publish the story?'

'Yes. The publicity will protect you, and prepare the ground for Millburn and others to be arrested.'

'For Red Dawn?'

'No. That was an official government policy, murky as it was. We can do Millburn for murder and attempted murder instead.'

'So he'll get away with everything else? With Red Dawn?' Vincent spoke for the first time, clearly outraged.

'In theory, yes, in practice, no. He'll go down for this, lose his career, everything. He'll pay, but in other ways.'

'I want him to pay for Red Dawn,' insisted Vincent in a quiet, but very angry voice. Scott shrugged, not appreciating his reasoning.

'Difficult to bring a prosecution for something protected by the Official Secrets Act. His defence will also be that he was acting in the national interest. Don't worry, we can get him for something else instead.'

'You don't understand,' muttered Vincent, shaking his head in disgust. Then, after a couple of moments of thought, he turned and walked off towards the mine opening. Susannah made to follow him.

'Leave him,' ordered Scott. 'Give him some space.'

'But he's upset.'

'Leave him.'

There was an awkward silence. Susannah was minded to ignore Scott, but the steeliness of his tone gave her pause for thought, and she turned back to the group.

'You never told me how you found us in London,' asked Hudson.

'Well, I lost you in Stratford, after you escaped from the hospital. That's when I crossed paths with DI Brannigan here. I heard the police reports that you had been dropped off by a taxi at Doctor Terleski's house, but that was when I lost track of you. I explained the situation with Clive, who agreed to come under cover with me. We went to visit your editor, Donald Winston. Figured you'd probably get in touch with him.'

'Don was in on this?' exclaimed Hudson, shocked.

'We didn't give him a choice, I'm afraid.' Scott's thin lips broke into a glimmer of a smile. 'Anyway, we found out about your visit to the Guardian.'

Hudson nodded as it all became clear. But something still bothered him. There was something missing from Scott's explanation, he was sure. His subconscious detected an inconsistency in the story, but he couldn't place his finger on it.

'So we need to get back to the paper, get the story published?'

'Yes, the sooner the better. Especially now you have Vincent as a witness.'

'Where is he?' asked Hudson, looking around.

'He went up towards the mine,' replied Susannah.

'I'll go and fetch him, have a word with him,' muttered Scott, and headed off towards the mine entrance. There was another silence as they began to absorb what had recently happened to them all. Brannigan cleared his throat and tucked his shirt in over his prominent belly.

'I suppose I owe you both an apology,' he stated quietly, awkwardly. 'It seemed so obvious to us at the time, but that was before I knew about what your uncle had been involved in. Especially when you consider the altercation you had with Mr Warburton the day before he died. I thought it may have been an accident. He turned up at your flat, there was another fight, he was stabbed. You didn't intend to kill him. You would have got away with manslaughter. But I know that didn't happen. We know he was killed there, though.'

Susannah put her hands to her mouth in shock at the thought of it. 'The bloodstains?' she whispered.

'Yes. How did you know?'

'My flatmate called me. And the arresting officer at the hospital told James.

Brannigan nodded. 'We think he went to your flat to confront James, especially after his arrest for assault. He probably wanted another pop at you. He was that type of person, by all accounts. He may have disturbed the people looking for evidence of your uncle's involvement in Red Dawn. They killed him for that. It was probably the same two back there.'

'Oh my God,' breathed Susannah. 'The tapes. They were after the tapes. My uncle wrote to me, with a clue. He said that he had evidence to support his dossier, the one he emailed to James. That's why we went to his house.'

'Even though your flat had been burgled?'

'Yes, but we didn't know about Alex then. After my flatmate called me, we just thought it was another break-in. There are loads in that area. The important thing for us was to find the evidence, so we didn't go back.'

'You see, to us it looked like you were running away. Then when James was admitted to hospital with a suspected gunshot wound, it seemed obvious to us. We thought Mr Warburton may have had a gun, James acted in self defence but ended up killing him, then you both panicked and disposed of the body and gun, and ran.'

'No. They found us at Doctor Terleski's house,' stated Hudson. 'That's when I was shot. They were trying to steal the evidence off us.'

'The same two men?' asked Brannigan, nodding towards the mine shaft.

'Yes.'

This thought prompted them to glance at the mine opening, which contained the two bodies, to see Scott re-emerging with Vincent. He was visibly distressed, and they could see Scott put a consoling arm around his shoulders. They all felt for him. All of them had been through a terrible time together. Although Vincent initially seemed to have coped better than Gregory, who was still shaking, the revelation about Millburn and the slim likelihood that he would be charged over Red Dawn seemed to have tipped him over the edge. Scott steered him gently towards the group, where both Hudson and Susannah consoled him. It helped take their minds off their own problems. Hudson glanced at Scott, as if to ask what the hell Vincent had been doing inside the tunnel but Scott, reading Hudson's mind, just shrugged. He had no idea.

'Right, we need to get out of here,' Scott stated. 'We need to get to London as quickly as possible.'

*

Dunscombe was still at his desk when the call came through. He snatched up the handset.

'Yes?'

'Alan Dunscombe?'

'Who the hell is this?'

'I'm with Gregory, Susannah and James. They're all safe, but they've been through a lot.'

Dunscombe sat up.

'They're alright?'

'Yes, they're fine, but they've been through a very bad experience this afternoon.'

Dunscombe felt the relief wash over him, and gave Amarjit Chohan and Terry Gallimore a thumbs-up.

'Who did you say you were?'

'I didn't. The name's Scott. I'll explain the rest later, but I thought you should know - we have a witness, so you can publish the story.'

'Brilliant! Bloody brilliant! Who is it?'

'Vincent Markham. The cooling system engineer.'

'He can corroborate what actually happened at Sellafield?'

'Yes, I believe so.'

'We need to get him here as soon as possible. Where are you now?'

'The Lakes. We're flying down by helicopter, should be with you in an hour or so.'

'Can I speak to Gregory?'

'He's not too good. I'll put you on to Hudson.'

There was a clattering noise as the headset was transferred. Dunscombe could hear the whine of the helicopter engine over the telephone.

'Mr Dunscombe?' shouted Hudson.

'Glad you're all okay, we were getting worried.'

'We're okay now, but there's another chapter to the story. Tell you about it when we get there. We have the witness, so get ready to print. The story's a go.'

'We're on it. Well done. Hurry up and get down here.'

Hudson finished the call and passed the headset back to Scott, who sat up in front with the pilot. He had invoked his authority at the small airfield near Lake Ullswater, requisitioning a helicopter on the spot. Fortunately, one was already cleared and ready to fly down to the helicopter port in Battersea, central London; the airfield provided a regular London service, so it was a routine flight.

On board the helicopter, they felt safe for the first time in what seemed ages, but which was in reality only a couple of days. Susannah sat next to an exhausted Hudson, holding his hand. Gregory was ashen-faced after his ordeal and had barely spoken since. Vincent seemed calm, simply staring out of the window. But only he knew what he had been doing in the cave before Scott had retrieved him, and his mind worked over the opportunity that now presented itself.

39

'You still want to do this, Alan?' cautioned Chohan.

'We don't have a choice. My family is being threatened, Gregory, Hudson and Susannah are all in danger, and the public has a right to know.'

'This engineer is subject to the Official Secrets Act too. You could both go to prison.'

'I'm willing to take the chance. Once this becomes public, they wouldn't dare.'

'But what about you and your family?'

'Let me worry about that.'

Chohan sighed. Once the fiery editor had made his made his mind up on something, there was generally little anyone could do about it. Dunscombe had the unstoppable inertia of a supertanker. It was Chohan's job to make sure he didn't crash into anything.

'What about the courier?'

'What about him?'

'He's waiting downstairs. You have to hand over the tapes, all the copies, and the rest of the documents.'

'You must be fucking joking! Now we have our witness, they can't touch us. Get security to throw him out of the building.'

Chohan shut his eyes, while Gallimore grinned. This was more like it. Dunscombe clapped his hands together, relishing the situation.

'Right, we've got work to do. The helicopter will be landing at Battersea in an hour's time. We need to be ready to run Vincent Markham's story as soon as we've interviewed him. Tidy up the front page and get the web release ready. We publish online as soon as we can. Make sure that we upload the audio files as well.' He tapped the flash drives on his desk, which contained the recordings of the threatening phonecalls he had received. 'They'll regret the day they threatened Alan Dunscombe.'

Just then the phone rang. It was the IT manager.

'Yes…I see…*What?* You're absolutely sure?' Dunscombe exclaimed in surprise. 'It's a definite match? Well done. Good work.' He sat back in his chair with a triumphant look on his face.

'Well, gentlemen. The stakes just got higher. The voice on the first call. We've got a match.' He looked at an expectant Chohan and Gallimore, savouring the moment in anticipation of the stunned silence which would follow.

'It's Giles Devereaux. The PM's Director of Communications.'

40

Peter Kroll realised that something had gone seriously wrong. His repeated attempts to contact Trevor and Julian were in vain. Since they had called him from Vincent Markham's house to receive their final instructions and confirm that they had retrieved all the evidence against Millburn, he had heard nothing. Hudson, the girl, Markham and the other journalist should all be dead by now, their bodies hidden where they would never be found, at the bottom of one of the myriad disused mine shafts that litter the Lake District. So why hadn't Trevor called him to confirm this fact? It was inconceivable that Trevor would not seek to report that the mission was accomplished. No, something had gone dreadfully wrong. It must have. With a mounting sense of panic he called Jeremy Langham.

'Jeremy? Peter Kroll…No, I'm not fine…we might have a problem…'

Langham was pale when he hung up. Moments earlier, Giles Devereaux had also reported that the courier had returned empty-handed from the Guardian's offices, having been forcibly ejected from the building by security staff. He was in the process of considering his response to Alan Dunscombe's petulance when Kroll had called him. Coincidence in the two matters was inconceivable. Langham was also in no doubt whatsoever that something had gone very badly wrong with the operation to dispose of the journalists and their witness.

Collecting his thoughts, he realised that there was only one way to put his suspicions beyond question. He picked up his phone. What he was about to do was highly illegal, though not unprecedented. It was only illegal if the wrong people found out.

'I need immediate surveillance, all media apart from mail…yes, right away…my eyes only…Alan Dunscombe, Guardian Newspaper. Focus on the last two hours. Report to me direct.'

Minutes later, the first report arrived on his computer screen, a breakdown of Alan Dunscombe's email, internet and telephone calls, including his mobile phone records over the past two hours.

One received phone call stood out like a sore thumb: A re-routed radio communication, from a private airfield in Cumbria.

Shit.

'Get me details of the flight plans of all flights from the Ullswater Airport this morning,' he ordered into his telephone. 'And hurry up! It's urgent!'

Langham waited an agonising ten minutes before the phone rang. He snatched it up.

'Yes?'

'The flight plans, sir. There aren't many, just a few routine tourist trips and training flights. Mainly helicopters.

'Are any of them headed for London?'

'Just one, sir.'

'Details?'

'Headed for Battersea heliport, due to land in approximately fifty minutes.'

'Passengers?'

'None recorded, sir.'

'Call the airfield, find out and get back to me. Now.'

'Yes sir.'

Langham rubbed his forehead. It was a longshot, but his intuition was screaming at him. If his hunch was correct, it could mean only one thing: Dunscombe's team had been successful and were on their way back to London with a witness. Somehow they had escaped from Kroll's men. He racked his brains. What the *hell* had gone wrong, and what could he do about it?

The phone rang.

'Sir, the airfield report that the helicopter was requisitioned over half an hour ago by a member of the Security Service.'

'*What?* By whom?'

'The name given was Andrew Cowdry. He had four companions.'

Langham felt a brief wave of nausea, his forehead prickled with perspiration. Without a word, he hung up. He could feel his control of events slipping away as he turned to his computer and accessed the Human Resources database. His maximum level security granted him global access to the system. He stared at the screen as the records were displayed.

Andrew Cowdry. *What the hell are you up to?* Langham eyes flicked through the file, and almost laughed.

Nothing. Operational status inactive, currently on an extended sabbatical until further notice.

Bullshit. This had Sir Mark Wellesby's fingerprints all over it. The wily old Director General had set himself up with an extra pair of eyes and ears, probably in anticipation of his health-enforced early retirement. Langham scanned through the notes. The extended leave of absence for Cowdry was authorised by Wellesby on the advice of medical personnel. Stress, apparently.

So why the hell was Cowdry suddenly requisitioning helicopters in Cumbria? And why the hell was he in communication with Alan Dunscombe in London?

There could only be one explanation.

Langham felt the nausea return as he picked up the phone and called Giles Devereaux at the Cabinet Office.

Devereaux was appalled by what he learnt, and was adamant on the course of action that had to be taken. Langham baulked at first, knowing that it would be his authority and position on the line, but Devereaux was insistent. If Vincent Markham made it to London and the sanctuary of the newspaper, then they were finished. Millburn would be destroyed, the Prime Minister's flagship energy policy would be in tatters, the government would be brought to account, and those held responsible would be punished.

It mustn't happen.

Langham sighed as he considered his options. He kept coming back to the same idea. There was a solution. A solution borne of desperation. He brought up another file on his computer. The dark unflinching gaze of a very brave man stared back at him. Abdul Samad was a top informer with access to the leadership of several extremist Islamic groups based in the UK. Acting as a discreet liaison between them, he was in an unparalleled position to glean information of interest to the UK authorities. Trusted implicitly by the men he secretly despised, he was party to some of the most hideous outrages ever conceived in the UK. Many successes against incipient terrorist actions could be attributed to the quiet, loyal and unassuming Abdul. His identity was known only to a tiny handful at the top of the intelligence community. Which made him ideal for Langham's solution.

The secret inquiry would attribute it to a simple error, a mistake, but one which had to be taken in good faith at the time, leaving Langham with little choice in the matter. There simply wasn't time to verify Abdul's startling new information which, sadly as it turned out, had transpired to be wrong. The brilliant agent had made a simple mistake. He was only human, after all. His star would shine less brightly afterwards, but Langham knew it would recover its lustre. They couldn't blame Langham for acting on the information, whilst Abdul was too important to censure for the mistake. It would be brushed under the carpet. Yes, the plan would work.

41

Following the September 11th attacks on New York in 2001, Britain had modified its structure for air defence. Whilst aircraft were still routinely scrambled to shepherd Russian aircraft away from their increasingly common habit of probing UK airspace defences, the chain of command was modified to accommodate responses to terrorist attack by air. Under the Quick Reaction Alert (QRA) element of UK air defence, Tornado F3 fighter aircraft were kept in a state of permanent readiness at RAF Coningsby in Lincolnshire and RAF Leuchars in Fife. Since incorporating the terrorist threat into its procedures, RAF Coningsby had responsibility for defending London from attack. An aircraft could be airborne within ten minutes of notification. Without any advance warning. From March 2007 onwards, the aircraft of No. 3 Squadron had been steadily replaced and upgraded by the highly advanced Eurofighter Typhoon F2, arguably the best fighter aircraft in the world with the exception, perhaps, of the US-built F-22 Raptor. At the end of June, these new aircraft had assumed responsibility for the Quick Reaction Alert.

Flight Lieutenant Cliff Morland was bored stiff. He wished the Russians would come out and play, just to give him something to do. During the good old days of the Cold War, his predecessors had been kept on their toes by regular intrusions into British airspace by long-range Soviet reconnaissance aircraft. The purpose was to probe and test UK air defences, the results being fed back to the military planners in Moscow. But there had been an extended drop in such activities during the chaos following the collapse of the Soviet empire. However, that had all changed now as a newly resurgent and aggressive Russia was flexing its military muscles once more. Long-range Tupolev 142's flying out of their base at Murmansk, on the Kola Peninsula, were taking a renewed interest in NATO maritime exercises. The number of airspace intrusions was increasing and Flt Lt Morland was hoping there would be one on his watch, to give him a chance to prove what the Typhoon was capable of, and hopefully give Boris a fright, or a good run for his money at the very least.

Morland's flight support team was equally bored and hopeful of some action tonight. As soon as satellites and radar detected the planes on a course for UK airspace, they would scramble and intercept the Russians, flying alongside them until they changed course and headed back out of UK airspace. Occasionally they would exchange waves. However, sometimes the Russians would be more aggressive, ignoring the fighters for several minutes, to the point where weapons were armed and locked on to target. Of course, that was precisely what the Russians were after, an important part of the exercise. The electronic information would be carefully harvested and returned to Russia. That the antiquated Russian reconnaissance aircraft were no match for the Typhoons was irrelevant. It was information, not combat, that they were interested in. For the time being, at least. It was all part of the new Great Game that would soon come to dominate the first half of the twenty first century. The sleepy, complacent populations of Europe had yet to wake up to the changing geopolitical reality driven by energy resources rather than competing ideologies, yet the seeds of conflict were already being sown.

Meanwhile, as long as Morland got to play with his multimillion pound machine, he didn't mind.

He had just sat down in the operations room with a cup of coffee when the alert came through. Highly trained men and women snapped to full attention, focused, professional. This was no drill. The grim-faced squadron intelligence officer tersely informed him that information had been received about a potential terrorist attack on London. The information was deemed utterly reliable. A helicopter had been commandeered. The exact intended terrorist target was unknown, as intelligence sources had been unable to verify that information, but was heavily suspected of being a Premiership football stadium. There were several playing host to mid-week games that night, with attendances in the tens of thousands. The potential for carnage caused by an explosive-laden helicopter flying into a crowded stadium did not bear thinking about: The detonation would be concentrated within the structure, packed with thousands of people, the shrapnel flying in all directions faster than the speed of sound. It had to be stopped.

Intelligence sources had obtained the flight plan of the helicopter, which listed Battersea as the final destination. They believed this was a ruse to get the helicopter close to central London before anyone realised the true intention of the flight. Once over the city, the sudden change in the course of flight would raise alarms, but shooting the craft down then would be fraught with danger. Many innocent people would be killed by falling debris and possibly by the explosion itself.

It had to be stopped before it reached London flight space.

Morland raced to his aircraft and went through the quick start-up procedure. The engines were ignited and he taxied to the end of the runway, receiving final clearance from the tower. Nine minutes after the alert came through, Morland pushed the throttles through their gates, taking the massive twin EH1200 engines to maximum power; the jet roared down the runway, the afterburn flame streaking out behind.

Full weapons release had been authorised.

On board the helicopter, a quiet mood had descended. As the adrenalin subsided, Hudson's wounds ached painfully, in particular the torn stitching in his side. Susannah was leaning into him, asleep, which added to his discomfort but he couldn't bring himself to move her. She had been through a terrible ordeal. They all had, but Hudson found that thinking of others stopped his own demons, helping him cope with it. He reclined his head on the headrest, hoping that the constant whine and vibration of the engines would lull him to sleep, but sleep eluded him. In the reflection of the window he could see Gregory fast asleep in the seat opposite. He had taken the experience very badly. Vincent Markham was awake, staring out of the window, a grim look on his face. He noticed Hudson was looking at him and glanced up. Hudson averted his gaze, but not before he had seen something odd in Vincent's expression. The man wasn't traumatised. Or frightened. He seemed possessed of a strange serenity and calmness, yet his eyes were angry, burning with rage. Perhaps Hudson was misreading the anger for determination of some sort. But whatever it was, Hudson found the expression disconcerting.

He looked out of the window to see that they were already over the open countryside of Oxfordshire. The industrial sprawl of the Midlands was disappearing behind them. They would be in London soon, and some semblance of normality, hopefully. Detective Inspector Brannigan had returned to his force in Manchester, but had assured Hudson and his companions that he would do everything in his power to help them, and would be working closely with the man they knew as Scott, who was now sitting up front with the pilot. Hudson studied the back of the man who had rescued them from their two would-be murderers. What sort of man was he? He had shot the two killers as though it was part of his normal working day, and seemed completely unconcerned about it. It suddenly occurred to Hudson that Scott may not be who he said he was. What if he was part of Red Dawn? Sent to tidy up loose ends? Kill the killers, who perhaps knew too much?

He was just considering this awful possibility, when his reverie was shattered by the scream of a jet roaring across the windscreen of the helicopter. The pilot jumped and the helicopter jerked and wobbled until he brought it back under control.

'What the hell!' exclaimed the pilot, wrestling with the controls.

The jet made another close pass, causing the helicopter to swoop in the turbulence. Scott cringed in the co-pilot's seat as it flashed in front of them. 'What's going on?' he shouted at the pilot.

'I don't know! It's a military jet, looks like a Typhoon. He nearly hit us!'

'Please identify your aircraft, please identify your aircraft!' the radio crackled on the open communications channel.

'We are flight tango lima zulu two four nine, over,' replied the terrified pilot.

'Are you in distress, over?'

'Er, no, over.'

'What is your destination, over?'

The pilot gave the details for the helipad in Battersea. On board the Typhoon, Flt Lt Morland checked against the information he had. It all tallied with what he had been given. The only niggling doubt was that he was expecting no communications at all. He had the right helicopter, his orders were clear: Shoot it down over open countryside before they had a chance to crash it into an urban area, or where falling debris could injure people.

But it didn't feel right to Morland. It was one thing toying with Russian Tupolevs flown by professional aviators who knew the risks and took their chances, quite another shooting down a small civilian helicopter over your own country. Morland had acquired the target from over seventy miles away using the CAPTOR radar system. Then he should have accelerated to Mach 1.8 to provide maximum kinetic energy for the optimum release of his Advanced Medium Range Air to Air Missiles, ensuring the complete obliteration of the target. However, he wanted to be absolutely sure, so went in close. He could afford to make sure. The extreme manoeuvrability of the aircraft, coupled with the Head Mounted Symbiology System, which allowed him to acquire targets merely by turning his head and looking at them, meant that he could respond instantly to any hostile intent shown by the helicopter. At any one moment, it was just seconds away from destruction.

Morland contacted base for clarification.

On board the helicopter, Scott/Cowdry was gripped by fear. There was only one explanation he could think of to account for the presence of the jet. Langham had found out about the flight and was going to shoot them down. Destroy the evidence. Destroy the witnesses.

'Get the helicopter down, now!' he shouted at the pilot. 'They're going to shoot us down!'

'What?'

'Don't argue, just do it!'

'I can't see where to land!' the pilot protested.

'I don't care, just *do it*!'

Cowdry snatched up a headset and frantically tried to contact the jet.

'Unidentified jet, please respond, please respond. Do not open fire, repeat, do not open fire. The information you have is *incorrect*! Repeat, the information you have is incorrect. We are not hostile, repeat, we are not hostile.'

Morland noted the helicopter descending. Trying to evade him? He heard the frantic message come over the radio, and spoke to base on his intercom.

'The target is descending rapidly, possible evasive action. I have received communications from them; they claim they have no hostile intent. Target is still acquired, please advise,' he requested.

Morland could kill them with one click of a button but one thought still nagged at him as he brought the Typhoon around in a shallow arc: *What if it's a mistake? What if I'm killing innocent people?* It didn't bear thinking about, especially after some of the so-called friendly fire incidents in Iraq. Some of the pilots responsible had suffered complete breakdowns as a result, their careers and lives in tatters.

On board the helicopter, the passengers were terrified. The helicopter descended rapidly towards the ground, the pilot panicking. It was an exceedingly dangerous situation.

'This is Andrew Cowdry. I am a Security Service agent. You have been given the wrong information. We are not a hostile aircraft. Do not open fire!'

The new information startled Morland. *Could it be true?* He banked the jet into another turn to bring himself back within close range of the target. The helicopter was very slow in comparison to the Typhoon, so he kept overshooting it at such close range.

'We are landing. I repeat: We are landing. This will demonstrate our peaceful intention. Do not fire!' shouted Cowdry.

'It looks like he's landing,' Morland reported back to base. He would have to select different weaponry to hit an object on the ground. But then if it was on the ground and stayed there, it was no longer an immediate threat warranting lethal action. Then his intercom put paid to any further reflection on the matter.

'Destroy the target, over,' came the confirmation.

'Roger. Over and out.'

He banked the Typhoon into its final approach, the target clearly illuminated in his helmet display. The weapons control system indicated that the target was acquired. Then he flicked the safety catch off his joystick, his finger squeezing the missile launch trigger.

42

'Where the hell are they?' Dunscombe demanded impatiently.

'They should arrive at Battersea in half an hour,' replied Gallimore.

'Go there and meet them. Now!' shouted Dunscombe, pacing nervously. 'I don't want to risk anything.' He lit another cigarette, unable to control his nerves. As soon as they were all back in the building, safe and sound, they could publish Vincent Markham's account of the accident. The rest of the Red Dawn cover up could be extrapolated from that. But they needed Vincent Markham's account first.

Gallimore left the office in a hurry, leaving Dunscombe and Chohan in anxious silence. The tension in the room was palpable, with Chohan drumming his fingers by way of release. Everything was ready to go; the frontpage and background stories, coverage of the government's nuclear generating proposals, analysis of Sellafield, the mysterious deaths of the Civil Servants. They had electronic copies of the Red Dawn meeting tapes ready to upload to the website. They even had a copy of Giles Devereaux's threatening phone call to upload. But that would be a last resort, to be used when all else failed. Dunscombe wanted to make sure he retained leverage of some sort, so was keeping that option open as a last resort.

Dunscombe had not told Chohan or Gall about his excursion that morning. It was only a few hours ago, but felt like weeks. After he had received the menacing phone call from whom it now transpired to be Giles Devereaux, he could think of only one person he had left to turn to.

When Dunscombe had first come to the attention of the Security Service during the industrial strife of the late 1970s, a young case officer had been sent to interview him. Although Dunscombe had been both flattered and outraged in equal measure by the interest of the security service, it soon became clear to the young officer that Dunscombe was no threat to the Establishment, just a journalist with perhaps a little more idealism than others. Against all the odds, the two men became friends; it went beyond simple professional acquaintance. They liked and respected each other, despite the vast political gulf separating them. Nevertheless, they met up occasionally to exchange information. The young officer would divulge some of the more controversial activities of the new Thatcher government, whilst Dunscombe would give him the inside track on Fleet Street. Over the years both careers had flourished, the irony being that one of the fastest rising stars within a paper traditionally regarded as the scourge of the Establishment was in fact on very close terms with one of the fastest rising stars within the security apparatus that protected the very same. But it was a mutually beneficial arrangement, and Dunscombe saw no problem or contradiction with it. He got good stories which advanced his career and reputation, whilst his friend was able to gauge the mood in Fleet Street and call in favours when expediency required it, even encouraging Dunscombe to be as scathing as possible about the activities of the Security Service.

Dunscombe had been sad to learn of his old friend's lung cancer, regretting the brutal finality of the prognosis. Mark Wellesby, now *Sir* Mark, did not deserve to die so young. Dunscombe had been meaning to visit him in hospital since he had learnt of his collapse and admission earlier in the week, but he had been so busy. That was until the phone call from Devereaux that morning. Dunscombe realised that he needed Wellesby's help and advice.

He had found Wellesby in a very poorly state and it was obvious that, barring a miracle, he would not be leaving hospital again. The private side room, with its rather grim view of a less than salubrious air conditioning unit, would be his last place of rest. Propped up in bed with an oxygen mask and various tubes protruding from him, he was able to talk, but weakly; the brilliant mind failed by the body which he had abused with such dedication for much of his life. Dunscombe had sat down and explained the situation carefully to him, revealing all he knew about Red Dawn and the attempts to find a credible witness from the list supplied by the now deceased Terleski. Wellesby had nodded with understanding when Dunscombe mentioned the threatening phone call, and the visit by the courier.

'There's no point denying it,' he whispered. 'It's all true…I've known for years,' his voice faded away and he closed his eyes, struggling to fight the soporific effect of the morphine drip. Dunscombe was shocked but said nothing. Now wasn't the time or place.

'You have to be careful,' Wellesby continued, forcing himself to carry on. 'They won't let this come out…There's too much at stake.'

'So what can we do?'

'Carry on as you are…'

'I don't understand.'

Wellesby smiled weakly. 'I'm already ahead of you, Alan…I've had an officer following your people all week…'

Dunscombe's eyes widened in surprise. 'What? He's with them now?'

Wellesby shook his head. 'He was onto Hudson and the girl, but lost them last night. Now I understand why…I need to tell him where they are, he'll keep an eye on them.'

Dunscombe couldn't ignore this. 'You *knew*? And you did nothing to help them?'

'I had no choice. We needed Millburn to make a move, catch his men in the act. Red Dawn is or was official government policy. Plus we had no idea what evidence Terleski was holding. We needed the girl to find it for us, and I only had one man I could trust…But it seems we lost control of events…'

Dunscombe stared at him for a moment, before letting his anger pass. He handed Wellesby the mobile phone, which sat on the bedside table in direct contravention of hospital policy, and explained as much as he knew about Gregory's location. Wellesby placed a very brief call, giving the terse message to his agent.

'It's done. He should be able to find them soon.'

'Thank you, Mark. As soon as you're out of here, we'll have a beer together.'

'We both know that's a lie…' His eyes opened, and were sad. 'Good luck, Alan.'

'You too, Mark. You too.' Dunscombe felt a lump in his throat. There was no point making platitudes about incipient recoveries and miracle treatments. Wellesby's ticket was stamped, and they both knew it. Dunscombe shook his hand, feeling Wellesby grip hard, the unspoken understanding passing between them.

'Don't worry about their threats, Alan. Just make sure you publish the damn story. Fuck them.' Then Wellesby let go and collapsed back into his pillow, overcome by the exhaustion of the brief conversation.

As Dunscombe waited for the arrival of the helicopter, he thought about that conversation he had had with Wellesby. The man who had phoned him from the helicopter, Scott, must be the officer assigned by Wellesby. Everything should be alright, he thought. Everything *would* be alright.

43

The bus full of schoolchildren headed down the narrow country lane, faces pressed against the window in excitement at the helicopter which flew low over their heads. Even the driver could not help but be distracted. The helicopter was very low: Perhaps it was in trouble. They rounded a bend to find the helicopter coming down fast in a field right next to the road. The helicopter was coming down fast. Too fast, thought the driver, who braked instinctively, bringing the bus to a shuddering halt in a cloud of dust. Mesmerised, they all gaped at the machine hurtling towards the ground in the field.

Flt Lt Morland spotted the brightly coloured school bus at the last moment and broke off the attack against the helicopter, replacing the safety catch on the joystick. He could hear desperate shouting from the helicopter over the radio, having kept the channel open.

'Brace! Brace! Brace!' shouted the pilot in warning as the ground proximity warning alarm sounded. He prayed they would avoid any unseen overhead power lines, which are notoriously difficult to spot from a vibrating helicopter. The passengers gripped hold of whatever they could and hung on for dear life. In the pilot's desperation to land, the helicopter slammed into the ground too hard, breaking the landing gear. Fortunately, it remained upright, preventing the rotors from shearing off on contact with the ground. They were jolted heavily in their seats, but not seriously injured as the seats absorbed most of the impact. The lights went out and objects bounced around the cabin. Quickly, the pilot initiated his emergency shut down procedure and cut fuel to the engines. As the rotors wound down, they could hear Scott still shouting into the radio, instructing the jet not to open fire. They heard the pilot respond:

'Tango lima zulu two four nine. Remain in your current position. Do not attempt to fly otherwise we have instructions to open fire… Do you have any casualties, over?'

'Negative, over. I repeat, we have no hostile intention. Do not open fire.'

'We've radioed your position to the emergency services. They'll be with you soon. I'll keep an eye on you until then, over. Do not attempt to fly or leave the scene.'

Bathed in sweat, Cowdry slumped forward and held his head in his hands. That had been close. Too close. As the rotors came to a halt, there was complete silence for a few seconds.

'We'd better get out. There might be a fuel leak.' He was also worried that the fighter pilot might receive fresh instructions.

Dazed and bruised, they climbed out of their seats and headed for the exit. With the collapsed undercarriage, there was no need for a ladder, so they just hopped the short distance to the ground. Outside, the jet could be heard circling above them, and they could make out its distinctive form as it banked around again. Cowdry suggested they move a good distance away from the machine. Just in case. None of them needed any encouragement, and they scrambled out of the fuselage as fast as they could, to put as much distance between the helicopter and themselves.

It seemed that they had put down in a field full of cattle; the herd gathered some distance off and regarded them with considerable, but entirely understandable, wariness. In front of them, they could see the top of a school bus over the top of the hedge, a row of little faces pressed against the windows staring at them, so they headed towards it. Cowdry stopped them, realising the potential risk to the bus passengers, but then it occurred to him that was probably what had saved them. The bus driver climbed out and headed towards them, pulling a mobile phone from his pocket, as Cowdry silently thanked him. As he got nearer, they could hear him calling the emergency services. Once they were a safe distance from the stricken helicopter, they sat down in the grass to await help. There seemed little else they could do.

44

Langham stared at the water in his glass, still unable to absorb the enormity of what he had done: Using false intelligence to order the shooting down of a helicopter. He ran over the story in his mind: He had been forced to act. The information came from their top informer. They had no time to verify it. Too much was at stake. It was a tragic error, but in the War Against Terror, no chances could be taken.

The board of inquiry would be conducted in secret, so as to protect the informer. The matter could be covered up. The helicopter had crashed, mechanical failure, pilot error. Whatever. The secret board of inquiry would find a good reason. As far as the public was concerned, it was a tragic accident. Yes, the incident could be covered up.

He sighed deeply. Red Dawn was safe now. For the time being at least. Langham had succeeded in protecting the government and his own organisation, an outcome which would surely increase his bargaining power. Favours were owed. He would call them in when he needed to.

He checked his watch. The shooting down of the helicopter would be confirmed at any moment.

As if reading his mind, the telephone jangled. *RAF Conigsby*.

'Yes?' he snapped aggressively, forcing the nerves from his voice. As he listened, he felt the blood drain from his face. 'It can't be,' he croaked, feeling his world fall apart. 'I don't understand...I gave specific instructions. I want that helicopter destroyed! *NOW!*...What do you mean, it can't be done?... A *bus*?...' his voiced trailed off, the shock of the failure hitting him. It was over. Pale-faced, he replaced the handset.

Think! He needed to *think*.

There was only one option left, but he had to act fast. He snatched up the phone and barked instructions.

*

Alan Dunscombe listened in stunned silence as Cowdry explained what had happened. On the other side of the desk, Amarjit Chohan was hunched forward, straining to hear Cowdry's voice as it crackled from the loudspeaker on the telephone: The mobile phone connection was poor, but not poor enough for Chohan to misunderstand what Cowdry was saying. His intelligent forehead was creased with a deep frown of concern, his eyes betraying his alarm at the development.

When Cowdry hung up, having assured him that they were all uninjured, Dunscombe was also very frightened man. The full power of the people they were up against had been made very manifest by what had just happened. This was no game. He glanced at Chohan, whose face said it all: They were playing for very high stakes.

And the stakes were about to get even higher.

Hudson heard the sirens converging on their location. The nightmare was nearly over. The emergency services were here to help. The man he had previously known as Scott, but who had dramatically revealed himself to be Andrew Cowdry in his frantic conversation with the fighter plane, was talking to the bus driver and helicopter pilot. He was explaining the situation, whilst keeping an eye on the jet still circling their position above.

The first of three fire engines raced down the lane, and pulled into the field, closely followed by ambulances and police cars. Within minutes, the field was swarming with fluorescent jackets, the new uniform of British authority. Before Hudson could stop them, two paramedics had unnecessarily wrapped him in foil and were treating him like an invalid. He angrily dismissed them, and told them to concentrate on Susannah and Gregory, who were in far more need of attention. A policeman strode across the grass and attempted to take control of the situation, barking orders until Cowdry had a quiet word with him. The firemen gathered around the helicopter, foam fire retardant at the ready, whilst someone else went to check on the children on the bus, who were gaping out of the windows, utterly enthralled.

In the chaos, no one spotted the unmarked cars creeping down the lane towards the field, followed by a large van. The cars pulled up, and eight men in dark overalls leapt out and fanned across the field, advancing rapidly on the unsuspecting group.

Hudson was tending to Susannah when he saw the movement first. His sixth sense alerted him to the anomalous behaviour.

'Cowdry!' he shouted at the agent, but it was too late.

'ARMED POLICE!'

Hudson froze to the spot as eight Heckler & Koch MP5 submachine guns were levelled at them.

'PUT YOUR HANDS UP!'

Hudson did as he was told. The others followed suit, including the shocked emergency workers. One of the armed policemen gestured for the paramedics to move away, which they did, terrified, their arms still raised.

Then the unthinkable happened.

With lightening speed, Cowdry grabbed the bus driver and pulled out his pistol, pressing it into the man's neck. He held the terrified man in a tight embrace, moving around to present a harder target. Everyone froze.

'BACK OFF!' he shouted at the armed policemen, cocking the pistol. There was a pause as everyone absorbed the situation. Cowdry looked around in panic, aware of the guns now trained on him. He kept moving to make the shot harder to take, the risk of hitting the hostage higher. One of the paramedics began moving away.

'Not you! You stay here!' Cowdry shouted at the petrified woman. The armed police trained their guns at him, unsure of what to do. 'Everyone on the bus!' he ordered, inching towards the entrance of the field. Slowly, the group headed towards the bus, hands still raised, surrounding Cowdry and effectively blocking a clear shot at him. After what seemed an age, they reached the bus and started climbing on. The children were by now equally terrified. Cowdry forced the driver into his seat and sat behind him, with the captive paramedic between him and the window. Susannah, Gregory and Vincent were herded into the seats opposite.

'What the *fuck* are you doing?' hissed Hudson into his ear, as the children started whimpering.

'They would have killed us. This is our only chance,' Cowdry murmured.

'These are *kids*!'

'I know. Call Dunscombe.'

'What, and tell him we've got a busload of kids held hostage? You're *insane*!'

'No, I'm not. Do you want to live? Tell Dunscombe what's happened. This is the plan…'

*

'WHAT?' roared Dunscombe into the phone. 'Has he lost his fucking mind?'

'Someone sent armed police to arrest us,' Hudson explained. 'Cowdry reckons they weren't police. He thinks they were sent to kill us.'

'They will now! Have you *any* idea what you're doing?'

'Cowdry says it's our only chance.'

'What is?'

Hudson explained Cowdry's plan, and Dunscombe whistled down the phone. 'It's very risky, could backfire completely. But I'll try.'

45

At his Surrey estate, Charles Millburn reclined in his custom-made leather chair, savouring his cigar. Kroll had assured him that everything would have been taken care of by now and, having heard nothing to the contrary, he had no reason to believe this wasn't the case. The journalists and their evidence would have been destroyed by now, the bodies hidden where they would never be found, certainly not in his lifetime. The government was doing all it could to help. After all, there were several people with a vested interest in burying Red Dawn for good, including the Prime Minister.

Millburn wondered whether the PM knew what Devereaux and Langham had been up to. Probably not specifically, but it was inconceivable that he had no inkling at all. But then deniability was everything in politics. Unless you wanted to claim responsibility for success. But Millburn couldn't care less about that now. The nuclear programme contracts were in the bag; his forward share options were in place through his discreet broker; the Gencor Energy share price was rising, realising a potential paper profit of several million for him already, and his mistress would be visiting later on that evening. Life was looking very comfortable for him.

He checked his watch: it was time for the early evening news. He flicked on the plasma television in his office and took another long drag on the fine cigar, rolling the sweet, aromatic smoke over his tongue.

'A gunman has taken thirty schoolchildren and six adults hostage on a bus in Oxfordshire. The drama unfolded earlier in the afternoon, following an as yet unexplained helicopter crash. It is thought that the some of the adults were passengers on the helicopter...'

Millburn's attention wandered. He didn't really care much for the minutiae of life. He had more important issues to worry about.

'...It is thought that one of the hostages is a journalist with the Guardian Newspaper, and he is being held with another journalist believed to be working on assignment from a regional newspaper in the north...'

Millburn blinked, his subconscious registering something, but he couldn't quite put his finger on it.

'...and I believe we can now cross live... yes, we can, to our regional correspondent on the scene...Ben?'

The screen switched to a reporter wearing trendy urban outdoor clothing, standing in a rural lane which had been sealed off with police tape, forming the dramatic backdrop of his piece to camera. The reporter was clearly very excited by the drama he had to report, the words pouring out breathlessly.

'Thank you Matthew. Yes, as you can see, the bus is surrounded by armed police in this truly extraordinary and terrifying hostage drama. No demands have been made, and it is not clear exactly what is going on here, but we understand that trained negotiators are trying to make contact, but so far have been unsuccessful.'

'Any news on the condition of the children, Ben?'

'No, Matthew. But we can only guess that they must be going through a terrifying ordeal…hang on…Matthew, I've just been told that we have one of the hostages on the telephone…this is an extraordinary development…'

Millburn listened idly, waiting for the business news, noting the red banner scrolling across the screen pronouncing BREAKING NEWS.

'…Hello? Hello?...this is the BBC…can you hear us?'

'Hello?'

'Yes, hello, this is the BBC, you are live on air, whom am I speaking to?'

'My name's James Hudson…'

Millburn sat bolt upright. What the *hell?*

'James, you're one of the hostages, can you tell us what is going on?'

'I'm not a hostage and I want you to know that the children will be released immediately. We have been forced to take this course of action to attract your attention.'

'Sorry, can you repeat that? The children are being released?'

'Yes, as I speak, they are leaving the bus. All of them are safe and well, and we are very sorry for any distress this has caused to them and their families.'

'You said that you're not a hostage? Are you the gunman, er...
.kidnapper?'

469

'No, no. Please listen. We were forced to do this. I am a journalist from the Preston Advertiser, working on special assignment for the Guardian, with a colleague, Samuel Gregory…'

The scrolling banner changed to HOSTAGES FREED.

'…we have a story the world has a right to hear. The remaining hostages will be released once you have heard what we have to say. The government has tried to stop us, but we have the evidence and a witness to support it…'

Millburn listened aghast as Hudson described the leak from the Sellafield storage facility, and the subsequent cover-up programme known as Red Dawn, using the Chernobyl fallout to explain any illnesses that resulted.

'These are substantial allegations, James. Can you provide any evidence now for the benefit of our listeners and viewers?'

'Yes. The man behind the programme is Sir Charles Millburn, Chairman of Gencor Energy PLC, but previously the Minister for Trade and Industry. A recording of the secret meeting in which he set up Red Dawn can be found on the Guardian's website…'

'We will try to bring that to our viewers as soon as we can, James…'

The scrolling banner changed to ALLEGATIONS OF NUCLEAR ACCIDENT AT SELLAFIELD.

'…You say that the government has tried to stop you telling this story. Can you describe how?...'

Millburn stared at the screen in a daze. The ash on the cigar grew slowly as he remained motionless, in shock. Finally, he mustered the energy to pick up the phone and call Peter Kroll.

The phone rang out. No answer.

Kroll had disappeared.

46

By nine o'clock in the evening, the news channels were dominated by the story. The bulletins were sensational.

"Survivors of a freak helicopter accident south of Oxford are currently helping police with their enquiries into an armed stand-off involving a coachload of schoolchildren…"

"All hostages in the Oxford bus hijacking have been released without harm amid allegations that the hostage-takers were journalists investigating a nuclear accident at the Sellafield plant…"

"The Guardian newspaper has released secret recordings and transcripts of meetings held between Charles Millburn and senior figures in the nuclear establishment in which details of a major nuclear accident and cover-up at Sellafield are discussed…"

"As the political storm surrounding Charles Millburn grows amid allegations that he was involved in a government sanctioned nuclear cover-up, unsubstantiated rumours are circulating that he might also be investigated in relation to an ongoing murder enquiry.…"

"Sources close to today's growing police investigation into allegations of a major leak at Sellafield have revealed that the role of Britain's intelligence services is also being questioned. It is thought that a high ranking officer is helping with the investigation. Attention is being focused on links between the intelligence services and Gencor Energy PLC, the FTSE100 company chaired by Sir Charles Millburn…"

"Police sources have disclosed that they are opening an inquiry into the suspicious deaths of five senior civil servants. It is thought that they were members of the top secret Red Dawn programme, the nuclear cover-up allegedly orchestrated by Charles Millburn in 1986.…"

"The Guardian newspaper is carrying allegations that its editor was threatened by a senior member of the Cabinet Office. Evidence has been passed to the police as part of the growing investigation into the activities of Charles Millburn, who has been arrested at his Surrey estate in the last half hour…"

The story continued throughout the night, growing in momentum. By the following morning, it had spread around the world. Hudson, Susannah, Gregory and Vincent Markham were placed in protective custody, but were advised that none of them would be charged for any offences relating to the hijacking of the school bus. It was felt that they would be safer in the protection of the police, especially after Detective Inspector Carl Brannigan of Greater Manchester CID intervened on their behalf. The man they knew as both Scott and

Andrew Cowdry mysteriously melted away, and no mention of him was made by the police.

At half past eight in the morning, the London Stock Exchange was forced to suspend trading in Gencor Energy shares following panic selling by institutional investors who feared that the revelations about the Sellafield accident would scupper the Prime Minister's plans for a revived nuclear energy programme. The Stock Exchange also began an investigation into suspiciously large volumes of options trading over previous days. Whoever had sold the options would have faced ruinous losses, running into hundreds of millions of pounds, as a result of the dramatically falling share price. The Exchange wanted to know whether whoever had purchased the options had known in advance that information was likely to emerge that would cause the share price to fall so sharply. In the end, the investigation would show that the options were sold by a Mr Simon Goldstein, a broker of dubious merit who appeared to operate as a front for wealthy individuals who preferred to remain anonymous. Either he or his client had suffered vast losses, which would surely not have been his or their intention when they put the options up for sale. Therefore, the inquiry would find no evidence of insider dealing.

At nine o'clock in the morning, a spokesman for the Board of Gencor Energy released a statement outside the company's Canary Wharf headquarters. The steps were already crowded with reporters and photographers, who had latched onto one of the fastest growing stories of the moment:

The spokesman cleared his throat nervously, knowing he was probably on the live breakfast news channels.

'I am authorised to read out the following statement on behalf of the Board of Directors of Gencor Energy PLC: Following the arrest of Charles Millburn, the Chairman and Acting Chief Executive, and in light of recent events, the Board has decided to ask Sir Charles to step down from his duties with immediate effect. He will be replaced by the current Finance Director, who we hope will restore confidence in the Board and allow share trading to resume. We understand that Sir Charles denies the accusations that have been made against him and will defend himself vigorously. However, the Board feels that he cannot continue as Chairman until his name has been cleared. Thank you.'

There was a momentary silence, before the kerfuffle began. A barrage of questions was hurled at the spokesman, who refused to answer them and beat a hasty retreat inside the building, where security guards barricaded the glass doors against press intrusion.

Later on that morning, an ashen-faced Millburn emerged from the front door of the magistrates court where he had been bailed for surety of £3 million, a staggering sum which had been hotly contested to no avail by the extremely expensive barrister hired by Millburn to defend him. The bewildered Millburn emerged to a phalanx of flash photography and excited journalists who bombarded him with questions. A police officer opened the back door of Millburn's chauffeured Bentley. It was only five metres away but it was the longest five metres of Millburn's life. The baying press demanded a comment, but Millburn fought his way to the car in tight-lipped silence, flanked by the barrister who almost seemed desperate not to let his lucrative new client escape his clutches. Although Millburn was quite capable of climbing into the car, the police officer insisted in pushing his head down roughly to clear the roof. Like a common criminal. Millburn was convinced he had done it deliberately, for the benefit of the cameras, which flashed with renewed frenzy. Bastard. But at the least he was no longer handcuffed. Once the door had been slammed shut, the interior of the car became a relative oasis of calm, though there was now a wall of camera lenses pressed up against the windows to snap him. The press delighting in the fall of a successful former politician and businessman. He could see the headlines already. It was all over. Millburn fought to maintain his composure, but he could not stop his eyes watering.

It was all over.

47

Two Days Later…

Peter Kroll was caught in Jersey. He had gone there quietly under a false identity as soon as he realised Trevor and Julian had failed to stop the journalists. The bank accounts set up by Millburn on his behalf were administered in St. Helier, the island's small but bustling capital. Keeping a low profile, he was staying at the Pomme d'Or, overlooking the harbour. The hotel had once been the administrative headquarters of the occupying Nazi forces during the Second World. It was quite apt, really. Kroll planned to stay for a few days while he sorted out his finances. There was nearly two million pounds in the account discreetly managed by one of the island's numerous small banks. The Gencor Energy shares which had constituted the bulk of his wealth previously were now utterly worthless, though the Director of Security had had the foresight to diversify at least some of his investments, and save any cash. The money needed distributing before he could set up a new life abroad. It wasn't much money by the standards of some of the bank's customers, but it was enough to enable him to live quietly off the interest. South America looked good. The pound was strong; it would go a long way in Argentina, still recovering from its economic collapse in the late 1990s. If he kept his head down, and lived modestly, he would be fine.

Kroll had just finished his breakfast, a continental affair of pastries and coffee served by one of the many itinerant Portuguese hotel staff, and had decided to take a walk around the new marina. The glistening powerboats were lined up in a strict hierarchy of wealth and importance. He strolled along the long jetty, idly admiring the boats and imagining his new life abroad. Indulging his fantasies, he failed to notice the two dark-suited gentlemen step onto the wooden planking behind him. At the end of the jetty, he looked out across the sea. Soon, by tomorrow he hoped, he would be gone, far, far away.

'Hello, Peter,' the voice murmured from behind. Kroll flinched, visibly startled.

'Can you come with us, please?' The two identity cards were flashed. They were genuine. Kroll turned away from them and looked out over the sea. The dream was over.

'How?' he managed, after a short while.

'Your friend, Mr Millburn. Or rather *Sir* Charles. He's been most cooperative. Especially as you deserted him. He was quite touched by your loyalty.'

Kroll nodded in understanding. *Charlie Fucking Millburn.* He should have realised, and fled without the money, but two million is a lot to walk away from, especially if it's all you have left in the world.

'Can I pack?'

The two men looked at each other and nodded. They escorted Kroll back to the hotel. In his room, Kroll seemed calm and dignified.

'Gentlemen, may I be alone for a short while?'

After pausing momentarily without a word, they left him and positioned themselves outside the door, on either side. Kroll's room was on the fourth floor, the window overlooking the marina. He couldn't escape. Inside the room, Kroll folded his clothes and packed them neatly into the small suitcase he had brought. Then he took off his shirt and folded that too, placing the monogrammed cufflinks carefully inside the collar. His trousers followed, then his socks, which he tucked tidily into his shoes. For the sake of modesty, he kept his underwear on. He took the belt he had removed from his trousers and headed into the bathroom. Quickly, he placed the belt around his neck and threaded the end through the buckle, pulling it tight under his chin. Then he tied a rudimentary knot in the end of the strap. Standing on the small bathroom seat, he placed the end of the belt over the top of the door and shut it, trapping the knot on the other side. Then he stepped off the chair.

After fifteen minutes, one of the men standing outside turned to the other.

'Do you think he's had enough time?'

'Best leave it another five. He might not have done it yet.'

The two officers knew that prison would not be a fun place for a former member of the Security Service. He also knew too many things that could prove embarrassing to others. Therefore, it had been quietly decided to give him an exit option. Fortunately, he had the decency to do the honourable thing, and save a lot of hassle, not to mention taxpayers' money.

48

One Week Later…

As befitted the occasion, it was raining. A steady drizzle soaked into the assorted hats and long black coats, producing an unpleasant musty smell. Again, it fitted the occasion. Dr William Terleski had a large extended family and many friends and acquaintances. The ranks of mourners had been swelled by the lurid revelations in the media, though the only journalistic presence was a hack from the local rag. The national media currently had bigger fish to fry, with the scandal threatening to engulf the government. The small church had been packed and several mourners had contributed eulogies. After the service inside was finished, the coffin had been borne outside to the prepared plot. A neat rectangular hole had been prepared next to the headstone denoting the last resting place of Mrs May Terleski, beloved wife.

As the coffin was lowered carefully into the dark, red earth, several mourners wept. Hudson put his arm around Susannah who was sobbing gently. The bruises on Hudson's face were slowly fading, though he still ached from the wound in his side. The stitches would be removed soon. The small cut to Susannah's ear had been expertly repaired, and already nearly healed perfectly. Besides, it was hidden by her luscious blond hair. She had recovered well from their protracted ordeal, and they had a tacit understanding that once their various court appearances as witnesses were over, they would not discuss it ever again.

After the brief interment ceremony by the graveside, the mourners trouped back slowly across the rain-soaked cemetery to their cars. Hudson took Susannah's arm and guided her gently away, hunched beneath an umbrella.

'Hello, James.'

Hudson looked up to see Cowdry falling in beside them.

'How are you both?' he enquired, with genuine concern.

'As good as we could be, I suppose.'

'You went through a lot.'

'So did you.'

They proceeded in silence for a while.

'Look, Scott, Andrew, whoever you are, we never thanked you. Without you we probably wouldn't be here.'

'It was nothing. Without Dr Terleski, and your help, we couldn't have stopped Millburn.'

'What's going to happen to him?'

'Well, as you know, Millburn's been released on bail but he's subject to a special order restricting his movements. He's not supposed to leave his country estate. He's ruined, but whether he'll ever end up in prison is another matter. He's got the best lawyers money can buy and they're already shredding the evidence against him. His right hand man, chap called Peter Kroll, was found dead at a hotel in Jersey a few days ago. Suicide. But that's strictly in confidence, you understand.'

'Suicide?'

'Yes. It seems he was tipped off that we were coming to arrest him. By the time our men got to him, it was too late.'

'Hope he burns in hell.'

'Quite.'

'What about you? What are you going to do?'

'The Service is in chaos over this. They've asked me to stay, but I think I want out. I've had enough. It's not what it used to be. There are a couple of risk consultancies in the City I could work for. The pay's better, the hours are better and it's a damn sight healthier!'

'Don't blame you. Did you hear that Gregory got a promotion? He only took a couple of days off work; apparently he was desperate to get back to normal. His boss has offered him a full contract, pay rise and bumped him up to Chief Reporter. He doesn't seem to be too badly affected by the whole thing. He did a big feature article on Vincent the other day.'

'Yeah, I read it. The shit's hit the fan up at Sellafield. Apparently they're going to build another vitrification plant to try to speed up the disposal of the waste.'

'It won't stop them building more nuclear power stations.'

'Probably not, in the long run. We never seem to learn, do we?'

'At least they're not going to prosecute him or Dunscombe under the Official Secrets Act.'

'Yes, well, don't assume that the country's going soft in its old age. I think it suits the current bunch to have this rumpus, means they can have a bit of a clear-out. They haven't done it out of the goodness of their hearts, believe me.'

Cowdry stopped next to a black Lexus. A driver sat at the wheel, waiting for him. 'Anyway, thought I'd pay my respects.'

'Appreciate it, thanks.'

'Take care, both of you.'

Hudson helped Susannah back to their car. He realised that he would probably never see Cowdry ever again, but that short time spent with him had established a bond that would last until the day he died. A camaraderie borne of shared adversity. And the man had saved his life.

As for Susannah, he didn't know what the future held. By any standard, it had been a difficult start to the relationship, but the fact that they had come through the experience together boded well. In the car he kissed her tenderly and she responded warmly to his embrace. Yes, he loved her and she was worth fighting for.

49

Charles Millburn stared into the flames of the huge open fire in his drawing room. A good metaphor for his career, he thought bitterly as he drained the glass which signified the half way point in the bottle of cognac he had opened an hour earlier. He hoped they had got that bastard Kroll, whose incompetence had caused his ruin. His wife had abandoned him as soon as the full implications of the story became clear. No doubt a hefty divorce settlement would ensue. Bitch.

His bail bond had been set at an eye-watering three million pounds, which had necessitated tapping his more discreet bank accounts. The terms of the bail conditions were draconian. He had been forced to surrender his passport and, for all intents and purposes, he was under house arrest, though his lawyers were campaigning hard for the conditions to be relaxed. His friends and allies had melted away and there was talk of his impending bankruptcy, courtesy of his indiscreet broker, Simon Goldstein. Goldstein was facing ruin too, and wreaking his revenge. The forthcoming realisation of the options on Gencor shares was going to wipe out his entire fortune, and leave him owing tens, if not hundreds, of millions to finance houses unless the shares staged a dramatic and miraculous recovery before then. But it was unlikely, now that the government had indicated a lengthy consultation period pending an inquiry into the Red Dawn programme. At least he wasn't the only one in the shit. Devereaux had been sacked on the spot as soon as the threatening tapes had been leaked to the media, and Jeremy Langham had been placed on extended gardening leave while a replacement was found. Peter Kroll was hopefully regretting his decision to jump ship by now. But all that, comforting as it might have been, did not get Millburn out of his predicament.

With nothing better to do, he was concentrating on getting thoroughly pissed, fuelling his brooding resentment glass by glass. All alone in a huge house in the middle of the Surrey countryside, a tracking device on his ankle to let the police know he was behaving himself. The shame of it.

His senses dulled by the expensive alcohol, he never heard the footsteps approaching until a floorboard creaked close by. Looking up, he felt a mixture of alarm and confusion. The man standing there seemed vaguely familiar, but he couldn't quite place him.

'Who are you?' he demanded, as imperiously as he could, though he was at a clear disadvantage.

The man did not answer, but moved carefully around the chair to face him. His expression was a mixture of triumph, sorrow and hatred. His cold eyes focused on Millburn's and, without a word, he pulled a gun out of his pocket. For several moments, he stood still, holding the gun down by his side. Millburn could feel his heart pounding. The man slowly reached into another pocket and pulled out a photograph. Millburn saw that it was of a happy little girl. He looked back up at the man standing over him. He was familiar, yes, very familiar. Then recognition dawned. Millburn had seen him on television a few days earlier, a survivor of a helicopter crash, a man who was going to testify against him, according to the newspapers. A key witness to what had happened at Sellafield all those years ago.

Then he knew he was going to die. The man saw the knowing realisation and fear in Millburn's expression, lifted the gun and shot him clean between the eyes.

Epilogue

The farmer drove his battered Land Rover Defender up the bumpy track up the side of the hill. The high Cumbrian grassland was unkempt and empty of livestock, all the sheep having long been carted away by the men from the Ministry. It was too contaminated to raise sheep fit for human consumption.

The radio was playing loudly, so that he could hear it above the noise of the diesel engine roaring from a damaged exhaust system. It was tuned into a local radio station. The news came on, and the farmer tweaked the volume a notch higher.

'….Police investigating the murder of Charles Millburn at his country estate say they are following up a number of leads. It is thought that the gun used was similar to one recovered from a Cumbrian slate mine where two unidentified bodies were found this earlier this week. Many senior politicians have expressed their shock at the incident and have criticised the security arrangements in place for the disgraced former Minister and prominent businessman. Mr Millburn was currently on police bail whilst the investigation into the Red Dawn nuclear scandal continues. It was also thought that the Crown Prosecution Service was on the verge of receiving a file from the police detailing Mr Millburn's association with the perpetrators of several murders involving key members of the plot to cover up the alleged Sellafield leak in 1986. The scandal is now threatening to engulf the government, with the Prime Minister being forced to answer questions in Parliament about the extent of his knowledge of the Red Dawn programme, and whether the Security Services were involved in recent events.

In response to the allegations that radiation test results were deliberately falsified, many farms across Cumbria are being subjected to fresh soil and livestock testing. A moratorium on livestock movements in and around potentially affected areas has been imposed, though critics have argued that contaminated products must have already entered the food chain. A full review of storage at the Sellafield nuclear installation is being conducted, though ministers are insisting that the plant is now one of the safest in the world. Spokesmen for environmental groups have condemned the facility, claiming that Britain has become the world's nuclear dustbin.

And on to local news. Police have announced that they are not searching for anyone in connection with the death of a local man found dead in a cemetery. It is understood that the middle-aged man died from a single gunshot to the head. A firearm has been recovered from the scene, though police sources have indicated that they do not believe there are any suspicious circumstances. The Coroner has been notified and it is likely that formal identification will take place later today once the next of kin have been informed. It is believed that the dead man was found dead next to the gravestone of his daughter, who died tragically several years ago from cancer....'

The End.

Jonathan Pennant Guppy, Shropshire, July 2008

Author's Note

Energy 'realists' will point to the growing energy requirements of the planet and note that the projected demand cannot be met with fossilised carbon or renewable sources alone, certainly in the short term. In this observation they are no doubt correct.

It is highly likely, probably inevitable, that the energy shortfall will be met through increased provision of nuclear power, in the short-to-medium term at least. However, familiarity with the technology should not breed complacency. The capacity of a single accident to contaminate vast swathes of an increasingly densely populated plant cannot and should not be underestimated. Modern waste storage (not disposal, as this option does not yet exist) techniques, such as vitrification, address many of the concerns associated with the storage of highly radioactive liquid waste at Sellafield, though it should be noted that the waste still has not 'gone away'. It has merely been transformed into a more stable medium.

The available evidence suggests that fallibility, as an intrinsic component of the human condition, has not yet been overcome or eliminated by progress or science. Whilst safety procedures have undoubtedly improved in recent years, particularly in the advanced democracies of the world, the potential for mistakes cannot ever be eliminated. An examination of incidents at nuclear facilities around the world suggests that the vast majority are the result of human error, either in the form of accidents, poor design, or substandard construction. It is up to energy consumers, politicians, and humanity in general, to decide whether the rewards of nuclear energy are worth the risk, however small it may be, of catastrophe. The design of Russian nuclear power facilities has improved dramatically since the Chernobyl disaster, though the country has a lamentable record for nuclear materials' storage and security. As the global nuclear club expands, such concerns will become ever more salient. The advanced democracies have to decide whether to share their expertise or deny it, thus forcing new entrants to the club to learn through experimentation. And mistakes.

Whilst this book has referred to some real events, institutions and people, the central plot concerning a leak from the storage facility at BNFL Sellafield is entirely fictional and is a figment purely of the author's imagination. The owners of BNFL Sellafield will no doubt be pleased for me to state unequivocally that there is no evidence whatsoever to suggest that a leak of the sort described in this book has ever occurred. This is not to state that matters are perfect, though. In the year in question, a minor leak from a Magnox flask did occur at 23:15h on 26th July 1986, resulting in 2.1Mbq of radiation being released via a ventilation stack. No casualties were reported. More recently, a leak of acid containing more than 20 tonnes of dissolved uranium and 160kg of plutonium occurred when a pipe fractured at the Thorp reprocessing complex in January 2007. The leak remained undiscovered for three months, because discrepancies in material inventories were not investigated. Various environmental protection groups maintain a log of such incidents, for those interested in researching them, whilst the Freedom of Information Act allows the public access to information not dreamed possible a generation ago.

The events in this book have also been partly inspired by a report prepared in December 2000 by the Radiological Protection Institute of Ireland (RPII), which examined the latest safety analysis prepared by the Sellafield authorities, known as the Continued Operation Safety Report (COSR). Ref: "The Storage of Liquid High-Level Radioactive Waste at Sellafield – an Examination of Safety Documentation" by FJ Turvey, Consultant, former Assistant Chief Executive, RPII and C Hone, Manager, Nuclear Safety, RPII, December 2000 (Doc. Ref. RPII-00/3).

The description of the Chernobyl disaster has been simplified for literary effect, with the words, identities and descriptions of individuals, and the actions attributed to them, are a figment of the author's imagination. There are numerous accounts of the disaster, both official and unofficial. A useful starting point for the casual enquirer would be the compendium of resources listed by the World Nuclear Association at: www.world-nuclear.org/info/chernobyl/inf07.html